The Lady

by Judy Higgins

G
GOSSART
PUBLICATIONS

Gossart Publications

Washington D.C.

First Gossart Publications Edition, October 2013

Copyright © by Judy Higgins, 2013

Published in the United States in 2013

Photo Credits

Cover: Nat Jones
Author Photo: Studio Walz

First Gossart paperback edition October, 2013
First Gossart ebook edition October, 2013

Printed in the United States of America

Judy Higgins
The lady : a novel / Judy Higgins

Summary: "The Lady tells the story of how Quincy Bruce jeopardizes her future when she explores her aunt's past." --- Provided by publisher.

ISBN-13: 978-0615878089
ISBN-10: 978-0615878083

For my family

Julia, Stephen, Jim, Erin, Kyle, Jon, and Karina

That evening I had been invited to a gathering which I was much of a mind to shun due to a particularly long run of London's abysmal mizzle. But the promise I'd made to attend moved me at last to set aside my book and don my despised rain gear. I traversed London's dour streets to be among the last to arrive at the premises. Upon entering the parlor, I stopped short. Across the room, in the flickering shadows of the hearth fire, sat the most enchanting lady I'd ever seen.

- *From* The Lady *by Nathan Waterstone*
Published in London, England. May,1943

London, England

June 1, 1943

BBC Radio

Partial Transcript of Amanda Blakeley's Interview with Nathan Waterstone

Amanda Blakeley:

Your first two books were mild successes, and now you've just published *The Lady.* I have to say I was quite taken with it. You fleshed out the woman in the book beautifully. By the time I got to the end I had begun to think of her as a real person.

Nathan Waterstone:

She *was* a real person.

Amanda Blakeley:

Yes, I suppose she must have seemed very real in your mind. Otherwise, how could you have been so successful in making her come alive for the reader?

Nathan Waterstone:

You're not hearing me. My Lady was an actual person, not an invention of my imagination.

Amanda Blakeley:

The lady in your novel, Lady Isabelle Duncan, was based on a real woman?

Nathan Waterstone:

Yes. I changed her name, of course.

Amanda Blakeley:

Since the story is told from the perspective of her lover. Were you, . . . I'm not quite sure how to ask this.

Nathan Waterstone:

If you're asking if I was the man, the main character, who loved her, the answer is yes. We were both very real.

Amanda Blakeley:

But . . . but, you've presented this as a novel.

Nathan Waterstone:

Yes. Names were changed. And details. I was never a journalist, for example, but I presented myself as one in the novel.

Amanda Blakeley:

Will you tell us who she was?

Nathan Waterstone:

Of course not. Never.

Amanda Blakeley:

Since you gave her the title *Lady*, can I assume she's someone important? Or the wife of someone important? A member of the aristocracy, perhaps? . . . You're not answering. . .Well, Mr. Waterstone, I must confess my astonishment at your revelation. Are you prepared for when someone out there discovers her identity and announces it to the world? Or more to the point, is *she* prepared for that? I assume she's the one who would want anonymity.

Nathan Waterstone:

No one will know.

Amanda Blakeley:

How can you be so sure? . . . I take it from your smug smile that you really don't believe anyone will discover her identity. Come now, that's a bit naïve, isn't it? It stands to reason that someone knew. That someone saw you with this woman.

Nathan Waterstone:

She wasn't just a woman. She was a lady. She embodied every good grace one expects in a true lady.

Amanda Blakeley:

At least tell me this: did she have the title *Lady*? Or do you mean she was the epitome of a lady? . . . You're shrugging. I see that you won't answer that question either. But I reiterate: I'm sure you were seen many times with your lady.

Nathan Waterstone:

We would have been seen together by people who didn't know us. My friends were busy fighting the Germans. Busy being killed. She was a stranger in London, so her friends lived elsewhere. As to the people around us, they weren't interested in what I was doing, or who I was with. Many had lost their homes and loved ones to Luftwaffe bombs, and those who hadn't were consumed with the fear of that happening.

Amanda Blakeley:

Yes, it has been a terrible time. I'm sorry about your friends. And all the others. Unfortunately, too many people have lost friends, husbands, fathers, sons. Their homes. It has been a dreadful nightmare . . . But still, there were people who knew who you were. Your book went on sale three weeks ago. After this interview some will be reading it with a view to figuring out who she is. I'll wager that before the week is out, we'll know. Ah, you're shaking your head.

Nathan Waterstone:

No one will know.

Amanda Blakeley:

I take that as a challenge. Since you yourself have revealed that she was a real person, I feel free to pursue this. I predict that within a few days someone will discover her identity. But our time is almost up for today, and I have one further question. You left us hanging at the end of the book. What actually happened? . . . You're shaking your head again. Can't you at least tell us that? . . . No? . . . Come on, Mr. Waterstone, at least let us know what happened on that train. . . .

Nathan Waterstone:

I miss her terribly.

Amanda Blakeley:

I'm very sorry, Mr. Waterstone. I didn't mean to upset you. Ladies and gentlemen, our time is up. Perhaps another day Mr. Waterstone will clear up the ending of *The Lady* for us. But for now, buy it, and curl up for a good read. As you just heard, I've challenged Mr. Waterstone by claiming that before the end of the week, someone out there among our listeners will let us know who the woman . . . excuse me, who the Lady was. Tune in again next week and find out.

CHAPTER 1

May, 1956

Ellerbie, Georgia

Late afternoon, a few weeks before my sixteenth birthday, I'm two-thirds of the way through my Carnegie Hall debut. I've already performed selections by Haydn, Beethoven and Brahms to wildly enthusiastic applause. Now I'm playing my most glorious piece: Chopin's Polonaise in A-flat. My audience sits spellbound. When the last note dies away, when the last magnificent reverberation fades, the hall will rise as one for a standing ovation. *Bravo, bravo,* they'll shout. Fabulous reviews of the amazing new pianist, Quincy Marie Bruce, will fill tomorrow's papers.

At the most exciting part of the polonaise where the key switches to E major, and the left hand thunders out octaves, E D C B, E D C B, in the lower register, fast, furious, and over and over until you feel like your hand is about to fall off, Daddy opens the door, sticks his head through, and calls out, "Quincy, we need to talk to you." Then the door thwacks shut behind him.

Without so much as a tremor of the earth, or an *Excuse me, I'm sorry to interrupt,* I'm back in the sanctuary of the smallest Baptist church in Colquitt County, Georgia, seated at a nicked-up, out-of-tune Chickering

8

upright. My Carnegie Hall audience evaporates, and empty, hose-snagging pews replace the red velvet seats filled with my imagined admirers.

I slam the lid down over the keyboard, gather my music, and storm toward the door at the rear of the sanctuary, slapping at the pews with the palm of my hand as I pass. *Slap, slap, slap.* How silly! Imagining that I perform in Carnegie Hall. *Really!* I'd never play in *any* concert hall.

ॐ   ॐ   ॐ

"Hey, Liberace, Baby."

I tried to ignore Vernon Slappey as I traipsed down the church steps and headed toward our house next door. If there was one thing I couldn't stand, it was being made fun of.

"You ain't even gon' say *hello?*" He called to my back.

I stopped and turned around. "Hello, Vernon." I grimaced at him and then continued on toward home. Vernon had been hired to keep the pine straw in the church yard swept up, but he spent about as much time leaning on the rake as he did raking. He wore a frayed dress shirt, sleeves rolled up and buttons unbuttoned. His white chest hair hung on his chest like corn tassels.

Vernon had once accused me of being *hoighty-toighty* because I liked classical music. I tried to explain to him that I didn't *choose* to like that kind of music. That came with the package: Quincy Bruce, red, wrinkled, squalling baby girl born six weeks early to ex-high school basketball player and former cheerleader. Baby girl with brown hair and brown eyes, who despised collard greens, and who loved Schubert more than Elvis. That's just the way I was.

Mrs. Swisher, watering her pansies next door, waved at me as I started up our front porch steps. "Hello, Quincy dear. You been over to the

9

church practicing?"

"Yes, Ma'am." I continued up the steps. If I gave her a chance, she'd start talking and not stop until she'd talked my ear clear off. At least she didn't call me Liberace-baby.

"How's your Aunt Addy? I ain't seen her for a while." Mrs. Switzer let the hand in which she held the water hose go slack so that the stream of water puddled around her feet.

"She's just fine. Mama and I went over and saw her last week." I stepped over Buster, our spoiled-rotten-hound, who slept at the top of the steps. Like everybody else in town, we had a wood frame house with peeling paint, tin roof, front porch swing, ice tea in the refrigerator, and a dog sleeping in an inconvenient place.

"Well, you tell her I said *hello* the next time you see her, you hear? Yo' Mama's sister is such a fine lady."

"Yes, ma'am, I sure will."

I wasn't ready to go inside and hear what Daddy had to say, so I leaned against the front door and watched Mrs. Switzer turn off the water hose, wipe her hands on her apron, and then lumber up the steps to her front door. Over in the church yard, Vernon, having no one to talk to, swiped at the pine straw. There must have been ten thousand pine trees surrounding Ellerbie. Where there wasn't a field, there were pine trees, and Ellis Turpentine Company had attached collecting buckets to every tree big enough to hold one. The town stunk of turpentine.

If you could even call Ellerbie a town. From the city limits sign on the end where the road headed north, you could see all the way to the city limits sign at the other end where the road headed south toward Wilson, where Addy lived. There were three stores, one gas station, two churches (Baptist and Methodist), and about four hundred sinners (so said Daddy) living in two rows of houses, one on this side of the highway and one on

10

the other. Daddy's sinners owned several hundred cows, pigs, and chickens, a motley collection of mutts of unknown parentage, and a few mules stagnating in their stalls because everyone had tractors now. That was Ellerbie: pigs, chickens, turpentine, and sinners. And not one single concert pianist.

I'd begun to feel like one of those sparklers I got in my Christmas stocking every year. I'd light one and watch it flame down to the last weak sparkle. I was on my last sparkle, and, short of a miracle, my last sparkle was about to flame out. All the famous pianists began serious study long before sixteen. Usually with the support of their parents. Mine kept prodding me to stop wasting my time. To be reasonable. They reminded me on a regular basis of what a crazy notion I'd gotten in my head, and that I should set my sights on something useful, like becoming a teacher or a secretary. But if Abraham Lincoln could go from log-splitter to President of the United States, I didn't see why my notion was so crazy.

Nights, before I drifted off to sleep, I imagined the dream collector, gnarled and slobbering with greed, shambling toward me, his fingers twitching, about to snatch away my dream. I could hear him dragging his feet. *Scritch, scratch. Scritch, scratch.* Like Vernon's rake. What did he do with his stolen dreams? Give them to other people? Bury them in a graveyard on the far side of the universe?

ॐ　　　ॐ　　　ॐ

I hated *talks. Quincy, you need to help more around the house. Quincy, what you did yesterday was conduct unbecoming of the preacher's daughter. Quincy, your uncle Roger needs help with the tobacco.* But what was I to do? My friends had to endure the same thing. Only they had brothers and sisters with whom to divide up the talks. As an only child I had no one to help take the load off.

I went to the kitchen and stood, shifting from one foot to the other, waiting, reviewing my actions of the past few days, trying to determine what I might have done wrong or what I should have done that I didn't do. Daddy sat at the table. Mama had her back to me. She stirred something on the stove which I knew to be turnip greens because of the smell. Outside, the March wind whipped at a branch of the chinaberry tree, drumming it against the house. *Thud, thud, thud.* I willed them to hurry so I could get back to the book I'd started the evening before. I liked to read almost as much as I liked to play the piano, but I didn't let on to any of my friends how much I read. It was bad enough being different because I was the preacher's daughter and because I liked my kind of music. I sure wasn't going to set myself further apart by admitting how much I read. Once, Bobby Souter told me I sounded like a book when I talked. After that, I tried to remember to sound like everyone else. Mama was the only one who knew how much I read, but some of my reading I kept secret even from her. Like the book I'd just started — *Lady Chatterley's Lover.* I hid the books I didn't want to be caught with on the shelf with the Sunday hats I hated to wear.

Mama turned around, wiped her hands on her apron, and came over to stand beside Daddy. A shiver ran down my spine. She looked ten years older than she had at breakfast, and Daddy wore his preacher face even though it was only Tuesday. Had someone died?

Daddy cleared his throat, took a deep breath, and blurted out, "Quincy, your Mama and me are going to Africa as missionaries." He swallowed, and then added in a softer tone, "You'll have to stay here."

My mouth fell open. I looked at Mama expecting her to explain that I hadn't heard what I thought I'd heard, but she breathed in a quick breath, squeezed her eyes shut, and then let her breath out in a long shaky stream. Her forehead gathered into deep folds as she opened her eyes and

12

tilted her head toward me. "Honey, There's no high school for Americans where we'll be in the Congo."

They were teasing, weren't they? *Going to Africa?* I failed to see the humor, but I almost laughed anyway, thinking I needed to acknowledge the bit of fun they were having with me.

"Sometimes we have to make sacrifices to do the Lord's work," Daddy said.

So I was going to be a sacrifice? Like Isaac?

He pulled back his basketball-player legs from where they sprawled underneath the table, sat up straight, and after setting his preacher face more firmly in place, began explaining how they hadn't wanted to tell me until they'd worked out the details. They'd checked on the school situation with other missionaries and with the Southern Baptist Convention Board, and . . .

Dread spread through me from the tips of my toes to the hair on my head as I began to understand they weren't teasing. Where would I live while they traipsed around Africa? One choice was too nightmarish to think of, and the other about as likely to happen as a concert pianist from Ellerbie. Drops of perspiration trailed down my face and collected in my armpits as I considered the hellish prospect of living with Daddy's sister, Aunt Mildred. She and Uncle Roger lived out beyond the cotton field bordering our backyard. Sometimes, I'd glance over at their house and see the sun reflecting off their tin roof like hell fire. That was fitting, I guess, since Aunt Mildred preached a lot about Hell. She'd also been gifted with the ability to read between the lines of the Good Book. What God meant to say and didn't, Daddy's sister knew, and she was more than glad to share that information. She preached to anyone who would listen that Methodists and Presbyterians had strayed from the true faith, and that Catholics . . . Well, Catholics had fallen so far from grace there was no point in even

13

talking about them. She hated Negroes, Jews, and Japanese war brides. She despised Yankees who sped through town on their way to Florida, as well as the ones who didn't.

And she couldn't abide Addy.

Mama's sister was all the things Aunt Mildred scorned and all the things Aunt Mildred envied. Addy had beauty, intelligence, and wealth. She was *Vogue*; Aunt Mildred was rumpled up *Sears and Roebuck*. Aunt Mildred was meatloaf; Addy was caviar — not that I had any idea what caviar tasted like or even looked like, but I knew it was supposed to be elegant. Addy met President Franklin D. Roosevelt when she was hospitalized in Warm Springs with polio, and she'd worked for the famous author, Nathan Waterstone. Aunt Mildred had never met anyone famous, although she did meet Mrs. Switzer's Yankee niece who was the only Republican ever to visit Ellerbie. Addy lived in London during the war and experienced the excitement of bombs and Luftwaffe planes. Aunt Mildred had never been more than fifty miles in any direction from her tin roof and didn't see why anyone would want to.

I didn't meet Addy until I was five, because she'd gone to Germany to study languages before I was born. In Heidelberg, she married Warren Simmons, another American studying there. When the war broke out, Warren wanted to fight the Nazis even though the United States hadn't entered the war, so he joined the French Resistance. Addy moved to London to wait for him, remaining there while the Luftwaffe dropped bombs on the city, and U-boats blew up ships in the Atlantic. When the war ended, she returned home a widow.

One sunny afternoon, shortly after the end of the war, someone knocked on our front door. Mama opened the door and gave an excited cry. I ran to see and found Mama clenched in a tight hug with a beautiful woman. Like Mama, the woman had color-crayon brown hair and milk-chocolate eyes. When they finally let go of each other and stood back, each examining the other, I knew the woman was Addy because she looked like a shinier version of Mama. In my five-year-old mind, she seemed as warm as a fireplace in the middle of January and as twinkling bright as the Bethlehem star. She smelled like roses. Mama usually smelled like something in the kitchen.

"My beautiful niece," Addy said, stooping and holding out her arms. I went to her. She hugged me tight, pressing my cheek against something hard. When she let go, I lifted one hand to my face where the hard thing had made an imprint, and at the same time, looked to see what had pressed into my cheek. A locket hung around her neck. When I reached out to touch the locket, she pulled my hand gently away, and didn't answer when I asked if there were pictures inside. Instead, she gave me a birthday gift she'd brought from London — a teddy bear dressed like one of the King's guards. In a flash of understanding, I knew I shouldn't ask about the locket.

There were lots of things I was told to keep my hands off of, so I wasn't offended. Instead, I imagined a mystery. Mama had read the Bobbsey Twin books to me, so I knew about mysteries, and secrets hidden inside drawers and cabinets and lockets. I thought I was lucky to have a beautiful aunt who traveled to faraway places and wore a locket with something mysterious inside!

In London, Addy worked for Nathan Waterstone, famous for his novel, *The Lady*. Aunt Mildred didn't like Addy for a whole bunch of reasons, but her having worked for Nathan Waterstone stood near the top of the list, right underneath Addy being way more beautiful, educated, and rich than she was.

Addy Simmons helped that Nathan Waterstone write a book glorifying adultery, Aunt Mildred would snarl. *No, no, no* I always want to shout,

15

although I never did; I'd been warned too many times about speaking back to my elders. I wanted to say to Aunt Mildred: *Addy didn't help him write* The Lady. *She typed the manuscript and helped him edit grammatical errors.*

The Lady tells the story of an affair between an American journalist stuck in England during the Blitzkrieg and a married woman. After the novel's publication, Nathan scandalized people by announcing in a radio interview that he'd based his story on an actual affair, and that he was the guilty man in the story. He didn't name the woman. *A war waged, yet a sleazy American had the gall to have an affair with a married woman whose husband gallantly sought to defeat a heinous enemy*, one newspaper article said.

The interview set off a flurry of speculation. *Who is she? What kind of woman would be unfaithful to her husband in times such as these?* The names of many women were mentioned, but no one succeeded in proving any of them guilty of being the Lady. The interview also set off a flurry of sales, catapulting Nathan's novel into best-sellerdom.

In many a sermon, Daddy accused the famous author of being a sinful and vile person. "Not *famous*," Aunt Mildred always corrected. "*Infamous!* God forgives people who sin," she'd proclaim. "But them that don't do nothing about sin when they see it are worse than people who sin. Addy Simmons seen it all and she didn't do nothing."

After the war, Addy moved to Wilson, ten miles south of Ellerbie. Nathan, originally from Macon, Georgia, decided to settle there, too, because Addy had described Wilson as a nice, quiet town, and a good place to work. Addy continued to work for Nathan until his death. He wrote four other novels while living in Wilson. I was very proud of my aunt. Working for a famous person sort of made her famous, too.

Nathan died in 1950, but Aunt Mildred couldn't leave off about Addy having worked for someone who confessed his adultery to the world and appeared to be proud of his sin.

They hadn't wanted to tell me until they worked out the details, Daddy had said. I knew, of course, which detail he referred to, and that they would have argued long and hard over that particular detail, Mama wanting me to live with Addy, Daddy wanting me to live with Aunt Mildred. So when Mama told me I'd live with Addy, every cell in my body broke out into a rousing rendition of the Hallelujah Chorus. I had no idea how she'd talked Daddy into letting me live with her sister, but I didn't care. My life was about to turn perfect. Addy was the only person in the entire world that supported my wish to become a pianist. My only ally. And I loved her dearly. Not just because she supported my *outlandish notions*. She was fun. She laughed a lot. She told fascinating stories about life in London and Germany. Life was going to be perfect.

The weeks of packing and making arrangements went by in a flash. I knew I'd miss Mama and Daddy, but parting anxieties didn't trouble me. I was sixteen after all — old enough to live without them, and the pleasure of living with Addy far outweighed any pangs of separation. She had a big, beautiful house, and I'd get to attend Wilson High School, a bigger and better school than Ellerbie High. I'd no longer have to be known as the preacher's daughter, always worried about whether or not I was reflecting well on my Daddy. I wouldn't have to walk out the church door and hear Vernon Slappey call me *Liberace Baby*. And the icing on the cake (or maybe it was the cake itself): Addy had a Steinway grand in her living room.

17

The day of my parents' departure and the day I was to move in with Addy came quickly. Right after lunch, as hellish-hot as the afternoon was, I brought my two battered suitcases and the cardboard box with my books and music to the front porch, and sat down in the swing to wait for her. I guess I thought the sooner I sat down to wait, the sooner she'd come, and the sooner my perfect life would begin. I spread my skirt across the swing slats so as not to wrinkle it; I wanted to look nice for my new beginning. Neighbors hung out on their front porches — something they didn't usually do in the heat of midday — but the Bruces leaving town was an event they didn't want to miss. There weren't many *events* in Ellerbie, so when one happened everybody paid attention.

Later, I realized that at the very moment I sat down to wait, Aunt Mildred started toward our house with a view to stabbing me in the heart. She was about to ruin my perfect life with an accusation that would set off a stream of events that, like a snowball, got bigger and bigger.

Not that I knew anything about snow from first-hand experience. Snow was about as rare in South Georgia as an ice cube in Hell. We were fresh out of ice cubes that day. We'd cleaned out the refrigerator and left the door open so the next tenant — the preacher who was replacing Daddy at his church — wouldn't find mildew inside. With no ice cubes, it was a given that the weather would turn stinking hot. Not one pine so much as fluttered its needles.

Mama and Daddy were busy with last minute packing. They'd subdued whatever guilt they felt over leaving their only child as they packed bags, gathered their wits and maps, and made endless arrangements. I had the notion they might throw in a few words every now and then about missing me, but they were too busy worrying if they had enough mosquito repellant, whether Daddy needed to wear a tie when he preached to the natives, and if they needed to bring along a supply of toilet paper. I thought

18

it might be sort of nice to hear them say, "Quincy, you know we're just going to miss you sooooo much."

Then I saw Aunt Mildred plodding toward our house. My chest tightened. When she was around, she had a way of breathing up all the air, leaving none for anyone else. There'd been a going-away dinner at church the evening before at which Daddy thanked everyone and explained we'd leave quietly the following day. "No fuss. No fanfare." But what applied to others apparently didn't apply to Aunt Mildred.

Darrell had given me an inkling that something was brewing when he'd come over the afternoon before to fetch Buster. He'd agreed to take care of our dog while we were gone. Darrell, Aunt Mildred's middle child, was fourteen years old, and the only cousin I cared to spend much time with. His sister Patsy, a year older than me and as boring as a haystack, had two interests: movie star magazines and fingernails. Every night she cried and moaned over broken nails and chipped nail polish. Then she repaired and repainted. *What color nail polish? Oh, I just can't decide. What do you think, Quincy?* I failed to understand anyone spending so much time on nails. I kept mine short for playing the piano. Bobby, only two years old, was the baby of the family. Even though Darrell was my favorite of the three, I thought he listened a little too often to what he shouldn't be listening to, and repeated a little too often what didn't need repeating.

He tracked me down in the kitchen while I was finishing up the supper dishes.

"Hey," he said, entering and letting the door slam behind him. "Tomorrow's the big day. Y'all going off to Africa!" He had his baseball glove tucked under his arm.

"You know perfectly well I'm not going." I put the last dish in the dish drain and turned around to lean on the sink.

"Yeah, I know. I meant yo' mama and daddy. And what else I

19

know is you gonna git too big for your britches when you go and live with Addy Simmons."

"It's a good thing that's none of your business, isn't it?"

"Mama says you're gonna' be spoiled rotten when you go live in that big house with a maid, all that other stuff."

"I don't know what other stuff you're talking about."

"Her and that man."

"Why can't you call Nathan Waterstone by his name, instead of saying *that man?*" I felt my face grow warm.

"Because that man was sinful. Mama says . . ."

"I don't want to hear what she says. Sin isn't contagious."

"Well, who's to say?" He shrugged. "Anyway, I come to get Buster and to say goodbye." He slipped on his baseball glove and pounded it with his fist. "Me and that ol' hound are going to have us a good old time while you folks are gone." He pounded the glove again. "We're gonna' go hunting and find us some partridges and some squirrels. Maybe even a coon."

"And throw rocks at them?" I went over and sat at the table.

"Nope, I'm getting a BB gun for my birthday."

"That's just grand. Now we'll all be dodging BBs. It doesn't bother you that BBs can put someone's eyes out?"

"You ain't gonna be here so you got no call to worry. You could of lived with us. Don't you like us?"

"Of course I like you; don't be silly. And don't say *ain't.*"

"Well, *la de da.* Like I said, you gonna git too big for your britches when you go and live with that woman."

"And like I said, that's none of your business."

Darrell smirked. "Everybody knows what that Nathan Waterstone she worked for done."

"I guess they should since he wrote a book about what he did." My shoulders tightened.

"And that woman he took up with . . . I can't believe he wrote a book about such goings on. *The Lady*! She sure wasn't no lady. I bet your Daddy don't even let you read that book."

"I read what I want to. Not everybody has to know what I read, do they?"

"Nah, I guess not. Do you want to go pitch a few baseballs? One last time?"

"Sorry Darrell. Not tonight. I'll miss you."

"Yeah, I'll miss you too. Well, I guess I'll go track down somebody else. I'm going to go get Buster now. I guess you already said goodbye to that ol' dog." He waved and headed toward the door. "Bye now."

ॐ   ॐ   ॐ

Whenever Aunt Mildred came to our house, which was a little too often, instead of coming across the cotton field behind us and entering through our back door, she skirted the edge of the field to enter the street several houses down. That gave her the opportunity to stop along the way and hand out advice to whoever was outside pulling dandelions or raking pine straw. I watched as she stopped to talk to Mr. Boomer. Then she meandered to the house next door and exchanged a few words with Mrs. Switzer before continuing in my direction, squinting her eyes against the sun. She waved at me. I wiggled my fingers back at her. When she reached the bottom of the steps, she leaned on the railing and huffed a few times, trying to catch her breath. Her dishwater-blonde hair, streaked with gray and cut in a blunt line, lay plastered to her head. Sweat stains spread like pancakes around her armpits. She wiped her brow with her sleeve, and, after blowing out a *whew*, came up onto the porch, stopped a few feet from me and propped her hands on her hips. She smelled of sweat and buttermilk.

"If it just ain't hot enough to fry eggs on the pavement," she said. "Y'all got any ice tea left?"

"No ma'am, the tea's all gone and we've already washed up the dishes."

She studied me for a few seconds and then shook her head. "Don't know what come over your Daddy to let you go off and live with that woman. Some people are just too high and mighty for the rest of us. That woman is prideful, and she ain't the right person to be raising no teenage girl. Not when she worked for that shameless man."

If she thought one person's sin became another's, then what about Jesus consorting with that prostitute? But Jesus was Jesus, and Addy was Addy. I guess what applied to Jesus didn't apply to her. I crossed my arms and hid my clenched fists in my armpits.

Aunt Mildred narrowed her eyes and blew out a breath that rattled her lips. "You ought to of lived with us and helped us out a bit. Roger could of used some extra help when the peanuts come in, and I ain't forgetting . . ." She pierced me with her steely blue eyes, ". . . you promised to help with Vacation Bible School."

The old crow! I'd never promised any such thing. She reminded me of the flat characters we studied in English class, like Uriah Heep in *David Copperfield* or the aunts in *The Mill on the Floss*. Miss Bailey told us that flat characters weren't representative of real people, but she'd never met Aunt Mildred.

"She don't even make you show proper respect," Aunt Mildred said. "Letting you call her by her first name. *Addy.*" She gave a snort, stared at me for a few seconds, and then let out a huff as she turned toward the front door. "Well, I'll just go on inside and see if I can't help 'em finish packing."

Was I going to be spared a long-winded advice session full of warnings? I blew out a stream of air and felt my shoulders relax.

With Aunt Mildred safely inside the house, *helping* Mama and Daddy, I walked to the edge of the porch and looked down the highway in the direction of Wilson hoping to see Addy's car. When I heard the door slam behind me, I turned to see Daddy setting two suitcases down. Mama, with Aunt Mildred on her heels, followed with two smaller ones.

Mama, looking peeved, collapsed onto the swing. She laid her head back and closed her eyes. "Don't forget to take the left-over food, Mildred. It's on the table, already bagged." She opened her eyes and looked at Daddy. "Winnie, why don't you help her?"

"I wanted to say our goodbyes without her," Mama said when they'd gone.

"Me, too." I sat down beside her.

"Honey, you need to study hard this year." She ran her hand over my face. Her hand smelled of onions.

"I always study hard." She irritated me, and not for the first time, or even the hundredth time. *Behave yourself. Study hard. Make us proud.* My voice must have given away my annoyance; she flinched and lowered her hand to her lap.

"I'm just reminding you that unless you want to be stuck in a college where the Southern Baptist Convention will give us a financial break, you need to earn a scholarship. Your Daddy expects you to take typing classes so you can be a secretary, but I think you can get a scholarship to a good college."

"I'm not going to be a secretary, and I'm not going to a southern Baptist college. I'm going to be a musician."

Mama gripped her forehead in a vise-like grip. "When are you going to be practical, Quincy?" She spit out the words. "Playing the piano won't get you very far in South Georgia. You need to concentrate on earning a scholarship."

I bit my lips. There was no point arguing with her.

She put her hand on my leg. "Quincy . . ." Her voice had softened but I refused to look at her. "It's no fun to be poor. Do you really want to be just a piano teacher earning fifty-cents an hour?"

"*Just* a piano teacher!" I glared at her. "You really don't understand, do you? I want to be a concert pianist, not just a piano teacher."

"People like us don't get to be concert pianists," she snapped.

The sound of a car pulling into the yard put an end to our argument. I pressed my lips together to keep from smiling. I didn't want Mama to see how glad I was to be moving in with Addy. Although, I'm not sure why I cared how Mama felt. She was abandoning me, after all.

Addy parked, got out, and waved as she came toward us, swaying her hips in a way that made her limp barely noticeable. A peach-colored dress fit snugly around her slender waist, and she wore high heels with ankle straps. At the bottom of the steps, she stopped to remove a clump of pine needles impaled on the heel of one shoe, and then came up onto the porch. She'd just returned from Florida, and her skin glowed with a Daytona Beach tan. Her eyes sparkled. The sun had streaked her hair with gold.

"Finally, the big day is here," she said smiling as she came over to hug Mama and me. "I'm sorry I'm late, but making plans for a little surprise took more time than I anticipated." She winked at Mama and then teased me with a raised eyebrow and a twinkle in her eye. I didn't have time to wonder about the surprise, because just then Deacon Bradford, who was to drive Mama and Daddy to Savannah to board their ship, drove into the yard and parked behind Addy.

What happened in the next few minutes blurs and twists in my memory like time caught in a whirlwind: Daddy throwing my suitcases into the trunk of Addy's car; Aunt Mildred rattling off advice to Mama and Daddy; neighbors, in spite of being asked to let us depart without a fuss, showing up to see us off.

Addy and Mama were saying their final goodbyes, and Daddy and Mr. Bradford were checking to make sure the lights in the house had been turned off, when Aunt Mildred sidled up to me with narrowed eyes. My heart skipped a beat, and I took a step backwards.

"When you go and live with that woman, the devil will pluck you up as easy as pulling a rotten tomato off the vine." She glanced over to where Mama and Addy stood, their heads bent together. "Your mama got herself in trouble not keeping her legs together, and now they're sending you off to live with that woman who had the same problem." My breath caught. Aunt Mildred nodded at Addy. "She was just lucky and didn't get caught like your Mama did." Turning back to me, she paused to run her tongue over her lips. "With Addy Simmons to guide you, you're going to wind up in the same fix as your Mama. Pregnant, if you ain't careful."

Heat surged through my body. "I'm not winding up in any kind of fix," I spat back at Aunt Mildred. "And Addy is a good person."

Slowly, slowly, Aunt Mildred cocked her head at me. "She ain't no good person. Not after what she done. Just ask her who the Lady was." She curled her lips in a sneer. "She herself was that sinful woman."

CHAPTER 2

I couldn't think of anything awful enough to say to Aunt Mildred, but even if I'd thought of something, I couldn't have said it. My body shook. My tongue was paralyzed. Had we stood on the edge of the earth, I'd have shoved her over and cheered while she plunged into hell. I was barely aware of Mama and Addy finishing their conversation and coming over to me, and then of someone steering me toward Addy's car. I barely listened when Mama echoed Daddy's words as he gave me a last minute lecture — something about being good, behaving myself, and signing up for typing class. As we said our good-byes, no one noticed how my body rattled with anger.

Addy and I drove away. I watched Aunt Mildred grow smaller and smaller in the rearview mirror until, after a turn in the road, she disappeared behind a clump of pines.

Addy flitted her glance at me. "You'll miss them," she said.

She'd misinterpreted my clenched hands and ragged breathing, but I nodded. How could I tell Addy that someone had accused her of adultery? Or that the same someone predicted my downfall? Mama had done what she'd done; there was no way to change that. But Aunt Mildred had shamed me for something I'd never done, that I'd never do, that I'd never think of doing. And as for Addy . . . How dare Aunt Mildred accuse her of something so vile? Addy was the best person I knew. I'd never known her to do anything mean or sinful. I vowed I'd discover who the real Lady had been, and when I did, I'd grind the truth into Aunt Mildred's every pore.

"Are you going to be all right?" Addy rested her fingers on my arm.

"Of course I'm going to be all right." I forced a smile and made myself take long deep breaths.

"I have a couple surprises for you."

That was so like Addy: planning something to ease me into my new life. Not that I needed easing; I was quite happy to jump in head first. "Are you going to make me guess?"

"Of course. My only hint is that the first surprise is going to keep you ver-r-r-ry busy." She waved at the Ethridge sisters clunking past in their old Ford.

"You got me a puppy?"

"Certainly not. I'm a cat person. You know that."

"You signed me up for crochet classes?"

"Right." She laughed. "*You* crocheting? *You* who talked Darrell into collecting Mildred's crocheted masterpieces and nailing them to the cow stall?"

"She has those awful things on every stick of furniture in her house. I thought I'd relieve her of a few and let the cows enjoy them." I smiled at the memory. "That wasn't as bad as when Darrell and I streaked around the church in the nude to entertain the Women's Missionary Society."

Addy laughed. "I'll say not. How old were you then?"

"Six." I'd enjoyed that bit of mischief, not because I liked running around naked, but because I'd dared to rebel. "Tell me what the surprise is. You know I'm not good at guessing."

"Florida State University in Tallahassee is only about thirty minutes south of Wilson."

"Yeeeesss." I didn't know why she was telling me what I already knew.

"FSU has a program for talented high school students. I've arranged an audition."

I caught my breath, and a huge smile engulfed my face. Only minutes from home and Addy had given me what I wanted most. While she focused on the road, giving me time to digest her news, I relaxed and stretched out my legs. My whole body felt light, and hope tingled through my veins like liquid candy. Within five minutes I'd gone from being so angry I wanted to cry, to being so happy I wanted to cry. I knew the anger would reappear, but right then I wanted to conjure up my magnificent future. I closed my eyes and, leaning my head back to rest on seat leather soft as a baby's skin and smelling as sweet, I imagined the course of my life. After studying with a fabulous teacher at FSU, I'd go to a conservatory. Then, after suitable experience, I'd perform at Carnegie Hall. Instead of a ghost audience in a church sanctuary, I'd play for a real one.

I worried, though. My piano lessons so far had been about as serious as a monkey at Sunday dinner. Mrs. Todd listened for the first few minutes. Or pretended to. Then she'd trot off to the kitchen to see to supper. I'd hear the clank of a spoon hitting the sides of a pot as she stirred collard greens. *Just keep playing, dear,* she'd say. I'd keep playing. *That's just fine dear. You're sounding right good.* Once, when she asked me to play *The Skater's Waltz,* I played *Malaguena* instead. She didn't notice.

I knew that talent and craft are two different things, and that I lacked craft. Sometimes, too, I feared my talent might not be as magnificent as I imagined. No matter how much I tried to brush away that fear, the thought kept reappearing, hissing at me like a Halloween ghost: *You haven't an ounce of talent. You haven't an ounce of talent. You haven't . . .*

I became so engrossed in my thoughts that, for several minutes, I didn't realize we were traveling in the opposite direction from Wilson, heading north toward Tifton instead. "Where are we going?"

"Did you forget I have a couple surprises for you? I only told you about the first one."

"But, what else?"

"You'll see."

We reached Tifton, and after a few blocks Addy pulled into the parking lot of *Glover's Hardware*, and parked between two Ford pick-ups. I looked at her for an explanation.

"Get out," she said, opening her door. "Bring your suitcases."

Puzzled, not to mention feeling rather stupid lugging my suitcases into a hardware store, I followed her.

The sales clerk at the front counter stopped weighing out nails for a customer and looked up at us. "Why, good afternoon, Miz Simmons. What brings you to Tifton?" A flush spread over his freckled face.

"Hello, Sam. We need to visit that big box you have back there in the corner. "

"Well, go right ahead, and if there's anything I can help y'all with, just holler."

"Sure will, Sam."

We headed to the rear of the store. I looked back to see Sam and his customer watching Addy. She often had an effect on men that left them staring or stuttering. Mr. Hodges over at the drug store always dropped whatever he was doing to rush over and take care of her, and I could name a few others who did the same. Like Mr. Sutton at the Five and Dime who riveted his eyes on her like she was the last peppermint in the candy store. I often wondered why she hadn't married again.

29

We walked past the faucet display, the shelves of hand tools, the stacks of light bulbs, the electric cords, back to where the Salvation Army collection box stood among stacks of paint cans.

"Dump your clothes in the box," Addy said. "Save a change for tomorrow but dump everything else. Shoes and all." She propped her hands on her hips. "We're going to Atlanta. You're getting a new wardrobe for your sixteenth birthday."

∼ ∼ ∼

We set out on the five-hour drive to Atlanta, my thoughts see-sawing between auditioning at FSU, and owning a closet full of new clothes. I tried to focus on the clothes, because the idea of auditioning scared me silly. Rose was my favorite color, so I wanted to buy something that color. An emerald green dress and a blue wool skirt and matching sweater would be nice, too. Gathered skirts were popular. I could use several of those as well as a new crinoline. Mine had gone limp. And Bermuda shorts. Everybody wore Bermuda shorts except for me. Daddy had somehow gotten it into his head that bare legs were sinful. Arm skin was fine; leg skin wasn't. But he was on his way to Africa. What could he do? I wondered if Addy would offer to buy me a winter coat. Sara Miles had a pink cashmere coat; I wanted a blue one like hers.

I expected students in Wilson to be dressed more like Sarah Miles, the only student in Ellerbie who looked like she could have stepped out of *Seventeen*. Sarah's father owned one of the largest farms in the state and sold enough tobacco, peanuts, and hogs for Sarah to have a brand-spanking new wardrobe every September. She and her mother made a trip to Atlanta at the end of each summer to replenish Sarah's wardrobe at Rich's, while the rest of us made do with home-sewn outfits, or clothes from Sears and

Roebuck and Belk-Hudson. Or in my case, with hand-me-downs from Daddy's congregation.

On the other side of Vidalia, Addy turned on the radio and we sang along with Little Richard. When she spied a watermelon stand just before the Warner Robbins city limits, she slammed on the brakes, veered off the road, and screeched to a halt in front of the stand. "Want some watermelon?" she asked.

Addy never carried on about whether she should or shouldn't do something. If she wanted watermelon, she jammed on the brakes at the first watermelon stand and strolled up with a *We'd like some watermelon, please.* When she graduated from Agnes Scott College and wanted to continue her language studies, she found scholarship money and took off for Heidelberg, Germany. She didn't ask anyone's opinion or permission, and she went with no more fanfare than stopping at a watermelon stand. The same thing happened when she decided to get married. In Heidelberg, Addy fell in love with another student, Warren Simmons from Decatur, Georgia. They married, and informed the family after the fact. When the war broke out, Warren joined the French Resistance. Addy, ignoring Grandma's pleas to return home, moved to London. In spite of the bombs, she preferred being in London, closer to Warren. Addy vexed my late grandmother no end. *That girl's always been too impulsive,* she complained.

So my beautiful, impulsive aunt and I sat on a bench, eating slices of watermelon. Juice ran down our chins and necks and seeped down our dresses. We spit the seeds at the ditch and joked about what the people at the check-in desk of our hotel would think when two Georgia peaches showed up with watermelon stains on their dresses.

"Do you think I can be a concert pianist?" I asked when we climbed back in the car. I wanted confirmation that one of those teachers down at FSU, assuming I got into the program, could teach me to sound like Addy's records.

"Sometimes what others think impossible, turns out to be possible after all. I'm the living example of that. The odds are against *anyone* becoming a concert pianist, but you'll work hard. You're going places with your music, Quincy." She dabbed at her mouth with a tissue, cleaning away traces of watermelon juice. "Hand me my lipstick, honey. It's there in my purse somewhere."

I rooted around for the lipstick, found it, and handed her the tube. "Tell me about Nathan Waterstone," I said, watching her steer with one hand while applying Ruby Rose Lipstick with the other.

"Well, that's a broad topic. Exactly what about Nathan Waterstone do you want to hear?"

"How you met him." me, changing the subject.

She laughed. "How many times have I told you that story?"

"All you've told me is that you met him in London. I want to hear every tiny detail."

"All right, then." She took a deep breath and, after handing me back her tube of lipstick, began. "I'd been in London only a few weeks and barely knew a soul. I was scared. Every time that bloody siren went off, we had to scurry to bomb shelters, and I'd wonder if Warren was safe. To be truthful, Warren infuriated me when he joined the French Resistance because the U.S. hadn't entered the war at that point." Her lips twitched and she stared straight ahead at the road.

"Did he really love me?" she asked at length. "I asked that a thousand times. If he was so eager to go off and fight, he must not. But then I'd remind myself of men sacrificing themselves in other wars for home and country, and I'd feel guilty. My thoughts went round and round. Warren loved me. Warren didn't love me. If only I had someone to talk to.

"I tried working on my master's thesis, but how frivolous is working on a thesis when things are exploding around you? Late one afternoon, when I couldn't bear staring at the typewriter another minute, I left my tiny flat and wandered the streets. I walked and walked. Eventually, I became hungry and stopped in front of a pub. Even with black-out curtains I detected a fire blazing in the hearth. A customer opened the door to exit, and a gust of warm air washed over me. I smelled good things to eat. Roasting potatoes. Melting cheese. Something frying. I went inside. A few people sat scattered: some old men in a corner; a couple of soldiers at the bar; a pair of dour-faced middle-aged women near the door."

"I didn't want to put my sad face on public exhibition, so I sat in a dark corner in the flickering shadows of the hearth fire and didn't notice the man at the next table. Not at first. After the waiter took my order, I happened to glance over. Considering the times, I'm sure he'd have caught anyone's attention with his long, blonde hair tied back in a ponytail. Practically every young man I'd seen in the past weeks had the requisite crew cut and wore a neatly pressed uniform, but he wore a rumpled, striped dress shirt with the top few buttons unbuttoned and the sleeves rolled-up. I'm afraid I stared. Thankfully, he didn't notice. A book, a pad of paper, a teapot and cup sat on the table in front of him. Ignoring them, he lounged back in his chair with his body twisted so that one arm fell across the back of the chair while the other rested on the table. He seemed deep in thought. Periodically, his lips would curl in a smile as though he'd just thought of something wonderful.

"A waiter approached him and said something. When the man answered with a Southern drawl, I was astonished and delighted. I rose, went over, and introduced myself, and discovered that he, too, was from Georgia." Addy bit her lip and waited a few moments before continuing.

"Anyway," she said, resuming, ". . . when Nathan invited me to join him, I did. At first we carried on about the war and about growing up in Georgia. He was so easy to talk to, and so willing to listen, I'm afraid I did more than my share of the talking. For weeks I hadn't had anyone to confide in, or to have a serious conversation with. Eventually my worries came pouring out." She shook her head. "I can't believe how I went on and on about how I missed Warren; how sometimes I cursed him for joining the French Resistance; how I feared his not coming back." She forced a laugh. "I'm still embarrassed. But Nathan behaved like a gentleman. He didn't pry. He didn't judge. He just listened. He didn't tell me he was writer until later that evening."

Addy took her eyes off the road long enough to give me a sad smile. "You have no idea how kindly Nathan treated me that evening. When he learned I'd been in Germany working on a master's thesis and thus must be relatively literate, he told me he'd recently published his first book and needed someone to type the manuscript for his second and to help with editing. He confessed he had a problem with commas and everything else that came under the heading of 'punctuation'." She laughed. "He spoke truth when he said that. He offered me the job."

"You typed *Himalayan Adventure.*"

"Yes. Three years had passed since the publication of his first novel. In the interval he traveled: India, Thailand, Nepal, Burma. Nepal provided the inspiration for his second novel." She sounded like she was giving one of the presentations she gave when schools and civic groups invited her to speak about Nathan Waterstone. She had once given one to my class. "I spent the year typing Nathan's manuscript and helping him edit. Sometimes we had difficulty staying awake because of spending the previous night in a bomb shelter. But . . ." She grinned at me. ". . . as scary as those times were, I think you'll have to admit that living in London during the Blitz made for a lot more excitement than living in South Georgia."

"Wouldn't almost anything be more exciting than living in South Georgia?"

We laughed.

"Especially when you spent the years between ages nine and eleven in a hospital bed. Anyway, we finally finished the book, and Nathan sent the manuscript to a publisher."

"Then you waited for the publisher to reply."

"It wasn't a pleasant wait. Nathan had just turned twenty-seven. His parents were pushing him to go to medical school, but Nathan didn't want to be a doctor. He kept making excuses. First, he promised them he'd go after his travels; then he promised to go when he finished the novel.

"Nathan had no work for me after he sent *Himalayan Adventure* to the publisher. But I saw him often. Sometimes we met with friends for tea in the late afternoons. These were mainly other Americans too afraid of German U-boats to attempt the Atlantic crossing. Nathan's British friends had all gone off to fight. We entertained ourselves by slandering the Nazis and defeating Germany with words. Often, we had to dash for bomb shelters." She gave a little laugh. "We were loud and noisy. Rowdiness is a great stress reliever. Then . . ." She stopped.

"Then?"

"Nathan announced that he would never go to medical school. 'I shall either make my living by writing or starve to death trying,' he said. He asked me to return to work and I began typing *The Lady.*" She threw up her right hand in a theatrical gesture. "And that's the story of how Adelaide Simmons met Nathan Waterstone."

When Addy finished her story, we were still two hours away from Atlanta. We rode in silence for a few minutes, and then I lay my head back and napped. When I awoke, the traffic had become heavier. Pine forests and fields of cotton, tobacco, and peanuts had given way to rows of identical houses. They looked like the paper doll cut-outs I made from folded paper when I was little.

"Look, we're almost there." She pointed to Atlanta's skyline looming gray against the dimming sky. The sun, trailing tentacles of rose and lavender, had dipped below the horizon.

"Shall we stop for a bite to eat or would you rather eat at the hotel?"

"I've never eaten in a hotel restaurant. Let's eat there."

$\approx$ $\qquad$ $\approx$ $\qquad$ $\approx$

Had Daddy known that Addy drank wine I'd have spent the next two years with Aunt Mildred. "Just a little secret between us," Addy said when she ordered Riesling. She'd changed into a mint green dress with a low neckline and wore a string of pearls and pearl earrings. I'd changed into the only dress I hadn't stuffed in the Salvation Army box.

The waiter returned with the wine and placed a small stand with an ice bucket next to our table. I watched, intrigued, as he inserted and twisted a device to pop out the cork. I'd never seen a bottle of wine, much less a gadget for removing the cork. He poured a swallow in Addy's glass. She took a sip and nodded her ok. The waiter filled her glass half-full, placed the bottle in the container of ice, and went away.

I memorized the routine — twist out cork, pour out a few swallows, taste, fill glass half-full, place bottle on ice, and finally, drink wine in tiny sips. I felt my level of sophistication edge up a notch. I definitely wanted to be more sophisticated. Except for music and books, I felt about as worldly-wise as a carrot, and my clothes didn't help. When I'd walked into the restaurant in my faded dress, which was god knows how old, and looked around at all the silks and satins, I felt like I'd just wandered in from the swamp. I half expected to look down and see webbed feet. I fantasized about how I'd look wearing something fine the following evening. Maybe the rose-colored dress I hoped to find.

Addy, giving no hint that sitting at the table with an ill-dressed nobody bothered her, sipped her wine and smiled at me over the rim of her glass. I felt delightfully wicked sitting so close to a bottle of wine. I wondered where the Bible said we weren't supposed to drink wine. If Jesus was allowed, then why not everybody else?

The waiter returned with menus. Addy urged me to try new things, so I ordered asparagus soup, boeuf bourguignon, and crème brulee. I had no idea what *bourguignon* meant, or *brulee*, but I was sure both ranked several steps above the peanut butter and jelly sandwich I'd had the previous evening.

Addy was saying something about asparagus when my mind took off in a different direction. I'd tried all afternoon to forget, but in spite of the glamor of being in a restaurant rich with white linen, sterling, crystal, and waiters in tuxedos, my thoughts went back to Aunt Mildred's accusations, and a shiver ran down my spine. *Just ask her who the Lady was.* Except for the Bible, her Sunday school lesson book, and the occasional article in *Ladies Home Journal,* Aunt Mildred didn't read. Had she bothered to read *The Lady,* she'd have seen that the description of Lady Isabelle Duncan — the name Nathan gave to his Lady — didn't fit Addy.

I don't know if Addy was an expert at reading my feelings, or if I was just bad at hiding them. "What's wrong?" she asked.

She'd drag it out of me sooner or later, so I decided I might as well tell her. Not everything, of course. I wouldn't repeat Aunt Mildred's accusation about her being the Lady or her prediction that I'd follow in Mama's footsteps. "Aunt Mildred," I said and sighed.

"What has she done this time?"

"She said I should have lived with them and helped her with Vacation Bible School and Uncle Roger with the peanuts."

"The nerve of the woman. Of course, you shouldn't. You should be practicing. Now don't you worry about Mildred Perch." She waved her hand in dismissal.

"She thinks the devil is going to grab me and cart me off to hell."

"Oh good lord." Addy let out an exasperated sound. "The devil doesn't grab people and cart them off to hell. People commit themselves to the devil with purpose and forethought." She reached over and patted my hand. "Come on, honey, we're going to have fun for two whole years."

In truth, the idea of the devil didn't bother me that much. I'd begun to classify him in the same category as the boogey man: a character invented to keep people in line. Aunt Mildred was the one that bothered me. "I hate the way she judges people."

"I suppose that's one of the most neglected verses in the Bible. *Judge not that ye be not judged.*"

"That must be the one verse she doesn't know."

"Mildred Perch needs to worry about her own sins."

"What are those?" Aunt Mildred's sins fascinated me.

"You just mentioned one. She judges people. Without much evidence, I dare say. She claims murder is wrong, yet she, and people like her, promote war. Often in the name of religion. And the spoils of war go to the victors, don't they? That's stealing."

While we talked, a Negro waiter placed a basket of rolls on the table and then went away without speaking. "There's another of her sins." Addy nodded toward the waiter. "She condemns a whole race of people because of skin color."

"You have a Negro maid."

"Yes, I do. But do you know any other jobs Earlene can get? Other

38

than working in the fields?" She reached for a roll.

I shook my head.

"I hope she's better off working for me than she would be picking cotton. Especially since she has to support a son in college." Addy opened the roll and buttered one side. She took a bite, put the roll down, and then lifted her glass of wine, holding the glass in front of her for a moment, studying it. "The cream will rise to the top," she said at length.

Confused, I examined her glass of wine. Was part of the wine called *cream*?

Seeing my puzzled look, she laughed. "Wait another hundred years. Negros will be like us. The smart ones will rise to the top, while the ignorant ones remain at the bottom. Both races will have their share of highly successful people, and we'll have *poor white trash* and *poor black trash*."

I found that hard to imagine.

"And so much for Mildred Perch." She waved her hand in dismissal, winked at me, and held her glass toward me. "Here's to the next two years, and to you becoming a musician."

We clinked glasses — water tumbler to wine glass.

"Can I have a sip of wine?" I suddenly felt reckless.

"Well . . ." She raised her eyebrows and leaned toward me with a look of conspiracy. "I could slip you a taste, but if they arrest me for providing alcohol to a minor, you'll have to live with Aunt Mildred."

"Forget that I asked," I said and threw up my hands in mock despair.

Her eyes twinkled. "For someone who has the devil after her, I wouldn't . . ."

A shadow fell over us, and we looked up to see the tall, red-headed woman who had appeared beside out table.

"Aha, she still speaks of the devil," the woman said in a throaty voice.

"Elizabeth Walker! You didn't tell me you were coming to Atlanta," Addy exclaimed, rising. She hugged her friend. I'd met Mrs. Walker before. She'd dropped by on many occasions when I visited my aunt.

"I didn't tell you because I haven't seen you, my dear. Don't forget you were in Daytona enjoying the beach while the rest of us were sweltering in Wilson. My wardrobe needs a Richs' fix," she spread her arms in a dramatic gesture, ". . . so here I am. And here's your pretty niece. Hello, Quincy, sugar." She patted me on the shoulder. "Don't tell me you're here to help buy out Rich's, too?" Her husky voice resonated a little too loudly and heads turned in our direction. As usual, Addy's red-headed friend wore flamboyant clothes — a low-cut, clingy red dress, large hoop earrings, and a necklace with the pendant nestling in her cleavage.

"Sit down, Elizabeth." Addy motioned to a chair. "Or should I call you Scarlet?" She nodded at Mrs. Walker's red dress.

"Hon', I have one more husband to go before you can call me Scarlet." She sat down and propped her arms on the table. "What's this about the devil?"

"One of Quincy's lovely relatives thinks the devil is hiding around every corner, ready to snatch her up."

"Oh Lordy, sugar, I can tell you that isn't so or he'd have snatched me up ages ago. If you don't believe me just ask your aunt here." Unlacing her fingers, she held her palm toward Addy. "She's *the* leading South Georgia expert on the devil."

"What do you mean?"

"You didn't know she spent her time in Germany studying the devil? Waiter!" Mrs. Walker held up her hand to stop a passing waiter. "Bring me grilled chicken and a salad, please." She turned back to Addy and grinned. "You haven't told Quincy about your stint with the devil?"

I tilted my head toward Addy. "Tell me."

She gave a dismissive wave as though her *stint with the devil* lacked importance. "I did my master's thesis on *Faust*, that's all."

Our waiter appeared, balancing two bowls of soup on a tray. He placed the soup in front of us and then looked at Mrs. Walker. "Can I get you something, Ma'am?"

"Honey, I already flagged down that cute little waiter with the black curls and asked for grilled chicken and salad. Just bring me some ice tea and a wine glass." She pointed at his vest. "You're about to lose your button there."

His hand flew to the bottom button of his vest which hung by a thread. "Yes, Ma'am. Thank you, Ma'am. Ice tea. Wine glass. Grilled chicken." He scribbled on his pad and then disappeared.

"Don't wait for me," Mrs. Walker said, fluttering her fingers at us. "Eat, eat. Don't let your soup get cold."

Addy and Mrs. Walker talked as though they hadn't seen each in years, even though it had been only days. I ate my soup, and then the main course when it arrived, half-listening to them until, during a lull in the conversation, I asked Addy about *Faust*.

"Faust sold his soul to the devil," she said, scooping up a glob of something called aspic. "You've heard of Goethe?"

"The German Shakespeare, you told me once. But I guess nobody else in South Georgia has heard of him. Except for Mrs. Walker." I nodded at Addy's friend who had followed our exchange with dancing eyes.

Addy laughed. "Oh, I imagine there are a few others who have heard of Goethe. Or at least they've heard of *Faust*, his best known work. Faust has several academic degrees, but he wants more than just degrees and knowledge. He wants something to make him truly happy. He signs a

41

contract with Mephistopheles, another name for the devil, in which he agrees to be Mephistopheles' servant in hell in exchange for true happiness."

"Does he find true happiness?"

"You'll have to read the play."

"I can't read German."

"You can read a translation."

I looked at Mrs. Walker who had followed our exchange with obvious enjoyment, her mouth puckered in a teasing smile. She looped a finger around her pearls, and slid the finger back and forth as though polishing them. "Tell her about Faust and Gretchen," she prodded Addy.

Addy rolled her eyes. "Elizabeth, sometimes I think you have a one track mind. I'm sure Quincy has no interest in Faust and Gretchen. She has new clothes and a piano audition on her mind." She winked at me.

At this point, dinner had lasted a little too long. Exhaustion weighted every muscle from my toes to my ears, and I wanted to go to bed. I'd have to hear about Faust and Gretchen another day. Addy looked tired, too. A few minutes later, declining dessert, we said good night to Mrs. Walker and went to our room.

❧   ❧   ❧

I snuggled in between starched white sheets, pulled the navy bedspread over me, and managed one more question before sleep took me away. "Did Goethe really believe in the devil? Once, I heard someone say the devil doesn't exist. That the people who translated the Bible didn't translate that word correctly."

"Use whatever word you like, honey, evil exists. Think of Hitler! Think of Stalin." She turned back her bedcovers and arranged the pillows, but instead of crawling in bed, she sat down on the edge. "I think *Devil* means anything that prevents a person from following his rightful path. And nothing will deter you from yours. So forget about that character." She leaned over and ruffled my hair. "Think about new clothes, not the devil."

CHAPTER 3

I jumped out of bed the following morning and, in about the same amount of time needed to play the *Minute Waltz*, slipped into my dress and ran a comb through my hair. Addy dressed with excruciating slowness. She spent forever choosing her dress, styling her hair, putting on makeup, filing her nails. I looked conspicuously at my watch.

"Rich's doesn't open until ten." Her eyes teased. She removed a jewelry case from her luggage and, after rifling through it, withdrew her gold locket.

"That seems to be your favorite piece of jewelry," I said, watching as she fastened the locket around her neck.

Ignoring my comment, she checked her appearance in the mirror, running her hands down her hips to smooth her dress. "I should have brought along a copy of *Faust* for you to read while I dress."

"No thank you. I'm interested in clothes this morning, not the devil."

"Thank goodness."

ೞ   ೞ   ೞ

We returned at the end of the day loaded down with shopping bags.

"Oh, Lordy, I'm tired," Addy said, dumping bags on my bed. "I need to get into something comfortable," She kicked off her shoes, one landing next to her suitcase in the corner and the other clumping against the nightstand. She began unbuttoning her blouse.

I added my shopping bags to the pile on my bed. When I'd protested her generosity, Addy countered with: "Don't be silly. You're like my daughter. Besides, I have no one else to spend money on." Thanks to her, I had a whole new wardrobe: dresses, blouses, skirts, underwear, night gowns, Bermuda shorts, and a cashmere coat — a blue one exactly like I wanted.

My legs ached from all the walking around and standing on hard floors. I was pushing aside packages to make room to curl up on the bed, when the phone rang. Addy froze. She'd finished unbuttoning her blouse and had pulled one arm out of a sleeve. She let the blouse hang there, one arm in, one arm out, her white lace slip showing.

"Can you answer that?" she asked after the second ring. "Say I'm not available." She turned her back to me and waited.

"Call for Mrs. Simmons," the hotel operator said.

"She can't come to the phone right now."

"I'll tell the gentleman to call back."

"Who …?" But the operator had already hung up. "A man," I said to Addy. "The operator didn't say who."

At first she didn't respond. "Call room service," she said then, still without looking at me. "Get hamburgers. Or whatever sounds good." She slipped into the bathroom, leaving the door ajar. I heard the click of buttons as her clothes dropped on the floor and, a few seconds later, the sound of water running in the bathtub.

A man had called and she didn't want to know who?

I called room service. I was ravenous. At lunch I'd limited myself to a chicken salad sandwich and a few chips because I didn't want to be seen overeating in a fine place like Rich's Magnolia Room. Especially since on my first visit to a dressing room I'd discarded my old dress in the waste paper basket and come out feeling elegant wearing a new one. When we went to the Magnolia Room I thought a chicken salad sandwich on a small croissant and five chips were about as much as elegance would bear.

Thirty minutes later a waiter wheeled in a service cart with our food and a bouquet of flowers. "For Mrs. Simmons," he said, pointing to the arrangement of white roses, baby's breath, fern, and purple heather.

I signed the check, adding a tip of five percent and dating it like Addy had instructed me. As soon as the waiter left, I pulled out the tiny envelope stuck between sprigs of heather. The card inside was blank. Who would send flowers without saying who they were from?

I slathered my hamburger with ketchup and mustard and sat down on the end of my bed to eat, and to wonder about a phone call from a man Addy didn't want to talk to and a bouquet of roses with an unsigned card. When she finished her bath, Addy barely glanced at the flowers. She pulled a chair over to the cart and began eating and chattering about our day.

After supper, I left the bathroom door partially open when I went in to brush my teeth. I hadn't meant to spy; I just hadn't bothered to close the door. I saw Addy's reflection in the bathroom mirror as she bent over to smell the bouquet. She closed her eyes and buried her face in the blossoms for a few moments. Then she drew back and, running a finger over the petals, smiled.

In the ninth grade we had to make a scrapbook for Georgia history class. I'd pasted in pictures of famous Atlanta attractions, wondering if I'd ever get to see them. Addy surprised me the morning after our shopping spree by taking me on a tour of those sites. She hired a taxi and off we went to see the Coca-Cola Building and the house where Margaret Mitchell wrote *Gone With the Wind*. Then we drove out to Stone Mountain. When we'd had our fill of staring at the unfinished sculptures of Robert E. Lee, Jefferson Davis, and Stonewall Jackson carved into the largest piece of exposed granite in the world, we returned to downtown Atlanta and lunched in a restaurant on Peachtree Street before going to Grant's Park to see the Cyclorama.

I felt an ache in my chest as we gazed at the dead and wounded soldiers in the gigantic circular canvas depicting the Battle of Atlanta. Addy folded both hands over her heart as she stared with downturned lips at the mutilated soldiers. I suspected the Cyclorama reminded her of Warren's death and of what she'd seen during the London Blitz.

"There's one thing that puzzles me," I said, trying to divert her attention to something more pleasant than dying soldiers as our taxi took us away from Grant's Park.

"What's that?" Her voice was flat, and she stared out the window.

"Why did Nathan decide to announce in a radio interview that the affair in *The Lady* really happened?"

She shrugged. "Who knows why Nathan did what he did? At any rate, his announcement created sales. Everyone talked about the book. *Who was she? Who could she have been?* People were glad to have something to think about other than the war."

After a quick visit to the Georgia State Capitol building we returned to our hotel in a happier mood.

"You know who Arthur Rubenstein is, don't you?" Addy asked as she fumbled in her purse for the room key.

"Of course I know who he is. He's one of the most famous pianists in the world."

"He's giving a concert tonight. . . ." Along with the room key, she pulled two blue tickets from her purse and waved them in front of me. ". . . and we're going."

My eyes widened. "Rubenstein is in Atlanta?"

"Yeesssss." She unlocked the door. "You didn't think we were going to fly off to New York or Paris to hear him, did you?"

I laughed. Then I laughed again. If I'd been forced to make a choice, I'd have chosen hearing Rubenstein over new clothes any day.

♫   ♫   ♫

We stood at the entrance to the amphitheater in Chastain Park and looked down to where the piano stretched across the stage.

"I see why they call the piano *grand,*" I said. "I've never seen one so huge."

"A concert grand. Maybe you'll play one on a stage like this someday."

"I *will.*"

"I admire your determination, Quincy. I hope your ambition never wanes." A cloud drifted over her face — a tiny tightening of jaw, the merest narrowing of eyes. "Let's find our seats," she murmured, looking away. She led, and I followed her down the long flight of steps to our seats. What had that look been about?

The amphitheater began to fill. The shiny black ebony of the piano reflected a symphony of colors — red from an usher's jacket, the yellow of a lady's dress, turquoise, white, pink. God answered my prayer when I pleaded for tall people to sit behind me and only short ones in front. A dwarfish woman smelling of cough drops lowered herself into the seat in front and had the good grace to slouch, leaving me a full view of the stage.

The lights dimmed. A hush fell over the audience. A burst of applause erupted when Mr. Rubenstein walked onto the stage. Such a little man to play such a huge piano. I'd expected him to look more like a god than an ordinary mortal, but despite his black tuxedo, he looked as common as the butcher down at Winn-Dixie. He had a big nose, a triangular face, and his hair stood up in one spot. However, his ordinariness faded away when he straightened from his bow. His eyes crinkled, and his lips broadened into a magnificent smile. I barely breathed as he positioned himself on the bench, turned to the audience, and smiled again. Then, after looking at the keyboard for a few seconds, he lifted his hands, brought them down, and when he played . . .

I crashed and broke into a million pieces from the beauty. From the awfulness. For the first time, I heard how a piano should be played, and I understood then that I knew nothing. A few scratchy recordings, a student recital here and there, a piano tuner rippling chords and arpeggios up and down the keyboard — that had been my schooling in music. Not Beethoven played like that. Nor Mozart. Nor Brahms. And no prayer had ever seemed more prayerful than the Schubert Impromptu. The Raindrop Prelude hypnotized: a repeated bass note — an *a-flat*, then a *g-sharp*, and then the *a-flat* again — persisted as steadily as raindrops. At first, a gentle rain. The rain intensified and then grew gentle again until finally, it ceased.

I was in agony. I'd never play like that.

           ى   ى   ى

I couldn't sleep. I forced myself to lie still until I heard the evenness of Addy's breath, the rhythm of her sleep, and only then, knowing that she slept soundly, did I give way to fitfulness. But I woke her. In the darkness I saw her silhouette as she lifted her head from the pillow.

"What's wrong, honey?"

"Nothing."

She sat up.

"I can't sleep."

"Do you want a back rub?"

"No."

She shifted. The bed springs squeaked. She waited.

"I want to play like Rubenstein, but I can't," I blurted then.

She burst out laughing. "Is that the reason you're tossing and turning? Because you can't play like Rubenstein? When he was your age he couldn't play like that, either."

I didn't think that was true but said nothing.

"When we get home you can practice all day and all night until you sound like Rubenstein. You're not born playing like that."

She rose, came over to my bed, and kissed me on the forehead. "Goodnight, honey. Stop worrying. You're going to be a wonderful pianist."

❧   ❧   ❧

Addy stashed the bouquet of flowers in the backseat when we left Atlanta the next morning. I wondered why, since they'd wilt before we reached Wilson. Especially since we had to stop and visit Warren's aunt who lived in a nursing home in Decatur. I'd heard Addy talk about her husband's aunt, but I'd never met Aunt Rosy.

"If that miserly brother of mine hadn't left his money to all them

50

charities I'd not be living in such a miserable place," Aunt Rosy said, motioning to her drab room. She'd sent Addy to the nursing station to get a box of tissues, so her remarks were addressed to me. "We'd all of been better off. Your aunt, too. That boy Warren didn't have two nickels to rub together. He didn't leave Addy a thing." She popped a cough drop in her mouth.

Her remark surprised me. Mama had told me that Warren's Uncle Samuel made a fortune in lumber and willed part of his fortune to Addy because of her being Warren's widow. I had assumed this inheritance made Addy's big house, expensive car, and my new wardrobe possible.

"No, sirree, instead of leaving his family fixed, every cat hospital and orphan's home within fifty miles of Atlanta got ahold of his money. And here I sit in this miserable place." Aunt Rosy huffed and knitted her gnarly fingers together.

"I thought he left Addy a lot of money."

"He left her what he left the rest of us. Five thousand dollars. I sat in that lawyer's office and heard him read ever' single word of that will and that's what we all got. Five thousand dollars. We could of lived right well on what Samuel had if he'd seen fit to give it to us." She shook her head. "That brother of mine always did act selfish."

Addy returned from the nurses' station with the box of tissues. Shortly after, she made our excuses and we left.

Aunt Rosy's claim puzzled me. If Addy had only inherited five thousand dollars in Uncle Samuel's will, then where had her money come from? But as we set out for home, I decided not to worry. Not that it was any of my business anyway. There had to be a perfectly good explanation for Addy's wealth. Maybe Aunt Rosy had gotten hard of hearing and hadn't heard what the lawyer said.

Just beyond Decatur I fell asleep and didn't wake up until we stopped at a roadside stand near Cordele. Addy bought a carton of Vidalia onions, a dozen cantaloupes, and a couple of watermelons. As we continued our journey south, telephone poles marched toward us in a never-ending parade. The smell of onions and stale roses filled the car. I wore a pair of my new shorts and the sun burned the leg and arm nearest the window. By the time we arrived in Wilson I was bored to death with riding in the car, and the right half of my body had turned blister red.

ری   ری   ری

Lawns spread around the houses on Addy's street like green carpets. No weeds. Grass cut just so. Trimmed hedges. Oaks, looking as old as Methuselah, loomed over the street, stretching gnarly boughs across the road to intertwine with those on the other side creating a tunnel of leaves, limbs and Spanish moss. The scent of freshly cut grass, honeysuckle, and jasmine mingled — summer perfume.

The street was the kind where people sat on their porches at the end of the day in swings and rocking chairs, sipping ice tea, talking to neighbors, smoking, or doing nothing. Addy waved to them as we passed.

I'd been to Addy's sparkling-white, two-storied house with the wrap-around columned porch hundreds of times, but I could hardly believe my good fortune in getting to live in such a place, so when I got out of the car, I stood in the driveway marveling at my new home.

"Why are you staring at the house?" Addy stretched her arms and then arched backwards to loosen muscles.

"Because I live here now."

"Welcome home." She began removing suitcases and shopping bags from the trunk.

Loaded down with a suitcase and bags, I followed her across the

52

lawn, skirting the camellia bushes and the azaleas, where a few burnt-crisp petals lingered. Addy had tucked her parched bouquet under one arm.

"Y'all just in time. I just got done frying up some chicken." Earlene's face, shiny with sweat, poked out the front door as we climbed the steps to the porch. "Miss Quincy, I'm so glad you going to be living with us," she said flinging the door all the way open and stepping out. She squeezed me to her bosom which felt like two overstuffed pillows. "We need a little noise and activity in this big old house."

"Well, I'll make plenty of noise as soon as I get to the piano. Right now, I'm ready for some of your fried chicken. Nobody makes fried chicken like you."

"I got talent, honey. Y'all just come on in now." She held the door open.

We stepped into a vestibule smelling of fresh wax. Ten feet wide, the vestibule extended back to where a curved staircase with mahogany railings led to the second floor. To the left of the entry lay the dining room, then the kitchen, and beyond the kitchen, a combination laundry room-pantry. A stairway in the laundry room led to Earlene's quarters over the attached garage. The living room was to the right of the vestibule. A hall began where the vestibule ended. The first door in the hall opened into a small TV room on the right, then came the powder room and, at the very back of the house, Addy's study. From the front door, you could look through the vestibule, and down the hall, all the way to the back door where Tar Baby and Lucifer, Addy's cats, lay on cushions. Tar Baby sat up and looked at us. Lucifer stretched lazily.

"I'll pour y'all up some ice tea," Earlene said as she bent down to pick up a rose petal that had fallen from Addy's bouquet.

"Anything to go with the chicken?" Addy handed Earlene the Vidalia onions.

"Yes'm. Potato salad and butter beans and there's some shucked corn ready to pop in the pot." She gestured to the suitcases. "Now, y'all jus' leave them suitcases and I'll take them up later. Come on out to the kitchen and cool off while I cook that corn."

"Thanks, Earlene. I think I'll take you up on that. But we'll carry up our own suitcases later. You're not going to wait on us." Addy walked toward the powder room, but stopped at the door. "Any messages?"

"Yes'm. Reverend Stewart dropped by. Wanted to know when y'all would be home. I don't think the poor man's wife is doing so good. And that Yankee. That one that lives up in New York City. He called."

"Adam Johnson?"

"Yes'm."

"I just don't like that man. Nathan Waterstone done been dead a while now and that agent of his keeps poking his face around here. Ain't no call for that." She took a deep breath. "I'm going to put the food on the table."

She shuffled off toward the kitchen, and Addy went into the powder room leaving me standing alone in the hallway.

Unlike our house in Ellerbie, dull, dreary, and drowning in the shadow of the church steeple, Addy's sparkled with light and color. She'd painted the walls a pale yellow. On shiny wooden floors, Oriental rugs swirled with patterns of blue, black, and several shades of reddish-pink on cream backgrounds. Cushions, embroidered with the same reddish-pink color, nestled on cream-colored sofas in the living room. Her walls looked like an art gallery. The painting that both Addy and I claimed as our favorite hung over the living room sofa. The painting showed two black rams, heads lowered and held close together as though conversing.

My favorite thing in the house was, of course, the Steinway. I went in the living room and ran my fingers across the keys without sounding them. Tar Baby, stark black except for one white paw, padded over and brushed against my legs, while Lucifer, the mottled gray tomcat, settled on his haunches in the doorway. He eyed me as though he dared me, an intruder, to disturb the quiet of his house.

But I didn't want to play just then. I needed a little more space between Arthur Rubenstein's performance and Quincy Bruce's attempts at piano playing. I headed to the kitchen, along the way collecting petals fallen from Addy's bouquet. I passed her in the hall, where she stood checking the messages Earlene had recorded on a pad of paper.

"I'm starved," I said to Earlene, entering the kitchen and throwing the petals on the counter. "I loved Atlanta, but I'm glad to be home and back to home-cooked food." I pulled out one of the Bentwood chairs that surrounded the old oak table in the corner of the kitchen and sat down. Except for when company came, and I didn't count as company, Addy ate her meals there. I slipped off my sandals, propped my bare feet on one of the table legs that projected from the pedestal, and waited for Addy.

The kitchen glowed with color: light blue walls, darker blue floor tiles, shiny white cabinets, mauve and cranberry colored pottery on the floor by the window and on the window sills. Geraniums bloomed in some of the containers; in others, vines cascaded over the edges. Addy's collection of English teapots was displayed on the top of the cabinets.

"So, your Daddy and Mama done gone off to the Congo," Earlene said. She stood beside the table, hands propped on hips. She'd prepared enough to feed a large number of those starving Chinese my parents reminded me of at least once a week, although I assumed their interest had now shifted to the starving Congolese.

"Yes, Ma'am."

"I guess they'll be saving the souls of the godless."

"That's what they mean to do."

"All that soul-saving and they won't let us sit in the same church with the white folk. I guess some souls are better than others." She turned away and, after wringing out a dishrag, swiped at the stove top, cleaning away spills.

I didn't understand any more than Earlene did. Aunt Mildred would probably have explained that Heaven was segregated, too, and that's the way God meant things to be. She could probably even point out the place where the Bible said so.

"It's good to be home," Addy said walking in, saving me from having to respond to Earlene's comment. "Shall we eat?"

Needing no urging, I reached for the fried chicken. Addy sat down, propped the newspaper beside her, and glanced over the front page as she and Earlene chatted about what had gone on in her absence. I half listened until, in the middle of a conversation about neighbors' lawns — I guess I was too tired to be polite — I interrupted with an off-the-subject question: "Why would Adam Johnson be calling now that Nathan is dead?"

"He calls occasionally just to say hello or to ask about Nathan's house." She frowned at the drumstick she'd been about to take a bite of.

"Why does he care about Nathan's house?" Nathan Waterstone's house, now a museum, was located a few blocks from Addy's.

"Advertising the house as a museum is one way to promote Nathan's books."

"Do lots of people visit the house?" I held a fork full of butterbeans suspended in front of me. Earlene's butterbeans weren't bland like Mama's. Once I made Mama mad by suggesting she take a cooking lesson from Earlene.

"More come every year. President Eisenhower visited the house when he came down to play golf last spring."

"I guess y'all heard he's coming again," Earlene stopped clattering pans in the sink and looked up.

"I read the story in the *Constitution* this morning."

"You read about what they got to do over in Montgomery? About them buses?"

Addy looked up. "The court decision? I applaud the Supreme Court. There's no reason some should have to sit in the back." Frowning, she pushed the newspaper aside.

"Eisenhower sent military advisors to help train forces in South Vietnam. Why in the world did they decide to do that? Is this the prelude to another war?" She sounded like she was talking to herself.

"No, ma'am, I don't think we be getting in no war any time soon." Earlene had never been shy about offering her opinion.

Addy shrugged and helped herself to more butterbeans. "Let's hope not. You said Reverend Stewart dropped by. Was his visit about church business or did he just want to talk about poor Fiona?"

"Didn't say." Earlene's upper arms jiggled as she scrubbed the frying pan. Suds slathered up her wrists.

I moved my feet from one location on the table leg to another — a cooler spot. "What's wrong with Reverend Stewart's wife?" Addy had mentioned her minister several times in the past, so I recognized his name.

"Fiona has multiple sclerosis." Addy looked up and sighed. "I'm on too many committees at that church. I should learn to say *no*." She looked at Earlene. "Did you tell Adam when we'd be back?"

"Yes'm. Said y'all would be back tonight."

As if on cue, the phone rang.

Unlike the unknown person who called at the hotel, Addy seemed eager to talk to Adam Johnson. "I'll get that," she said, rising quickly.

Three days of shopping, traveling, and sightseeing had exhausted me. I put my elbows on the table and rested my head on one hand while I ate.

"They finally done something right," Earlene said.

My mind had drifted to nowhere, so I didn't know what she referred to. "Who is *they*?"

"Over in Alabama, about them buses."

"Oh, that."

"Ain't fair them people has to ride in the back when they been working all day." She removed Addy's plate and glass from the table. "Do you want some lemon icebox pie?"

"You made one?" Lemon icebox pie was my favorite desert.

"Wouldn't have offered if I didn't."

"A big piece, please."

Tar Baby brushed against my legs. As I reached down to pet her, Addy appeared at the kitchen door.

"Just going to close this while I talk," she said. "Don't want to keep disturbing you with all this chatter." She flashed a fake smile and then closed the door, leaving me to have my dessert alone and wonder why she didn't want me to hear her phone conversation with Nathan Waterstone's former agent.

      ∝   ∝   ∝

After supper I scooped up Tar Baby and took him to my room. Lucifer followed, but stopped at my door where he sat on his haunches like he was king of the kingdom — a furry ball of mottled colors posed on the red rimmed white medallion of an Oriental rug, licking his paws and staring at me.

The room had always been *my* room. To celebrate my twelfth birthday, Addy painted the walls a deep rose, bought a canopied bed and things that went with canopied beds: ruffles, flounces, cushions, matching curtains. She brought a big easy chair up from her study — the kind you want to sink into and never leave. Then she let me choose paintings from her collection. I chose prints of fairy tales she'd bought in some forgotten antique shop.

I crawled onto the bed and sank back against the pillows. Tar Baby jumped up and snuggled against my thigh, his breath ruffling across my skin. He closed his eyes, tilted his head back, and purred while I stroked his fur. Addy had kept me so busy for the past three days I'd hardly thought of Mama and Daddy. I knew that had been her intention. Buying a new wardrobe could have waited, and we could have bought one in Wilson or Albany just as well. I'd never have known the difference. But thinking I might be upset over being left behind, she'd wanted to distract me.

I wondered what Mama and Daddy were doing. Having dinner in the ship's dining room? Standing at the railing watching the waves? Getting sea sick? I had a hard time imagining Mama on the way to Africa to be a missionary. What had happened to her? Like me, she'd once had a dream. Now she'd turned down so many roads she'd never find her way back to what she once wanted. Certainly, not from Africa. How could she even think of going off *to do the Lord's work*? She pretended. I *knew* she pretended for Daddy's sake. Sometimes I'd catch her staring out the window during a sermon, her eyes glazed over, and then everybody would stand for a hymn and she'd be jolted back to thumb hastily through the hymnal to find the right page. She didn't like hymns. I saw how she widened her eyes to keep from rolling them and then set her jaw as she mouthed the words. Once I caught her checking her grocery list during a prayer. She fed the deacons when required, attended Women's Missionary Union, and never said one word against religion. But I knew she pretended. Now she planned to go traipsing around Africa, pretending some more?

Everyone expected me to miss them, and I supposed I would eventually. But so far, all I felt was a tinge of guilt at being glad to be away from Daddy's preachiness. I loved those rare times when he forgot about the Lord, and the Church, and the Good Book, and turned into a normal person. Once, when I was little, he chased me around Uncle Roger's watermelon patch spitting watermelon seeds at me. We ran around like goonies and I laughed until my sides hurt. Much too soon, he became Preacher Bruce again, spitting out quotes from the Good Book, condemning sinners, and pitching for higher offerings in the collection plate.

Another time, Aunt Mildred and her family came for Sunday dinner. Between helpings of corn bread and chicken-fried steak, she got on her high horse about some sin I'd committed. I ran away in tears and hid down by the creek. I'd never go home again. I'd sit there until a big 'ol rattlesnake bit me. Then I'd lie down and die. Aunt Mildred would be sorry. They'd all be sorry they let her talk to me that way, and I'd show them.

After a while Daddy came, bringing a book. He sat down on the bank beside me and began reading *Hans Brinker and the Silver Skates*. He said nothing about Aunt Mildred, or what I'd done, or what she thought I'd done. He just read. When he finished, he took me by the hand and led me back to the house and became Preacher Bruce again.

Surprised by a touch of loneliness, I rose and went to Addy's room.

The only light came from a lamp on her dressing table where she sat brushing her hair, surrounded by deep indigo shadows. She wore a sky blue robe that matched the walls and blended with a darker-hued bedspread. Blue and blue and blue. A rhapsody in blue. Contrasting cushions in navy, purple, and lilac lay scattered on bed and chairs.

Lucifer reigned at the head of her bed, reclining royally against the brass headboard, his body stretched out where Uncle Warren's head would have been had he not been killed in the war. Lucifer gave me a disdainful look and flicked his regal tail. I sat at the foot, away from his royal highness and close to where Addy brushed her hair. She smelled of Jergen's and her face was shiny with cream. I reached out to feel the satin of her robe.

"Do you have a boyfriend?" I knew I wouldn't be able to contain my curiosity about flower bouquets and phone calls for long, so I decided I might as well ask and get it over with.

She gave me a surprised look.

"Is Adam Johnson your boyfriend?"

She laughed. "Oh, good heavens! Certainly not. Why would you think that?"

"He called you."

"People call me all the time."

She put down the brush and turned for me to see her real face, not her mirrored one. For a moment, for two moments, her eyes appeared to see neither me nor the room, but something else. I thought she looked sad.

"Adam Johnson isn't my boyfriend, honey." Her voice told me the look *had* been a sad one. "He calls because we have things to discuss regarding Nathan's estate and the publication of his books. I'm so glad you're here, Quincy." She reached out and touched me, her fingers lingering light and warm, on my arm.

"I'm glad, too."

"It won't be so lonely now."

Addy lonely? I'd never have guessed her to be lonely.

"Well," she said then, rising. She went to the head of the bed, pushed Lucifer aside, and turned back the bedcovers. "I'm going to bed. What about you?"

"I'd like to go downstairs and play the piano." I could no longer resist. Even knowing I sounded nothing like Rubenstein, I couldn't resist.

"Do you mind? I'll play softly."

"Of course, I don't mind. Play to your heart's content."

And I did. Phone calls were just phone calls, and flowers sent from the florist were just flowers — things to entertain me with imagined mystery. Like her locket. But at the piano, I didn't need any other entertainment. I played far into the night.

CHAPTER 4

"You need to meet some girls your age. Shall we have a party?" Addy asked when we came down for breakfast the next morning. She was dressed to go out; I had on a pair of my new shorts. "We can't have you poking around here all summer with just us adults."

I liked her idea. I didn't want to start school in September not knowing anyone. "Do you know any girls to invite?" I slid into my chair and unfolded my napkin.

"I know several. Mary Watson, for one. Her father is the attorney for the Nathan Waterstone Foundation. And there are some girls at church. We'll ask them to bring their friends."

I piled scrambled eggs on my plate. "What about Alice Worthington?" I knew the answer to that before I even asked, but I asked anyway. Just in case something had changed. It hadn't.

"We'll not be inviting Alice Worthington. How does Thursday of next week sound?"

I nodded, and reached for the bacon. Thursday sounded as good as any other day. It wasn't like I had a full schedule. Or any schedule at all. I decided Addy must be glad to be home again. In spite of her quick answer to my question about inviting Alice Worthington, she looked relaxed and happy.

"And speaking of the Nathan Waterstone Foundation . . ." She began to butter a piece of toast, ". . . the Foundation board will be meeting here tomorrow evening."

Addy had helped set up the Nathan Waterstone Foundation after Nathan's death and then become an employee of the Foundation. One of her jobs was to supervise Nathan's house which had been turned into a museum.

"What does the board do?"

"Nathan set up a trust fund for the upkeep of the house, so they oversee those funds and the royalties that still come in."

"I thought you oversaw the house."

"They set guidelines and make decisions. I carry them out." She reached for the fig preserves. "You haven't been to the house since Nathan died, have you?"

I shook my head. While Nathan was still alive, Mama would bring me along when she had errands to do in Wilson. We'd stop at his house and ring the doorbell. Pearl, his housekeeper, would open the door and lead us down the hall to Nathan's study where Addy did her editing and typing. Nathan's last three books were written in his Wilson study. Early every morning, Addy drove the few blocks from her house to his and worked with him until mid-afternoon.

"He never seemed to mind that we disturbed you at work."

"I think he rather enjoyed the diversion." She spread fig preservers on her toast and took a bite. "It's my morning to go over to the manse and help with Fiona." She wiped away a fleck of fig from her mouth.

"Fiona?"

"Reverend Stewart's wife. Maybe you can work on choosing pieces for your audition."

"I wish I could snap my fingers and sound like your recordings."

"That's why you need a new teacher. So you can learn to sound like the recordings. Or like Rubenstein." She tilted her chin up, raised her eyebrows in a friendly challenge, and smiled. "You have the talent, honey." She reached over and squeezed my hand. "But achievement comes after years of hard work." Her hand slid away then, and she looked over to Earlene. "Earlene, are there any more of those fig preserves from Mrs. Thompson? I should take some to Fiona."

"No'm, they all gone."

"Too bad. We'll have to beg her for more."

     ✍   ✍   ✍

After breakfast, I looked through my music, trying to decide what to play for the audition. I'd read that people always included a Bach Invention for auditions. I played numbers one and eight well enough. I'd choose something by Mozart. Maybe the Sonata in C — the one they call the "easy" one, or Sonata no. 5. And a Chopin waltz.

I worked on the *Raindrop Prelude* for nearly an hour — not because I intended to play the prelude for the audition; I just wanted to try and imitate Arthur Rubenstein. My rendition, however, sounded like a bumpy ride in Uncle Roger's Ford pickup compared to Rubenstein's mesmerizing performance. For sure, the notes I played didn't sound like raindrops.

I should have sat at the piano all day because as soon as I rose from the bench, a smidgen of independence and a bit of defiance took root and grew, finally luring me out the back door. If Addy could have secrets — like phone calls and flowers from a secret boyfriend — then so could I. If Mama and Daddy could have secrets — like not telling me they were going to Africa until the last minute — then so could I. And anyway, what was wrong with Alice Worthington?

I stood on the back steps shifting from foot to foot. Earlene sat in the swing under the pecan tree snapping string beans and sweating. "I'm going for a walk," I said. She didn't answer. Maybe the sun made her deaf or else snapping beans sent her into some sort of trance. "Earlene, did you hear me?"

While I waited for Earlene to spring to life, not that Earlene ever did anything with a spring, I watched Tar Baby playing with a beetle that attempted to cross the bottom step. Every time the poor thing made any progress, Tar Baby brushed the beetle in a different direction. Finally, I picked up the beetle, set her in the grass, and then walked over to Earlene. "I'm going for a walk," I repeated.

"Uh-huh. Your aunt ain't back yet?"

"No, ma'am."

"Ain't it a little hot for a walk?" She wiped her sleeve over her brow.

"If you're so hot why don't you go inside in the air-conditioning?" She didn't respond.

"I've been practicing for two hours. I need a break. See you." I walked away before she could answer.

❧   ❧   ❧

The previous summer when I came for a visit, Addy had taken me to the municipal pool one day. She sat in a lawn chair beside the pool reading while I swam. I splashed about for a while — I wasn't such a good swimmer — until a skinny, freckle-faced girl with dish-water blonde hair, bumped into me. She apologized for nearly knocking me over and then introduced herself as Alice Worthington. Discovering that we were the

66

same age, we talked about school and boys and clothes. I told her I wanted to be a pianist; she told me she wanted to be an artist. "Anytime you visit your aunt," she'd said, "come on over."

On the way home from the pool, Addy advised me that Alice Worthington was not a suitable choice for a companion. When I asked why, Addy waved her hand in dismissal and changed the subject.

So I felt a bit sneaky going to visit Alice. But not sneaky enough to turn around and go home. What harm could come from one visit? I trudged along, following the directions Alice gave me when we met. Even though I walked underneath the canopy of oak limbs, my body swelled with heat — probably enough to warm an igloo for a year. Addy once told me that people in Sweden built little rooms called saunas, which they heated up and sat in for the purpose of sweating. They'd run out and throw themselves in the snow when they got too hot and then go back into the sauna to get hot all over again, she explained. That was one story of Addy's I found hard to believe. If they wanted to be hot, they should have moved to South Georgia.

Alice's face lit up when she opened the door and saw me standing there. "Quincy Bruce. My gosh, I'm surprised to see you. Come on in." She wore a man's shirt with rolled up sleeves and a pair of cut-off jeans.

I stepped inside. The Worthington's living room would have fit four times over into Addy's. The furniture crowded together like gossiping women; newspapers lay scattered on furniture and floor; cigarette ashes meandered across the coffee table, and the air stunk of tobacco and mildew.

"You're visiting your aunt, I guess." Alice closed the door, plunging the room into gloom. Yellowed shades shut out the sunlight. One shade had become unattached in a corner and flopped down to let in a triangle of light.

"I'm living with Addy for two years while Mama and Daddy are in the Congo."

Her eyes widened. "In Africa?"

"They went there as missionaries."

"My gosh, Africa! What kind of house will they live in?"

I shrugged. "I don't know."

"Maybe a hut? Will they have to go outside and squat in the bushes to pee?"

"I hope not." Chalk up one reason Addy didn't want me hanging around Alice. *Pee. Squat.* Her parents let her talk like that?

"A bathroom in the bushes." Alice laughed hysterically. "Good gosh, girl. No wonder you stayed here. There're probably snakes out there waiting to bite people on their hineys. Does this mean you'll be going to Wilson High?"

"Yes." What *were* the bathroom facilities like in the Congo?

"Hey, come on back to my room and see the stuff I've been working on."

I followed her. She stopped when we came to the kitchen.

"Want some ice tea?"

"Sure." So many dirty glasses cluttered the sink and the area around the sink I wondered where she'd find a clean one. A lard can on the stove overflowed with drippings, infecting the air with the smell of rancid lard.

"Just let me hunt up a clean glass." Alice opened and shut cabinets, searching. "Mama is doing the morning shift at the diner and my brother is gone off somewhere, so we're alone. I'm supposed to do the dishes but I didn't get to them yet."

A roach ran from a cabinet, crossed the counter, and disappeared behind a peanut butter jar. I wondered if the Worthington's lack of cleanliness was the reason Addy considered Alice an unsuitable companion. But how would Addy have known about the dirty house?

"Ah, here we go." Triumphant, Alice held up a Welch jelly glass pulled from behind a box of Ritz crackers. "And here's mine." She took a glass half-full of watery tea, dumped the contents down the drain, and then removed a pitcher from the refrigerator and filled both glasses. "Bring the tea with you," she said, handing me mine.

Alice led me to her room behind the kitchen. She'd made her bed, giving some order to an otherwise disordered house. The bed, covered with a green chenille bedspread, took up most of the room. She'd taped drawings and paintings — human figures, landscapes, still lifes — to the walls

Surprised at how good they were, I spent several minutes looking at them. "I'm impressed," I said, motioning to the pictures. "I don't know anyone else who can draw and paint like that."

"Sit." She pointed to the floor. "I'll show you my latest work." She plopped down on the rag rug next to the bed and patted the floor beside her, indicating where I should settle. She rolled the sleeves of the oversized shirt up one more roll and then pulled a cardboard box from beneath the bed and removed the lid. Crayons and colored pencils lay scattered over a stack of papers.

"Are you signing up for art class?" She pushed aside the pencils and crayons and lifted a sheaf of papers.

"No. Are you?"

"Yeah. These are some of my illustrations." She handed them to me.

I leafed through the drawings depicting gnomes, fairies, a collection of friendly looking pigs, chickens, and goats. While I looked, she pulled her pony-tail over her shoulder and ran her hand up and down, fingering and twisting the strand.

"They're really good," I said when I handed them back to her.

"Daddy says I have talent. He thinks I can get a scholarship to some big college like the University of Georgia. What about you? Do you still want to be a concert pianist?"

I nodded. "I want to go to a conservatory when I graduate from high school."

"A conservatory?"

"Like Peabody or Julliard, where you study classical music."

"I guess a conservatory costs lots of money." She swatted at a fly buzzing near her face. "But your aunt has lots of money, doesn't she?"

Chalk up another reason Addy wouldn't want me hanging out with Alice. *You never ask someone about their age, weight, or wealth. Or lack of wealth.*

"Her husband must have left her a bunch when he got killed in the war."

"I suppose," I said even though I knew that to be untrue. "What else do you have in the box?"

She raised her eyebrows. "You might not want to see."

"Why not?"

She set her glass down, stuck her hand under the stack of drawings she'd just shown me, and felt around. When her hand stopped moving, she raised her eyebrows again, igniting my curiosity.

"Come on, show me."

"Promise you won't tell."

"I promise."

She withdrew a roll of papers fastened with a rubber band. Sloooowly, she removed the rubber band, unrolled the papers, and then lowered them inch by inch until they lay in her lap. She slid the first paper off and held the picture out for me to see.

"Alice. I don't believe . . . ." I stared. A man and woman lay in an embrace — reason number three why I shouldn't be there. "Let me have

70

them. I can't see very well when you're holding them."

I was sixteen, after all, and interested in the facts of life and love, and more than a little bit intrigued with sex, even though I'd never even said the word out loud. Nice girls didn't. But some day I'd marry, and I wondered how *that* would be, and whenever I wondered, a throbbing began between my legs, and I'd get warm there. I didn't want Alice to guess my feelings, so I acted silly. One by one, she handed me the drawings and we giggled, becoming sillier and sillier, until we heard someone coming through the kitchen.

"Alice." The female voice that called out sounded like gravel.

"Oh, gosh. Mama's home." Alice grabbed the pictures and shoved them back in the box.

We looked up to see her mother in the doorway, a lemon-sucking look on her face. Like Alice, she had dish-water blonde hair and pale blue eyes, and looked as tired and wilted as the waitress uniform she wore. Smoke spiraled from the cigarette clenched between her fingers. She flashed a glance at me before settling her sour look on Alice. "You didn't do the dishes."

"Sorry. I lost track of time. Quincy wanted to see my pictures."

"Quincy?"

"This is Quincy Bruce. She's living with her aunt, Mrs. Simmons. You know . . . the one who worked for that writer."

I rose. "Hi." I tried to smile but Mrs. Worthington wore such an unwelcome look that a genuine smile got caged somewhere inside my ribs.

She glared at Alice. "I know who Mrs. Simmons is." She blew out a little puff of air. "This is the second time this week you didn't do the dishes."

"I'll do them. I didn't know you were coming home early."

Mrs. Worthington shifted her gaze to me. "I guess you don't have

71

to do dishes at your aunt's, what with her having a maid and all." She flicked ashes on the floor and then puckered her lips around the cigarette while she took a long drag.

"No, ma'am." I didn't tell her that I'd hoed a lot of cotton for Uncle Roger, or that I'd handed tobacco until the black from the leaves clung to every part of my body, forcing me to scrub my skin raw to get the black off. The time had come for me to exit. "I'm glad to have met you, Mrs. Worthington. I have to go now. I have to practice."

"She's going to be a concert pianist," Alice explained. "She wants to go to a conservatory."

Mrs. Worthington's brows rose. "Big house, live-in maid, new car, and now a niece going to conservatory." She sniffed, and then turned and walked away.

❧   ❧   ❧

"Was Uncle Warren rich?" I asked at supper. Earlene had gone off somewhere, so Addy and I were alone.

"Good heavens, no. Why do you ask?" She gave me a puzzled look.

"Just wondering." I'd hoped that by bringing up the subject, she'd drop some hint about where her money came from.

"He was as poor as a church mouse." She reached for the tea pitcher. "We were both poor students trying to survive on student grants, living in neighboring garrets in Heidelberg. Then we married and lived in one garret, and we were still poor." She filled her glass. "Want more tea?"

"No, thank you. Did Warren write about Faust, too?"

"No, Warren had no interest in the devil. He wrote about a German poet called Novalis." The ice clinked as she lifted the glass to

72

drink.

"Did you finish your thesis?"

A wry smile twisted her lips. "No, I never did finish with Faust and the devil."

﮼   ﮼   ﮼

Earlene whipped up four masterpieces for the board meeting: a caramel cake, a pecan pie, a sweet potato pie, and a batch of divinity. You could practically lick cinnamon and sugar out of the air. Then she squeezed lemons for lemonade, while I made two pitchers of ice tea.

"He don't like ice tea," she said, stirring sugar into the lemonade.

Who was she talking about? I began arranging the divinity on a platter.

"Don't make no sense. He likes cold lemonade but his tea has to be hot." Her spoon clanked against the side of the pitcher. "Over there they drink milk in their tea."

"Over where? Who are you talking about?"

"The Reverend Stewart. He came from Scotland." She opened the door to the refrigerator and, as she put the lemonade inside, Lucifer inserted himself in the opening and sniffed at the contents. Earlene pushed him away with her foot. "Milk in tea don't sound right to me, but he's a real nice man, anyway." She took a deep breath and looked around. "We better finish up. Won't be long before they'll be here."

She began folding napkins into fan shapes while I finished arranging the divinity. I cupped the lumps from a broken piece in my hand.

"Reverend Stewart is on the board?"

"Yes'm." She folded a napkin, pressed her fingers along the crease, and added the napkin to the stack. "His wife be in a bad way. Has multiple

73

skeerosis. Miz Fiona can barely hold her head up. Can't go nowhere without a wheelchair."

"I guess that's why Addy helps at the manse. Who else is on the board?"

"Miz Walker. You know Miz Addy's red-headed friend. And Dr. Whiddon. He came when you took with the strep throat that time."

I remembered tall, skinny, slump-shouldered Dr. Whiddon prodding in my mouth with a wooden tongue depressor during my fifth-grade spring vacation which I spent with Addy. "And there's Mr. Watson and Mr. Chapman," Earlene continued. "Mr. Watson's a big deal lawyer. He has a daughter your age, and he talks all the time about how smart that girl is. But I expect my James probably be just as smart as Mr. Watson's Mary. Mr. Chapman owns all them fertilizer mills and the John Deere place, and who knows what else. He's verrrrrry rich." She folded the last napkin.

I followed her into the dining room and set the platter of divinity beside the other refreshments. She arranged the napkins and then stepped back to view the table. "Don't look too bad," she said, brushing away crumbs of divinity that had fallen on the white lace tablecloth. "That librarian over at the school is on the board, too. You be seeing plenty of Miz Burke next year, I imagine. Sour old lady. I need to put some mints and sugar pecans out, then we'll be finished."

She shuffled off to the kitchen. A few seconds later I heard her yelp. "Scat, you darn cat," she screeched. I ate the broken divinity while I listened to Earlene, exclaiming and panting, as she chased Lucifer around the kitchen. I knew it was Lucifer. Tar Baby had better manners. I heard the backdoor slam as Earlene threw Lucifer into the yard.

"I'm gon' kill that cat, she said, returning to the dining room." She wiped the back of one hand across her brow. In the other she carried a gold rimmed crystal bowl filled with toasted pecans. "Darn animal was on the counter sniffing at them pecans. You better chase down Tar Baby and lock them both outside. Lucifer for sure be up on the table licking the icing off the cake if he gets back in. I declare, that cat has a sweet tooth."

I found Tar Baby stretched out on the sofa in Addy's study. When I put him on the back steps, I saw that Lucifer had wandered over to Mrs. Thompson's back yard where he sat on the concrete bridge that spanned her egg shaped gold fish pool. Only about a foot wide, the bridge was barely broad enough for a person to walk across but big enough for Lucifer to perch on to eye the fish. The way he sat on the bridge, leaning over with one paw up ready to snatch up a golden snack, I half expected him to fall in one day.

I shut the back door — cat tight — and returned to the dining room to find Addy standing in the half-dark, staring absently at an arrangement of yellow roses and purple heather which the florist had delivered earlier in the afternoon. She picked up a fallen rose petal and, for a few moments, looked down at the bit of yellow before dropping it back on the arrangement. The petal landed on a piece of heather, balanced there a moment, and then slid off to land in the same place as before.

"It looks like we're ready," she said in a voice as shadowed as the room.

"What's the matter?"

She gave me a sharp look, but followed the look with a quick smile. But she smiled with her mouth, not her eyes. "It's always sad when we meet to discuss Nathan's business and have to acknowledge he's no longer with us."

"But you look wonderful." I turned on the light to see her better. She wore a cream-colored dress, fitted tightly at the waist, and with a rounded neckline that dipped low. Instead of her locket, she wore a gold chain on which hung a pendant set with a single opal. Earlier in the day she'd gone to the beauty parlor and had her brown hair bobbed to perfection. I smiled at the idiocy of Aunt Mildred's accusation that Addy had been the Lady. In the first chapter of the novel, Nathan describes Lady Isabelle Duncan's hair:

> *She didn't follow the fashion favored by most women of pinning up their hair into complicated "dos." Rather she chose to drape her long tresses over one shoulder, allowing them to flow across a breast. Unable to decide if her hair was blonde or red, for the color fell somewhere in between, I chose to call it golden.*

A loud knocking, followed by the ring of the doorbell interrupted us. "It's Elizabeth!" Addy said. "Impatient, as always. Come with me to the living room. You know Elizabeth and Dr. Whiddon, but I want to introduce you to the other board members before you go off and do whatever you're going to do. What *are* you going to do?"

"Read," I said.

I followed her into the living room and leaned against the back of a chair while she opened the door for Mrs. Walker who entered flapping her hands in front of her face, fanning herself.

"Lordy mercy, it's like a furnace outside." She closed her eyes, tilted her head back, and breathed deeply. "Hmmmmm, this air-conditioning feels fabulous." She wore a white dress imprinted with big purple flowers and, as usual, bright, red lipstick. She opened her eyes and gave Addy an approving look. "You look smashing tonight, Addy, my dear." She turned to me then. "Sugar, did your aunt get around to telling you about Gretchen and Faust?" Her eyes flickered with amusement.

"No, ma'am."

Addy rolled her eyes.

"Lordy, Addy. Why haven't you told the poor child about Gretchen? You do have something cold to drink, don't you?"

Earlene appeared with a tray of glasses filled with ice tea and one with lemonade. The ladies were about to settle on the sofa with their drinks when the doorbell rang again.

A burly man with faded red hair and a protruding stomach entered, followed by a tall, dark-haired man. The dark-haired man looked suave in a meticulously pressed, beige summer suit. He reminded me of Rhett Butler. There were hugs and *How are you's* and rapid fire comments about the weather and the torn up road in the middle of town. I watched and listened until Addy motioned me closer.

She introduced the red-headed man as Mr. Watson. "You didn't tell me how pretty your niece is," he said, grabbing my hand in his pudgy, freckled one and squeezing. For a moment I feared missing my audition due to a broken hand. "I have a daughter your age. I should have brought her along so you two could get acquainted."

Mr. Chapman, more restrained, nodded to me, and in a deep bass, mumbled something about being glad to meet me. For an older man — older, as in a few years older than Addy — he wasn't bad looking. I imagined Addy with such a man.

"You're going to have to meet my Mary," Mr. Watson said. "I'm sure you'll be in some of the same classes. Smart girl, Mary. She's at the top of the class in all her subjects."

Addy saved me from having to hear more about Mary's academic talents by asking Mr. Watson to deliver an invitation for my party. He'd announced his daughter's brilliance with such an air of superiority, I wondered if Mary would turn out to be the academic version of Aunt Mildred, knowing everything in the textbooks the way my aunt knew everything in the Bible. Even what wasn't there.

The group migrated to the dining room. In the midst of *oohs* and *aahs* over Earlene's caramel cake, Miz Burke, the tight-faced librarian arrived. She shook my hand limply.

"I look forward to seeing you at school, Quincy," she said, in a raspy voice. Wiry hairs stuck out from her chin.

Dr. Whiddon arrived a few minutes later with a downturned mouth and a frown that pulled his eyebrows together. Had one of his patients died? "Good to see you again, Quincy," he said nodding at me. Then he turned to the others. "Robert said to start without him. Fiona is having a bad day and he needs to tend to her first."

I used that as my excuse to slip away. I'd meet the Scotsman, the Reverend Robert Stewart, another time.

و   و   و

The phone rang as I passed through the hall.

"Hey, it's me," Darrell said when I answered. "How come you ain't called us? We been talking 'bout you at supper tonight and we think you done forgot about us."

"Sorry. We went to Atlanta for a few days and just got back."

"Atlanta? What'd you do there?"

"Uh, well, we . . . Addy had some stuff to do there and we saw one of her friends. Then we went to see her husband's aunt." I didn't mention my new clothes. If Aunt Mildred found out I'd discarded the clothes given to me by members of Daddy's congregation she'd bombard me with lectures about ungratefulness the next time I saw her.

"I thought you might want to know Buster is ok. We went coon hunting last night."

"Did you get a coon?"

"Nah, we didn't see no coons."

"Darrell, I'm really glad you called but I better hang up. Addy has a

78

meeting going on here and I don't want to disturb them."

"What kind of meeting?"

"The Nathan Waterstone Foundation Board."

"You watch out for them Nathan Waterstone people, you hear? You never know what they might be up to."

I thought about retorting that a minister was on the board, and ministers don't usually do things that need watching out for. But when I remembered that Reverend Stewart was a Presbyterian minister, not a Baptist minister, I said nothing. Other denominations were always suspect with Aunt Mildred.

"Good-bye, Darrell," I said instead and hung up.

Darrell provided a perfect example of ignorance being handed down from one generation to the next. I imagined Aunt Mildred holding forth at the supper table. *There ain't no doubt, that Adelaide Simmons is a big time sinner hooking up with that writer. All that education and she don't know no better. And him following her to Wilson, of all things. And them other people that run that Foundation. 'Ever' one of them ain't got no morals if they support what that man did.*

Something else struck me, and the very thought made me nauseous. Had Aunt Mildred repeated her accusation about Addy being the Lady to other people? If she hadn't already, she was sure to do so soon. I needed to squelch the rumor before the thing spread all over creation. I'd start my quest to find out who the Lady was by asking Addy questions. I wouldn't ask direct questions about her identity, because Addy would clam up. I'd ask about other things related to Nathan, hoping she'd drop some tidbit to set me on the path to discovery.

Meanwhile, I needed something to read. The voices in the living room had fallen into the monotonous rhythm of a meeting. I pulled off my shoes and went barefoot down the hall so they wouldn't hear the clacking of my shoes. In the study, I found Earlene standing in front of the book shelves, hands on hips, head tilted to one side, reading titles.

"I'm looking for a book," she said.

"You like to read?"

She swiveled her head to look at me. "You think I can't read jus' cause I'm black?"

"Of course not. I just didn't know you *liked* to read. Not everybody likes to read. Aunt Mildred doesn't like to read."

"Anybody who don't like to read ain't going to get nowhere in life."

"Aunt Mildred doesn't have to get anywhere; she's already there. She's God's spokeswoman. Didn't you know that?"

"There're a lot of them about. They sure do have some mixed-up messages."

I pulled a book from the top shelf. "Have you read *A Tree Grows in Brooklyn?*"

She looked sideways at the book and shook her head.

"I really liked the story." I handed her the book.

"Maybe I'll just give this a try while I sit out in the kitchen." She brushed her hand over the jacket wiping away a speck of dust, opened the book, and then shuffled away, reading as she went.

Floor to ceiling bookcases lined three walls of Addy's study. One wall contained her fiction collection arranged alphabetically by author. The section to the right of the door held nonfiction. Addy's German books filled the shelves along the left wall farthest from the door. Intrigued by a language of which I hardly understood a word other than *Gesundheit*, I'd sometimes browse through the titles wondering how to pronounce them — *Buddenbrooks, Tod in Venedig, Deutsche Barockforschung*, and of course, *Faust*.

The furniture looked like furniture in a study was supposed to look: a brown leather Chesterfield sofa underneath a set of windows opposite the door, two matching armchairs, sturdy lamp tables. Addy's desk stood a few feet in front of the shelves containing her German books. When she sat at the desk, her back was to the German books and her face toward the door. A French armoire stood near the far corner of the wall opposite the door. The antique armoire had a couple minor nicks and scratches from a previous owner, but otherwise reigned in the room like a royal among commoners. Leaves were carved into the panel along the top as well as along a center board where the two doors met. A row of fancy metalwork ran along the center edge of the doors. The cabinet was always locked. As a child, I liked to imagine that the cabinet contained secrets. Maybe Addy had been a spy during the war and locked away the evidence in the cabinet. Or she had a secret document that revealed the identity of the Lady which she'd sworn to keep hidden until a certain distant year. Or love letters sat on one of the shelves.

I browsed among the books, finally choosing *The Yearling*. Back in my room, I yanked a pillow from underneath the spread to use as a prop against the headboard, and settled down to read. Tar Baby jumped up beside me.

I read the first two pages. Then I reread the first two pages because I hadn't concentrated the first time. I was suddenly impatient to ask Addy questions that would lead to discovering who the Lady had been. I pushed Tar Baby away, got my autographed copy of *The Lady* from my desk drawer, and crawled back onto the bed.

Nathan named the man in the book *George Atkinson*, but because of the radio interview, everyone knew that *George* was really Nathan. I opened the book to the beginning and reread the passage where *George* meets Lady Isabelle Duncan for the first time and describes her hair.

Unable to decide if her hair was blonde
or red, for the color fell somewhere in between, I

81

chose to call it golden. She was my fairy-tale princess.

Beside me, Tar Baby stretched and yawned as I ran my fingers down the lines of print, looking for the reference to the Lady being married. I found the place and read the lines out loud.

No husband or lover attached himself to her that evening, and so conceiving the idea that she was available, I fell completely under her spell. One of the last to leave the party, I was retrieving my rain gear, when Smithers approached and laid his hand on my shoulder.

"Be careful, old chap," he said, "Get too cozy with Lady Duncan and her husband will have you drawn and quartered.

I leafed through the pages until I found where *George* visits Isabelle for the first time in her flat. She'd invited him to tea, wanting to hear about his adventures in the Himalayas.

When the day finally arrived, I set out for her accommodations with mixed emotions. I had never been a philanderer, a scurrilous seducer of married women; yet, throughout the previous week I had been beset with feelings and imaginings of a most ungentlemanly nature. As I waited to board a bus in Trafalgar Square I almost walked away, but after a few steps, I stopped and turned slowly back. I would go. I would keep the appointment. Away from the flicker of party candles and a blazing fire in the hearth; away from the drinks and the merriment,

I'd view her differently. Just a woman, I'd see. Just an ordinary woman. Then I'd go back to my writing, cured of this crippling attraction.

But I wasn't cured. That afternoon over scones, miniature sandwiches and several pots of tea, and while I related my travel experiences and writing travails, I fell completely, hopelessly, in love.

Isabelle, for I shall call her that now, sent me away finally, but with an invitation to return the following week. "Indulge me," she begged. "I need something, someone, to turn my thoughts away from this dreadful war."

"But why don't you leave London for a safer place?" I asked.

"I can't bear that either. I grew up so far away from everything, in a place where nothing ever happened. I was cocooned from the world for so long, that I prefer danger to boredom." Of the absent husband there was no mention.

Addy, I supposed, could be said to have been *cocooned* when she spent two years in a hospital bed, but I thought Lady Isabelle referred to geography, not a hospital bed.

I continued to leaf through the pages, reading here and there, until I came to the section about Lady Duncan's birthday.

I searched for the perfect gift. But what is appropriate for the woman you will love for the remainder of your life, but to whom you can never be

bound in wedlock? In the end, I chose a gold pin with
an opal in the center. I chose the pin, not because of the
opal's ancient significance as "Gem of the Gods," or
because the opal is also known as the gem of love, but
rather because of the gem's mythical power to strengthen
the memory. We shall never forget each other.

Another reason I knew Addy hadn't been the Lady came in a paragraph about a third of the way into the book. After an especially bad bombing, George goes to Isabelle's street to make sure the building where she lives hasn't been destroyed. As he stands there, relieved to see the building untouched, she exits the building. He is surprised to see her in a nurse's uniform.

"Three times a week I volunteer at the
hospital," she said, explaining the uniform. I do
what I can: change dressings, administer
medications, sponge foreheads, and hold hands."

Addy hated hospitals. After spending two years in one, who could blame her?

In the last pages of the novel, George searches through the wreckage of trains for Isabel's body. Her husband had insisted that she leave London. After a tearful farewell with George, she boards a train for Cambridge. George watches the train fade away. Shortly after he returns to his flat, a rare daytime bombing raid destroys two trains. Not knowing if one of the trains is hers, he searches frantically for her body among the corpses lined up at the wreckage sites and in the morgues where some of the bodies have already been taken. Not finding Isabelle among the dead, he goes to the hospitals where the injured have been taken. He never finds Isabelle.

She's alive. I feel it in my heart. When

I find her, and I will, I vow to remain near her for always. Even though we may not speak to each other, or touch, or even acknowledge that we know each other, I will go wherever she goes and be near her. Always.

I closed the book. Addy couldn't possibly be the Lady. Did no passage in the Bible deal with false accusations?

ல   ல   ல

When everyone left, I sat on Addy's bed watching her perform the nightly ritual of brushing her hair one hundred strokes. Lucifer lounged in his usual place on the pillow. "How'd the meeting go?"

"Like them all. They're as much about socializing and eating Earlene's caramel cake as about taking care of business."

"Tell me about Gretchen and Faust."

"Gretchen became pregnant."

"By Faust?"

"Yes, by Faust."

"Like Mama."

Addy gave me a startled look and twisted around to face me.

"Don't look so surprised. I've known for a long time."

"How . . . ? Who told you?"

I shrugged. "I don't remember. Maybe Aunt Mildred."

Addy rolled her eyes.

"Did Faust marry Gretchen?"

"No." She turned back to the mirror and resumed brushing.

"Did the Board settle all the problems of the Nathan Waterstone Foundation?"

85

Addy's eyes settled on me, but without actually seeming to see me. After a few seconds, she looked down at her brush and began removing strands of hair entangled in the bristles. She wadded the hairs into a little ball and threw the ball in the wastepaper basket next to her dressing table.

"When we get one problem solved another pops up," she said, still looking down. "We have to install a new heating system, and we need to replace the fixtures in the visitors' bathroom."

Heating systems and bathroom fixtures sounded about as interesting as Wednesday night prayer meeting. "I guess I'll go to bed," I said, rising. Tomorrow I'd start making a list of questions to ask Addy about the Lady.

CHAPTER 5

On Sunday, I met the last member of the board, the Reverend Robert Stewart.

The day dawned bright and hot, which is the only way a South Georgia summer day dawns except for rainy and hot. A persistent knocking on my door jarred me awake — *awake* being a relative term because my eyes remained stubbornly closed. Addy and I had spent Saturday evening watching television until the wee hours. Or trying to. Mostly we watched a bunch of wavy lines rippling across the screen. Reception in South Georgia was awful.

When the door squeaked open and I heard Addy walk over to my bed, I knew I'd have to rise and shine. I sat up.

"You need to dress fast. The time got away from me. Sunday School starts soon."

I swung my feet to the floor. "What I really want to do this morning is go to some Baptist church where I don't know anybody and listen to more stuff about the devil."

"Who said you were going to a Baptist church? I promised you'd go to Sunday School. I didn't say which one."

"Which one am I going to?"

"Mine, of course."

"First Presbyterian?"

"Yes. Make haste and get ready."

ʁ   ʁ   ʁ

The Reverend Robert Stewart spoke with a Scottish burr — that's what Addy called his dialect, a *burr*. His speech alone would have guaranteed my attention, but even before he spoke, my heart skipped a beat as he stepped up to the pulpit. He wore a welcoming face, not a pious one. And it was a perfect face — even featured, with sparkly eyes and straight, dark eyebrows. He had thick brown, almost black, hair. I couldn't see the color of his eyes because we sat ten rows back from the pulpit, but I saw the way they crinkled when he smiled, and he smiled often. His smile, I decided, must have conquered many hearts.

His wife, Fiona, sat in a wheelchair near the organ, sagging like a rag doll.

"She looks poorly," Addy's pew neighbor commented.

For a few moments, I examined Fiona's bloodless skin and vacant eyes, pitying her, but she didn't hold my attention long. There were too many other things to examine on my first Sunday in Addy's church. During the hymns and prayers, I examined the congregation, studying their clothes and behavior, hoping I fit in.

I never listened to Daddy's sermons — I always wound up daydreaming — so when the sermon finally began, I surprised myself by actually paying attention. Reverend Stewart's voice, his tone, his sincerity compelled me to listen, and he seemed to look at every man, woman, and child as he spoke. As though he spoke privately to each of us. Several times I thought he looked directly at me. Addressing the congregation in a quiet

88

voice, he described the battle between good and evil, not as a monstrous battle in the sky between angels and demons as the poet Milton portrayed, but rather as a battle that took place every day in the heart of each man, woman, and child. His sermon reminded me of what Addy said in the restaurant: *The devil doesn't grab people and cart them off to hell. People commit themselves to the devil with purpose and forethought.*

At the end of the service, Reverend Stewart shook hands at the door of the sanctuary. Once, while we waited in the line that snailed toward him, I glanced back to where Fiona still sat. My view was partially obliterated by someone's hat, so I saw only a sliver of her profile — a ribbon of brow and cheek and nose. And a tress of red-gold hair that brushed her cheek. Except for her hair, she looked so pale and vulnerable that I quickly looked away.

"I'm glad to finally meet you, Quincy," Reverend Stewart said when we came to the front of the line. He shook my hand and then brought up his other hand to hold mine between both of his. He looked deep into my eyes with his blue-grey ones, and smiled. "I'm told much talent resides in these hands, and that you have an audition scheduled at Florida State. I wish you the best of luck."

God only knows what stupid thing I mumbled. He held my hand sandwiched between his for what seemed a long time. But not nearly long enough. "How did he know about the audition?" I asked when we walked away, my hand still warm and pulsing.

"I told him, of course. How else? Come, I want to introduce you to people." Addy introduced me to more people that day than I could possibly remember. She invited Penny Martin and Jessie Buchanan, whom I'd met in Sunday school, to my party.

Penny, a cheerleader, had short, curly brown hair, a perfect nose, and long shapely legs that she kept crossing and uncrossing during the

Sunday School lesson.

Jessie, head majorette in the high school band, wore her blond hair in a single braid that hung halfway down her back. She'd stormed into Sunday School late, flung herself onto a chair, and thrown up her hands. "I'm going to kill him," she hissed.

The teacher, who had been going on about the prodigal son as if we hadn't already heard that story five hundred times, stopped.

"I'm going to kill him," Jessie repeated.

The teacher gave her a stern look.

"Sorry."

"You're going to kill Devilstiltskin?" A boy who'd been introduced as Buddy Simms whispered. Buddy had the largest freckles I'd ever seen.

"You bet."

"Who is Devilstiltskin?" I asked Jessie after church. Addy had invited her and Penny to my party and they'd both accepted.

"My devil of a little brother." She pointed to where a platinum-headed, freckle-faced boy of seven tore around the church yard, bumping into people and stepping on toes.

Addy drew me away to meet others. But during all the introductions, the chit-chat, and the questions about how I liked Wilson, I remembered the pleasure of having my hand resting between Reverend Stewart's hands and found myself looking forward to Sundays.

᪣   ᪣   ᪣

Before I practiced that afternoon, I sat cross-legged on the living room floor and listened to Schubert Impromptus played by Lily Krauss. I'd just about worn out that record. After a phrase that I especially loved, I'd pick up the needle, and then put the needle down to listen to that part again. And again and again. I'd actually destroyed a couple of Addy's records doing that. But she never fussed. She'd just go out and buy a new one. Or rather order a new one. Classical music wasn't big in Wilson either, although I think there were more people in Wilson who could name at least three composers than there were in Ellerbie.

Addy's records were my gateway to Heaven. I loved the music on them so much that sometimes I found myself holding my breath, and I'd have to remind myself to breathe. When a record stopped playing, my skin tingled happily for a few minutes, but then frustration set in. I'd pinch my lips together and grab clumps of my hair as I agonized over my vain attempts to sound like the musicians on the records. And I had one really worrying question: Did I still have time to learn?

≈   ≈   ≈

Elizabeth Walker, who lived on a plantation five miles south of Wilson, had invited us to dinner that evening. Late in the afternoon, Addy and I got dressed up and headed south. Addy looked smashing. She wore a turquoise-colored dress with a scoop neckline and pearls. She seemed to prefer her pearls when she was around her Wilson friends. I didn't understand why, when the locket was the most beautiful piece of jewelry I'd ever seen, she'd prefer pearls.

"Mrs. Walker must be very rich to own a plantation," I said when we came to the mile-long lane leading to her antebellum mansion and turned in. Spruces lined both sides of the lane, shielding the fields from view.

"Very. She's been married three times to rich husbands and widowed three times by rich husbands."

I thought if Mrs. Walker could find three husbands, then Addy should be able to find at least two. "Why haven't you married again?"

She gave me a cocky smile. "Why honey, how many perfect men have you seen lined up at my door waiting to propose?"

"Well, I'm sure there must be plenty who'd like to marry you."

"I can't give up my freedom for just any man, you know." She spoke in her party voice. "Oh, my goodness," she said as the car hit a bump. "Elizabeth needs to have her driveway fixed. Keeping this place running must cost an absolute fortune. Just look at that." She waved her hand toward the huge white house that had just come into view. "Painting that must cost enough to send a man to the moon. If we actually could."

Chatty, chatty. She had her ways of avoiding what I wanted to talk about. Like Adam Johnson. After church, just as we finished lunch, the phone rang. Addy ran to answer. And guess who? Adam Johnson. Again, she closed the door between us while they talked. I saw no other explanation for her closing the door, except that she'd not been truthful about his being her boyfriend.

We parked in the circular driveway. Addy, as though she hadn't seen Mrs. Walker's home a few hundred times before, dawdled in front of the flower beds, touched a red rose, leaned over to smell a yellow one. Then she made her way to the veranda, sauntering as slow as a caterpillar on a Sunday stroll. She ooohed and aaahed over Elizabeth's impatiens and the colossal ferns lining the veranda at precise intervals. "I just don't know why mine don't look like that," she kept repeating.

Mrs. Walker met us at the front door and took us through the house to the back terrace. She wore a floor-length, emerald green skirt, a multi-colored Oriental style blouse, a stack of clattering bracelets, and a large opal pin on her lapel.

"Would you like ginger ale?" she asked me after she'd poured sherry for Addy. Each time she moved, her bracelets sounded like the

92

clanging of symbols in the percussion section in an orchestra.

"Yes, Ma'am. Thank you." I smiled sweetly and, crossing my legs at the ankles like I'd been taught a lady should, wondered how old I'd have to be before she offered me sherry.

She tonged ice from the silver ice bucket, clinking piece by piece into a glass with her bracelets clanging in accompaniment. From the assortment of bottles on her cart, she took a Schweppes Ginger Ale, filled a glass, and dropped in a cherry. "Perhaps you'll play for us this evening," she said, handing me the drink.

"Yes, Ma'am, I'll be happy to." On the way to the terrace, we'd passed the grand piano in her living room.

She turned to Addy. "How was your vacation, my dear? We haven't had much chance to talk about your visit to Daytona."

"Very relaxing. And yours? Did you enjoy London?"

"As always."

They seemed to forget me as they talked, and that suited me fine because I wanted to soak up the surroundings. Mrs. Walker's plantation house looked like it belonged in *Gone with the Wind*. A breeze, laced with the spicy scent of crepe myrtle, blew up from the pond. Crickets chirped. A dog barked somewhere in the distance, and from the stables, located just past the vast expanse of lawn, came the occasional neighing of horses. I had a hard time imagining Mrs. Walker on a horse, but, as the owner of a plantation, I supposed she had to keep up appearances by having them.

My thoughts drifted to Reverend Stewart. I'd managed to forget him while I practiced that afternoon. But later, while Addy napped, I went out walking and wound up at Alice's house. We spent nearly an hour looking at her erotic drawings. I tried to imagine being in an embrace with a man like Reverend Stewart. Boys my age were so boring and infantile. I'd sampled a few dry kisses and a bit of fondling. Kissing had been something of a disappointment, but I reckoned that practice makes it better. I imagined kissing Reverend Stewart. I imagined a kiss as warm and electric as his hands felt holding mine, and what had Mrs. Walker just said to me?

"Ma'am?" I'm sure I blushed even though she couldn't possibly have guessed my thoughts.

"I asked if you would like to see the house. Addy suggested you might enjoy a tour."

"Yes, Ma'am." I brushed aside thoughts of kissing.

Mrs. Walker called her maid. Annie Mae appeared in a black uniform and crisp white apron. "She'd like to have you show her around," Mrs. Walker said, motioning at me.

I followed Annie Mae from room to room, gaping at the fine antiques and carpets, admiring paintings, Chinese lacquer ware, silver tea sets, and so many other things that I can't even begin to name them. Two large wooden masks hung on the wall above a bookcase in the library. Both had jagged teeth and black eyes the size of tangerines. A revolting orange tongue hung from the mouth of one. The other had what looked like a peacock headdress.

"From Nepal," Annie Mae said, seeing me stare. She pointed to where a Buddha served as a bookend on one of the shelves. "That's from Thailand. And that Bedouin jewelry over there on the wall came from Arabia."

I looked to where she pointed and then stepped closer to examine the ornate, but clunky, silver jewelry mounted in black frames. I marveled at a maid in South Georgia who knew about Bedouin jewelry and Nepalese masks. Aunt Mildred probably had never even heard of the Bedouins. I'd barely heard of them myself — just a mention in geography class. I also marveled at anyone who'd had the opportunity to travel to those places and come back with such a collection.

The tour ended in the living room. In spite of that room being as full of treasures as the others, I only had eyes for the grand piano. "May I play?"

"Yes, ma'am, you go right ahead."

I played a Mozart sonata, the easy one in C — the one they say is too easy for a student and too difficult for a concert pianist. Enchanted with the sonority of the instrument, I rippled off a Brahms waltz and then one by Chopin.

When I looked up, Addy and Mrs. Walker stood a few feet away. I'd been so engrossed I hadn't noticed their entrance.

"Bravo, bravo," Mrs. Walker said, clapping her hands. "When you're famous I can boast that you once played in my living room." She touched Addy on the arm. "You make sure this child gets a good piano teacher down at FSU. All teachers aren't created equal, you know."

"I intend to make sure that happens," Addy replied.

Others came to dinner that evening, including Dr. Whiddon and his wife, and Mr. Rich-Fertilizer-Man Chapman, without his.

Mr. Chapman pulled out Addy's chair and then deposited himself to her left where he paid her far too much attention. But who could blame him? She was especially lovely in a turquoise silk dress that fit snugly around her waist and hips but flared slightly below her knees. I thought her locket would have been nicer than the pearls she wore, but when I suggested she wear it, she shrugged and fastened the pearls around her neck. Candle light reflected in her eyes and on her lips. I'd never noticed before how expressive her lips were as they parted slightly, or formed a little pout when she shook her head over some comment, or when she puckered them in a smile.

They discussed the Suez Canal and the advisors sent to Vietnam while we ate an appetizer of lobster salad. "No chance of that becoming a full-scale war," Mr. Chapman insisted, tapping his curled hand on the table for emphasis. Then the conversation turned to the bus problems in Montgomery, and after that, the torn up street in Wilson.

With the standing rib roast, the men argued over who'd win the football game between Georgia Tech and the University of Georgia in the fall. *Had anyone received his season tickets yet? No? Soon, maybe.*

During dessert — blackberry cobbler with rum-flavored whipped cream — they spoke of Fiona. *Too bad Robert couldn't get away this summer. He must be exhausted taking care of her and working full time. Fiona isn't long for this world, I think. Poor man. This is the first summer he hasn't been able to go hiking.*

"He hiked the Appalachian Trail all the way from Maine to Georgia twice," Dr. Whiddon explained to me. Then he said to the others, "I'll have to grab Robert and take him off fishing one day."

Great idea. Wonderful idea. The Scots do like their fly fishing. The ladies agreed to sit with Fiona while Robert fished with the men.

They attempted to include me in the conversation. *Had I enjoyed* "The King and I"? *What courses would I be taking next year?*

At last — at *long last* because the gathering had become rather tiring — the party moved to the terrace for after-dinner coffee. Before joining the others, Addy and I headed to the powder room. I let her have the first turn while I waited outside the door.

"Why doesn't Mr. Chapman go places with his wife?" I asked when she came out.

She considered her answer for a moment. "Well . . ." she paused. We stood close together and I felt her breath on my cheek. "They have four young children. She stays home to take care of them."

Well, that was lame. One of the richest men in town and he couldn't afford babysitters?

Addy and I were the last to leave. Mrs. Walker followed us out the front door and onto the veranda. We stood there for a few moments surrounded by Greek columns and a night black as sin. The moon hid behind huge oaks, and the stars concealed themselves behind clouds.

"I guess you haven't talked to Adam Johnson for a while," Mrs. Walker said. "Say *hello* to him the next time he calls."

"Sure will." Addy put her hand on my arm and gave a gentle push to urge me away.

How strange, I thought. I wanted to ask why she didn't tell Mrs. Walker that Adam had called that afternoon. But I kept my mouth shut. Something — maybe the complete lack of expression on Addy's face — silenced me.

CHAPTER 6

How do you tell when someone doesn't like you? They don't show up for your party! We invited people for three o'clock. At two o'clock, I was pacing up and down the hall, around the kitchen, in and out of the living room, fretting and whining, worrying about no one showing up, getting in Earlene's way and on Addy's nerves. Finally, Addy gave me another job to do. "Check the glasses for lip prints," she ordered.

As it turned out, I needn't have worried. Penny and Jessie showed up at three o'clock sharp with the entire cheerleading squad and half the band front. Mr. Watson's brilliant daughter, Mary, also honored me with her august presence. Miss Top-of-the-Class had a mop of red hair hanging halfway down her back. Unlike her father who was a smidgen on the portly side, Mary's ankles and wrists were skinny enough to circle with my thumb and middle finger. I didn't actually put that to the test, but I was sure they were that tiny.

Earlene came through with flying colors in the food department, whipping up divinity, a caramel cake, and a mountain of peanut butter cookies. She also roasted a bunch of peanuts and made a pitcher of lemonade. Addy bought potato chips and two cartons of Cokes.

Addy greeted everyone and then disappeared into her study. Fortunately, she didn't hold the same opinion as Daddy regarding the sinfulness of showing legs because everyone wore Bermuda shorts. I wore my new green and blue plaid pair and a white shirt with a matching plaid collar. We sat around eating, drinking cokes, and listening to Blue Suede Shoes and The Happy Whistler, to Eddie Fisher and Elvis. At first, the girls acted a bit shy and stiff. Legs crossed at the ankles. Cokes held primly between fingers and drunk in little sips. *Just one cookie, thank you. Oh, what a nice house,* and *How do you like Wilson? Don't you miss your parents? Tell us about Africa. What a nice piano. Do you play?*

Things loosened up eventually. The music got louder. Voices got louder. Cheerleaders propped their legs over chair and sofa arms. Or maybe it was band front legs that were draped over Addy's immaculate upholstery. Some found the floor more comfortable. Drinks and paper plates cluttered every surface.

They warned me which boys to watch out for; shared which teachers were the pits; told me about Mr. Harry Feldman, the handsome English teacher. *And oh, by the way, will you be in the smart classes? Yes, because you look smart. Smart people have a look, you know. And you must be smart because your aunt worked for Nathan Waterstone. Your aunt is pretty. Does she have a boyfriend? Do you think we'll have to go to school with the Negroes? They're making them sit together on the buses over in Montgomery. Maybe Wilson High will be integrated.*

"Oh, no, my daddy says integration won't happen for a while — not until after we've graduated," Mary Watson contributed.

A communal sigh of relief greeted her pronouncement and the chatter returned to happier topics: *Do you want to hang out tomorrow afternoon at Rittle's? That's the drugstore downtown. Why don't you meet us at the swimming pool some afternoon?* I was dizzy with invitations, with information, with new names.

Late in the afternoon, abandoning a clutter of glasses, napkins, and potato chip crumbs, and with Elvis still playing in the background, everyone left except for Penny and Jessie.

"We have someone for you," Jessie said, when the door slammed behind the last guest. Sinking onto the middle sofa cushion, she pulled her braid over her shoulder, spread her arms over the back of the sofa, and stretched her legs out beneath the coffee table.

"Someone?" I switched off the record player. I'd had enough of Elvis.

"You know. A boy. His name is Fulton Hodges."

"He's in Gatlinburg right now," Penny said. She sat on the arm of the sofa. "We're going to introduce you as soon as he gets back. His girlfriend moved away last year."

"Oh . . . well, what's he like?"

"Cute," they answered in unison.

They left me with an invitation to go with them to the Saturday matinee and with the promise that Fulton would be back real soon.

I was standing in the living room looking at the clutter of paper plates when Earlene stuck her head through the door to announce supper.

"I'm not hungry."

"Yes'm, but I done made a big pot of Irish stew and you needs your nourishment."

"I'm pretty well nourished on peanut butter cookies and potato chips."

"Miz Addy 'spects you to eat supper."

"OK. I'll be there in a minute. I need to clean up." I didn't think I could bear to look at more food.

"Don't you worry none about this mess. I'll take care of that later."

I sighed. I'd have to sit down and pretend to eat. If I didn't, Earlene would fuss and fret that I didn't like her cooking, or that I'd starve to death, which was about as likely as my growing a tail. "I'll help you with the living room after supper. You're not going to clean up this mess alone."

I didn't trot off to the kitchen immediately. Instead, I took a few moments to look at the music strung across the piano — Chopin Waltzes — Schirmer Edition in a bright green cover; Chopin Nocturnes — same bright green cover; Brahms waltzes and Bach Inventions in yellow covers. I couldn't decide which Chopin waltz to play for my audition, but favored the one in A-flat which began with several loud chords before going into a lilting melody followed by showy sections with runs of grace notes. I played the showy section rather well, I thought. The waltz also kept going from loud to soft and from soft to loud. Very dramatic. In one place, the music died away to a double pianissimo before suddenly bursting forth with a double forte. I sat down and played the first line. The line needed more life, so I repeated the line, trying to add sparkle. I didn't realize Addy had come in until she touched me on the shoulder.

"Come to supper, honey."

"I'm not hungry."

"Come keep me company. You can romance the piano for the rest of the evening."

Of course, I had to tell Addy my impression of every girl at the party. In the middle of my description of Mary Watson, the phone rang. Earlene went to answer, while I continued with my description of Mary. "She's allergic to cats, so every time Lucifer or Tar Baby walked in she got all squeamish. And she's so arrogant about how smart she is."

"She didn't really talk about how smart . . ."

"Alice Worthington," Earlene announced from the door.

Addy looked at me; I looked down at the lump of stew beef I'd been pushing from one side of my plate to the other. I felt her eyes piercing me with questions — little ovals of heat where her stare burned my cheeks.

For a few moments neither of us said anything. Earlene stood in the doorway waiting.

"Tell her we're in the middle of supper," Addy said finally.

The guilt I'd kept at bay when I pretended to go out for walks but went to see Alice instead swept through me like water from a broken dam.

Addy lowered her gaze and resumed eating.

I suppose I thought I'd look less guilty if I kept talking. So I did. I jabbered away a mile a minute. "Mary said she wouldn't be a cheerleader because she wanted to devote herself to academic pursuits. *Academic pursuits.* Can you imagine using words like that? Everyone else just rolled their eyes. She said she might run for Student Council though because she needs extracurricular activities for her college application." I knew I chattered, but I didn't stop. No sirree, I kept right on chattering like a magpie. I think I even told her about Jessie and Penny wanting me to meet Fulton Hodges.

Addy finished eating. She laid her fork across the top of her plate, sat up very straight, dropped her hands to her lap, and fixed me with a look that brought my chatter to a screeching halt.

"I can't control who you choose for friends," she said, in a voice cold enough to freeze ice cream. "But understand this: Alice is not welcome in my house." She rose, pushed in her chair, and walked away.

I was ashamed. I didn't understand Addy's reason for not wanting me to associate with Alice, but I vowed to honor her request from then on. When I went to her room before going to bed, and admitted to my sneaky visits, the look she gave me tore me apart. I'd disappointed her after she'd been so good and generous to me.

"There are things . . .," she began, and stopped. She took a deep breath. "Please, believe me when I say Alice isn't a good choice of friend for you." She touched my cheek. "Honey, you met some nice girls today. You don't need Alice."

Jessie, Penny, and I went to the swimming pool fairly often during the following weeks. We'd be sitting on the side of the pool, gabbing away a mile a minute, or lounging on our towels talking to boys, and I'd look up and see Alice. She'd poke her head up out of the water, look in my direction, and then swim away. Or she'd stare at me from the edge of the pool where she sat splashing her legs. I pretended not to see her.

I'd never known Addy to be prejudiced because of religion, skin color, or the size of someone's house, so her disapproval of Alice sent my imagination into overdrive. *Someone in Alice's family was a murderer or horse thief. Her father sold moonshine. Her uncle had been a German spy. Alice had somehow uncovered the secret of the Lady's identity.*

In spite of this one glitch, I called this my Garden of Eden Summer. Everything else was perfect. I felt like my lungs had expanded as I breathed easier and deeper. The knots in my neck loosened. I practiced for my audition three or four hours every morning, spent my afternoons having fun, and had the luxury of having someone actually listen to me when I had something to say. Addy, the best listener I'd ever known, always made time for me when I wanted to talk.

Mornings, she worked in her study while I practiced. Sometimes she wrote minutes for the Women's Club or the Garden Club. She'd been elected secretary for both organizations. She took care of correspondence and press releases for the Foundation. When none of those chores demanded her attention, she made lists — grocery lists, shopping lists, Christmas lists, things to do around the house lists, chores-relating-to-the-Foundation lists. Sometimes she wrote letters to old friends. There were so many letters going to so many different places, I think she must have had college friends scattered over the entire U.S. She was always writing one thing or another.

About once a week, she and Elizabeth Walker went for lunch or a movie. Or both. Sometimes they went antiquing, and Addy would return with some trinket: a bracelet for me; a ring or pin for her; another silver salt spoon to be polished and added to her collection in the dining room china cabinet; an antique perfume bottle for the curio cabinet in her bedroom.

My afternoons glided past in a blur of movies, parties, outings to the municipal pool, hanging out at the drug store. One day, I persuaded Jessie and Penny to come with me to a tobacco auction, something neither had done before. Surrounded by the pungent smell of tobacco, I explained how each morning at the crack of dawn, farmers brought in their bundles of freshly cured tobacco and laid them out in long rows in the warehouse. Auctioneers, spouting auctioneering garble that you couldn't make heads or tails of, shuffled their way down the rows followed by buyers bidding on the various bundles. The buyers came from Camel and Pall Mall, Winston and Phillip Morris. We trailed behind the buyers and auctioneers until we became bored and went off to see *Around the World in 80 Days*.

I also spent a fair amount of time being lazy — something I'd never done before. One of Daddy's favorite quotes was *Idle hands are the devil's tool*. How absurd, I thought. Addy, anything but evil, had no problem kicking off her shoes and stretching out on a chaise lounge on the back porch with a glass of lemonade or on the front porch with a tumbler of ice tea. She laughed and chatted with neighbors who dropped by. Sometimes she wandered over to their porches.

Lucifer always followed whenever she went next door to Mrs. Thompson's backyard. While Addy and Mrs. Thompson strolled about admiring Mrs. Thompson's day lilies, he'd perch on the bridge spanning the fish pond and stare into the water's murky depths.

Mr.-Rich-Fertilizer-Man Chapman, who I could also have named *second-best-looking-man-on the-board* (Reverend Stewart being the best looking) dropped by one day with watermelon, tomatoes, and corn from one of his farms. He not only owned fertilizer plants and the John Deere business, but three farms as well. He made several trips to the kitchen bringing in the produce, and then sat with Addy on the back porch. I heard them laughing and laughing.

A sub-committee of the Nathan Waterstone Foundation, consisting of Mr. Watson (brilliant Mary's daddy), Dr. Whiddon, and Addy met twice during the summer. They went in Addy's study, closed the door, and conducted their proceedings in secret. I supposed they didn't want the rest of the world to know what kind of roof they considered for Nathan's house, or what color they'd decided to paint his back door, or whatever it was that needed to be discussed behind a closed door.

Reverend Stewart dropped by several times. He and Addy always sat on the front porch. Even if his visits came during my practice sessions, I took a break and sat with them while Earlene rustled up lemonade. If she caught wind of Reverend Stewart's coming ahead of time, she whipped up a treat for him to carry home — chicken 'n dumplings, a lemon icebox pie, or her famous divinity. I decided Earlene loved Reverend Stewart almost as much as I did.

Sometimes Addy and I spent our evenings on the front porch watching the shadows grow long. Or on the back porch where, away from the giant oaks, we saw the sky change from gold and orange to indigo and purple, and then to navy. We played gin rummy until midnight about once a week. Or we'd read together in the study. Or separately in our own rooms. We almost never watched television because of the awful reception.

"What a waste of money that TV was," Addy complained every time we abandoned our attempts at watching.

Time passed in such routine contentment you'd think I'd have forgotten Aunt Mildred. But I didn't. Thank goodness, she didn't call me, because there was no way I could have been polite to her. Nor did Darrell call. They were too busy with various harvests: cotton, tobacco, peanuts, the garden. But I didn't need her calls or her actual presence to remember. She was a thorn imbedded so deep it pinched me every time I moved. I'd never be able to gouge her out.

Inside my desk drawer, at the very bottom underneath some pads of paper where no one would see, I'd started my list: *Hints as to who the Lady might have been.* I didn't have much on the list: *Her hair was somewhere between blond and red (Nathan called it golden.). She wasn't from London. She volunteered as a nurse. Her husband was away, doing something having to do with the war. Was he fighting or something else? Nathan gave her an opal pin.* Her hair color reduced the suspects to a few hundred million women. Adding the other clues didn't improve the situation much. I suspected that somewhere there was a document or letter that would lead me to the answer. Probably in Nathan's house, to which I had no idea how to gain snooping rights. Or maybe even in the locked cabinet in Addy's study.

As summer sauntered toward fall, I quizzed Addy, thinking that if she talked enough she might let something slip. I'd begin with questions about her living in Germany and in London, and then maneuver the conversation to her working for Nathan.

"You must know who the Lady was," I ventured one day when we sat in the backyard swing sipping lemonade. I was barely able to mouth the words because the crushed ice in my drink had numbed my lips and tongue.

She laughed. "Quincy, you must be the most persistently curious person I know. How many times do I have to say *No, I don't know who the Lady was* before you'll believe me? But persistence is good," she added. "You need that quality to be an artist." She ruffled my hair playfully.

"But didn't you wonder who she was?"

"Of course."

"You could have followed him."

She stopped pushing the swing back and forth with her feet and stared at me. "Do you really think I'd have followed Nathan around, spying on him?"

"No. I think you'd make a terrible spy."

She raised her eyebrows. "Why do you think that?"

"You're too pretty. You could never sneak around unnoticed."

She laughed again, shook her glass to distribute the ice, and changed the subject to my upcoming audition.

ى   ى   ى

Toward the end of July the weather became so hot it made your skin cry. Then a long, dry spell set in. The blue sky changed to beige, and lawns turned to hay.

"It's going to be the ruination of the cotton crop," Earlene said. "Everybody's saying there ain't going to be no cotton to amount to a hill o' beans this year."

But I didn't have time to worry about cotton or parched lawns. August 10, my audition day, was crashing toward me. I spent my mornings in a frenzy as I struggled with Mozart and Brahms, Bach and Chopin, trying to get the fingering right, the phrases fluid, and the dynamics . . . Well, I tried to get them *dynamic*.

I worried. Would my hard work be enough to make up for never having had a good teacher? Was I too old at sixteen to begin the rigorous training demanded of a musician? Sometimes I'd be stretched out on the living room sofa on a lazy afternoon reading, while Addy read in her study.

About every third page I'd start fretting about the fingering in the Bach Invention. Or I'd be sitting with friends in a booth at Rittle's and remember a passage in Chopin or Mozart where I couldn't coax out a tuneful sound in spite of hours of practicing. My stomach would start churning like a washing machine and my foot tapping the floor in a nervous rhythm. Jessie always knew. "Ah, our Miss Quincy is thinking about her audition," she'd say. "Her face has turned purple and her feet are twitching!"

I'd laugh. Thank goodness for Jessie. She always made me feel better and helped me get through a million moments when my nerves were about to explode.

૮ઃ   ૮ઃ   ૮ઃ

Earlene's son, James, came for a visit during the first week of August. Earlene was very proud of her only child. "That boy, he dreams big," she told me. "He's going to be a doctor." James attended a college for Negroes in Albany and performed brilliantly (according to Earlene).

When James wasn't with his mother or visiting friends, he did a list of chores for Addy. He removed the wasps' nest from under the eaves at the back of the house, pruned dead limbs from the wisteria, dug up a flower bed, helped her clean out the garden shed, and painted the walls of the downstairs bathroom. I realized Addy had saved these jobs for James so she'd have an excuse to give him money.

"Added to the wages he earns from his summer job he should have enough for spending and book money next year," she said one day.

"Can he really be a doctor?" We were sitting at the kitchen table. I ate chocolate ice cream while Addy polished her latest salt spoon purchase.

"Why not?"

"Are there medical schools that admit Negroes?"

108

"Up north there are." She frowned at the spoon, focusing her efforts on a particularly stubborn spot. "But it's difficult for them to get in. We'll just have to hope for the best."

Addy gave Earlene a week off to visit with James, so at mealtimes we had to fend for ourselves. But Addy didn't cook. "No sirree," she said. "Not unless that's the only thing standing between me and starvation and maybe not even then."

"I can cook," I offered.

"Honey, that's what restaurants are for. So we can be ladies of leisure."

Aunt Mildred once accused Addy of being spoiled. "It's what come of having people wait on her, spoiling her rotten for two years," she said.

"Addy can hardly be blamed for having polio," Mama retorted. "Have you forgotten she nearly died, and when she didn't, how they thought she'd be crippled for life?"

Aunt Mildred had no answer for that.

I suppose Addy's near loss-of-life, or the threat of being a cripple, affected her outlook on life. She understood what was important and what wasn't. If you didn't like to cook and could afford to eat out, then why not?

We had cereal for breakfast, made sandwiches for lunch, and, except for three evenings when people invited us to dinner, went to restaurants for supper.

One evening we dined at Elizabeth Walker's. At Mrs. Walker's you *dined*; you didn't *eat*. We had enormous fun because Mrs. Walker spent the evening telling jokes and laughing so uproariously at her own nonsense that we couldn't help but do the same.

Miss Burke invited us another evening. During most of the meal she complained about the school board not giving her money for new library books, the principal refusing to hold back reports cards for students

109

who didn't return books, and naughty boys sticking gum underneath library tables. When she finished complaining about library matters, she and Addy talked about Foundation business.

I stopped listening after a while and went off into a dream world. I imagined sitting in Addy's front porch swing with Reverend Robert Stewart holding my hand, heat surging through my body, heart drumming. When I'd expressed my opinion to Addy that he was the most handsome older man I'd ever seen, she pointed out that forty could hardly be considered old.

"Well, old or not," I said, "He's handsome."

The third dinner took place at his house. We bought fried chicken, coleslaw, and sweet potato pie at Dupree's Diner and took the food to the Stewart's. Addy put the food into proper dishes while I made ice tea and set the table.

"I'll go and get Robert," she said when everything was ready.

"Where is he?"

"In his office next door at the church. You can tell Fiona we're ready."

I went to the screened-in back porch where Fiona sat in her wheelchair, half dozing. Every few seconds her head would jerk, and then she'd roll her head to face in the opposite direction. Tiny blue veins marked the lids of her closed eyes and her chalky-white hands lay thin and motionless in her lap. The nurse sat nearby reading a magazine.

"Supper is ready," I announced.

Fiona's eyelids fluttered. Then, in spite of the temperature being in the upper eighties, she shivered.

"She's cold," the nurse said, looking up at me as she massaged Fiona's arms. "Would you mind bringing a shawl? There's one in the bureau drawer — the third drawer down. The bedroom is on the left."

When I entered the bedroom, my hand flew to my nose and pressed against my nostrils to block the odor of medicine. Rows of medicine bottles and vials lined the bedside table. How could Reverend Stewart bear to sleep in such a smelly room? In such a depressing one? Heavy drapes blocked the outside light as well as any whiff of breeze that threatened to seep through the windows. The furniture was dark and massive, the walls a dreary beige.

A lamp, a glass, several framed photos, and a box of tissues stood on the bedside table along with the medicine containers. I turned on the lamp and dallied for a few moments looking at the photos. In one, a handsome Robert Stewart in military uniform stood next to Fiona in her bridal gown. She looked nothing like the Fiona on the back porch. I recognized her in the photo only because she stood next to Reverend Stewart. Another picture showed them sitting on a beach holding hands. Reverend Stewart stood with three friends on top of a rocky outcrop in a third photo. Pictures of people that I guessed to be parents or grandparents hung on the wall above the bureau.

I opened the third drawer. A gold pin with an opal embedded in its center rested on top of several shawls. Etched into the gold background surrounding the opal was a fanciful design of twining leaves and stems. I walked over to the mirror and, holding the pin to my blouse, admired myself. The opal caught a reflection of light and gleamed back at me. Someday, a handsome man would give me jewelry. Opals and emeralds. And of course, a diamond. But I had an errand to do. I put the pin down and returned to the drawer.

A red wool shawl and a plaid one both looked too hot. Underneath these lay a third one made of cotton. With its wide fringe and red flowers on a black background, the shawl looked like something for a Spanish dancing lady, not a sick Scottish one. However, Fiona would probably be more comfortable with a cotton shawl than wool ones in the heat of the afternoon.

About to replace the wool shawls, I noticed a large photo in the bottom of the drawer. Holding the photo up to the lamp, I recognized a younger Fiona with big, bright eyes and a lovely smile. Her hair slid over one shoulder, falling half-way to her waist. How long had it been, I wondered as I traced the pattern of her hair, since her smile disappeared, her skin paled to blue-white, and the sparkle evaporated from her eyes? How long since she changed from being the beautiful girl in the photo?

A door slammed. Footsteps clattered from the front door toward the back porch. I stuffed the photo underneath the shawls, returned the pin to the top of the stack, and hurried to the porch in time to see Reverend Stewart kissing his wife lightly on the forehead.

"Hello, Quincy," he said, turning to me and smiling his heart-stopping smile.

"I brought a shawl."

He took the shawl and wrapped it around Fiona, rubbing her shoulders lightly as he did so. "Ready for supper, Fiona?"

She gave her husband an expressionless look.

"Sure, she's ready. Aren't you, dear?" The nurse answered for her and then complained about one of the wheels on the wheelchair.

While Reverend Stewart bent down to adjust the wheel, Fiona lifted one hand a few inches above her lap, and moved her fingers as though communicating in a secret language. I watched, fascinated.

I could have done without the meal that evening. Pretending not to notice Fiona's bad humor at being fed like a baby, Addy chatted a mile a minute, bearing the entire burden of conversation. The few times she managed to get Fiona to say something, I barely understood her slurred speech.

I'd looked forward to hearing Reverend Stewart's Scots accent, but, except for an occasional response to Addy's monologue, he ate in silence. When fragments of sweet potato pie fell from Fiona's mouth and landed on her housecoat, he watched with a pained expression as the nurse wiped them away. Once, Fiona moved her head so that her hair caught a beam of light and reflected red-gold. For just a moment — the tiniest of moments — I imagined her as the woman in the photo. I wanted to reach over and touch Reverend Stewart. To run my hand over his arm to comfort him. My heart clenched as I tried to imagine the agony of seeing your beloved wife die — every day, a few more drops of life dripping away.

We left as soon as we finished washing the dishes. I was glad to leave. Glad to get home. Glad to get back to my piano. And to my rosy room with Tar Baby curled up beside me. Back to normalcy.

ൟ   ൟ   ൟ

A few days later, as the sun dipped toward evening, Reverend Stewart dropped by. They didn't invite me to join them when he and Addy sat on the front veranda.

"He's worried about Fiona," Earlene said when I complained about the exclusion. "He needs to talk to someone and Addy's right good at talking to people what needs sympathy. You just go off now and find something to do and leave them two alone."

I didn't. When Earlene went to the backyard to bring in clothes off the line I slipped into the living room and peeked onto the veranda through the slit where the drapes met. Shadows crept across the porch. Addy sat in the swing without swinging, and he sat in a rocking chair without rocking. He propped his elbows on the arms of the chair and leaned forward, resting his chin on templed hands. His mouth drooped.

What he said was lost to me for his voice was no louder than Tar Baby's purr. Addy spoke softly too, her words vanishing into a windless twilight. Mainly, she just listened. Once, frowning, she looked down at her lap and swatted away a fly that had settled there.

Earlene caught me.

"You're eavesdropping!" she hissed.

I moved away from the drapes. "No Ma'am. I'm not eavesdropping."

Her eyes opened wide.

"I couldn't hear. They speak too softly. I was just . . ."

"You were just . . .?"

"Well, you see, the Reverend Stewart looks so different from any minister I ever knew . . ."

"You get away from that window." She motioned me away.

I followed her to the kitchen where she pointed to a chair. "Sit. Your aunt sure be upset if she knowed you listened in on her private conversations, and what you mean that man look different?"

I sat down. "To tell the truth, Earlene, I think Reverend Stewart is the handsomest older man I know, and I just wanted to look." I stretched my mouth into a whopper smile, hoping for Earlene to take my truth as the silliness of a sixteen-year-old. "How in the world did he get from Scotland to Wilson, Georgia?"

She bared her teeth in a smile that outdid mine in size. "Yeah, he sure be a looker of a man. He come to Wilson because Nathan asked him to."

"Nathan?"

"They got to be friends over there in Nepal."

"You're kidding. Reverend Stewart was in Nepal?"

"Yeah, the Reverend, he likes to hike and such. He and Nathan met and went hiking around them mountains. Then they met up again in London, and they've been friends ever since. Leastways until Nathan died."

&ch; &ch; &ch;

Later that evening I stood beside the piano, staring down at the keyboard as though staring might help me play better. I wanted so much to be accepted in the program at Florida State, and I wanted to show Mama and Daddy that, even if they didn't, others recognized my talent. Or at least the talent I *hoped* I had. The audition had become the Great Divide in my life. If I succeeded my dreams would march forward. If not . . . Sometimes, I preferred being on the side of the Divide where I didn't know the outcome. At least I could still dream. If only I could hold back time; if only I could put out a hand and stop the passing of days. But I couldn't. The day came.

CHAPTER 7

Picture this: a nearly bare room filled with neon light — one light blinking and humming. A grand piano in the middle of the room. Me, standing beside the piano. Three metal folding chairs lined up in front of the piano. A tall lady — grandmother age with white braids pinned across the top of her head — sitting on one chair. A man with pursed lips and receding hairline on another, a pen clutched in one hand and a pad of paper resting on his lap. On a third chair, a younger woman with thick glasses and a bush of unruly brown curls. Her pen is stuck above her ear. All three silent. All three staring at me.

My knees shook. My hands sweated — a bad sign. Sweat makes piano keys slippery.

"Tell us what you're going to play," the older lady said. Her voice was husky, but in a pleasant way. She smiled at me, and I relaxed one-tenth of a degree. The curly-haired woman with thick glasses crossed her legs and swung her upper leg back and forth like a metronome. The man, who had been staring at me with blank eyes, tilted his head up and looked at the ceiling. Jutting out his chin, he stroked his neck.

I told them my selections. I wished that Addy had come in with me instead of sitting in the next room reading a magazine. Maybe she was nervous, too, and only pretended to read.

I sat down at the piano, wiped my sweaty palms on a handkerchief, and then placed the handkerchief next to me on the piano bench. I shouldn't have come. Being able to play loud and fast didn't make me a musician. I'd pressed my ear to the door and listened as the boy who auditioned before me played a Chopin etude. He played far better than I. The three jurors stared at me. *You're here, Quincy,* I prodded myself, *pick up your hands. Play. Bach, first. Just play.*

I forgot what I intended to play and played Bach Invention Number One instead of Number Four. Halfway through, I realized what I'd done, faltered, but then managed to keep going.

"I'm sorry," I said, when I finished. "I'm nervous. I forgot what I was going to play."

"That's quite all right," the white haired lady said.

I tried to remember her name. Mrs. Rich? I'd been so flustered when introductions were made, I hadn't paid much attention to names.

"You're supposed to be nervous," she said. "It gives your performance life. Why don't you play number four now. Consider what you just played as a warm up piece." She fluttered her hand, motioning for me to play.

The only kind of life my nervousness gave Bach Invention number four was a very shaky one.

I played the Mozart Sonata next. The man wrote on his pad. The woman with the thick glasses uncrossed her legs to sit askew in her chair, one arm draped over the back. "Nice," she muttered. She sounded insincere. She didn't write anything. Did that mean I wasn't good enough for her to write about?

I paused before I began the Brahms Waltz, trying to calm myself. I wiped my hands on my handkerchief and then dropped the handkerchief

117

on the floor. I bent over to pick it up and then thought I shouldn't have. Poor stage conduct. Only I wasn't on stage. I was fighting for my life — the only life I wanted. Hitting all the right notes in any Brahms piece requires concentration because of all the accidentals and octaves and big chords. I knew I'd die if I messed up and played too many wrong notes.

Ask and ye shall receive. I asked, but I didn't receive. Nope, God didn't help me out with the Brahms. I played a multitude of wrong notes. I hated myself. But I played loud and fast. Yes sirree, Quincy Bruce knew how to play loud and fast.

Deciding that I just needed to get the audition over with, I prepared to launch into the Chopin. I wouldn't be a pianist; I'd be a school teacher. Oh God, I'd wanted so much to be a pianist. I lifted my hands to play but then let them drop to my lap again.

Every noise in the room shouted. The humming light stopped humming and drummed instead. The man moved in his chair and the chair moved with him, screaming as the legs scraped the floor. I heard every breath of my three judges.

They waited.

The piano waited.

Then . . . A messenger whispered in my head. "Try to remember, Quincy," the messenger said, ". . . when late at night, when everyone else has gone to bed, how you feel playing the piano for fun. Have fun." If I was going to blow the audition, I might as well at least have fun. I lifted my hands to the keyboard and played the Chopin waltz.

Caressing the keys, I persuaded them to sing. I put my hands in my lap when I finished, but only briefly. Before the jurors could say anything, I lifted my hands to the keyboard and my fingers danced across the keys as I played the Waltz in E-flat major. I hadn't planned to play that waltz. But I did. Because I wanted to.

When I finished they clapped politely and smiled. Real smiles? Fake smiles? I didn't know which.

"Why don't you join your aunt in the other room," Mrs. Rich said. "We'll talk to you in a moment."

I nodded — my voice refused to work — and walked the ten miles across the room into the next where Addy waited. I shrugged when she gave me a questioning look. She closed her magazine and rose to give me a hug.

From the other room we heard the occasional raised voice, followed by a stretch of silence. Maybe we waited only a few minutes, but the time seemed to drag on forever. If they rejected me, then what? Expire and die?

Eons later, Mrs. Rich appeared.

"Congratulations," she said. "We're going to accept you into our pre-university program, and I would like to be your teacher."

I don't know what I did then. Something really silly, I'm sure. Like screaming, or jumping up and down. Or maybe I just stood there with my hands clasped in front of me and my mouth hanging open. Or maybe I did all those things. Or none of those things. Without my remembering how we got there, Addy and I found ourselves seated in Mrs. Rich's studio.

Her studio was at odds with her neat appearance. We sat on cracked leather armchairs in front of a desk littered with music books and notepads. A coffee cup, smelling of stale coffee and with brown stains dripping down the sides, sat in the middle of the mess. A bust of Schubert anchored a stack of music on one corner of her desk, while behind the desk, a bookcase overflowed with music and books. The grand piano on the far side of the room didn't look as shiny and new as Addy's but appeared regal, nevertheless.

"Quincy," Mrs. Rich said, and then paused to take a breath. "I have to be honest with you. Your background in music leaves a lot to be desired." She looked at me as though waiting for a response. I had none. She continued, "I think you play with a spirit that can't be taught, but you lack discipline, technique, and God knows what else." She gave a little wave with her hand. I guess the wave represented all the things I lacked. "There are a few things you have to understand and agree to," she said.

I nodded.

"You'll practice two hours every day, no exceptions." She smiled then. "Perhaps you can take a break on Christmas, Thanksgiving, and your birthday." Her face became serious again. "I will choose what you play. The succession of repertoire is very important for your development, and you might not like what I'm going to say next." She paused, and narrowing her eyes, studied me. "You're going to have to begin at the beginning."

"The beginning?"

"You have faults that need to be corrected. We'll begin with easy Bach pieces, some other primary pieces. Kabalevski, Clementi. Then we'll move on to one of the easy Haydn sonatas. Maybe a Mozart sonata or some variations. If you do as instructed you'll move rapidly through those and soon be back to more difficult pieces. You exhibit a lot of raw talent, Quincy, but we have to work to develop that talent. Are you willing to do that?"

"Yes, ma'am." I would have licked the floor if she'd asked me to.

೪   ೪   ೪

"I should get a job to help pay for lessons," I said when Addy and I were half-way home. Blown-up with happiness, I was half afraid of floating out the car window like a balloon.

"You're not going to get a job. How could you possibly think you'll

120

have time? Two hours practicing everyday plus homework?"

"But, Aunt Addy. . ."

"No *buts*. Enough of that."

CHAPTER 8

One morning a few days later, when I paused between endless repetitions of the g-minor scale and wiggled my fingers to relax them, the phone rang.

"Hello," I heard Addy say. A period of silence followed while the person on the other end talked. Several minutes passed before I realized she was speaking with Adam Johnson. Addy interjected only occasionally in the mainly one-sided conversation with Nathan's former agent. I'd hear a *no . . . , but Adam . . . , but we . . ., please, you said . . . , you're not being fair.* Finally, she banged the phone down on the receiver, stormed down the hall, and slammed the back door as she exited the house.

A creeping cold clawed down my spine. I went and peeked out the door and saw her sitting in the backyard swing, her hands covering her face. Had she been truthful when she claimed Adam Johnson wasn't her boyfriend? The conversation and her reaction sounded suspiciously like a lovers' quarrel.

Or did they argue about some mystery having to do with Nathan Waterstone? Something unrelated to the unidentified Lady? Or something related to the Lady other than her lack of identity? Maybe the Lady, whoever she was, bribed them to keep quiet because she was now happily married. Or maybe they bribed *her* to keep quiet. Nathan portrayed her as refined, but what if she'd been that way only in his imagination? She could have been a slut. How would that make Nathan look? Laughable, I thought.

∞   ∞   ∞

We scheduled my piano lessons for Saturday mornings. At the first one, I learned some of the reasons I didn't play well. I could play loudly, but not softly — at least not softly enough. I didn't give notes their proper values, holding some too long, letting others go too soon. My playing tended to be uneven and the phrasing sometimes nonexistent.

I began a disciplined practice routine. I worked on lifting my wrist at the end of a phrase so that the sound dwindled instead of ending abruptly. At the beginning of phrases I practiced dropping my fingers onto the note with wrist raised and then quickly lowering my wrist to balance my hand-weight for what followed. I did scales. Mrs. Rich said my notes didn't sound even and that I had to learn to listen. *Learn to listen. Learn to listen.* But no matter how much I listened, my thumb still thumped and my fourth finger played weakly. My scales went *thump*, two, three, *thump*, two, three, *weak fourth finger, thump.*

I practiced more than two hours every day, because I had a new worry. If I had to begin at the beginning, would I move up to difficult compositions in time to audition for college?

I practiced only in the mornings. I knew Addy was right when she insisted I take breaks so I wouldn't burn out. I filled my afternoons with friends and fun, reading, chatting with Addy. Sometimes I hung around the kitchen and talked to Earlene. Fulton Hodges returned from his vacation, and Jesse and Penny introduced us. In spite of being a football player, he was funny and perpetually cheerful. Cute, but not as good looking as

Reverend Stewart, he had short brown hair and a scattering of freckles across the bridge of his nose. Best of all: he liked me.

We went to a Saturday matinee on our first date and then afterwards to Jessie's with a bunch of people, including Miss Top-of-the-Class Mary Watson, where we roasted peanuts, danced, and talked. One afternoon, he drove me around town, showing me spots of interest, including the gigantic oak tree Wilson was famous for, and his daddy's tobacco warehouse and cotton gin.

"I have to work at the warehouses next summer," he said when we stopped at Ship Ahoy for hamburgers. "Daddy expects me to learn the business. Would you believe he's making me take typing classes? Typing classes! He says I have to work first in the billing department and learn how to charge people and collect money. But, jeez, typing classes!"

I didn't tell him my daddy expected me to take typing classes too and that I planned to disobey him.

We spent several afternoons at Rittle's drinking cherry smashes before slipping out the back door to go over to the Rose Theater, where we sat in the back row holding hands, or with his arm propped on the back of my seat and his hand caressing my shoulder. Fulton knew the rules. No petting below the neck. I wondered how Mama and Daddy had managed to forget.

One evening before school started, Elizabeth Walker and Reverend Stewart came to dinner. They had to decide on a new heating system to replace the defunct one in Nathan's house, so the dinner conversation revolved around fuel efficiency, service costs, ducts, and leakage. If Reverend Stewart hadn't been there I'd have eaten my meal in the kitchen with Earlene. Her conversations weren't half as boring as what I endured. But instead, I sat at the dining room table, watching the handsome minister discussing the merits and drawbacks of oil, gas, and electric heating systems with the two ladies. His voice that evening was restrained, and his face reflected what everyone knew: Fiona was deteriorating.

"I guess a former nurse like Fiona must have difficulty when she becomes the one having to be nursed," Mrs. Walker commented when Reverend Stewart left.

"Fiona was a nurse?" I asked.

"And a very good one, I'm told," she replied.

ممم   ممم   ممم

The day came when I had to switch piano practice from morning to afternoon: school started.

I wanted to put my best foot forward, so on the first day I wore what I considered to be my most attractive outfit: a full skirt with butterflies in a dozen different shades of pink imprinted on a navy background; a navy blouse; a long pink scarf tied around my waist as a belt; and penny loafers with navy socks. I knew I looked good. I had a boyfriend. I'd already made several girlfriends. And my musical career was off to a start. Life was perfect.

Then, during second period, the world changed.

I walked into English class and chose a front row seat. Jessie grabbed the one behind me. Only after flopping my school supplies onto the desk and sliding into my seat did I glance at the teacher. In one second flat, the handsome Reverend Stewart went skidding to the back of my mind.

Mr. Feldman stood beside the battered and scarred wooden teacher's desk, one hand in a pocket, the other tapping the desk. He had wavy blonde hair and eyes blue enough and big enough to swim in. He smiled at me and the heat wave of the century surged through me. My cheeks turned the color of pomegranates. I knew they did because I felt

125

how hot they were. Did I breathe? I'm not sure. I remember smoothing my skirt over my knees and uttering a quick prayer: *Please God, don't let my face stay red.* I'm sure my heart beat loud enough to be heard all the way to the gym.

When everyone, including Mary Watson who took a front row seat beside me, had sat down, Mr. Feldman began. He spoke with eloquence, explaining that we'd be studying American literature from beginning to end. A great deal of reading would be required — several hundred pages each marking period. He'd give us lists from which to select the readings. He required that we write a three page essay each week. *Please have the essay ready to hand in at the beginning of the period on Fridays.* Although today was only the first day of school, we'd be prudent, he advised, to begin thinking of a subject for our big project of the year: a research paper on an American author. We would, of course, read a sizable portion of that author's works.

There were the usual sound effects that greeted that sort of announcement: groans, shuffling of feet, sighs. I, however, sat quiet as a mouse on Christmas Eve. I vowed to make my paper the best he'd ever seen — good enough to set him raving in the faculty room about what a marvelous student Quincy Bruce was. Wonderful enough to win his heart. I'd ask for Addy's help. She knew about research because of her work on *Faust*. Not only did I vow to present Mr. Feldman with the best research paper he'd ever seen, but I planned to be his best student ever. Mary Watson didn't stand a chance. No, sirree, Quincy Bruce was about to rocket to the top of his list of all-time great students.

He stopped tapping the desk and moved over to stand in front of me. Inches away. "Quincy . . ." he said, and smiled down at me. A light danced in the vast blueness of his eyes. ". . . I believe you must know quite a bit about our local author, Nathan Waterstone. Miss Burke told me Adelaide Simmons is your aunt."

I managed a hoarse "Yes sir."

"When we come to modern American writers perhaps your aunt will speak to the class."

No, I decided in a flash. I wouldn't allow Addy to come and charm him and have him going gaga over her like other men did. "I'm sure she'd love to," I said, struggling to sound normal. When the time came, I'd find an excuse for her not to come. I wanted Mr. Feldman all to myself even if the having existed only in my dreams.

❧   ❧   ❧

Addy quizzed me about school during supper. Parents, and aunts acting as parents, *have* to ask about school. As if you'd really tell them the important things. Like how I ignored certain people at lunch — Alice Worthington, to be specific; or how Fulton kept leaning all over me in the two classes we had together because he wanted to make sure the other boys understood I'd been taken; or how a certain man teacher had come to dominate most of my thoughts.

"School was good," I said. "It's going to be a lot more work than my old school. But I'll do fine. Don't worry."

"I'm not worried, honey. I know you'll do well. Tell me about your teachers." She leaned back to listen.

"Miss Ellsworth teaches algebra. She's about two hundred years old and verrrrry strict. She makes you keep a math notebook which has to be just so or she makes you do the pages over again. That's what everybody said. You know, the ones with older brothers and sisters who've had her."

"I've heard about Miss Ellsworth. Her students do well in college."

"I have Mr. Mann for American history. He's skinny and ugly and has a beak instead of a nose. They say he's really hard." I hated history to

127

begin with, so I expected his class to be a challenge. "Mr. Kirkland is my physics teacher. He's funny."

"Who do you have for English?"

I toyed with my fork, hoping my face hadn't reddened at the mention of English. "Mrs. Richards is my French teacher. I wish I could take German."

"You can take German in college. Most high schools don't offer German. Who is your English teacher?"

"Mr. Feldman." I'd been told spearing food wasn't polite, that one should always scoop food. But I looked down, letting my hair slide over my cheeks, hoping to conceal my blush, and speared my peas. I watched how they made their way up the tines of the fork as I added others at the bottom. Spearing took longer than scooping, and I didn't want Addy to notice my face.

"Ahhhh, Mr. Feldman."

I gave her a sharp look and wondered about the smile that crept across her lips.

"I've heard about Mr. Feldman." She rested one arm on the table and let the other dangle over the back of the chair. "He's every female student's dreamboat, isn't he? I need to meet this legend."

"He's too young for you, Addy. And he's too young to be a legend."

She laughed. "A good-looking man is never too young for any woman, my dear. At least as long as you're only admiring. You aren't going to let him distract you from what you're supposed to be doing, are you?"

"Nooooo." I stretched the *no* out as long as a boa constrictor. *Please don't let my face be red*, I implored. *Oh, dear God, please don't let Addy notice.* "We have to do a research paper on an American writer. I thought you might give me ideas on research, and writing, and stuff."

"Stuff?" She raised her eyebrows.

"You know. Whatever stuff I need to know so I can write a good paper."

"Of course I'll help you, but begin by not using *stuff*." She pushed her plate back and leaned on her elbows. "You need to remove that word from your vocabulary, honey. *Stuff* isn't a word a concert pianist wants to use when she's speaking to people sophisticated enough to enjoy good music. Speaking of music, are you going to have time to practice and do all this studying?"

"Yes, ma'am. I just won't be able to hang out very much during the week."

"Well, I'm sure your friends won't be able to either. What other classes do you have?"

"Art," I groaned. "I wanted to take something else but that's the only thing that fit in my schedule. Don't expect too much from me there; my talents lie elsewhere." I didn't tell Addy that Alice Worthington had enrolled in the same art class, and that we'd been seated next to each other, or that she'd spent most of the period snarling at me.

"Just do your best."

In a sudden change of mood, Addy frowned down at the table and rubbed her forefinger back and forth along the handle of her knife. "Adam Johnson will be here next week," she said. Her voice sounded flat.

"Why?"

"To meet with the Board and look around Nathan's house." She stopped massaging the fork and looked at the far wall. "As long as Nathan's books continue to sell, Adam will be down occasionally to deliver his opinion and advice." She turned to Earlene who had just walked through the door with a pile of clean dish towels. "Is there any pound cake left, Earlene?"

"Yes'm." Earlene set the towels on the counter beside the cake stand. "You want a piece, missy?" She looked over her shoulder at me as she lifted the cover from the cake.

"No, thank you," I said, rising. "I want to finish my homework so I can practice a little more."

Tar Baby followed me to my room and leaped up beside me when I settled in the chair with Hawthorne's *The Fawn*, the first of my extra reading in English. So, I'd finally get to meet Adam Johnson. My gut feeling told me his trip to South Georgia had little to do with poking around Nathan Waterstone's house and meeting with the board.

∾   ∾   ∾

The following Friday after an excruciating day at school, I staggered through the front door to find Adam Johnson standing in the living room, hands planted in the pockets of his expensive looking suit. He stood around six foot two, about the height of my daddy. He had gray eyes and dark hair, and thanks to liberal amounts of Murray's Pomade, his hair lay sleek and ordered. He spoke like a Yankee. I guess that makes sense since he *was* a Yankee — one of that breed that invaded Georgia with Sherman and burned Atlanta. He wasn't bad looking, but he didn't measure up to Fulton and Reverend Stewart, and he was leap years away from Mr. Feldman. He must have heard my footsteps when I crossed the veranda because he acted like he had nothing better in the world to do than stand there waiting for me to walk in. He couldn't have chosen a worse day.

To begin with, I came home exhausted. Our English themes had to be handed in on Fridays, so I'd gotten up extra early to go over mine even though I'd spent ages the previous evening doing the same thing — checking and rechecking. I aimed for perfection. I guess I thought something might change while I slept — like maybe the devil dropping in during the dark of night and replacing periods with commas, or putting singular verbs with plural nouns.

On top of that, Alice Worthington had been particularly obnoxious in art class. It wasn't bad enough that we sat next to each other where I had to watch Alice turn out amazing drawings while mine looked like a pile of rubble. But after shunning me all week, she suddenly decided to taunt me with the fact that I'd ignored her during the last half of the summer; that she was beneath me because the "in" crowd had befriended me; that she wasn't good enough for the likes of me because of my rich aunt.

"Would you stop that about my rich aunt. She isn't rich," I snapped.

"Realllly." She arched her eyebrows and stopped sketching the bowl of fruit Mrs. Arness had placed on a stand in front of the room. "Your aunt owns a big, fancy house; she drives an expensive new car; you told me she has a Steinway grand piano. If that's not rich I'd like to know what is." She turned away and resumed her drawing.

"Alice, I'm sorry I ignored you most of the summer, but I had to practice for my audition."

"You don't have to explain." Her voice would have registered down around zero on a voice thermometer. "I thought we were going to be friends. I saw you at the pool and at Rittle's with those other girls, and you pretended you didn't see me."

"Addy wanted me to get to know them." We had to end our conversation because Mrs. Arness came and stood over us, scorching us with her dragon glare.

Things went downhill after that. Unable to do all the problems on the algebra quiz, I had to watch Mary Watson gloat because she got an A+. Mr. Mann sprang a pop quiz with impossible questions about colonial settlements in New England. Mary Watson did fine, of course. Mrs. Richards spent part of French class yelling because Thomas Burns didn't have his homework for the third day in a row. It didn't seem fair that the rest of us had to listen to a screaming teacher because of one student. To make matters worse, Buddy Simms held his nose and, in a nasal voice not quite soft enough, made fun of the way she spoke French. Mrs. Richards can hear an ant peeing, so we had to endure another round of yelling. I was zonked by the time we got to the pep rally at the end of the day.

Ellerbie High didn't have a football team, so pep rallies were new to me. I had no idea how much noise can be generated at one. But I did my share of screaming, stomping, and clapping. No, sirree, nobody could accuse me of lacking school spirit. Fulton, being on the football team, made my enthusiastic participation sincere. After the rally nobody went home, at least nobody that was anybody. We all went down to Rittle's, where the noise almost equaled that of the pep rally.

So, I wasn't overjoyed to come home and find Adam Johnson planted in the middle of Addy's living room, holding out his hand out and saying, "Hello, I'm Adam Johnson." All I wanted to do was grab a cookie and get to the piano. But there he stood, right in front of the Steinway, smiling his Yankee smile, waiting for me to acknowledge his greeting.

"I'm glad to meet you," I said, and shook his hand.

"It's my pleasure. I've heard so much about you."

What do you say to that? *I've heard so much about you.* That statement always made me feel like I was hanging upside down on the jungle gym with my underpants showing.

"I've heard so much about you too." Actually, all I knew about him was that he'd been Nathan's editor, and that he called Addy a little too often, and that sometimes he upset her. I shifted from one foot to the other, weighed down by my gargantuan stack of textbooks.

"Why don't you put your books away and come chat with us," Addy said. She sat on one end of the sofa, legs crossed, and a cigarette posed between two fingers. Tar Baby lay on her lap. She stroked him with her free hand.

Addy smoked? I stared at her. In disbelief I watched her put the cigarette to her lips, inhale, and then blow out a long stream of smoke. "I'll just take my books up to my room," I said and glared at the spiral of smoke curling toward the ceiling.

I trudged upstairs and flung the books on my bed. Secrets! Addy smoked; Addy whispered on the phone; Addy drank wine. Someone sent her flowers. Who? Had she, by any chance, forgotten that tomorrow was Saturday, my piano lesson day? She wouldn't cancel my lesson because of a tall, slick-haired Yankee, would she?

I returned to find him sitting on the other end of the sofa. I plopped down in a wing chair. They both looked at me like I was the centerpiece on a banquet table until Addy finally looked down and stubbed out her cigarette in an ashtray I'd never seen. Some people had secret stashes of chocolate; Addy had a secret stash of cigarettes and ashtrays.

"Addy's been telling me about your piano playing," Adam said. "Can I hope to be so fortunate as to be treated to a little recital?"

"I don't think you'd really enjoy hearing me now. I have a new teacher and I'm working on some easy stuff to improve my technique. I need to learn to apply my improved technique to the easy stuff before I can move on to more difficult stuff. And I'm practicing a lot of scales, and finger exercises, and stuff like that." *Why am I going on like this,* I wondered. *Adam Johnson doesn't care about my technique or my scales, and I just said stuff four times.*

"You can play the pieces you played for your audition," Addy's voice was a mite sharp.

I relented. "I'd be happy to play for you, Mr. Johnson. Just not today. Tough day at school, you know." I tried to fake a pleasant look. "How long will you be here?"

"That depends." He gave Addy a meaningful look. "It depends entirely on how well and fast my persuasive abilities work."

My heart crashed to the floor. He wanted to marry her. Why had she lied to me? A lump the size of a watermelon grew in my throat. Would she go away with him to New York? Of course she would. What about me? What about my piano lessons? My career? I wanted her to have a husband, but someone who lived in Wilson, not a Yankee who'd take her away.

"Would you mind if I go to the kitchen for a drink?" My voice trembled.

"Of course, honey. I'm sorry. Go and relax. We'll talk later. Adam and I will move to the study so you can practice."

ʔ   ʔ   ʔ

"You look like you been run through the mill," Earlene said, when I came drooping into the kitchen. "But I got just what you needs." She opened the cupboard and brought out a platter of peanut brittle and held it out to me. "Go ahead; supper ain't for a while yet. Little sugar do you good."

I took two pieces. "How long will Adam Johnson be here?"

"Don't know. Them two's being whispering all afternoon. Can't figure what they're up to."

"Where's he sleeping?"

"Down at the Park Hotel."

"I didn't know Addy smoked." I took the pitcher of ice tea from the Frigidaire and poured myself a glass.

"She don't hardly never smoke. Just when she get nervous about something." Earlene dumped a five-pound bag of potatoes in the sink and began scrubbing them.

"What is she nervous about?"

Earlene shrugged. "I ain't got no idea."

"I've known her all my life and didn't know she smoked."

"I expect there's lots of things about your aunt you don't know. Sit down before you drop crumbs all over the floor." Her arms jiggled as she attacked a potato with a paring knife. "I just don't like that man," she muttered. "Ever' time he visits, out come them cigarettes and she gets all funny acting."

Too tired to pry information out of Earlene, I sat there eating peanut brittle, drinking ice tea, and watching her peel potatoes. Two bottles of wine stood on the table. A gift from Adam, Earlene explained when she saw me staring at them.

Four pieces of peanut brittle later, I sat down at the piano and stormed into a Brahms waltz, pounding the piano like I was about to storm the Bastille — too loud, too fast, too passionate. After a couple more stormy pieces, I relaxed. School faded away. Adam Johnson faded away.

Too bad he couldn't fade away permanently, I thought when we sat down for supper in the dining room. The Wedgwood china and the Waterford crystal were laid out for Adam. And linen napkins. A bottle of wine. A vase of roses. The fragrance from the roses harmonized with Addy's gardenia perfume. When she lit the candles and turned off the chandelier my heart cried. My soul cried. In fact, I cried everywhere except from my eyes. Was I going to have to witness romance in bloom — looks and sighs and veiled comments? But the conversation turned to mundane subjects. To the upcoming presidential election, for one.

"There's no way," Adam said, and tapped the fingers of his left hand on the table for emphasis, ". . . that Adlai Stevenson can beat Eisenhower."

"Of course not. That would be too good to be true."

"At least you'll still have your moment of fame in Wilson every time Ike comes down to play golf." He took a sip of wine.

"I wish he'd pick a better looking vice-president."

"You don't like Dick's looks?" Adam seemed amused.

"I like neither his demeanor nor his politics." Addy didn't seem amused. Nor hungry. She toyed with her food, pushing peas around with her fork, tearing off a bite of bread but then letting the bread drop to her plate uneaten.

"Well, Stevenson won't win."

Addy sighed. "I know. Are they still rehashing the sinking of the Andrea Doria up there?"

"Yes. I imagine they'll dwell a while on that tragedy. Don't you like the wine?"

"Of course. Thank you for remembering that I like German wines." She lifted her glass and smiled at him. She looked like a million dollars in her dark red dress, gold locket, and gold earrings, her perfectly applied makeup. Her hair dazzled with hints of gold.

Adam raised his glass, too. "Drink up. Perhaps when you've had enough you'll see things my way."

Hope flamed. She must have refused his proposal. When he suddenly remembered that I sat at the table, I felt better about talking to him. He asked me about school, about music, about boyfriends. *My favorite subject? English.* I didn't tell him I loved English because I had a passionate crush on the teacher. *The subject I liked least? History. He couldn't understand why; he'd enjoyed history immensely. Had I thought about where I might study music? Julliard? Curtis? I'm not that good. Oh, you're just being modest. What about boyfriends? How many? A pretty girl like you must have them lined up at the door. Was there one in particular? Oho, A football player. So Miss Quincy Bruce was not only pretty, smart, and talented, but popular, too.* Good God! He was disgustingly Uriah Heepish.

"Did you like *David Copperfield?*" I asked.

"Why yes, I liked *David Copperfield.*" A look of confusion spread over his face at the sudden change of subject, and at his failure to make the connection between his own groveling behavior and that of Uriah Heep. "Can't say that was my favorite book, though. I prefer Hemingway and Steinbeck and some of our more modern writers."

The conversation dwindled to unimportant things: more talk of Eisenhower and Stevenson, and of something going on over in South Africa that had to do with removing people from their land to make room for other people. As soon as possible I excused myself and went back to the piano.

ৡ   ৡ   ৡ

I lingered in the archway to the unlit living room. From somewhere outside — a street light, or a porch light, or a fairy's twinkle — a tiny glow touched the piano and reflected from the darker than night ebony. I crossed the room and, instead of sliding the piano bench from beneath the keyboard, I lifted the bench and without making a noise, set the bench down at a proper distance for playing. I didn't want to destroy the blessed quiet by scraping the legs on the floor.

I played. In the dark. From memory. And something magical happened. Things I'd worked so hard on suddenly fell into place. The upward and downward movement of my wrists at the beginning and end of each phrase became a natural movement, correctly timed, and for the first time I understood how each phrase "spoke."

Thrilled, I played all the Mozart I knew and then switched to Chopin. I played on and on, until finally exhausted, I crept shoeless — my shoes lay under the piano — to the study to say good night to Addy.

I'd forgotten about Adam until I heard their voices. The door to the room stood open the barest of cracks. Standing in the dark hallway I looked at the thin line of light coming from the study and, God forgive me, I stepped closer and listened.

"It isn't fair, Adam. The last time, you said . . ."

"I made no promises last time. You know that."

"But you implied . . ."

"The implication was of your imagining. Come on, Addy. Look at what you've gotten out of this."

"Yes, just look. What I've gotten is . . ."

"Shhh, not so loud."

I leaned closer to the door. They whispered. Then their voices rose again.

"There were no promises last time." Adam sounded angry. "But this time there will be. Please . . ." he said more softly, ". . . once more. Then, you'll get what you want."

"Everything?"

"Of course not. You know that's impossible. We'd be ruined." I heard the panic in his voice.

Then: a lingering, deepening silence.

Barely breathing, I pressed closer to the open slit. Until I heard a sound — a chair scraping or a foot shuffling. I couldn't tell. Frightened that I'd be caught, I tiptoed away.

In spite of awakening the next morning to a sunny-delicious day, a bird chirping outside my window, and the smell of cinnamon buns baking, I had a heavy feeling in the pit of my stomach. *Promises? Ruined?* What had they been talking about? But grown-ups talked that way, didn't they? Like the slightest little thing might ruin them. Mama and Daddy had those conversations. *The offerings in the collection plate weren't enough to make our car payment this month,* Daddy would say. *We're going to be ruined,* Mama would reply.

I sat up and swung my feet to the floor. Surely their argument had to do with money. The subject of money made adults pessimistic. I'd forget the conversation, go downstairs and have a nice breakfast that included fresh cinnamon rolls, and then I'd go to my piano lesson. Maybe the Foundation treasury didn't contain enough money to replace the ancient heating system in Nathan's house. Or something like that. I shouldn't have been listening in the first place.

CHAPTER 9

When I walked through Mrs. Rich's studio door every Saturday morning, my stomach fluttered in happy anticipation, and I put everything else out of my mind. The mysterious conversation between Adam and Addy disappeared somewhere in the jungle inside my head.

Not only did I love playing the piano, but I loved Mrs. Rich.

I loved the way she sat beside the piano, listening, narrowing her eyes as though that helped her hear better. When she found something she didn't like, she stopped me and made me go back and do the measures or phrases again and again until I got them right. She didn't hand out compliments freely, so when I got one, my head swelled a few sizes.

I loved her melodious, cello voice and the way she enunciated her words, turning every syllable into a jewel.

I loved the way she looked: tall and slim, dressed with easy elegance. She always wore a simple skirt and blouse, a strand of pearls and pearl earrings. If someone had asked me to describe what a *lady* looked like as opposed to just a *woman*, I'd have described Mrs. Rich.

That morning we exchanged the usual pleasantries — *How was your week? How did school go?* Then we got down to business. She turned on the piano lamp. I sat down at the piano. After positioning her chair to my right, she put on her glasses, arranged her arms, and we began.

I played the F-major scale and then the F-major chords and arpeggios. She gave me a drill to make the scale smoother and asked about the Hanon exercises. *Yes, I'd been doing those faithfully. She could tell. My fingers were working quite well, independently of each other, strong. I needed to learn to play all the notes equally, however. I still clunked on some. Listen, listen, listen. Ears must be trained as well as fingers. Let's hear the Clementi.*

"My dear, my dear." I heard the excitement in her voice when I'd played the last note of the Clementi sonatina. "You've mastered the phrasing. I'm very, very pleased."

My playing of the Kabalevski and Bach pieces pleased her too. "We're ready to move on," she said, and reached for my book of Mozart Sonatas. She turned to the easy sonata in C; the one that isn't as easy as it looks. "Let me show you."

I slid off the bench and she slid on. Her playing warmed me like a fire in the hearth on an icy winter day. "If I played like that I'd be the happiest person in the world," I said when she finished.

"Every note must be even. These phrases . . ." she pointed to a run of notes, ". . . should sound like a string of pearls, and that isn't easy. Keep practicing your scales."

I begged her to play the sonata again. I wanted to memorize every nuance, every movement of her hands. "I'll play something else for you instead," she said. She went to her bookcase and ran a finger along the spines of music books until she found what she was looking for. Returning to the piano, she placed a book of Shubert sonatas on the music rack and sat down. When she opened the book to a sonata and played, I felt my eyes water.

"How long will it be before I can play Schubert like that?" I wanted to know.

"Schubert is demanding. But you'll get there. Keep practicing."

        ꝺ   ꝺ   ꝺ

Our football team smashed Albany High's that afternoon. Still hiding the fact that I didn't completely understand the game, I jumped up and down when everyone else did, hollered, waved my flag, and groaned when things didn't go well. Fulton made three touchdowns.

"What are you wearing to the dance tonight?" Jessie asked as we pushed through the crowd exiting the stadium after the game. She clunked along in her majorette boots, baton clutched firmly to her body so as not to poke anyone.

"A lavender dress I bought last summer. What about you?"

"Mama made me a strapless dress with a tulip skirt. Oh, look there's Mr. Feldman." She waved.

Ten feet away, heart-breakingly gorgeous, Mr. Feldman was making his way toward the exit. When he saw Jessie wave, he wove through the crowd to join us.

"Enjoy the game?" he asked.

"Immensely," Jessie answered.

"What about you, Quincy?" He smiled down at me.

My brain went dead. I couldn't think of anything intelligent or witty to say.

"I enjoyed it." *I enjoyed it.* I gave him a big, stupid smile and wanted the earth to cave in under me because I felt like such a klutz. I wished I were like Addy; she always knew what to say to a handsome man.

He walked out of the stadium with us, chatting and dazzling us with his smile.

Still in a romantic daze when Jessie dropped me off at home, I floated through the fallen oak leaves cluttering the yard. The perfume of summer had disappeared and that of fall tinged the air. I wiped my feet on the mat at the front door, discarding a leaf that clung to my shoe. Others had collected there — the signature of fall: a little pile of brown and yellow leaves at the front door.

Silent, dark, empty — the house felt abandoned. Earlene wasn't in the kitchen. The door to Addy's study stood ajar. I looked in. No one. Upstairs, no one. Even the cats had vanished.

I found Addy in the back yard swing — without a book or the pad of paper on which she made her endless lists. She had one arm draped over the back of the swing and the other resting in her lap while she stared off into space.

Swishing through the fallen leaves, I went to join her. "What are you doing?"

"Nothing. Sometimes doing nothing is quite nice."

"Where's Adam?" I leaned against the trunk of the pecan tree.

"At Nathan's house. Doing whatever he does when he's there."

"And what's that?"

Her gaze drifted. "I expect he just hangs out and talks to Pearl and Jonas. You remember Pearl and Jonas, don't you?" She sounded tired.

"Of course. When Mama brought me to Nathan's house to see you at work, Jonas gave me candy. He sang out of tune when he mowed the lawn and snipped shrubbery. But he sounded happy. Does he still do that?"

She nodded. "He still sings out of tune." She moved over in the swing and patted the space next to her.

I squeezed in. A leaf floated down from the pecan tree and landed on her hair — a yellow leaf on her brown hair.

"And Pearl?" Addy asked. "You remember her?"

"The housekeeper. Of course. Jonas gave me candy, but she

frowned at me and wouldn't let me run in the house."

"You shouldn't run in houses." She sounded less tired, and a smile played at the corners of her mouth.

"Does Jonas still keep a bottle of whiskey hidden away?"

"Ah, yes. The whiskey. I'm sorry to say that sometimes he still treats himself to a drink, or several.

Neither of us said anything for a few minutes. She was right. Doing nothing felt good. Addy moved the swing back and forth with her feet. The swing creaked — a comforting, friendly creak. I dragged my feet on the ground, making parallel paths.

"How long will Adam be here?"

"Until he gets what he wants."

My breath caught. "What does he want?"

"Adam has an agenda, honey." We were sitting so that our arms touched. I felt her muscles tighten, until, in a sudden movement she sat upright, bringing both hands to her lap. She looked straight ahead. "I might as well tell you."

My stomach tensed. Fearing what she was about to say, a lump rose in my throat. My mind told me I had no right to decide who she fell in love with, but my heart told me that Adam Johnson wasn't the right one.

"Adam wants to do another novel."

I let out a whoosh of air as relief rushed through me. So he wasn't her boyfriend after all. "You mean, like the posthumous novel you already did? Like *The Mistress*?"

"Yes. Now you know why Adam came."

"But that's wonderful." I felt a rush of adrenaline. How exciting to be present when Addy worked on the last Nathan Waterstone novel that would ever be published. Clearly, she wasn't experiencing the same excitement as me, however. "Why do you look unhappy?"

"We began the final editing of *The Mistress* before Nathan died, but now Adam proposes publishing a novel from a sketchy draft. And Nathan had terrible handwriting." Looking down at her lap, she massaged the back of one hand with the fingers of the other.

"So you have to edit, rewrite, and still make the book sounds like Nathan's work."

"Exactly." She drew the sweater she'd thrown over her shoulders tighter around her. "What are you wearing to the school dance?"

"The lavender dress. The one we got in the store next to Rich's."

"You look good in lavender." Lucifer, who'd wandered over, rubbed against Addy's legs. She reached down and lifted him onto her lap. "Who won the football game?"

"We did. Thirty-five to six."

"Great. What time is Fulton picking you up?"

"Seven o'clock. But, Addy, I want to hear about the new novel."

"I'm not ready to talk about the novel yet. The setting is Scotland; that's all I'm going to say. When Nathan died, my only thought was of finishing his last novel. But now, I know that every time I struggle to decipher his accursedly bad handwriting I'll hear his voice the way I used to, chiding and teasing because of my inability to decode his squiggles." She gave a little laugh and wiped away a tear. A shadow from a drifting cloud passed over us. "Quincy . . . ."

"Yes?"

"What I just told you can't be repeated. For now, the novel must be just a little secret between us."

Another secret.

"I won't tell anyone."

＊ ＊ ＊

The board members met with Adam before he returned to New York. I didn't hang around to greet them, but during a study break when I slipped downstairs for a brownie, I ran into Mr. Watson who had just walked into the dining room for a piece of peach pie.

"I hear you and Mary have several classes together," he said.

"Yes sir." I put the biggest brownie on a napkin to carry back upstairs.

"My Mary is a right smart girl." I guess he forgot he'd already informed me of her brilliance. Peering at me from over his glasses, he picked up a fork. "You two must be real good friends by now."

"Yes, sir. Well, I have to go. Lots of homework." I smiled and escaped to the kitchen for a glass of milk.

＊ ＊ ＊

I had the dubious pleasure of having Mary in all my classes except for art and French. She took Latin and music appreciation instead. I'd walk into class, and there'd be Mary sitting in a front row desk, her text-book open to the right page, her gaze fastened on the teacher, her mouth open waiting to devour every tidbit coming out of the teacher's mouth. Her notebook — unlike everyone else's — had no loose pages falling out. Neat and orderly homework, done in precise handwriting, lay ready to hand in at the drop of a hat, and she had her assignment book out and her pencils sharpened.

"I'm going to medical school," she explained a few days after my encounter with her daddy. "I need to make the best grades in every subject. Getting into med school is sooooo competitive."

We were standing at our lockers outside the second floor boys' toilets, close enough to smell sanitizer and urine every time the door opened. Unlike the jumble in everyone else's locker, the contents of Mary's looked as neat as my late grandmother's china cabinet. Big books lay at the bottom, middle-sized books in the middle, smaller books on top. Goldilocks and the Three Bears popped into my mind.

"So far I've been successful in achieving that goal," Mary continued. "When I go to college, I know making the best grades will be more difficult, but I will. My father — he's an attorney, you know — graduated at the top of his law school class at Mercer University. If he can, then so can I." She paused to remove a book from her locker. "I think we have something in common, Quincy." She didn't look at me because she was busy closing her locker door. Everyone else slammed theirs. But not Mary. She closed hers with two fingers, pressed to snap the locker shut, and then ran her finger along the edge to make sure she'd done the job properly. While she went through her ritual I waited to hear what we had in common. Finally, she finished closing her locker to perfection and turned to me. "Let's talk while we walk. I don't want to be late to class."

"We both have a goal," she said as we wove our way through the hall, which was like a can of sardines with all the sardines trying to move from one side of the can to the other. "You want to be a concert pianist, so you're sacrificing things so you can practice." She glanced at me. "I hear that you practice two hours every day. Is that true?"

I nodded. I didn't know when the word had gotten out. Now everybody wanted me to play for them. I never did. They wanted to hear things like *Love Me Tender, Love Me True.* They definitely didn't want to hear Mozart.

"I'm giving up things too, for the sake of my grades. As a woman, I have to be exceptional to get into medical school. Did you know that fewer than ten percent of medical school classes consist of women?" She raised her eyebrows and waited for me to acknowledge that I didn't know.

"No, Mary, I didn't know that." At least she had a ten percent chance. I wondered what chance Earlene's son had.

We arrived at Mr. Feldman's class to find him bent over his desk, shuffling papers. He pushed a stack to one side, picked up a couple papers, put them down, and then shuffled through some more papers. The tingling feeling I always had around him tingled away.

The bell rang. He straightened and looked around the class. I could almost read his thoughts: *Well, everybody seems to be here, so let's get started.* He got started all right, and I hated Mary Watson from that day. The papers he'd been shuffling turned out to be the themes we'd handed in the previous Friday. He took one, leaving the others in a disorderly pile. The theme was Mary's, and he read it to the class as a fine example of what a theme should be: interesting subject, well-organized, no trite phrases, and the punctuation was mostly right. Mostly? Good, I thought. She messed up something — a comma somewhere, or a hyphen.

"You also wrote an excellent theme," he said to me a few minutes later as he passed out the graded papers. But mine hadn't been good enough to read to the class. Mary had the biggest gloat I'd ever seen. I wanted to squish her face in a cider press and squeeze out every smidgen of her arrogance.

"I've decided to do my research paper on Ferlinghetti," she said, when we walked out together at the end of the period. She *had* to walk out with me so she could rub in her superiority.

Who in the world was Ferlinghetti? I felt hopelessly unsophisticated. I'd been considering Mark Twain or Ralph Waldo Emerson. How could I compete with someone doing a paper on a man with a name like Ferlinghetti? Or was Ferlinghetti a woman? I imagined the

148

rest of us turning in boring, hum-drum papers about ordinary famous people while Mary Watson wrote a smashingly successful paper on someone I'd never heard of. I agonized when I thought of Mr. Feldman looking at her with that look in his eyes: *Oh, you've done a splendid job on your research paper, Mary Watson, and aren't you special!*

I must have still had that good-god-I'm-jealous look smeared across my face when I walked into Addy's study after school. She observed me with raised eyebrows — her silent, questioning, raised eyebrow look.

"What's the matter?" she asked. She sat in a chair, feet curled up under her, pen and pad of paper on her lap. Adam sat on the sofa reading *The Atlanta Constitution.* He glanced up for about a tenth of a second and then went back to reading his paper.

"Nothing," I said. She should have known not to ask me things like that with Adam around.

"Everything ok at school?"

"Everything's fine."

Silence. Her eyebrows still raised. Adam still reading.

"How's Fulton?"

"Fine."

More silence, but a lot of questions coming from her eyes. I shuffled from one foot to the other. "I'm going to get something to eat," I said finally.

She caught me before I got to the kitchen and gave me a long, intense look, the kind that said *Ok; we're alone now, so tell me.*

"It's just that I haven't decided who to do my research paper on. You know, the one we have to do in English class about an American author."

"Were you supposed to decide that by today?"

"No."

"So why are you worried? I thought you'd chosen Mark Twain."

"He's so ordinary."

"By no stretch of the imagination is Mark Twain ordinary."

"But everybody knows about him. Mary Watson is doing hers on Ferlinghetti."

"I see." A hint of amusement flickered in her eyes.

"I want my paper to be better than hers."

"Because she's writing about Ferlinghetti doesn't mean her paper will be better. I had no idea you were so competitive, Quincy."

"Well, I am." I wasn't — except where Mary Watson was concerned. I wanted Mr. Feldman to think I was the best. I wanted him to look at me the way he'd looked at Mary.

"Adam leaves tomorrow. We'll talk about your paper when he's gone."

"Thanks, Addy."

      ও   ও   ও

When the idea hit, I was sitting at the kitchen table eating peanut butter smeared on vanilla wafers and listening to Earlene hum, accompanied by the thump of the rolling pin as she rolled out dough. I watched her flatten the dough and then cut the dough into long strips for dumplings. Chicken simmered in a big black iron pot waiting for the dumplings.

"Early supper tonight," Earlene said. "So Mr. Johnson can go back to his hotel and get a good night's sleep before he leaves tomorrow. He says he loves my chicken 'n dumplings."

There aren't too many things that smell better than chicken 'n dumplings. The aroma from the cooking pot and the monotony of listening to Earlene thump the rolling pin lulled me into forgetting Mary Watson and her paper on Ferlinghetti.

"What else are we having?"

Earlene straightened, arched backwards, and rubbed her back. "My back sure been hurting lately. I ain't getting any younger."

"What are we having for dessert?"

She hummed a few more bars before answering my question, but her answer didn't register because that's when the thunderbolt hit. Just like that. Whack. I almost fell off my chair.

Of course. Why hadn't I thought of him before? *Nathan Waterstone*. I'd do my paper on Nathan Waterstone! Addy knew things about him that nobody else knew, and I could announce the new book in my paper. Surely, by the time the research paper was due, the time would be ripe for revealing the news. And maybe, just maybe, I'd figure out what people had been trying to figure out for years: the identity of *The Lady*. So, watch out, Mary Watson! Ferlinghetti, whoever he/she was, was going to look like cold mashed potatoes to my filet mignon.

Adam left, and Addy began hibernating in her study, the pages of the new novel piling up on her desk as fast as the brown and yellow leaves piled up outside. The pages continued to accumulate as the leaves disappeared, swept up by Addy's occasional yardman, or blown away by remnants of hurricanes blowing up from Florida, of which there were two that year. First came the strong winds and then the rains, which began as a patter on the roof but quickly turned into a pounding.

Soon, chilly mornings demanded that coats come out of closets, and the bleachers in the football stadium grew cold enough for cushions and blankets. Frost glittered on the Spanish moss and, one day after school, sleet bounced off the windshield of Jessie's old Studebaker as she drove me home. Hot chocolate replaced ice tea as my after-school beverage. Earlene had the good grace to have the hot chocolate simmering on the stove when I walked through the door every afternoon.

Addy kept working, oblivious to changes in the weather, but she often joined me in the kitchen for a few minutes before she went back to her editing and I to my practicing. We sat shoeless at the round oak table. I slipped off my shoes as soon as I sat down, while she didn't have any on to begin with. When she wrote, she dressed comfortably. Comfortable, she claimed, meant no shoes, just a pair of warm socks, a pair of baggy pants she'd saved from her London years, and an over-sized sweater. "Women wore slacks to work during the war," she explained when I saw her in slacks for the first time. "They wore them because they were doing men's work while the men were fighting."

Addy became a different Addy. No longer dressed like she'd stepped out of *Vogue*, she shunned make-up and left her hair disheveled. Her focus had changed to something deep inside her mind. Only when we went out did she take the time to reconstruct her former self.

Neither Earlene nor I were allowed in Addy's study, nor did she invite Elizabeth Walker in when she came to visit. Nor her other friends. I'd peek through the door from time to time to see her sitting at her desk, the glow from a single lamp burnishing her hair with streaks of reddish gold. She'd be hunched over the Underwood, pecking away, or frowning over something written on a page, or reading a secret message written on a far wall while she tapped her pencil. I guess she was waiting for inspiration when she gazed at that wall. Or clarification. "Nathan's handwriting is sooooo difficult to read," she complained at least once a day, and she'd pat the stack of handwritten papers that sat beside the typewriter. "Just look at this," she said once when I peeked in. She motioned me over and handed me a page. After laboring to decipher a few lines of Nathan's spidery handwriting, I understood her problem.

When I asked about the board's reaction to the new book, Addy flabbergasted me by saying they didn't know about the new book. "You didn't tell the board?"

"Preparing a manuscript for publication isn't their concern. At least, not yet. They're charged with operating the house as a museum and taking care of financial issues."

There was one board member, however, who knew. Reverend Stewart dropped by one day to pick up chicken soup Earlene had made for Fiona. Addy followed him to the front door when he was ready to leave, and I heard them talking about the book. "If the book is a secret from everyone else," I asked when he'd gone, "why does Reverend Stewart get to know?"

"Robert proofread Nathan's last four books," she explained. We were standing in the hall outside her study. "He's an excellent proof reader. He found errors and inconsistencies that both Nathan and I missed. And because he knew Nathan longer than either Adam or I, he understood Nathan better." She leaned on the doorframe, rubbing her hands together to warm them. A cold wind had blown in while she stood at the front door talking to Reverend Stewart. "Besides, Robert's a minister and accustomed to keeping secrets."

In answer to my question as to why the book had to be a secret, she shrugged her shoulders and said there was a right time for everything. The right time for telling about the new novel, I knew, needed to be at the same time my research paper came due. I wanted to be the first to announce the publication of another posthumous novel by Nathan Waterstone. I pictured the scene:

"Miss Bruce, what is this about a new novel by Nathan Waterstone?" Mr. Feldman would ask. He'd be standing there, handsome as ever, dangling my paper in his hand, focusing his big blue eyes on me.

"They'll make the announcement to the public later this week," I'd say. Then I'd look over at Mary Watson and give her a coy smile before turning back to Mr. Feldman. "My aunt is in the process of editing Nathan's notes. I expect the novel will be ready for publication within the year." Or within two years. Or six months. I wondered how long a publisher needed to get a book ready for publication.

I'd already figured out a strategy, or rather a framework, for my paper. First, I'd start with a paragraph about my aunt writing in her study — my aunt, Nathan Waterstone's . . . What was she? His typist? That didn't sound special. His secretary? Too ordinary. His assistant? I didn't like that either. I'd figure out what to call her before the final draft. So anyway, she's in there typing. But what is she typing? Something special to be revealed at the end of the research paper!

While I practiced, I kept a notebook beside me and recorded the hours she spent writing. I'd be agonizing over a difficult passage in a Bach Invention, or working on the a-minor scale when Addy emerged for a drink of water or a cup of coffee. I'd stop and make a note. *November 10, 1956 and Addy Simmons, Mr. Waterstone's ?????, takes a refreshment break from the secret undertaking she's been involved in for the past few weeks. What could all this writing be about? A biography of the writer? Who would be better qualified to write the biography of the man who knocked the socks off the literary world with his novel,* The Lady, *and then went on to win prizes for two of his novels. Mrs. Adelaide Simmons spent four years in London working with Mr. Waterstone on* The Lady *and* Himalayan Adventure. *After the war, they both came to Wilson where he wrote the remainder of his novels.*

After writing something of that sort, I'd go back to factual things about Nathan. How he grew up in Macon and went to a private school.

How his parents expected him to be a doctor. Then I'd intersperse more about the writing that went on in Addy's study. I'd describe her sitting at the desk with the sleeves of her cardigan pushed up. Her ink-stained hands. Her hair in disarray. I'd tell how she got up from her desk and went to sit in her favorite chair to struggle over the wording of something, pulling at her ear while she sat deep in thought. How sometimes she bent over the typewriter until late at night, papers strewn about. How the desk lamp shone on her work and her hair, but left her face, which was bent over the typewriter, in shadows. By the time I got to the end, I'd have everyone wondering if Addy was writing a book about Nathan. Just when my readers (Mr. Feldman and the other students, because surely he'd read my paper to the class) thought they were about to hear the announcement of a biography, I'd proclaim the issuance of another posthumous novel edited by my aunt. Try to top that, Mary Watson, I gloated.

CHAPTER 10

"I'm glad to see you're still among the living," Elizabeth Walker complained to Addy at church. "It's been ages since we've done lunch, and you missed both the Garden Club meeting and the Women's Club. You haven't been sick, have you?" Fingering her long strand of coral beads, she tilted her head to one side and widened her eyes in a question.

"I'm doing some sorting. You know how things pile up." Addy gave a dismissive wave. "I've been tossing and organizing. Sometimes I get so busy I forget which day of the week it is."

"Well, my dear, I hope you won't forget to come to dinner on Friday." She began pulling on a long, black leather glove. "Leland Chapman is coming and he's actually bringing that mouse of a wife with him. And I persuaded Robert to get away for an evening, so he'll be there."

Addy assured Mrs. Walker she wouldn't forget.

Reverend Stewart dropped by later that week. We were halfway through November, and the weather had become too cold to sit on the veranda, so Addy brought him inside. For a few minutes he ignored Addy and talked to me. "How's school?" he inquired. Then he asked about piano lessons. Adults could make a recording. They all say the same thing. *How was school? How is this? How is that?* But there was a difference between

156

Reverend Stewart and other adults. He actually listened to the answers. No wonder Nathan confided in him.

In spite of the restrictions on the rest of us to keep out except when invited in, and in spite of the fact that the study was a mess, Addy took him there. Papers were strewn everywhere — on the floor, the sofa, the chairs, the tables. So much for secretaries (?), typists (?) being neat and orderly. Whenever she left the room she shut the door behind her to keep me and Earlene out, claiming she'd never find things if someone moved them.

"I'll close the door so we won't disturb your practicing," she said and left me standing alone in the hall.

I practiced while they talked. Mrs. Rich had assigned me a Chopin Waltz. "Some call this the two-three waltz," she'd explained, "But that isn't correct. The right hand plays a six-eight rhythm while the left hand plays a three-four rhythm."

Try putting that together! I'd turn on the metronome and practice the left hand; then I'd practice the right. Then I'd try putting the two together and fail completely, so I'd go back to practicing hands separately. The piece fell apart every time I tried to play with both hands together. Tar Baby sat on the sofa flicking his tail like a metronome. I guess he was trying to help me with the rhythm.

During a break I crept down the hall to the study to eavesdrop and was surprised to hear angry voices. Two people I liked very much were angry with each other? Disturbed, I didn't stay to hear what they said, but returned to the piano. I pulled my legs onto the bench and sat for a few minutes with my arms wrapped around them.

When Reverend Stewart left, I still sat at the piano; I wasn't playing because my hands shook. Why were they arguing? He didn't say goodbye, but strode past the living room, his head down and face flushed.

By the end of the week, I still hadn't gotten the waltz right.

"Don't worry, you'll get the hang of complicated rhythms," Mrs. Rich said. I must have looked doubtful because she patted me on the arm. "If everything was easy, then everybody could accomplish all things, and as you know, they can't. But you will."

She took her book of Chopin Nocturnes from the bookcase, motioned for me to rise from the piano bench. "Chopin has bedeviled many a young pianist by writing a constant rhythm in the left hand and a phrase for the right where you have to intertwine an odd number of notes." She slid onto the bench, opened the book, and pointed to a passage. "Look! Fifteen notes in the treble played against four bass chords. It's a dickens of a job to coordinate that." She played the nocturne, stopping to replay the passage where the fifteen notes were. Then she played another passage where seven treble notes intertwined with two bass notes.

"Keep practicing," she said.

And I did. Between school, football games, dances, movies, I practiced like a Banshee. I had no idea what a Banshee was, but Addy often used that phrase. "I worked like a Banshee today," she'd say sometimes as we sat in the kitchen after school, spreading peanut butter on vanilla wafers or having a piece of pound cake with a hunk of cheddar.

Refreshed and fueled, we'd both go back to our work: she, to adding more pages to the pile destined to become the new book; me, to working on becoming a famous pianist and writing a research paper to win Mr. Feldman's heart.

Around the first of each month, a letter from the Congo fell through the letter slot in the front door and clunked to the floor along with the other mail. Descriptions of life in Africa and tales of saving the natives, or of not saving the natives, filled the letters. Mama reported how she and Daddy learned the Binga language bit by bit. Daddy, with help from another missionary, managed to put together simple sermons in Binga. Mama taught an English class in the village. A shipment of clothes from Ellerbie Baptist Church had arrived at their mission, but they found the natives reluctant to wear them. Some made the effort but discarded them after a few days. "I think western clothes don't fit their lifestyle," Mama wrote. "But Daddy keeps trying."

In one of the early letters she described their living quarters as harsh: a house that was nothing more than a hut; no running water; a toilet in the bushes with the snakes; a bathroom in the river with the crocodiles. I shuddered.

Mama still had no interest in my music. She didn't congratulate me when I wrote saying that I'd been accepted in the program at FSU. *You're devoting too much time and too much of Addy's money to something you can't continue*, she answered. In our hearts, my parents and I floated apart on an ocean wider than the real one that stood between us.

In the November letter, Daddy asked me about my typing class — the one I wasn't taking.

The one Fulton *was* taking.

"Damn, I hate typing," he exclaimed one day as six of us sat crowded in a booth at Rittle's, slurping root beer floats. "Peck, peck, peck. Old Lady Fussell struts around the room and yells if we aren't sitting straight or holding our hands properly. Jeez, what a waste of time. Nobody else's daddy makes them take typing."

"Well, I guess you just need to learn all sorts of stuff to run that ol' cotton gin," Jessie quipped.

"I can run my Daddy's business without learning to type." Fulton jammed his straw up and down in the ice cream at the bottom of his float. "That's what you hire secretaries for."

We laughed.

"Well, y'all can laugh all you want, but y'all don't have to take typing."

ॐ   ॐ   ॐ

The subject of typing came up again at our pre-Thanksgiving dinner. Aunt Mildred had called one day to invite us for Thanksgiving dinner when Addy and I were both out. Earlene answered the phone, took the message, and relayed the invitation to us when we returned. We'd already accepted an invitation to Elizabeth Walker's.

"I don't think our previous invitation is going to hold much water with Mildred," Addy said. "At least where you're concerned. You haven't seen her since your parents left. She'll be insulted if you don't go."

"Addy!"

"It won't be that bad."

I gave her an *oh-yes-it-will* look.

"I guess you're right. You'll definitely have more fun at Elizabeth's." She looked at me for a moment, thinking. "We'll invite them here the evening before Thanksgiving," she said, finally. "We'll tell her we've already accepted an invitation for Thanksgiving dinner and can't be rude by turning down an invitation we've already accepted."

I didn't want to have pre-Thanksgiving dinner, or any other kind of

160

dinner with Aunt Mildred, but my mind was at ease on that score. I knew Aunt Mildred wouldn't accept an invitation to eat at a sinner's table.

Addy issued the invitation.

Aunt Mildred accepted.

But Addy, I wanted to cry, *you don't know what Aunt Mildred thinks you did; or what she thinks I'll become.* But how do you tell your favorite person in the whole world that someone thinks she's an adulteress?

∾   ∾   ∾

Addy laid out her best for Aunt Mildred's family: the Wedgwood, the Waterford, the Towle, the Irish linen napkins. They arrived on time, dressed up in Sunday-go-to-meeting clothes. I wanted to ask Aunt Mildred why she'd come for a meal at Addy's when she seemed to think you caught sin the same way you caught chicken pox, but she wouldn't have understood the logic. Seeing her standing there behind her chair, cloaked in self-righteousness, waiting to eat at Addy's table, while thinking that Addy had been the Lady galled me so much I didn't think I'd be able to swallow turkey or pumpkin pie.

Addy piled Sears and Roebuck catalogs on a chair for Bobby. "You don't need a booster seat; you're a big boy, now," she said, and tweeked him on the cheek. At the last minute, after everyone had taken a good look at the pre-Thanksgiving table in all its glory, she replaced Bobby's Wedgwood plate and Waterford crystal with an ordinary plate and glass.

"It sure looks grand," Aunt Mildred said. The finery must have made her nervous because she kept pulling at her suit jacket. I'd seen the suit in one of the Sears catalogs that Bobby sat on. The pea-green color of the material reminded me of the Wicked Witch of the West. Uncle Roger looked nervous, too. He jammed his thumbs into his pockets, rocked back and forth on his heels and shifted his eyes around, checking out the finery. It was his first time in Addy's house.

"This food smells pretty darn good," Darrell said leaning over the table and sniffing. "And I sure do love turkey, Mrs. Simmons."

"I'm so glad you do, Darrell." She lit the candles and then flicked the light switch. "The blue in that dress you're wearing suits you right well, Patsy."

"Thank you, Mrs. Simmons. My Mama bought me the dress special for today."

"Well, the dress is very pretty. And that's such an interesting shade of nail polish you're wearing." She nodded at Patsy's nails which were the color or ripe persimmons. "Shall we sit?"

Addy asked Uncle Roger to sit at the head of the table and give thanks. Even though he looked uncomfortable sitting at such a fine table he managed to produce a lengthy and pious blessing in which, among other things, he asked God's help in beating the Commies wherever they needed beating.

"What about Cuba?" Addy asked when he finished. She unfolded her napkin and laid it in her lap. "Whose side do you think God should be on down there? Castro's or Batista's?"

He looked at her blankly.

She smiled sweetly at him. "Shall we pass you our plates and have you serve the turkey from there, Roger?" For the first time, I became aware of Addy's mask — the sweet, dripping-with-sugar mask.

"How's Buster?" she asked Darrell, her mask cast aside. She liked Darrell.

"He's fine. We go huntin' just about ever' day after I'm done my chores." Darrell passed his plate to Uncle Roger. "Fill me up with plenty of dark meat, please. Maybe, I'll just take one of them big ol' drumsticks." He turned back to Addy. "Buster is a fine hunting dog."

"Do you kill any game on these hunting trips?"

"No ma'am, we just go traipsin' around. I shoot my BB gun sometimes, but we ain't never brought nothing back. Maybe I'll get me a squirrel or a possum one of these days."

Addy passed her plate down to Uncle Roger and then turned to Patsy who sat next to her. "What about you, Patsy? Are you enjoying school?"

"It's ok." She shrugged. "I don't 'specially like my teachers, and I have to take algebra. I can't see why we have to take such useless stuff. And we're all pretty worried about having to go to school with the niggers."

Earlene had just walked in with hot rolls. Her face remained impassive, but Addy's expression froze. My cheeks turned hot. If Darrell hadn't sat between us, I would have kicked Patsy in the shin. Mortified, I wondered if one could divorce relatives.

"I can't see what them people in the courts are all about when they allow such," Aunt Mildred said, ignoring Earlene's presence. Did she not realize that Earlene was actually a person? "The Bible says . . ."

"Do try some of the corn pudding, Mildred," Addy interrupted. Her eyes looked like a film had slid down over them. "How are your clothes collections for the Congo coming along?" she asked in a practiced, even tone.

So went the conversation — Addy trying to steer the talk to unobjectionable subjects; Aunt Mildred and Patsy finding their way back to objectionable ones. Including my not going to the Baptist Church.

"You're going to the Presbyterian church?" Aunt Mildred asked, narrowing her eyes and cutting me with her steel-blade gaze. She held her fork suspended between plate and mouth. "Even though your Daddy is a Baptist preacher?" I held my breath. Glancing around the table, I saw that everyone else did too, as we waited for Aunt Mildred to launch into one of her sermons. She merely raised her eyebrows, and gave me one of her looks before going back to eating. Who else, other than Aunt Mildred, could express so clearly with a look that Presbyterians ranked below Baptists?

Next, she brought up the subject of typing. "I just can't believe in another year and a half you'll be out on your own earning a living," she said, as she crunched into a stick of celery. "I remember when you were running around with diapers hanging down to your chubby little ankles." She picked a celery string from between her teeth and put the string on the side of her plate. "Pretty soon now, you gon' be graduating and going to work." She took another bite of celery. "Your daddy says you're learning typing. I was pretty darn good. I could type sixty words a minute with no more'n two, three errors. Since you just got started, I guess you ain't doing that well yet." She fell silent for a moment while she swallowed. "With all that piano playing, your fingers must be nice and limber for typing." She looked at me questioningly. "Well, how *are* you doing?"

What could I say? If she told Daddy I'd refused to do what he told me to, he might give her permission to yank me away from Addy's and take me to her house. Then, goodbye, music.

Addy came to my rescue.

"She's doing well in all her courses," she said. "A fine job. You just wouldn't believe how much homework she has. And she never complains. Try some more cranberry bread, Roger." She handed the bread plate to Patsy. "Pass this down to your daddy." She turned back to Aunt Mildred. "I've been wondering what you do with all those beautiful pot plants on your front porch when winter comes, Mildred. I declare, you have about the greenest thumb I ever saw. You're going to have to give me lessons in plant care one of these days."

I went to my room when they left and curled up in my easy chair to read. Tar Baby jumped up and stretched out in my lap. I ran one hand up and down his silky fur; in my other I held an English translation of *Faust*.

"That's heavy reading for a holiday."

I looked up to see Addy standing in the doorway.

"I guess. But I wanted to read *Faust*. How weird is that — someone selling his soul to the devil?"

She came in and sat down on the bed. "People sell themselves all the time."

"What do you mean?"

"For one thing, people sometimes take shortcuts to get what they want."

"Why shouldn't they take a shortcut if that gets them where they want to go faster?"

"Not all shortcuts are good, but that subject is too serious to tackle on a full stomach." She waved her hand in dismissal. "I came to talk about typing. To keep your daddy and Aunt Mildred off our backs, you're going to have to learn."

I closed my eyes and slapped my forehead in frustration. Why couldn't we just tell him that I took typing? Would one little lie hurt? By the time he got back from the Congo, I hoped to be enrolled in a university with an outstanding music department. Or maybe even a conservatory like Julliard. It wasn't like I'd be selling my soul with such a tiny lie. "I can't take typing now. Not after the school year has already begun."

"You don't have to take typing at school. I'll buy you a typewriter and an instruction book. Typing isn't major brain work. You just practice.

That's how I learned. I taught myself. During your Christmas vacation you can start."

And lo, it came to pass, with the advent of the Christmas season I bent my head over a Royal Portable Typewriter — an ugly black one — and learned to type. As I pecked away, the charm bracelet Fulton gave me for Christmas jingle-belled in four-four time, and in the background my new record player, a gift from Addy, played a selection of Chopin favorites performed by Arthur Rubenstein, another gift from Addy.

CHAPTER 11

The big announcement day in English class rolled around: January 10, the day we had to tell whom we'd chosen for our research reports. Outside, the weather had turned cold enough to freeze your gizzard; inside, the central heat worked overtime and we sweated, although some of the sweating had more to do with people not being prepared. Like Buddy Simms.

While he waited for the bell to ring to start class, Mr. Feldman positioned himself in front of the blackboard where, for his previous class — the twelfth grade— he'd written a list of reasons why Shakespeare was really Shakespeare. The top of his head reached the first item on the list and his blonde hair underscored the words: *Shakespeare is really Shakespeare because genius appears from time to time irrespective of education or social class.*

The bell rang. One by one Mr. Feldman called on each student to tell who he planned to write about. Then a short discussion followed with Mr. Feldman commenting on the choice of authors.

"So, Mr. Simms, you're going to write about Nathanial Hawthorne. What can you tell us about Hawthorne?"

"Uhhh. He wrote some books."

Laughter.

167

"Which books did he write?" Not amused, Mr. Feldman pressed his fingers against his forehead.

"Uhhhh, I can't remember the titles." Beads of sweat appeared on Buddy's forehead. In the last seat, in the last row, as far away from Mr. Feldman as he could get, Buddy lounged in his desk, one arm thrown over the back, legs sprawled into the aisle.

"We studied Hawthorne four months ago. You can't remember?" Mr. Feldman dug his hands into his pockets.

"Well, yeah. There was the one about the lady that got knocked up, and it was the minister that did it." He grinned at his friends.

"And the name of the book?"

Big pause. Shuffling of feet. Grin fading. Red creeping across Buddy's face as he pulled his legs from the aisle and stuck them under his desk. He frowned. "I can't remember."

"Let me give you a hint. Think of the alphabet. Think of colors. Think of Scarlet O'Hara."

"*Gone With the Wind?*"

Laughter.

Mr. Feldman gave him a look that should have killed, but that left Buddy unfazed. "Try again."

Silence. Except for the occasional suppressed tittering here and there.

"Lord, help us," Jessie whispered behind me. "He's got the brains of a chicken."

"Mr. Simms, I hope you'll be able to remember once you've done your paper." He sighed. "Miss Watson, let's hear from you."

Mary smiled smugly. "I'm going more modern than the author of *The Scarlet Letter* and *The House of Seven Gables*." She sat with legs primly crossed at her skinny ankles, hands calmly resting on the desk top. She'd painted her nails an awful shade of tangerine, and a reflection flickered off them like the twinkling lights on a Christmas tree.

Mr. Feldman smiled. I wanted the floor to open up and swallow Miss-Show-Off Mary Watson. "God, could you work a miracle here," I begged silently. "If making her disappear is too much to ask, at least let her say something stupid."

"For my research paper," Mary continued, "I'd like to tackle someone who has proven to be a prominent voice of the wide-open poetry movement that began in the early fifties."

The wide-open what? "Oh, please, this is too much," I whispered over my shoulder to Jessie.

Jessie expelled a noisy sigh. "Wake me up when she's finished."

I looked around the class. Some had gone glassy-eyed; others looked puzzled.

"Lawrence Ferlinghetti not only has written poetry, fiction, theater, art criticism, film narration, essays, and so forth, but he has countered the literary elite's definition of art and the artist's role in the world."

How long had she practiced that speech? . . . *countered?* . . . *literary elite?*

"And perhaps most of you don't know yet . . .," she twisted around to look at the class, ". . . Mr. Ferlinghetti, just three years ago, founded City Lights Bookstore which is the first all-paperbound bookshop in the country. Last year he launched City Lights Publishing House."

Yet? Probably nobody even knew who Ferlinghetti was, me included — except that I'd heard her mention him that one time.

She turned back to Mr. Feldman. Each time she turned her head she flung her mane of red hair away from her face with a jerk. "City Lights Publishers has just begun the Pocket Poets Series through which Ferlinghetti aims to create an international, dissident ferment."

Mr. Feldman's brow wrinkled, and he remained silent for a moment. Then, removing one hand from a pocket, he pulled at the end of his tie as though testing a fishing line. Embarrassment began in my toes and crept, inch-by-inch, to the top of my head. Did Mr. Feldman not know who Ferlinghetti was? Was Mary about to make a fool of him?

"I'm impressed, Miss Watson, with your knowledge of the Beat movement," he said at length. He let go of his tie and turned to pace a few steps toward the windows. "I'm sure you're aware of Mr. Ferlinghetti's arrest on obscenity charges when he published Allen Ginsberg's *Howl* last year." He turned and paced in the opposite direction toward the door.

Relief swept through me. He knew.

"I'm aware of that," Mary answered. "He was acquitted."

Mr. Feldman stopped pacing and stared at the door. "When I asked you to do a research paper I had in mind a more established literary figure."

"Prestigious literary and academic figures supported Ferlinghetti overwhelmingly in that trial. The trial turned out to be a landmark First Amendment case."

"This isn't a course in constitutional law." He turned to Mary. "Ferlinghetti could very well be nothing more than an upstart whose writings fade into literary oblivion in a few years."

"But, Mr. Feldman . . ."

"Choose someone else." A tired look crossed his face. "Miss Bruce, whom have you chosen?"

"Nathan Waterstone." A sudden concern hit me that Mr. Feldman might also consider Nathan Waterstone an upstart in danger of fading into literary oblivion.

"Terrific. You have access to a great source in your aunt. Good choice, Miss Bruce. I look forward to reading your paper."

Yes, there is a God, I rejoiced.

"I found out about military pensions," Alice Worthington said in art class that same day. We'd settled into a guarded companionship for the purpose of getting along in art class. "My uncle fought in France during the war and he knows about that kind of thing. You probably don't even know how much your aunt gets, do you?" She stopped sketching and gave me a sideways look.

My fingers tightened around my charcoal until the crayon broke. We worked at sketching round objects — lemons, apples, and oranges — trying to make them appear round by proper shading. Alice succeeded. Mine looked like cookies. Amazing. She could sketch round objects, do a fabulous job of making them look round, and pry into my aunt's income all at the same time. Determined to ignore her, I set the shorter piece of broken charcoal aside and continued to sketch with the longer.

"Nathan Waterstone must have paid her an awful lot for just being his typist, or . . ." She let her sentence trail off.

Would she never shut up? My will to ignore faded. "What do you mean, *or* . . .? I made short, angry lines in my lemon.

"My daddy says . . ."

"Your daddy says what?" I stopped pock marking my lemon and glared at her.

"That Pearl . . ., you know, that mulatto who worked for Mr. Waterstone? Anyway, that Pearl was supposed to get a bunch of money in Nathan's will, but she's still over there working in the house like some common nigger maid. And your aunt . . . Well, she doesn't get much from a military pension because they don't pay much."

"My aunt doesn't get a military pension," I snapped. I gave Alice a

171

slow, poisonous smile. "Uncle Warren was in such a hurry to fight Hitler he joined the French Resistance before the United States declared war." The look on Alice's face gave me joy. Miss Know-It-All didn't know it all, after all.

She recovered fast. "So, I guess you're agreeing that Nathan Waterstone must have paid her a huge amount for being his typist? That would be sort of weird because typists don't usually earn much."

What was she insinuating? "She was his editorial assistant, not his typist." *Editorial Assistant.* That was good. That's what I'd call Addy in my paper. "He paid her a good salary because of her advanced education. She was living in Heidelberg, Germany, working on a master's thesis about *Faust* when the war broke out. You know about *Faust*, of course." I could tell by the look on her face she'd never heard of *Faust*. "Nathan paid her well because she knew a lot about literature and writing. Besides, her husband's uncle willed Addy a lot of money." I turned back to my drawing. Now that I knew Warren's uncle hadn't left her much, I, too, still wondered where Addy's money came from.

❧   ❧   ❧

"What did Nathan call you when you worked for him?" I asked Addy when I walked into the kitchen after school. She was sitting at the table drinking coffee.

"He called me Addy."

"I mean, what was your job title?"

"I didn't have a job title."

"But what did he say to people when he introduced you? Did he say 'Hello, Mr. So-and-So, this is Mrs. Adelaide Simmons, my typist? My secretary? Or what?'"

172

"He said, 'Hello, Mr. So-and-So, this is Addy Simmons, she's helping with my manuscript.' Sit down, honey." She patted the chair beside her. "Want something to eat? I think Earlene's nap has gone into overtime. Supper might be late."

I sat down and propped my elbows on the table. "Did Nathan leave money in his will to people who worked for him? Like Pearl and Jonas?"

"Yes." She looked puzzled at my random question

"A lot?"

"He made adequate provisions for their future."

I nodded at the pad and pen on the table in front of her. "What are you doing?"

"Writing a grocery list." She rubbed her ink-stained forefinger along the pen. "You know what I love?" Her eyes looked dreamy.

"What do you love?"

"I love how you can guide a pen across paper and a black line comes out, curving this way and that, and this black squiggle of a line can say something beautiful, or powerful, or funny."

"Maybe you should have been a writer."

"Your mother should have been a writer. She was very talented and creative."

I stared at Addy. The most creative thing I'd ever known Mama to do was figure out what to serve the deacons when they came for dinner.

Addy looked amused. "Did she never show you her poems?"

I shook my head. "She told me once she'd written a few but that they weren't any good."

"They were good enough to be published. Three in the local newspaper, one in *Ladies Home Journal,* and one in that weekly paper we used to get as students. I forget what it's called."

173

"You're kidding!" I felt a surge of pride in Mama. "Why did she stop writing?" Mama had always told me she dreamed of being an English teacher not a poet.

"She fell victim to public opinion."

While Addy poured another cup of coffee, I puzzled over what public opinion had to do with writing.

"Some seem to think that women should give up their own interests as soon as they have husbands and babies," she said, returning to her seat. "But they shouldn't have to." She stirred her coffee. "When I returned home after the war, your mother told me that Aunt Mildred informed her that writing poetry fell into the category of *wasting time*."

"Like playing the piano."

"Yes. And then Mildred quoted the scripture about *idle hands*. Or is that really a scripture? Maybe someone just made it up. I'll have to ask Robert. Do you remember the first five words in the Bible?"

"*In the beginning, God created . . .*" I ticked off the words on my fingers, counting to five.

"And a few lines later . . . ?"

I shrugged, not knowing what she referred to.

"The Bible says God created man in his own image. If that's true, then it seems we should be busy creating instead of worrying about the devil chasing us around with a view to packing us off to hell. I wish that your Daddy had urged your mother to keep writing." Absently, she rubbed her forefinger around the rim of her coffee cup. "I'm told he was a good student," she said finally. "Especially in math. He could have gone to the University of Georgia on a basketball scholarship. Even married and with a baby, he could have gone. Others did. He gave up both his opportunity and your mama's. And then he bought into all that man-made religious stuff."

My mouth dropped open. Addy went to church; surely she wasn't an atheist. "Man-made?"

"I refer to the assertions of those who read between the lines in the Bible. Sometimes I think they're more interested in controlling everyone than they are in loving everyone. Too often, I get the feeling that people forget what Jesus said about loving your neighbor. Listen to Robert if you want to know what religion should be about. But enough of that." She waved her hand dismissively. "You'll never let anyone or anything deter you from your goal, will you?"

"Of course not. Never." We sat for a few moments in silence. "You always have a pad of paper nearby," I said then, nodding at the pad.

"That's how I entertained myself when I had polio. Drawing and writing."

"Did you have a pad of paper when President Roosevelt came to the polio clinic in Warm Springs?"

She laughed. "I can't remember, but probably not. I was too excited about meeting the President of the United States to think about drawing pictures." She leaned back and draped an arm over the back of her chair. "Tell me about school. Did Mr. Feldman approve your choice of authors?"

I smiled at the memory of my success and Mary Watson's humiliation. "He thinks I made a good choice. Tell me something interesting about Nathan."

"What do you want to know that you don't already know?"

"Who the Lady was."

She rolled her eyes. "You won't learn that from me."

"Tell me how Nathan looked."

"You saw him many times."

"I was little."

"You've seen his pictures."

"He wore a ponytail. He was thin and angular. He had prominent brow ridges and deep-set eyes. But pictures don't show everything. Like how he walked, or his mannerisms."

Addy propped her elbows on the table and leaned her chin on her hands. "How did he walk? I can barely remember. He just sort of appeared. You'd be in a room and suddenly he'd be there. He had long legs and, instead of bending his knees much, he sort of swung his legs feet first when he walked. His voice . . . definitely, a tenor. He spoke quietly and walked quietly. I think what first comes to mind when I think of Nathan are his hands. His long fingers. The way he moved them."

I thought of Fiona's fingers and the way she'd moved hers the day we'd taken supper over.

"So expressive," Addy continued.

"But he wasn't effeminate?"

"Good lord, no. There was nothing effeminate about Nathan."

"What did he do for fun? Other than hiking and traveling?"

"He read. I think what he enjoyed most was sitting in a pub, or in someone's living room, discussing issues, joking, gossiping. Men gossip too, you know." She winked at me. "In London, he entertained us with stories about Churchill and Chamberlain and some really good ones about Wally Simpson. Aren't you going to practice?"

"Yes, I am." I rose. "Do you write poetry?"

"No, I'm totally lacking in that talent."

"I don't suppose you're ever going to tell me who the *Lady* was."

"Nope."

Just when I thought I'd never learn, the timing on the Chopin waltz came together. Excited, I played the waltz over and over. Then I worked on the Brahms' waltz I'd been assigned. By supper time I'd almost mastered the notes in the first line.

"I think I'll conquer Brahms, after all," I said to Tar Baby as I closed the lid on the piano. Tar Baby had become my biggest fan. When I practiced, he sat in his special spot on the sofa, looking for all the world like he listened.

"Jessie is on the phone," Addy said, as I entered the hallway. She held the phone out to me. A stream of light from the kitchen door partially illuminated the unlit hallway, making Addy a study in light and dark. The smell of tomato soup and grilled cheese sandwiches wafted from the kitchen, reminding me that it was supper time.

"Edgar Allen Poe was some kind of pervert," Jessie blurted when I took the phone. "I can't believe I chose a pervert to do my research paper on. Do you know what he did?"

"What?"

"He married his own cousin when she was only thirteen. Thirteen years old! Can you believe it?"

I couldn't.

"Did you start working on your paper? I want to get started so I don't go bonkers at the last minute. Do you know who Mary Watson is doing hers on?"

"Not Ferlinghetti."

"Nathaniel Hawthorne. The Women's Club gives a prize every year for the best research paper. Mary says the judges won't understand someone like Ferlinghetti. Oh, my gosh, I can actually pronounce his name. Fer-lin-ghet-ti. I must be brilliant! Anyway, Mary doesn't think you'll win if you write about Nathan Waterstone because he's too modern."

"So who cares about some contest? I just want to get the thing done." I lied; I definitely wanted to win.

"Yeah, me too. Just want to get the thing done. Hey, do you want a little brother?"

"If you mean Devilstiltskin, *no*. What's he done this time?"

"Poured Dr. Pepper all over my homework. You can have him as your slave."

"No, thank you. I don't want Dr. Pepper on my homework."

≈   ≈   ≈

January and February crept past while I ate, slept, went to school, practiced, did my homework, and spent the remaining time learning everything I could about Nathan and his books. I reread some and skimmed through others; I read reviews; I looked up magazine and newspaper articles. I kept hoping that, while I gathered information for my paper, I'd also discover a tidbit leading me to discover who the Lady had been.

I participated in social activities only on weekends. Needless to say, I didn't have much time for Fulton, but in addition to playing football, he also played basketball, saving me from having to make excuses to not see him during the week. Our Friday night dates usually occurred after basketball games which, I discovered, I actually liked. Maybe because Fulton, like Daddy, had been elected captain of the team. However, unlike Mama, I didn't plan to engage in activities below the neck. Not that she *planned* what happened. Fulton showed interest in exploring, but I was firm on that issue. I didn't want to wind up like Mama and Hester Prynne. For sure, I didn't want to give Aunt Mildred the satisfaction of having predicted my fall.

As dreary as those winter days might sound, they weren't. Even though I spent so much time working, and even though the world outside lay cold, colorless, and mostly silent, I flourished in the warmth inside. Addy — always nearby, always generous with encouragement, and forever ready to be an audience to my music and chatter — contributed as much warmth to my days as did the furnace.

As did Earlene. She shuffled around in her slippers, supplying me with hot chocolate and sweets, and entertaining me with the various ways she'd like to do away with Lucifer. The tantalizing aroma of one of her masterpieces filled the kitchen almost every day: chicken 'n dumplings, sweet potato soufflé, fried chicken, caramel cake, corn pudding, peanut butter cookies.

Afternoons, I struggled to learn the notes in Brahms, to get the rhythms right in Chopin, to master the fingering in Bach. Mrs. Rich started me on a Schubert Impromptu — the one in B-flat major. That winter, playing Schubert the way Mrs. Rich did, became my greatest challenge.

After supper I'd go to my bedroom, put on my nightgown, housecoat, and a pair of warm socks, and settle into the easy chair with a shawl thrown over my legs. I'd read about Nathan, or reread something he'd written. I bridled my curiosity about the new novel — Nathan's eighth — and concentrated on his life and first seven books.

I'd include something about Nathan's background in my paper, naturally. I already knew the essentials from previous reading and from listening to Addy's stories. He grew up in Macon, Georgia. His father owned a cotton gin, a string of feed mills, three farms, and a canning plant. His mother *came out* at a debutante ball in Atlanta. Nathan attended Bakersfield Prep School and Yale University where he majored in chemistry. Emory University accepted him into their medical school, but he delayed admission for a year. His parents grudgingly gave him their ok to spend a year traveling. So off he went. Ignoring the threats of war, he spent the year in Europe. He upset his parents further by delaying medical school for a second year. He settled in London, living on a trust fund left him by his maternal grandfather.

During that year in London, he wrote his first novel about two young men hitchhiking in Scotland. They meet a mysterious girl somewhere between Inverness and Clyde. She invites them to spend a night in a castle — one owned by her uncle, she claims. The two men awake the following morning to find themselves locked up and held for ransom, but they escape. Not content with escaping, they decide to give the girl a dose of her own medicine. They go back, grab the girl, cart her off to London, and lock her up in their apartment. After much carrying on, one of the young men falls in love with her. I liked *Highland Deception* least of all Nathan's books. I found the plot boring and predictable.

Nathan's parents were not happy when a publisher accepted the book because there went medical school out the window for a third year.

While the publisher readied the book for publication, Nathan went to Asia. He traveled in Thailand, Burma, India, and finally Nepal where he spent several months traipsing around the Himalayas. According to Earlene, Reverend Stewart, who wasn't a reverend then but just plain old Robert Stewart, met Nathan in Nepal.

Nathan returned to London and wrote *Himalayan Adventure* in which he tells the story of an American couple who get lost trekking in the Himalayas. They meet a Sherpa and persuade him to lead them out. As the Sherpa guides the couple back to civilization, the woman falls in love with the Sherpa, and the husband starts to unravel. They make their way down out of the mountains eventually, and the husband is committed to a hospital. The Sherpa visits the woman's bedroom, makes love to her, and then leaves. She thinks he's waiting for her in the hotel lobby, but when she gets dressed and goes downstairs to find him, he's gone. She never sees him again. *Himalayan Adventure* was the first novel Addy typed for Nathan.

"Why didn't he give *Himalayan Adventure* a better ending?" I asked one cold, cold evening. Freezing air seeped through crevasses around the windows and under the doors. I'd looked into Addy's study to find her snuggled in a chair, a blanket drawn up around her. Instead of working on Nathan's manuscript, she'd buried herself in her favorite book, *Pride and Prejudice.* Tar Baby lay curled beside her. Lucifer slept on the sofa.

"You don't like the ending?" She closed the book and motioned for me to come in.

"Couldn't the ending have been more exciting, or at least nicer?" I pushed Lucifer aside and sat down. He opened one eye and gave me a quizzical look. Then he stretched his legs, yawned, and curled back up into a ball. "Nathan liked to write about married women having affairs, didn't he?"

"That's a pretty common theme in literature."

"I guess. Even in *The Scarlet Letter.*"

She pulled the blanket up around her neck so that only her head showed. The floor lamp beside the chair cast shadows under her eyes.

"Why do people like to read about sin? Like adultery?"

"Maybe because we want company in our transgressions. Or because reading about others who err makes us feel better." She leaned over and put her book on the floor. "Maybe the interest in adultery is wishful thinking. Life can be messy, you know."

"Who was the Lady, Addy?"

"You know I don't know."

"You must."

"Quincy, I don't know." She looked away and stroked Tar Baby vigorously.

At that moment, I knew for sure that she *did* know. I saw the truth

181

written all over her face. I pressed on. "How can you not know? You were there."

"What Nathan did after work was none of my business."

She sounded peeved, but I pestered her with more questions. "Why did Nathan move to Wilson? He grew up in Macon, his mother came from Atlanta, but he chose to come here."

She frowned. "He was looking for a quiet place to write. I talked a lot about Wilson. I guess he liked what he heard."

"It's because *she* lives nearby, isn't it?" I had no idea where that thought came from. The words jumped out of my mouth without first filtering through my brain.

"Quincy, that's ridiculous." Her face reddened as she pushed Tar Baby away. "You're assuming she was an American? Don't leap to such conclusions." She stood and bent down to retrieve the blanket which had fallen to the floor. Avoiding my eyes, she folded the blanket slowly, meticulously. Then she looked directly at me. "He did not follow a woman here and that's the truth. Get that idea out of your head."

~   ~   ~

Instead of getting the idea out of my head, the thought festered there until a few days later the answer practically knocked me off my feet . . . *she had chosen to wear her hair pulled over one shoulder . . . blonde or red . . . for the color fell somewhere in between . . . an opal pin for her birthday.*

The picture! The one I found hidden in Fiona's bureau drawer underneath her shawls. The one where Fiona wore her red-gold hair like Nathan described in the novel. Why hadn't I realized what I was seeing? An opal pin had also been hidden in the drawer. And like Lady Isabelle Duncan, Fiona had been a nurse. Addy told the truth when she claimed

Nathan didn't follow the Lady to Wilson. Fiona followed him.

I understood now why Addy would never tell. What kind of a horrible human being would hurt such a kind and sweet man as Reverend Stewart? Did he know? But how could he not know? Was he so naïve and right-minded that he failed to see the clues?

CHAPTER 12

I thought adultery only happened in books. Or in some other universe. Not to people I knew. As my suspicions about Fiona settled into a depressing certainty, I went to school in a dark mood, feeling like a vital part had been ripped out of my body. I tried to focus on other things, but without success. Fulton finally distracted me from the grim knowledge for a few minutes when he stopped me on my way to history class.

"What's the matter?" I asked, leaning against the lockers. He looked like a dog whose bone had been snatched away.

"I'm grounded." He hung his head. "I can't go anywhere this weekend."

Buddy Simms grinned as he passed. "Hey, great going, Fulton."

I directed a stern look at Fulton. "What did you do?" Penny had invited us to a party and I'd been looking forward to some fun after my sad discovery.

He rolled his eyes and grimaced. "I didn't think it would work."

"What wouldn't work?" I lifted my palm in a question. "Fulton, just tell me what you did. I don't want to be late for class."

"I set a typewriter on fire."

I flinched and took a step back. He'd spoken so fast I wondered if he hoped I wouldn't understand what he said. "You set a typewriter on fire?"

"Damn, I hate that class." He rubbed his nose and frowned. "Miss Bitch was being such a witch, I couldn't stand pecking away another minute. I sprayed Jane Howell's hairspray on the keyboard and lit a match. I didn't think I'd actually set a typewriter on fire."

"Fulton!"

"They called Daddy. I can't go to the party."

ꝛ   ꝛ   ꝛ

"How was school?" Addy asked, looking up from her newspaper.

"Fulton set a typewriter on fire and can't go to the party." I plopped into a chair on the opposite side of the table.

"He what?" She let the paper drop to the table.

When I explained, she burst out laughing. Considering the consequences to my social life, I didn't think Fulton's prank the least bit funny.

"I'm sorry, honey," she said, when she managed to control her mirth. "I guess that messes up your weekend."

"It looks like I'll be spending the weekend working on my paper."

"You can go to the party alone. I go to social events alone."

"Reverend Stewart goes alone too."

"Other than church, I don't think he goes anywhere anymore." She reached for her coffee and then looked at me over the rim of the cup, the laughter in her eyes gone.

"Nathan really liked Scotland, didn't he?"

"Whatever brought that up?" She set her cup down.

"Two books are set in Scotland. The first one and the last one —

the one you're working on now." I didn't mention that Fiona was from Scotland.

"I think the settings have more to do with his liking mountains — Scottish mountains, Himalayans, Appalachians."

"I'm going to practice." I rose abruptly, went to the counter, and after cutting a large slice of pound cake, headed for the living room. If knowing about Fiona made *me* unhappy, I hated to imagine how Reverend Stewart would feel if he found out.

I began with scales and Hanon exercises, and then moved on to Brahms. For a change, music didn't help me forget. The disturbing vision of Reverend Stewart being duped played in my head along with the Brahms waltz, which I performed without joy or energy. I'd known all along that Addy wasn't the Lady, but I wished the Lady had been someone other than Reverend Stewart's wife.

"The devil has played an interesting role in American literature," Mr. Feldman said. He stood in front of the room, one hand in a pocket of his khaki trousers, the other holding an open book. Although it was only the end of February, the weather had decided to do a trial run for spring. Sunshine flooded the room, sending us into a state of semi-somnolence. "Some writers have shown proper respect for the power of the evil one and written accordingly. Others have treated the devil with humor and derision. Today, I'm going to read you a story by one of the latter. Washington Irving was fond of ghost stories and quirky tales. Put your pencils and books aside and enjoy. Here is *The Devil and Tom Walker*.

He read. Sometimes he shifted his weight from one foot to the other; sometimes he paced. I didn't especially like the story, but I enjoyed listening to him read. His baritone voice rang with expression, and he pronounced every word with precision. For a few minutes his voice lulled me into forgetting about Fiona and Nathan.

When he finished, he closed the book and laid it on his desk. He took his hand out of his pocket and, reaching up, loosened his maroon tie and tugged at his shirt collar as he focused on the back of the classroom. Buddy Simms, head resting on one cupped hand and mouth wide open, slept soundly. Mr. Feldman opened his mouth to say something but then seemed to decide to let sleeping dogs lie, or rather, leave sleeping students alone.

Next to me, Mary Watson, waiting for the next opportunity to impress, kept her gaze glued on Mr. Feldman as he cleared his throat and spoke. "The idea of selling one's soul to the devil for some sort of benefit originates in European literature. Does anyone know the most famous example of this?"

Happiness filled my soul like hot water pouring into a cold bath. From the blank look on her face, I realized Mary Watson didn't have a clue. Deliciously slow, I lifted my hand to waver in the air a few feet from Mr. Feldman.

"Yes, Miss Bruce. Do you know the famous work of literature in which a man makes a contract with the devil and offers his soul in exchange for happiness?"

"*Faust*, which is a German play written by Goethe." From the corner of my eye I saw Mary staring at me. "Faust, a scholar, is unhappy, so he makes a deal with Mephistopheles. That's what he calls the devil: Mephistopheles. Faust agrees to be Mephistopheles' servant in hell in return for happiness. And Buddy Simms might be happy to know . . .," I turned to look back at Buddy, now awake, ". . . that Faust knocked up a girl named Gretchen."

The class laughed. Mr. Feldman raised his eyebrows and amusement flickered in his eyes. I blushed. Miss Prim-and-Proper Mary Watson never used words like *knocked up*.

"I'm impressed, Miss Bruce," Mr. Feldman said.

Mary glowered. At least I think she did. Reluctant to look at her directly because I couldn't guarantee I wouldn't smirk, I tried to see her in my side vision.

The bell rang, but Mr. Feldman held out his hand to keep us in our seats. "Tomorrow I would like each of you to give a synopsis of your research paper. Please come prepared."

I came prepared, all right. A little smugly, I admit, because I had come up with something to catch Mr. Feldman's attention. I didn't volunteer right away but let the others present first. Jessie made a big mistake when her whole synopsis turned out to be about Poe's life rather than his work.

"A little background is nice," Mr. Feldman said. "But what we really want to hear about is Poe's work."

"What I really want to hear is what he did with that little cousin of his," Jessie muttered to my back.

"Jessie!" I exclaimed over my shoulder.

"Well, I do."

Buddy Simms must have decided he didn't want to compete with Mary. He'd changed from Hawthorne to Hemingway. When Mary stood to give her synopsis, he sat in the back rolling his eyes and in general being rude until Mr. Feldman chided him. "The idea behind each of us giving a synopsis, Mr. Simms, is to learn something. If you bothered to listen instead of behaving like a clown, you'd realize that each of these synopses is a short review of the authors we've been studying this year, something which, I might remind you, will be on the final exam."

To tell the truth, I felt like rolling my eyes too. In fact, I wanted to gag when Mary started talking about sin in Puritan New England.

"Hawthorne focuses on the psychological effects of sin rather than sin itself," she said. She stood in front of the class, hands folded, chin jutting. "To Hawthorne the greatest sin in *The Scarlet Letter* isn't Hester's adultery but Roger Chillingworth's attempt to master the soul of Arthur Dimmesdale."

While Mary rattled on, I tuned out. Maybe Hester Prynne's adultery wasn't the greatest sin in *The Scarlet Letter*, but in the case of Fiona and Nathan I couldn't think of any greater sin. Reverend Stewart would be devastated and shamed. My semi-crush on him had evaporated, but I'd come to admire and respect him, and I couldn't bear to think of his being hurt and shamed.

Engrossed in my thoughts, I didn't realize Mary had finished until Mr. Feldman called on me. I pushed thoughts of Fiona out of my head and stood up. I gave four or five lines of background information and then talked about Nathan's books, especially the two that won literary prizes. Regret over what Fiona had done didn't interfere with my desire to be better than Mary, and so, because I wanted to upstage her, I concluded with my teaser: "Although Nathan Waterstone died a few years ago, his literary career hasn't yet officially closed. New information regarding Mr. Waterstone will come to light in the next two to three months." I sat down.

"What do you mean, Miss Bruce?" Mr. Feldman, who sat behind his desk, leaned onto folded arms and looked at me, curiosity dripping from every pore.

"I'm not allowed to say just yet, but by the time the papers are due,

I'll be allowed."

"Could you possibly have learned the identity of the Lady?" Mr. Feldman's eyes teased.

"I'm sorry, you'll have to wait."

The bell rang, saving me from further explanation. I escaped, leaving Mr. Feldman and Mary Watson, as well as a few others, staring after me. Could I do anything to speed up the writing of the new novel? I'd committed myself to announcing new information. If I failed to come through, I'd never be able to look Mr. Feldman in the eyes again. And Mary Watson . . . Well, I hated to think of her look of disdain if I didn't deliver. Revealing the identity of the Lady would certainly fall into the category of new knowledge but that was unthinkable. I imagined the headlines in *The Atlanta Constitution: A Scarlet Letter for the Minister's Wife.*

Mary caught me in the hallway after history class as we walked to our lockers. "How did you know about Faust? Did you study that in your old school?"

"No. My aunt wrote about *Faust* for her master's thesis."

We arrived at our lockers. Hers remained neat — big books on bottom, middle-sized books in the middle, little ones on top. Mine was as messy as ever. My math book fell out along with the pencil case I hadn't bothered to zip. Pencils scattered; some rolled into the midst of the between-class crush. I stooped to retrieve the book and the pencils that hadn't been smashed by stampeding feet.

"It's interesting," she said, as she watched me chase pencils.

"What's interesting? My pencils all over the floor?"

"The devil."

"What's so interesting about the devil?" I crammed the fallen items back in my locker.

"It isn't actually the devil that's so interesting. What strikes me as

190

interesting is that even though we attribute everything that's evil to the devil, they keep writing stories about how people willingly sell their souls in return for something they want. Like in *The Devil and Daniel Webster* and *Faust.*"

"Yeah. I guess that's kind of interesting." I shrugged — I'd had enough of the devil for one day — and went running off to meet Fulton for a thirty-second chat before the next class.

و   و   و

Schubert wrote the most beautiful music you can ever imagine, including the impromptu Mrs. Rich had assigned me. But the impromptu didn't sound beautiful when *I* played it. I played the notes correctly; I got the timing right; I got the dynamics right; I even got the phrasing right. Yet, something was missing. When Mrs. Rich played the piece for me, I watched and listened with every ounce of focus I could muster, but when I tried to copy her, my attempts still didn't measure up. If Mephistopheles had come along, I think I'd have signed on with him right then and there in return for playing the impromptu the way Mrs. Rich did. Addy bought a new recording of the Schubert Impromptus played by Lily Krauss, but in spite of listening to the record over and over, I still sounded nothing like Mrs. Rich or Lily Krauss.

"In time, you *will* sound as good," Addy said one evening when I complained for the umpteenth time about playing the impromptu so poorly. She was sorting laundry. "One day you'll sit down to play, and lo and behold: perfection."

"How many days do I have to wait?"

"A thousand and forty." She held up a pair of panties. "I believe these are yours. You can fold your own." She tossed them to me.

191

"Well, that sure makes me feel better. A thousand and forty." I folded the panties, although I didn't see why they needed folding. Wasn't getting them in the right drawer enough? "When do the thousand and forty days start? Now, or back when I first started trying to play the piece? And why not a thousand and one?"

"A thousand and one belongs to Scheherazade. Keep practicing, honey. Rome wasn't built in a day."

She pulled the last pair of panties from the dryer, threw them in the panty pile, and began folding her slips.

"How are you doing with the book?" I asked.

"I'm making progress. I'll be getting together with Adam soon."

"He's coming again?" I leaned against the washing machine.

"I'm going there."

"To New York?"

"Yes."

"You're leaving me here alone?"

"Earlene will be here. Or if you like, you can spend a few days with Aunt Mildred." She raised an eyebrow at me.

"No, thank you. When are you going, and how long will you be gone?"

"I don't know." She folded the last slip and added it to the stack. "I've finished the rough draft. I'll start fine-tuning after I meet with Adam."

"When will you tell the board members?"

"Soon."

I breathed a sigh of relief. That probably meant I could include the information in my paper. If the board was going to find out, I reasoned, then shortly afterwards they'd tell the world. I'd have to talk her into saving the announcement until after I handed in my paper.

Addy turned to carry her laundry upstairs. I followed with mine.

192

"I guess you worked for Nathan enough that you sort of know how he wrote, how he used words and all," I said to her back.

She looked at me from over her shoulder and rolled her eyes. "That's for sure. Sometimes he made me retype a page a dozen times because he kept changing things. Yes, I'm well acquainted with Nathan's writing style."

"Could I do some research in Nathan's house? I'd like to describe his study, talk about his things, stuff like that."

We were halfway up the stairs. She stopped and looked around at me. "*Stuff* like that?"

"*Things* like that."

She laughed and continued up the stairs. "I'll tell Pearl to let you have the run of the house whenever you want. Are you going to do homework now? I want to read a bit before I go to bed."

"I've finished my homework. I'm going to read too. Good night, Addy." I kissed her on the cheek. "Happy reading."

"Happy reading to you, too, and sweet dreams."

I felt a sudden spring in my step. I'd just received permission to snoop.

I woke up the next morning feeling like I'd been whacked in the head. I crept out of bed, washed my feverish face, and struggled into my clothes. I wasn't going to miss a day with Mr. Feldman because of a little headache. But when Earlene put a bowl of oatmeal in front of me my stomach rebelled, screaming *no, no, no* at the smell.

"What's the matter with you this morning?" she asked. "You just sitting there like you 'spect your breakfast to jump down your throat."

"I can't eat."

"You better hurry up cause it ain't gittin' any sooner." She dunked the oatmeal pan in the dishwater.

"I can't eat," I repeated.

"Why not?"

"I'm sick."

"You ain't sick. You look just fine."

"You aren't looking at me, so you don't know how I look."

She turned around and studied me for a moment. "You do look a little peaked. We better tell your aunt." She wiped her hands on her apron and shambled out of the kitchen.

Addy appeared a few minutes later with pillow wrinkles on one side of her face and bed hair. "What's the matter, honey?"

"My head is about to explode, and my stomach is upset."

She felt my forehead. "Oh, dear. You have a fever. You'd better stay home." She pulled out a chair and sat down. "You've been working too hard. Take a day off. No practicing, no studying."

I nodded, pushed aside the bowl of oatmeal, and lay my aching head on the table. She rubbed the back of my shoulders. In spite of my headache and sick stomach, a tingling warmth spread through me at the feel of her warm fingers on my shoulders

"Go back to bed," she said. "I'll call school."

I went back to bed and slept. Around ten-thirty I got up and trudged downstairs. Addy had gone.

"She went to deliver fried chicken over to the Stewart's, and then she had a meeting," Earlene said. "You just rest now. I'll bring you some ginger ale. That's always good for tummies what ain't acting right."

Forgetting that Addy's study had been designated as forbidden territory, I went in and stretched out on the couch. The leather upholstery felt cool against my fevered cheek. A clock ticked on the wall. Too loudly. When I glared at the clock, not that I expected my glare to silence the thing, I saw that it was time for English class. My seat would be conspicuously empty. I imagined Mr. Feldman missing me. Miss Bruce who knew about *Faust*. Miss Bruce who was about to reveal something previously unknown about Nathan Waterstone. *What could she know? What could she be about to reveal*, he'd be wondering.

I dozed. Around eleven I awoke to find Earlene standing over me with another glass of ginger ale.

"Your aunt called to check on you. She'll be home soon."

I sat up and gulped down the ginger ale. My throat felt like I'd been stranded in the desert for a week without water. I lay back down, and Earlene returned to the kitchen.

The study looked different. The notes strewn here and there had disappeared and the clutter of papers on desk, chairs, and floor had been put away or discarded. I dragged my body, aching head, misbehaving stomach and all, over to Addy's neatly arranged desk. The typewriter, the lamp, and a fancy pencil box with brass hinges stood in the same places they'd been before she began work on the novel. One thing had been added, however: a neat stack of paper next to the typewriter.

Dunfermline the top page said. By *Nathan Waterstone*. Dunfermline? What was that? A person? A place?

I removed the title sheet and began to read:

Chapter One.

> *I've crossed the ocean once again, my love. I have come back hoping that nothing has changed, or that everything has changed. When I first left, traveling far away*

The front door slammed. Quickly, I replaced the page on the stack as Addy's footsteps, at first muffled by a rug, but then clacking on the hardwood, moved from the front door toward the study. I scurried back to the sofa, lay down, and pulled an afghan over me.

A few seconds later she strode into the room. "How are you feeling?"

"Not good; but not quite as bad."

She leaned over and felt my forehead. "Ah, one of the blessings of being young. An illness overtakes you, but you outrun it fast."

"My head still hurts and my stomach still feels queasy."

"I'm sure you'll be fine tomorrow. Want to try some chicken noodle soup?"

I nodded. "Tell me what the new novel is about."

"Later." She patted my hand. "Let me check on things in the kitchen."

When she'd gone, I rose and walked over to the desk. Where were Nathan's notes? Underneath the manuscript? I looked. They weren't there. Perhaps in the cabinet? I listened for Addy's footsteps. Or Earlene's. I heard the clang of a pan from the kitchen but nothing more. I tiptoed to the cabinet and, pulling at the handle, found the cabinet locked as always. I imagined that museums or collectors might pay a fortune for Nathan's original manuscripts. She'd probably put the original in the cabinet for safe-keeping.

What else had she locked away in the cabinet? A revealing picture of Fiona and Nathan? A letter from Addy revealing the Lady's identity — one meant to be read after both Fiona and Reverend Stewart died? I pulled at the handle once more, but the door didn't budge.

"Quincy," Addy called. I jumped. "Your soup is ready."

I turned to see her in the doorway. She'd come so silently in her stocking feet that I hadn't heard her. She gave no sign of having noticed my attempt to open the cabinet.

I settled in a chair in the kitchen while Addy ladled soup into a bowl.

"Aren't you eating?" I asked when she placed the bowl in front of me.

"I had coffee and cookies at the church, and then I had more coffee and cookies at Fiona's."

"How is she?"

"Not good."

"What did you do at the church?" I watched the steam rise from the soup.

"Attended a meeting." She nodded at my soup. "Try to eat a little."

I took a sip. The salty broth trickling down my throat felt good. I had another spoonful. "When will you tell me about the new novel?"

She leaned back and let her gaze float to that non-place she stared at sometimes. "The novel tells the story of a woman — a Scottish woman — who leaves her lover and comes to America."

"Why does she do that?" I put down my spoon and folded my arms on the table.

"He's married to someone else."

The plot sounded like *The Lady* in reverse. "I'm not sure I like the subject of this story."

"Why? Because she leaves her lover, or because her lover married someone else?"

"Both. Nathan wrote too much about people being unfaithful."

"So did a lot of others. Anyway, she comes to America, lives, works, has other loves."

"Has other loves? She must not have loved him very much."

She cocked her head at me. "You think true love is eternal?"

"Shouldn't true love be eternal?"

She opened her mouth to speak, but didn't. I could have kicked myself. She'd lost the love of her life when Uncle Warren died, and there I was reminding her. I waited, despising myself for saying things that tore at her soul. The clock on the wall buzzed, and from the utility room behind the kitchen came the sound of the washing machine knocking during the spin cycle. At length, Addy put her elbows on the table, clasped her hands together, and leaned her chin onto them.

"Sometimes," she began, "when two people meet, they feel as though they knew each other already. They might even wonder if this whole thing about reincarnation is true. If they were lovers in a distant past. In *Dunfermline*, Ellie and Patrick meet, and they know they were meant for each other. Sadly, Patrick has already committed himself to another woman — his childhood sweetheart, the daughter of longtime family friends. Their parents have hoped for and planned their union for years. Patrick, being the kind of man he is, honors his commitment. Ellie goes to America. She marries and has a child. When her husband and child die in an accident she knows she can't survive alone; she must at least be near the person she still loves. She returns to Scotland. Being near him will be enough, she thinks. She can breathe the same air he does. Perhaps she will see him occasionally as he passes on his way to work. She can walk where he walks and know that on a stormy evening he's sitting beside his hearth reading as she, not so very far away, sits beside hers."

"That's so sad," I said, when she paused. "How does the story end?"

"The story hasn't ended yet."

"What do you mean, the story hasn't ended?"

"Nathan sketched out two possible endings."

"You mean the book isn't finished after all?"

"I've written out both endings. It's just a matter of choosing. I'll see what Adam thinks." She sighed. "Nathan was such a shillyshallier when he had to make up his mind about an ending. You should have seen him struggle with the ending for *The Lady*."

"Will the readers know you had to make a choice between endings?"

"Of course not. The readers won't know a thing."

"That's the reason you have to see Adam?"

"One of them. He'll pass judgment on the entire manuscript. So, very soon, I shall be off to New York."

CHAPTER 13

I missed two days of school. March blew in while I sat at my desk catching up. Algebra went quickly. I was good at math and thought the problems more like a game than work. In French I had to conjugate a list of verbs in the future perfect tense. What I despised most was the reading I had to do for history about the Great Depression and Hoover. I hated everything that had to do with politics, treaties, gross national product, and the other nonsense that filled history books. Thank goodness, I had no work in physics. Mr. Kirkland had the same bug I did, and his substitute didn't assign homework. I also had none to do in English because in that class I always worked ahead.

So I didn't get to Nathan's house, and I didn't practice enough.

"Well, my dear, sickness can't be helped," Mrs. Rich said. "Just stay healthy for the next ten weeks. The recital has been scheduled for the first Friday evening in May."

"The first Friday in May," I repeated dumbly. Our research papers were due the same day.

"Shall we get started?" She positioned her listening chair next to the piano and sat down.

Much to my surprise I played well. Like I'd taken a vacation and returned refreshed. When we finished, Mrs. Rich hit me with another bit of news. The two biggest events of my year happening within a hair's breadth of each other was enough to have me tossing and turning in bed, but when she told me whom she expected in the audience, I felt like an ant colony had taken up residence under my skin.

"Mr. Devenuto teaches at Peabody Conservatory," she said, scribbling in her lesson notebook. "He's an old friend. He'll be in Florida in May, so I've asked him to come. We'd love to have you study at FSU, but if you have a chance for a good conservatory, then . . ." Her voice trailed off as she closed the notebook and looked at me as though she expected me to say something.

What could I say? I wasn't ready for anyone important to hear me. My Schubert was pathetic. The more I tried to shape and color the notes in the Impromptu, the more frustrated I became. My Mozart and Haydn sounded reasonably good. As did my Chopin — or at least my Chopin sounded good to me, especially now that I was getting the hang of the tricky rhythms. But I wanted to be Rubenstein-good when I played for someone like Mr. Devenuto, and I was light-years away from that.

I began gathering my music. "Am I ready for this?"

"You sound better every week. But you still have much to learn, my dear. Keep practicing."

"What am I going to play?" Clutching my music books tightly to my chest, I shifted from foot to foot. If just the *thought* of playing for Mr. Devenuto from the Peabody Conservatory made me feel like ants crawled under my skin, what would actually performing for him be like?

"The Haydn Sonata. Perhaps the Schubert impromptu."

"But I don't play the Schubert impromptu well."

"*Well* is a relative issue." She went to her desk and picked up her coffee which was, by then, surely as cold as a buried bone. "You don't play the piece well enough to perform in Carnegie Hall, but you play it well enough for a recital."

"What about the Chopin nocturne? Or the Brahms waltz?"

"Oh, you'll play those, too. I want you to perform a varied selection."

❧   ❧   ❧

"You'll do fine," Addy said on the way home.

She always said that. *You'll do fine.* Her words didn't mean diddly, because I didn't always do fine. How had I come so fast to the point of having someone from a conservatory listen to me? What if he thought I wasn't conservatory material? What if he thought I wasn't good at all?

I wondered if Mr. Feldman would be impressed with my playing. Did he even like music?

Mary Watson liked classical music, she claimed. Beethoven was her favorite composer, and she especially liked the Pastoral Symphony. She liked that particular work so much, she bragged, that she played the symphony when she wrote to help put rhythm to her words. She'd been playing the Pastoral nonstop for weeks while she worked on her research paper, which, by the way, progressed beautifully.

But I didn't want to think about Mary Watson. I rolled down the window and propped my arm in the opening. The wind blew my hair into tangles and whipped and tore at the new leaves, which clung stubbornly to the branches that had borne them. The bleak, gray winter canvas was changing to color. Azaleas were about to burst into a dozen different hues. The scent of camellias hung in the air. The world was being born anew, and everything would turn out right. My recital. My research paper. What could possibly go wrong?

The following day when I should have been listening to Reverend Stewart, visions of his wife and Nathan Waterstone haunted me. I kept seeing Nathan running his hands through her hair; Fiona putting her head on his shoulder; Nathan and Fiona going arm in arm down a London street. I imagined them lying in bed together, and then her sitting up and red-gold hair cascading over bare breasts. I was sorry that she no longer came to church. I wanted to examine her in detail, imagining her as young and vibrant, with golden hair flung over one shoulder — an adulteress. Had her conscience bothered her as she sat Sunday after Sunday in a place of worship, listening to her husband preach about goodness and morality?

I planned to go to Nathan's house after school on Monday to search for material for my paper and, at the same time, look for proof that Nathan and Fiona had been lovers. I wanted solid evidence to flaunt in Aunt Mildred's face.

A problem occurred to me then — one so obvious, I wondered why I hadn't thought of it before. How could I clear Addy's name without revealing that Fiona had been the Lady? Aunt Mildred would have fun spreading *that* tasty tidbit. *Oh, them Presbyterians, I always did know they weren't followers of the true gospel! A minister's wife, of all things.*

Meanwhile, I had a paper to write. Using the hymnal as a lap desk, I jotted tasks and questions on the back of the church bulletin. I'd examine Nathan's original manuscripts and notes if I could find them, and describe their present location. I'd write something like: *Nathan Waterstone's original manuscripts reside in a locked cupboard in his study.* I had no idea where the manuscripts were kept, but a locked cupboard sounded logical. *Now, yellow and fraying around the edges, the manuscripts can be seen by special appointment with his former* . . . .

Addy gave me a questioning glance. I looked up and pretended to be interested in the sermon. Reverend Stewart was saying something about not needing rules to *love thy neighbor as thyself*. "If each person looks into his own conscience . . . ," he said ". . . he already knows the answers as to how he should behave." Fiona obviously hadn't looked into hers.

Addy appeared to forget me, so I resumed scribbling on the bulletin. What had I decided to call Addy? Editorial assistant? Yes, *editorial assistant. The manuscripts can be seen by special appointment with his former editorial assistant, Mrs. Adelaide Nunnemaker Simmons.* Or should I just say *Mrs. Adelaide Simmons* and leave out the *Nunnemaker*?

In my paper I'd give a brief summary of Nathan's novels, trying to find interesting details to begin each summary. I remembered the painting of the Himalayas that hung in Nathan's hallway. That could be the starting point for discussing *Himalayan Adventure*.

But what could I use as a beginning for the description of Nathan's fourth novel? *Runaway,* published a couple years after *The Lady*, tells the story of a Tennessee farm girl who marries at the age of sixteen, has two babies, and then runs away with a traveling salesman leaving the babies behind.

I'd start my description of *Game of Chance* by saying this novel won several literary prizes. Of all Nathan's books, *Game of Chance* was my favorite. In the first scene, two men gamble over a backwoods girl living near the Okefenokee Swamp. The winner takes her home and forces her to sleep with him and do his housework. The girl — smarter than the man thinks — discovers where he stashes the profits from his moonshine business, steals the money, and runs away. Several months later he finds her in Oklahoma. Unable to retrieve the money, he vows to *repay her for the evil deed she did him*. Before he can put his plan into action, she retaliates. I loved the way Nathan had her wreak her revenge.

The critics also liked the novel. "His best yet," one critic said, ". . . even though the plot begins as a variation of the plot in *The Mayor of Casterbridge*." I'd discuss in my paper how writers often borrow plots from other sources, Shakespeare being one of the best examples. If writers borrow plots from Shakespeare, then Nathan could borrow a plot from Thomas Hardy.

In Nathan's next novel, *Mary Moran,* two sisters living in the hills of North Georgia fall in love with the same man. He loves the older one, but the younger sister tempts him into running off to Chicago with her. They live in sin until their relationship turns poisonous. He returns to Georgia two years later to find the older sister married to a local businessman. His attempts to win her back are unsuccessful. Sales for *Mary Moran* skyrocketed when they made a movie from the book, and then again when Nathan won the Marshall Prize for the best novel of the year.

Nathan's last book, *The Mistress*, published posthumously, tells the story of Anna Readfield whose husband dies during World War II, leaving her with two young children. To survive, she becomes the mistress of a wealthy man. The people of the small town where she lives condemn and shun her until, in a strange twist, the mother of her lover comes to Anna's defense, claiming that the real sinners are those who promote war and killing.

The book received mixed reviews. An article in the *Atlanta Constitution Sunday Magazine* claimed the book to be one of the best published in twentieth century America, while a critic in the book review section of that same paper blasted the book for condoning adultery. Daddy and Aunt Mildred acted like Nathan Waterstone was Satan's disciple for having written such a story. Except for the few pages one of the deacons dog-eared, neither actually read the book. Daddy used those passages to construct a sermon around fallen morals in which he compared America to Sodom and Gomorrah.

I became so absorbed in my thoughts I almost forgot where I was until everyone stood for the last hymn. While I waited to shake hands with Reverend Stewart after the service, I couldn't help but think about the differences in Reverend Stewart and Daddy. Reverend Stewart never pounded on the pulpit or engaged in theatrics. In a quiet manner, he talked about love and being guided by your conscience. He even claimed, in one of his sermons, that circumstances sometimes have a bearing on what is right and wrong. He mentioned Jean Valjean stealing bread in *Les Miserables* as an example. I wanted to ask him what he thought about the circumstances in *The Mistress*. In *The Lady*, both the man and the woman were clearly in the wrong. But I wondered if the woman in *The Mistress* might be in the same position as Jean Valjean: she needed to feed her family.

"Other than practicing piano, what are you up to these days?" Reverend Stewart asked when the line brought me to him.

"I'm writing a paper on Nathan Waterstone for English class. Can I interview you sometimes about your friendship with him?"

"Of course, Quincy. I'd be more than happy. Why don't you call the church office and arrange a time. Or have Addy bring you over one evening."

It was then that I realized they hid the secret of the Lady's identity not from the world, but from him.

≈   ≈   ≈

Instead of paying attention in classes on Monday, a movie of myself at Nathan's house ran through my head. There I was in full

Technicolor: Quincy Bruce, sleuth extraordinaire, opening a drawer in Nathan's desk to find — Lo and behold! — a letter! Or a document! Something proving that Fiona was the Lady. Then I saw myself in Nathan's bedroom examining a diary I'd found in his bedside table. I still hadn't figured out how to use the evidence without revealing Fiona's identity to Aunt Mildred.

I willed the day to fly by, but time slowed to the speed of a turtle out for a Sunday stroll, and little annoyances kept popping up.

The first annoyance was Fulton.

"Want to go down to Terry's after school?" he asked, leaning over my desk. The bell to begin algebra class hadn't rung, and Miss Ellsworth busied herself writing problems on the blackboard. Instead of gliding her chalk over the board, she stabbed at the board, *rat-a-tat-tat, rat-a-tat-tat.*

"You'd better sit down before the bell rings."

"Yeah, I will. But what about after school?" He put his hands on my desk and leaned closer. He smelled of Aqua Velva.

"You know that I practice after school." I didn't tell him that I planned to delay practice until evening because of going to Nathan's house.

"Can't you practice later?"

"Did I ever ask you to miss a basketball practice?"

"I don't have a choice when basketball practice happens."

Miss Ellsworth turned around. Hands on hips she aimed her pop-eyed stare at Fulton's back. He must have felt her eyes burning holes in his back because he slid away and melted into his seat. Giving me a helpless look, he opened his math book.

I had a problem. With both basketball and football seasons over, Fulton wanted to spend time with me after school. He wanted to go to Rittle's. He wanted to go to the movies. He wanted to hang out. If I kept refusing, he might start looking at other girls. I needed to get him into track or tennis. I liked Fulton, but I couldn't let him interfere with my practice time.

The next annoyance reared its ugly head in history when Mr. Mann assigned us an essay for homework. "A three-page paper on the French and Indian War," he announced. Groans erupted. Mr. Mann crossed his arms and looked at Buddy Simms, waiting for the predictable objection. Buddy, thick-headed as always in the art of getting along with teachers, spoke up as expected.

"But, Mr. Ma-aa-aan," he began.

"No *buts*. You have a paper due."

"Couldn't we at least have a little time?"

"Mr. Simms, I contend that no matter when I give you an assignment, you'll wait until the last minute to do the work. As will most of the class, judging by the results I've seen in the past." He wore the same mocking half-smile I imagined the Lord High Master of a torture chamber might wear. He looked around the classroom until his gaze landed on Mary Watson. "Miss Watson, what do you think? Is one day too little to do a three-page essay?"

She shook her head. I joined the chorus of students casting evil looks at Mary. A red flush crept over her cheeks as she studied her nails. I let out an exasperated sigh. How could I go to Nathan's with so much homework?

I set myself to the grindstone during study hall and produced a rough copy of a reasonably decent paper on the French and Indian War. I knew my paper to be nothing like the masterpiece Mary Watson would present, but I had my priorities. Actually, I felt a little sorry for Mary. Mr. Free had set her up for class ridicule. Just because she worked hard.

By the time I got to art, my excitement at going to Nathan's had me just about jumping out of my skin. I walked into class, threw my books on the floor under the table, and grabbed charcoal and paper.

Alice gave me a surprised look. Usually the last person to get started, there I sat, everything in front of me, raring to go. As though that would make the class end sooner.

"You're perky today," she said.

"Yep, that's me. Perky Quincy." I positioned my sketch paper and grabbed a piece of charcoal. Squinting, I looked toward the front of the room at the wooden elephant we were supposed to sketch. *If you squint your eyes you can see the various shades and shadows* Mrs. Arness had taught us. To create better shadows she'd turned off the overhead lights and positioned a lamp to the side of the elephant.

"You shouldn't start out so dark," Alice said.

"So how do you draw white tusks on white paper with black charcoal?"

"Shade the area around the tusks."

She began her sketch, and I watched the lines flow onto her paper. The charcoal seemed to join her body as a sixth finger, performing a job as deftly as my fingers did at the piano. "I think I should stick with music."

"How is the music going?" She glanced at my clumsy drawing.

"Good. But sometimes the goal seems unreachable." I rolled the charcoal around my palm, leaving smudges that would eventually make their way to my sketch and my clothes.

"What is your goal?"

"To play like Arthur Rubenstein."

She stopped drawing and cocked her head at me. "Isn't that like me wanting to draw like Michelangelo?"

"Don't you want to draw like him?"

The idea of drawing like Michelangelo seemed totally foreign to Alice. She sat very still. Our eyes met and held for a few moments. On the other side of the room, Mrs. Arness bent over a table helping someone and took no notice of us.

"Yes, I guess I do want to draw like Michelangelo," Alice said, finally.

"Well, he practiced a lot. How much do you practice?"

"When nobody's home I draw. But Mama thinks I'm being lazy when I work at my art. *Just doodling your time away,* she says. *Like there's nothing to be done around here. You need to be helping around the house more.*"

"She sounds like my parents. What about your daddy?"

"He says I have talent, and that I can get a scholarship. But he's nothing but talk. When he's around, that is. When he's not working he's usually off cavorting in the wrong places." She shrugged and, holding her charcoal sideways, began shading the top and bottom of the elephant's torso to make the body appear three-dimensional. "One thing's for sure, my daddy will never help me pay for college or art school." She leaned back to study her sketch.

"I'm sorry, Alice." Without Addy, I'd have been in the same fix. I no longer bothered to include news of my musical progress in letters to Mama and Daddy. I might as well have reported the number of polar bears in Alaska for all they cared.

"You still working on that report about Nathan Waterstone?" Alice asked after a few minutes. She didn't look up.

"I'm going to his house this afternoon to do some research."

"You might want to look at his will."

"Why?"

"And you might want to find out how he died." She bent closer to her drawing, her face contorted in concentration.

I stared at her. "He died of a heart attack."

I must have spoken more loudly than I thought. Mrs. Arness,

who'd been making her way up and down the aisles between the art tables, stopped and looked at us. She drew back her shoulders, dug her hands into the pockets of her paint-smeared smock, and walked over to where we sat.

She always frowned at my work, so I wasn't surprised when she crunched up her forehead at my feeble attempt to sketch an elephant. She said nothing. I guess my elephant looked so pathetic, words failed her. She turned to admire and critique Alice's sketch, suggesting a lighter value here, a darker value there. *And oh my, weren't her lines good. Just look at the way Alice managed to bring out those tusks without using heavy lines. And the shadow! Why Miss Alice Worthington did shadows better than just about any student she'd ever had.*

When Mrs. Arness moved on to someone else's table, I put down my charcoal and faced Alice. "Why did you say that about the will and the way Nathan died?"

"My uncle drove the ambulance the day he died." Keeping her eyes on her work, but wearing a smug look, she continued sketching. "And my daddy talked to Pearl. He knows stuff."

"What does he know?"

She tilted her head to first one side and then the other, studying her drawing. "The feet aren't good," she said, and set about improving them.

"What does he know?" I repeated.

"Come over sometimes and we'll talk."

"I'm so busy during the week, I can barely find time to breathe. Maybe if you're around on the weekend, I might slip over."

"Slip over?" She scowled at me. "You can't just *come* over; you have to *slip* over. Your aunt prefers that you hobnob with people who live in big houses, doesn't she?"

"Yes." I didn't know why Addy wanted me to stay away from Alice, but letting Alice think her station in life was the reason was one way to shut her up on that subject. I jabbed at my elephant until the hide looked more like that of a reptile than a pachyderm. We finished the period without saying another word to each other. But she had me hooked. What did she know about Nathan's death and will?

⁂ ⁂ ⁂

Shivering, Jessie and I hurried to her car after school. South Georgia weather went back and forth during March and November, unable to decide whether to be warm or cold. We'd come to school that morning in March clothes, but around lunch time the weather had reverted to February temperatures. Jessie flung open the car door, slid in, and started the motor.

"Can you drop me at Nathan's?" I hugged myself to get warm.

"Sure." She turned on the heater, but it blew out cold air. "How come you're going there?"

"Research."

"Wish I could go to old Poe's house and be a fly on the wall. I'd like to research what went on there."

"Jessie!"

She laughed as she backed out of the parking space. "Come on; admit you'd like to see some of that stuff, too."

"I'd be too embarrassed."

She gave me her look. All Jessie had to do to start me giggling was give me her *look*. She'd draw her lips up at one corner, turn her head sideways, close one eye and peer at me from the corner of the other eye. I couldn't help but laugh, and when the two of us started laughing, all was lost. By the time we'd arrived at Nathan's, I'd transformed from a serious would-be researcher to a very silly sixteen-year-old.

I still felt giddy when I rang the doorbell of Nathan's huge

Victorian house, but when Pearl Latrelle — tall, slim, olive-skinned, and haughty as an English butler — opened the door and I stepped inside, the silliness vanished.

"Hello, Pearl. Remember me? Quincy? Addy said I could look around." My voice echoed in the long, dark hall.

Her eyes roamed over me. I'd grown a few years older and several inches taller since she'd last seen me. After an interval, apparently satisfied that I was really me, she nodded and closed the door, plunging us into semi-darkness.

The hall ran from the front door to the back door. Dark wainscoting covered the bottom half of the walls; the plaster above the wainscoting had been painted the color of Dijon mustard. Odds and ends of heavy, mahogany furniture loomed against the walls. Halfway down, a flight of stairs led to the second floor.

"Where do you want to begin?"

"Anywhere. Where should I put my books?"

She motioned to the sitting room on the left and then glided through the arched doorway into the darkness, leaving me to clunk along behind. I caught a faint whiff of cigar smoke. Like Nathan's ghost was there. I shivered.

Pearl switched on a lamp. "Put your books there." She pointed to the coffee table.

I put my books down and looked around. I'd been in the room many times, seeing, but not seeing. I examined the flowered rug, the black wrought iron grate in front of the fireplace, the leather upholstery, the brass Arabian coffee pots on the mantle, the painting of a Roman villa above the fireplace. Framed photographs stood on an end table. None contained pictures of women.

"What I'd like to do," I said, ". . . is wander from room to room

213

and write down what strikes me as interesting."

Pearl nodded but made no sign of going away. Hands folded together like a singer, she stood at the edge of the rug — an Aubusson, I'd heard Addy tell Mama once. Now that I found myself actually in the house, I realized I didn't have a clear course of action. Pearl breathing down my neck didn't help. I took pen and paper from my school bag and, after jotting down the words *sitting room*, described the room. *Dark burgundy leather couch and a matching chair. Two additional chairs upholstered in faded red plaid fabric. A wicker love seat with embroidered cushions, also faded. A camel saddle used as a foot stool.* I knew about the camel saddle because Addy had explained that to me years before. *A coffee table made from a door that came from India. A . . .*

I stopped. Going from room to room, writing down everything, was a waste of time. If I described the whole house, my paper would stretch from here to next year. Besides, who wanted to hear about Nathan Waterstone's furniture? Mr. Feldman had made clear that the main focus should be the author's work. On the other hand, I reasoned, if I stood there long enough writing everything down, Pearl might grow bored and leave me alone. I resumed writing. *Five framed photos on an end table. A big blue ashtray on the coffee table. A wooden elephant on . . .*

Alice's hints of something scandalous reverberated in my mind. What did her daddy think he knew? Or was he just a big gossip, inventing things like Aunt Mildred?

Pearl moved about, showing signs of restlessness. She ran her hand over the back of a chair, peered out from between the closed drapes, flicked a bit of dust from a picture frame. I kept writing, trying to look like I knew what I was doing, even though I didn't. I wrote: *Nathan Waterstone sat with his men guests in his sitting room, smoking cigars, laughing and joking, and recounting adventures.* I'd ask Addy later if that were true.

I walked across the hall into the living room. Pearl followed. How could I snoop if she attached herself to me like a leech? I sighed. Then I decided that my sigh might have sounded too impatient, so I smiled sweetly.

I scribbled, describing the living room and looking up occasionally to see if Pearl's boredom might be on the verge of driving her away. The room had a small fireplace with an intricately carved mantel. A gold framed mirror hung above the mantel. Doodads adorned various pieces of furniture: on a small bureau a large porcelain swan planter held a palm; an arrangement of flowers stood on the glass-top coffee table; a collection of small boxes that looked like they'd come from other parts of the world decorated various surfaces; embroidered cushions . . . I wrote everything down. Pearl still hung over me.

A sneaky idea occurred to me. When Addy went to New York, perhaps . . . Yes, I could do that: tell Pearl I had Addy's permission to go through Nathan's papers. Especially if Addy gave me permission to look at the original manuscripts. She'd shown me the manuscript for the new novel — or at least she'd shown me one page to illustrate Nathan's bad handwriting. Surely she'd give me permission to see the others. I'd extend that permission to include Nathan's private papers.

I went from room to room writing down what I saw, noting unique pieces of furniture, color schemes, decorative items. I took my time.

Pearl started to hang back when we went upstairs. She straightened pictures in the hallway, flicked dust from a table. Once — briefly — she left me alone in a bedroom but reappeared after a minute or two. She walked over to the bed and smoothed a wrinkle in the bedspread.

"How did he die?" I asked. Even though I knew. Which Alice obviously didn't.

"Heart attack," Pearl answered.

We returned to the first floor and went into the kitchen. I asked about his food preferences.

"Simple foods. Strong coffee for breakfast. At lunch, yogurt and a piece of fruit."

"Yogurt?" I'd never heard of yogurt.

"Made from milk." She pointed to a set of crockery jars. "Warm milk goes in those and sits until it thickens like clabber. He ate mostly vegetables for supper." She tore a banana from a bunch that lay in a bowl on the counter, examined the black spots, and then threw the banana in the trash. "He tried to be a vegetarian but didn't succeed. He liked curry."

"Curry?"

She wiped her hands on a towel hanging near the sink. "It's a mixture of spices. Something he learned in India."

When we came to Nathan's study, I stood in the doorway for a few moments looking at the room where Nathan wrote his last four books and where Addy sat every day typing his manuscripts. Unlike the rest of the house, the study was bright and airy, without curtains covering the wall of windows that looked out onto the backyard. Waning sunlight slanted through the glass, glazing the contents of the room with silver. The room moved, or seemed to, as light flitted and careened from clouds carousing past the sun, or from wind jostling the branches of the sycamore outside. Like a silly five-year-old, I stepped on a shard of light. The light moved and I stepped on another. Pearl remained just outside the door, boredom smeared across her face as obvious as grape jelly.

Floor to ceiling bookcases lined the wall to the left. Unlike Miss Burke's library, with book spines arranged evenly and pushed back exactly one-inch from the edge of the shelves, Nathan's books lay helter-skelter and were crammed into every available nook and cranny.

Two desks stood along the wall opposite the door, a Windsor chair in front of each. I remembered seeing Nathan working at the desk on the left and Addy at the one on the right, where an Underwood typewriter now collected dust.

A metal file cabinet with a pipe rack on top stood between the desks. The cabinet pulled at me like a magnet. What secrets lay inside? I glanced at Pearl. She still showed no signs of leaving me alone.

"Do you mind if I sit at his desk?" I put my hand on the back of Nathan's desk chair as though I were about to sit. "I want to describe how Nathan saw the room from his chair." Pearl looked at me like she thought I was crazy. "Pearl, I've been thinking, you know so much about Nathan, you could really help me with this paper. I have a whole list of questions I want to ask you." I held up my pad of paper and pencil like I was about to write down her answers to my imaginary questions. "How many hours a day did he work?" I looked at her expectantly.

She shook her head. "Don't remember."

"Did he write with a pencil or a pen?"

"I don't think I know much you'd want to hear about." She turned and went away, leaving me alone at last.

So that's the way to get rid of her, I realized: ask her to talk.

I pulled at the top drawer of the file cabinet. The drawer was locked. I tried the others. They, too, were locked. Disappointed, but not surprised, I went over and sat down on the Chesterfield sofa in front of the wall of windows. When Mama and I stopped to visit Addy at work, Pearl would bring us to the study. We'd find Nathan at his desk, sprawled in the chair, shirt partially open, sleeves rolled up. He'd draw his legs up from where he'd stretched them underneath the desk and lean forward as he rose to reach out his long, thin hand to Mama. He'd look down at me and nod a *hello*. After motioning in the direction of the sofa, indicating that we should sit, he'd reach for his pipe. Only after he lit his pipe and took a couple of puffs did he settle into the matching leather chair and ask Mama how the cotton crops were doing that year. Always the cotton. Even in the middle of the winter he asked about the cotton.

Mama gave the same answer each time. *Just fine, Nathan. Just fine.*

And the soul-saving business, how's that? he'd ask.

Addy interceded then with something like *Behave yourself, Nathan.* Or she'd give him a playful punch on the arm and say, *You be nice to my sister, you hear?*

At that point, I usually decided exploring the house sounded like more fun than listening to adult conversation. I'd run off, Pearl chasing behind and calling out *Don't run in the house.*

A wisp of cold air made me to shiver. Seeing that one of the windows stood open a crack, I walked over to close it and saw Jonas sitting in the backyard bundled up in several layers of cardigans. He sat on a bench under a mimosa tree puffing at a cigarette. Nearby, the lawn mower and various garden implements waited.

"From the window of his study. . ." I wrote, ". . . Nathan Waterstone could look out onto a backyard, lush with mimosa, azaleas, japonicas, and . . ." I didn't know the names of the other plants. I'd ask Jonas. He knew the names of everything.

But I wasn't after the names of trees in Nathan's backyard. Looking over my shoulder to make sure Pearl hadn't slipped back in to spy, I went over and pulled once again at the drawers of the cabinet. Where were keys to file cabinets kept? In a desk drawer? On a nail somewhere? In a jar in a kitchen cabinet?

From the dimming light, I knew the afternoon drew rapidly to a close. Thanks to Pearl hanging over me, my visit had been a complete waste. I had to come back.

218

CHAPTER 14

A freezing mist fell as I walked the six blocks home. I buttoned my sweater and hugged myself to keep warm. I passed yard after yard filled with Japonica blossoms about to expire from frostbite. Lights were coming on in windows, and smoke puffed from a few chimneys.

Earlene had hot chocolate waiting.

"It ain't good when the weather gets cold again like this," she said. "I expect poor Mrs. Thompson's going to lose some of her flowers." She stirred the Irish stew bubbling on the stove. "You find what you wanted?"

"No, ma'am." I wrapped my hands around the cup of hot chocolate to warm them. "I wanted to learn something new about Nathan."

"Well, you ain't going to find out who the Lady is. Ain't nobody knows that."

"I guess *she* knows."

"And *she* ain't telling." Earlene scooped up a spoonful of stew. She watched the steam rising for a few seconds before tasting. "Just right." She dropped the spoon in the sink and turned around. "Maybe the Lady ain't even still alive. Not after what happened at the end of the book.

"You've read the book?"

"Of course, I have. I told you, I ain't no ignoramus."

"Aunt Mildred hasn't read *The Lady*. All she reads is her Sunday School lesson book and the Bible."

"Well now, she must not of read the Bible any too good."

"Why do you say that?"

"Them God-fearing white folks go on about loving your neighbor, but they be real careful who their neighbors are. They keep us black folk in a different part of town so they won't have to have us as neighbors and love us."

What she said was true, so what could I say? "Did you like *A Tree Grows in Brooklyn?*" I asked at length.

"I sure did. Especially that Christmas tree scene." She wiped her hands on a dishtowel. "You better go get some of your practicing done. Supper's ready anytime now. All I have to do is put the biscuits in the oven."

I finished my chocolate and stood up.

"And forget about the Lady."

"Earlene, I do believe you seem a little worried about my finding out. Do you know who she is?"

"I don't know who she is and I expect there be a good reason why we don't know. You go on in there and practice now. I ain't got all night to finish up in here."

๑   ๑   ๑

Earlene held off baking the biscuits to allow me an hour of practice before supper. After we ate, I went to Addy's room before going back to the piano for my second hour. I sat in the rocking chair and watched her pack for her trip to New York. She'd turned on all the lamps in the room as well as the overhead light.

"So I can tell the difference in black and navy," she explained. Her suitcase lay open on the bed.

"When you get back will you walk me through Nathan's house?" I asked. "I have a lot of questions."

"Of course." She took a white lace blouse from her closet and added the blouse to her suitcase.

"How long will you be gone?"

She sat down on the bed, smushing the feather comforter so that it ballooned around her legs. "Maybe a week. Maybe two. Adam and I will go over everything. Then I'll come home and make changes. Will you be all right with Earlene?" She reached up to touch her gold locket.

"Of course. She'll cook my favorite dishes and try to stuff me until I can't stand the sight of food."

Addy laughed. "I can't imagine you not being able to stand the sight of food. You have Elizabeth Walker's phone number in case of an emergency, and there's always Mildred."

"I can't imagine what kind of emergency would make me call Aunt Mildred." I pulled my feet onto the chair and wrapped my arms around my legs.

"Robert will drive you to your piano lesson on Saturday."

"How did you talk him into that?"

"There'll be a payback, I'm sure. He'll rope you into playing the piano for some event at church." She reached over to pet Lucifer.

"I didn't finish at Nathan's house."

"What did you do there?" She rose and went back to the closet.

"I wrote down things about the house. Looked at photos. He had lots of friends."

"People liked Nathan." She pulled two skirts from the rack and held them up, examining them. "You know, honey, if you have any sort of problem you can call Robert. I mean, if Elizabeth isn't available."

"How long have you known him?"

"I met him in London. Which skirt should I take?"

"The black one. How did you meet him?"

She ignored me for a few moments while she unhooked the skirt from the hanger, folded it, and then put it in her suitcase. She went to her bureau, opened a drawer, and looked down at the contents. "Robert was in London doing research for his dissertation," she said finally, still looking down at the contents of the drawer.

"What was his dissertation about?"

"Something to do with comparing Christianity to other religions. What have I forgotten?"

"Was Fiona in London, too?"

"Briefly." The corner of her lip twitched.

"Do you think Reverend Stewart winding up here is strange?"

"Not strange at all." She closed the drawer and, turning around, leaned against the bureau. "Nathan notified him when there was an opening at the church. Actually, there were two openings. The first time, Robert declined. Then Fiona became ill. When there was a second opening, Robert came for Fiona's benefit. *A better climate in Georgia* he said. Anyway, lots of Scots immigrated to America; so no, his coming isn't strange at all."

"Fiona was sick before she came?"

"She'd been diagnosed, but the symptoms weren't evident to the rest of us." Addy walked over to the bed, snapped the suitcase shut, and sat down. "You know the house rules while I'm gone."

I let out a little puff of air and a long drawn-out *yes*. Adults were all the same; they couldn't resist moral lectures and reminders.

"No boys in the house when I'm not here. Go to bed on time. Don't be late for school. And you need to be in by midnight on the weekends. Go to church on Sunday. I don't want Mildred Perch claiming I shirked my duty on that score."

"Yes, ma'am." I stood and gave a mock salute. "I guess I'll march off and finish practicing."

"That's one thing I'll never have to remind you to do." She smiled. "I'm proud of you, honey."

I stopped at the door and turned around. "Did you know Fiona when you were in London?"

She looked to the side of the room. "Yes, I met her." She waited a few seconds before looking back at me, her smile translated into a weaker version.

❧   ❧   ❧

The Schubert began to sound hopeful, and I lost myself in the passion of playing the impromptu, unaware that Addy had slipped in and sat down to listen.

"That was beautiful, Quincy," she said when I looked up. She leaned toward me, her eyes glowing with pride.

"Sometimes I get so lost in the music I forget everything else. I forget that there *is* anything else." I'd played with such energy that my hands ached. I slid them between my thighs to warm them. "The house could probably burn down around me and I wouldn't know."

"That's the sign of a true artist, the ability to become completely absorbed in her art. You're talented, Quincy. Don't let anything ever come between you and your music."

"Why would I let that happen?"

She stood up and yawned. "It's time for bed. What happened to your nightly call from Fulton?"

223

Fulton? I'd forgotten about Fulton. What *had* happened to him?

 و   و   و

Addy dropped me at school on her way to Atlanta the following day. She planned to spend the night with a friend in Atlanta, and then catch a train the next morning to New York. I was a tad late getting to school, so I rushed to class and didn't see Fulton until after homeroom.

"Daddy wouldn't let me use the phone last night," he said as we walked to our third period classes. Probly' won't let me call tonight either. Says I have to stay out of trouble and study." He frowned.

"Well, that's a crying shame, having to study." The playful sarcasm in my voice didn't seem to register; Fulton still frowned. "Why are you in trouble?"

He rolled his eyes. "It wasn't that bad."

"What wasn't that bad?" I stopped and leaned against a locker. He huddled close enough for me to feel his breath on my face. I liked the warm feeling of standing together, touching, feeling someone else's breath. "Fulton, what wasn't that bad?" I repeated when he didn't answer right away.

"The chemistry experiment yesterday."

Fulton had chemistry last period. He and the chemistry teacher had locked horns before. "What did you do this time?"

He grinned. "Nearly burned down the lab."

"Fulton!"

"Hey, it was really cool. Mr. Rivers had to go piss . . ."

"Fulton!"

"Sorry. He had to go to the toilet. The door to the supply closet was wide open and Buddy and I couldn't resist."

224

"What couldn't you resist?"

He raised his eyebrows to keep me in suspense while I waited to hear what he couldn't resist. Up and down the hall, lockers screeched open and slammed shut. Next to us, a ninth grader opened his, letting out a whiff of smelly gym clothes and dirty socks.

I tapped my watch to remind Fulton that I didn't have all day. "Are you going to tell me or not?"

"We found a jar of sodium. We meant to take only a teensy piece and throw the piece in some water. But, well, what can you do?" He shrugged as though to say what happened next was a matter of fate rather than fault. "We pulled out a big hunk. Then we decided we'd probably get in trouble anyway, so why not make the thing worthwhile. We pulled out a bigger hunk." He leaned closer to me. We were almost nose to nose, lip to lip. "Do you know what happens when you put sodium in water?"

I shook my head.

"Sodium and water sparks and flames like the Fourth-of-July. You should have seen the fireworks." He pulled back and laughed, but then stopped and frowned. "The papers old man Rivers had stacked on his desk caught fire, so he went and called my daddy. He called him at his office, would you believe? The man's got no sense of humor."

I wavered between outrage and giggles. "You could have burned down the school."

"But we didn't."

"You could have been hurt."

"Hey, there's always a risk when you're engaged in scientific inquiry. Want to go down to Rittle's after school?"

"You know I can't."

"Ah, come on. One day won't hurt."

"No." I moved away from the lockers. "Why don't you go out for

225

track?"

"I don't want to go out for track."

"It'll help you run faster when you're trying to get that little ol' football down the field." We pushed our way through the thronging students.

"I'm already the fastest quarterback in South Georgia."

"Maybe you could be the fastest in the state."

"Right now I don't want to be the fastest; I just want to go hang out at Rittle's."

I quickened my steps. We'd dallied too long and the bell was about to ring. "If you study and make good grades, you can get into a good college."

"I don't have to worry about that. I'll get a football scholarship to the University of Georgia or Georgia Tech. Maybe even Alabama."

"Well, I need to practice and study so I can get into a decent college. See you later, Fulton."

It didn't seem fair. Football players had everything handed to them on a silver platter while people with other talents, like me and Alice Worthington, were invisible when they gave out college scholarship money. The only scholarship Alice would get would be just about enough to buy shoe polish. I had talent. I made good grades. I worked hard. But no one wanted to give scholarships to future concert pianists. My only hope lay in Addy's support.

When I walked into English class, Mary Watson was already there, notebook open, pencil in hand, poised to devour every syllable that floated from Mr. Feldman's mouth. I nodded at her and sat down.

I turned around to watch Jessie desperately ransacking her book bag. "I think I left my report at home," she moaned. I watched as she dumped the contents of her book bag on her desk and scrambled through them. Finally, she stopped her search, put her hands on her cheeks, and looked at me. "What am I going to do?"

"Calm down. Your report's probably there somewhere. Look again." The bell rang and I turned around.

Mr. Feldman had asked us to come prepared to present progress reports on our research papers. Most had very little to say and you could tell they hadn't bothered to prepare ahead of time. They'd say things like: "I went to the library last weekend; I have twenty-five note cards full of notes." Then Mr. Feldman would ask: "What sources did you use?" "I used the encyclopedia." "Which one?" "The *World Book* and the *Britannica*." "What do your notes pertain to?" "His (or her) life, of course."

Behind me, Jessie still shuffled through books and bag. "Devilstiltskin has been messing with my stuff," she muttered. "I know he has. I stuck my report in my book bag. I'm going to kill the brat."

Mr. Feldman wanted to know if anyone had actually bothered to read works of their chosen authors other than the ones we'd read in class. Except for Mary and me, the patent answer was that everyone intended to. *Oh, yes, this weekend in fact, they were going to read such and such and they'd already checked books out of the library, and the books sat on their desk at home just waiting, and yes, they'd read the books this weekend for sure.*

"I'm going to read that novel about the preacher that knocked up the broad," Buddy Simms said.

"We read *The Scarlet Letter* already, Mr. Simms."

"Oh, yeah. That's right. Well, I'm going to read *The Scarlet Letter* again."

I guess Buddy had forgotten that he'd switched from Hawthorne to Hemingway. Or maybe he thought they were one and the same since both names started with H.

Mary had a great deal to say about her paper. I wondered how she

227

failed to see the bored looks while she talked. Jessie had apparently found her report because I no longer heard her scrambling among her things. She kept expelling little explosive breaths while Mary spoke. "Lord help us," she muttered when she could no longer be quiet.

Mr. Feldman called on me when Mary finished. "Miss Bruce, how is your research going?"

"I've read all of Nathan Waterstone's books and I'm doing research in his house."

"That's wonderful. You'll still be giving us some previously unpublished information?"

A lump rose in my throat. What if I couldn't present new information? If Addy wouldn't let me write about the new book, was there something else? Mr. Feldman looked at me, waiting for my response, so I nodded.

"I'm intrigued. This might be the most interesting research paper I've ever gotten from a student."

A thrill ran through me. I *had* to put something new and exciting in my paper. Hands in pockets, he leaned back on his desk and focused on me as though there were no one else in the room. "Can you not give us a hint?"

"No, sir. I'm not allowed to say anything yet."

"Can you at least tell us what this new information relates to?" He wasn't giving up.

"I'm sorry, not yet."

"Well then," he said. "We'll wait with bated breath to see what new thing you divulge about Nathan Waterstone. Don't forget, I'd like to have your aunt come and speak to the class."

I had the perfect excuse to keep her away: her publishing deadline. If she didn't have one, I'd make one up.

But I worried. What if the timing of the publication announcement was all wrong? What if they announced the new novel right after New York? Or what if they decided to wait another six months until every comma and syllable was finalized? Mr. Feldman would think I was a liar.

I could identify the Lady. There *had* to be evidence. But without proof — something more than a picture and a pin, and the knowledge she'd been a nurse, and that Nathan had lured her to Wilson under the pretext of recommending a job for her husband — my suspicions, no matter how well founded, wouldn't be enough. Even with proof I'd never identify Fiona by name. How mean would that be — hurting someone like Reverend Stewart by announcing to the world that his wife had an adulterous affair with a famous American author? He'd be devastated, and Addy would be beyond angry. Wreaking revenge on Aunt Mildred wasn't worth paying that price. The new book was my only choice of previously unpublished information.

Unless Alice actually knew something.

"Tell me about meeting Addy in London," I said to Reverend Stewart as he drove me to my lesson on Saturday.

"Ahhhh," he said, and rubbed his hand across his neck. "Meeting Addy . . . That was one of the great pleasures of my life. I was down from the University of Aberdeen in Scotland doing research for my dissertation." His mouth curved in a broad smile. "I came out of the British Library one rainy day and bumped into her." He took his eyes off the road and turned to me just long enough for me to see his eyes dance. "When I say *bumped*, I mean that literally. After a particularly grueling session with the books, I bolted down the stone steps of the library. They were slick with rain. You know about London weather: rain, rain, and more rain. At the bottom, I slipped and crashed into her, and she landed in a wee puddle. She'd just bought *Burmese Days*, and her new book landed in the puddle along with her back side." He chuckled. "Addy cursed royally. Your aunt really knows how to put a chap in his place." He smiled at the memory. "Her anger wasn't as much about muddying her skirt as about her new book being ruined. I kept offering to pay the cleaning bill for her clothes, while she kept ranting about how I'd ruined her book. Finally, she calmed down enough to let me take her back to the bookstore. I bought her another copy of *Burmese Days* and then we went for tea, muddy clothes and all."

"You became friends."

"Indeed, we did."

I understood Addy hitting if off with Reverend Stewart. Talking to him was as easy as cutting warm butter with a butter knife.

He slowed the car to a crawl. Ahead of us a tractor pulled a wagon stacked high with empty cotton baskets. We'd crept along behind several tractors that morning. Farmers were plowing their fields, getting ready for planting. Soon, another cotton-picking season would be upon us. Reverend Stewart looked at his watch. "Not to worry. We have plenty of time."

"I thought Nathan introduced you and Addy," I said, puzzled. "Didn't you meet Nathan in Nepal?"

"I did." He leaned forward as he pulled into the passing lane and swept around the tractor. "But I met Addy on my own at the British Library. Nathan and I reconnected after I met her." He propped his left arm in the open window and steered with his right. "I spent a lot of time with Nathan. And with Addy. She was lonely with Warren off fighting. Nathan included her in many of his outings."

"He was working on *The Lady* then."

"Yes."

"You must have met her, too."

He looked intently at the road and said nothing. I felt mean, asking him about meeting the Lady when I knew that his wife was the Lady, but I wanted to see if I could detect a hint that he knew.

"I didn't meet her," he said, finally.

"But how could you not have? You were there and saw Nathan often."

"That's true. But the average man isn't going to let his friends know he's carrying on with a married woman. Certainly not his ministerial friends. You wouldn't let your minister know you were engaged in adultery, would you?" He looked at me.

I shook my head. "No, but then I wouldn't be."

"No, you wouldn't. But some do." There was no look of judgment on his face, only a sad smile. "We humans are a long way from perfect."

The black mood that descended on me following the realization that Fiona had been the Lady returned. I didn't care so much about Fiona's adultery as I did about the hurt Reverend Stewart would feel if he knew. Would he forgive his wife for committing adultery? In his sermons he spoke of forgiveness, but had he ever been put to the test?

We rode in silence for a few miles. The azaleas had burst into bloom. The landscape looked like fairies had taken paintbrushes and colored in every imaginable shade of pink and purple and then flung the sweet smell of azalea scent through the air like fairy dust.

"You know . . ." I said, struck with an idea, "Mr. Feldman wants Addy to talk to the class about Nathan, but she's so busy. Could you come and speak instead?"

"I'd be glad to if Mr. Feldman finds me acceptable. Addy would be better, of course."

"You'd be a great second choice. Besides, you speak so well."

"All right, then. When the time comes, let me know."

"There's something I've been wondering about."

231

"What's that?" He glanced at me — with his beautiful smile and his lovely crinkly eyes.

"How did Nathan persuade you to leave Scotland and come to Wilson?"

"It took no persuading at all. Fiona had begged to come for years. I finally gave in to her wishes."

My heart broke at knowing what he apparently didn't.

~ ~ ~

Mrs. Rich made a final decision on my recital pieces: Mozart Sonata in G-major, K 189; the Schubert Impromptu in B-flat; and now that I'd gotten the rhythm right, the Chopin Waltz, where the right hand plays a six-eight rhythm while the left hand plays a three-four rhythm. The idea of performing thrilled me; the idea of performing also sent me into a nervous frenzy.

"Next year there'll be more," she said. "You've come a long way since last August. Expect to play in my private recitals every two months. Play anywhere you can, my dear. I want you to have more experience in front of audiences."

Reverend Stewart must have heard her because on the way home he asked if I'd perform at the coming month's service in the nursing home. I agreed. What else could I do? Would he expect me to play *Amazing Grace*, or some such thing?

"Play whatever you like," he said, as though reading my thoughts. "Preferably, something cheerful." A horse fly buzzed around the window. He swatted, sending the fly hurtling toward the back window.

"Did you ever meet Warren?" I asked.

"No, I never met Addy's husband."

"Were you with Addy when he died?"

"No, I was in Aberdeen, just returned from my honeymoon. Nathan rang me up when the telegram came. Addy was vacationing near Inverness. We had to track her down."

The horsefly, after buzzing around the back seat, returned to the front and landed on the passenger side window. I rolled the window down and shooed the pest out. We talked then about mundane things. School. Boyfriends. Sports.

"If you need anything, money, help, or if you need a ride, give me a call," he said when he dropped me at home.

"I sure will, and thank you so much for taking me to my lesson."

"The pleasure was all mine. See you in church tomorrow."

    ❧   ❧   ❧

I made a beeline for Alice's as soon as Reverend Stewart drove away. My previous visits to her had been sneaky, but with Addy gone they felt more like vile deception.

Alice looked surprised when she opened the door. "Can't say I expected to see you." She motioned me in.

I followed her to her bedroom.

"Well?" she said, after we sat down cross-legged on the floor

"What have you been up to?" I wouldn't give her the satisfaction of begging for information. At least not immediately.

"Not much." She looked aimlessly around. "Do you want to look at my latest drawings?" I nodded, and she reached for the box under her bed. "After our talk about practicing I started copying things by famous artists." She pulled out a stack of papers and handed them to me. "These are copies of Hieronymus Bosch drawings."

I leafed through them, looking at sketch after sketch of demons and devils. Alice was very, very good, and I told her so. "But these are weird," I added as I handed the drawings back. "Why would you want to draw demons and devils?"

"I wanted to practice drawing people."

"These aren't people."

"They illustrate the evil in humans. Demons punish sinners."

"There's no such thing as demons."

"Of course there are. You just don't see them." She laid the drawings aside and wrapped her arms around her legs. "Everybody has a demon inside."

"I don't."

"Sure you do. Demons are like compulsions." She rested her chin on her knees and fixed me with a lop-sided grin.

I grinned back. "My only compulsion is to impress Mr. Feldman."

"You and every other girl in school." She gave me a sly look. "If you want something interesting for your paper, figure out what happened when Nathan died and how come they didn't honor his will."

"Alice, what do you know?" A sudden inkling of why Addy didn't want me to associate with Alice dawned. Addy must have known that Alice had heard rumors.

Alice took a deep breath. "I told you before, Uncle Frank drove the ambulance the day Nathan died. When they got to his house the doors were locked. Your aunt called out to them from a window, something about having to find the key. As soon as Dr. Whiddon came, she miraculously found the key and let him in, but Dr. Whiddon made the ambulance crew continue to wait outside while he went in."

I couldn't imagine where Alice's story was going.

"Finally, Dr. Whiddon came out and let them in. They found

234

Nathan's body lying on the floor at the bottom of the stairs. His eyes were wide open. 'He had a heart attack,' Dr. Whiddon told them. Then my uncle said something about calling the coroner, and Dr. Whiddon told him there was no need. There was something strange about the whole thing."

"He had a heart attack. What's strange about that?"

"Uncle Frank said he looked at Nathan's eyes and knew he didn't have no heart attack. And Nathan's shirt was all sweaty."

"Your uncle isn't a doctor."

"He drove an ambulance long enough to know a thing or two. He saw all sorts of stuff that I bet you don't even know goes on." Alice looked down at her fingernails, ran a thumb over the ragged nails of one hand, and then, after breathing a drawn-out sigh, put her hands on the floor behind her and leaned back onto her arms. "Dr. Whiddon rode in the ambulance. He wouldn't let anyone else near the body."

I put my hands up in a questioning gesture. "And?" A cold feeling crept down my spine.

Alice looked down at the drawings scattered across her lap and said nothing. For what seemed a very long time, the only sound in the room was a fly buzzing near the window.

"Your uncle told you this?" I asked finally.

"I heard him whisper the story to Mama." She fell silent for a moment, before continuing. "My daddy has heard talk." She gave me a fleeting look from the corners of her eyes.

"What talk?"

"He hears them niggers down at Jake's telling about how Nathan didn't die of no heart attack, and how the white folk had the wool pulled over their eyes. Pearl goes there, and she talks plenty. She says he didn't die of no heart attack."

Now I knew for sure somebody was making things up. Pearl barely

235

talked.

"Aaaand . . .," Alice flitted her eyes at me and then looked down at her finger while she doodled circles on her thigh. "Pearl was supposed to get a bunch of money from Nathan's will. Her boyfriend showed a copy of the will to everybody down at Jake's. My Daddy saw the copy, and sure enough, that's what the will said: Pearl was supposed to get Nathan's money." Alice looked up and narrowed her eyes at me. "But did she? No, sirree. She goes right on living in that house, cleaning and scrubbing, and they give her a measly little salary every month. What happened to all that money she was supposed to get?"

I felt my muscles go tight. "Are you saying someone is keeping money from Pearl?"

Alice shrugged. "I'm just trying to help you find something new and different for your paper. You said you wanted to impress Mr. Feldman. But if you don't want to hear . . ." She gathered her sketches and put them back in the box.

My legs seemed to develop a will of their own, wanting to run away. I clenched my thighs, willing them to be still. I had to hear.

"They say things about Pearl and Nathan," Alice said. "About her being his mistress. You must have heard that." She looked at me for confirmation.

I shook my head. Her tale sounded like a story someone invented to relieve boredom.

"They say she did a lot more than just take care of his house. Maybe she was the Lady."

"She couldn't have been," I lashed out. I knew who the Lady was, and she wasn't Pearl. "Pearl came from New Orleans and has never been near London. She started working for Nathan after he wrote the book."

"You're sure?"

"I'm positive. Nathan died of a heart attack." I glared at Alice. "People just like to make up scandals. None of that is true."

"Well . . ." Alice looked out the window. "Maybe you're right, and that's just all talk. The will, Nathan's falling down the stairs. After all, your aunt must know everything there is to know." Sarcasm dripped from her tongue like slime from a rotten onion. "I have to do the dishes before Mama comes home." She stood up.

"Well, thanks Alice for the info." My voice sounded slimy too. "I have to go. See you around."

I walked away. Through the kitchen, through the living room. Alice followed. When I reached the front door and grabbed the knob, I turned slightly — just enough to see her over my shoulder.

"He didn't die of no heart attack," Alice said. "Uncle Frank says someone poisoned him. That's the reason his eyes looked funny, and there was all that sweat."

I let go of the knob and turned around to glare at her.

"The money Pearl was supposed to get . . .," Alice tilted her head and narrowed her eyes at me. "They kept the money themselves — your aunt, Dr. Whiddon, and Mary Watson's daddy. He was Nathan's lawyer."

I ran. As though I could escape from Alice's horrible lies. As though the wind rushing through my lungs would erase what I'd heard. The memory of Addy meeting with Dr. Whiddon and Mr. Watson flashed through my memory. They'd gone into Addy's study, Addy leading. Hunch-shouldered Dr. Whiddon followed. Mr. Watson, the last to go in, had glanced at me as I stood in the hallway, watching. One corner of his mouth twitched in a poor attempt at a smile before he closed the door between us.

After two blocks I stopped running and slogged the rest of the way home in a daze. I went to my bedroom and threw myself onto my bed. Had Alice made up the dreadful tale to get even with me for choosing other friends?

CHAPTER 15

Jessie dropped me at Nathan's after school on Monday. I marched up to the front door, rang the bell, and without saying *Hello*, blurted out to Pearl, "I want to look at Nathan's original manuscripts." If I had access to manuscripts, then I could sneak around and look at other things. Death certificates. Wills.

"You have permission?"

"Yes."

"People don't get to touch them without permission."

"Addy is away, but I can call Mrs. Walker or Reverend Stewart if you need to hear direct."

She looked uncertain. I hadn't exactly asked Addy if I could see them, but I drew back my shoulders and, without flinching, looked Pearl straight in the eyes.

She tipped her head to one side and fiddled with her hoop earring while shifting from one foot to the other. "Well . . . all right," she said finally.

I followed her to Nathan's study. She went to the file cabinet, but then, hesitating, she turned and pursed her lips as she studied me through narrowed-eyes. I smiled and stood as tall as I could. As if I really did have permission. Finally, she tilted back the pipe rack on top of the file cabinet and removed a small envelope from which she took a key.

"The manuscripts are in the top three drawers," she said, unlocking the top one.

"Thanks. I'm going to sit at Nathan's desk and go through them." *And whatever else I can find.*

Pearl didn't leave. She stood a few feet away, fingering her earring. I sat down, took a pad of paper, and began writing. *I'm sitting in Nathan's study. Pearl is hovering over me. If I ignore her, maybe she'll get bored and leave. I'm looking for three things: information for my research paper, evidence that Fiona was the Lady, and as if that isn't enough, I need to find something to show Alice that her Uncle Frank is a liar. I can't concentrate on any of these with Pearl standing there.*

It didn't work. She remained, still playing with her earring. I'd just have to ignore her.

In the top drawer of the cabinet I found a stack of manuscript boxes. The label on the top box read *Highland Deception.* Two more, labeled *Highland Deception,* lay beneath the first one, and underneath those, lay three boxes labeled *Himalayan Adventure.* One by one, I opened the boxes. The first box for each title contained a typed manuscript, while the next two contained hand-written versions. The hand-written manuscript for each novel required the use of two boxes, whereas the typed ones only needed one.

When I opened the second drawer, Pearl finally slunk away. I found six more manuscript boxes: three for *The Lady* and three for *Runaway.* Expecting to find the same things in the third drawer — typed manuscripts followed by handwritten versions, I was surprised to see only one box each for *Game of Chance, Mary Moran,* and *The Mistress.* The handwritten manuscripts were missing. Nor were they in the bottom drawer. In that drawer, I found a jumble of odds and ends. I rummaged through the clutter, discovering nothing of interest. Where did Nathan keep his private papers? I didn't think they'd be in the desk drawers. Those were too public. I had to find a way to search the whole house, but I couldn't with Pearl around. Meanwhile, to gain her trust — at least as much trust as Pearl was capable of, I needed to do what I'd said I was there to do: examine the manuscripts. If she trusted me, sooner or later she'd relax her vigilance.

I removed the first half of the handwritten manuscript for *Highland Deception* from its box. The writing looked more like the rough draft of Fulton's weekly English theme than something done by a famous writer. Words, and sometimes entire paragraphs, were crossed out. Scribbles littered the margins and spaces between lines. Nathan's handwriting was practically unreadable in places. I leafed through the manuscript, stopping to read here and there. At the end, I found a page on which he'd written a synopsis of the plot and a comment entertaining the idea of using a different ending.

Next, I examined the handwritten manuscript of *Himalayan Adventure*. Again, sections had been crossed out. One of these described an incident during the trek down Mt. Ghoripani when the Sherpa was leading the lost couple back to civilization. The woman, Anna Wiley, reaches out to pet a goat and brushes her hand against a stinging nettle. A page and a half followed, describing how the Sherpa crushes leaves to make a poultice, and how he holds her hand to apply the treatment. Nathan droned on and on about the feelings aroused in Anna by his touch. He shortened the scene in the finished book. A little further in the manuscript, I found a scene not included in the final version, in which Anna searches for the Sherpa in Kathmandu. For four pages Nathan describes how Anna Wiley goes up and down Freak Street, looking for the Sherpa in opium dens.

When I removed *The Lady* from its boxes, I took a few moments to stare in awe at the original manuscript of the novel that made Nathan

241

Waterstone famous. Would the novel have been as successful had he not confessed the story was true? What a coup to identify the Lady in my paper! I envisioned Mary Watson turning pea green with envy. I couldn't give Fiona's name, but I could say the Lady was a Scots lady now living in America, and that I was honor bound not to reveal her true identity. Or I could say she was the wife of a minister — sort of a reversal of the *Scarlet Letter*. But if people thought I knew, they'd torment me until I told. And Addy . . . Well, who knew what she'd do.

I didn't realize how long I'd spent with the manuscripts until the light began to grow dim, warning me that the afternoon drew to a close.

"Are you finished?" Without a sound, Pearl had slipped up to stand in the doorway.

"No ma'am. But I'll come back another day." Something told me I'd better get my research done before Addy returned.

As I gathered my school things, I glanced out the window and saw Jonas in the back yard hunched on a bench. I went out the back door instead of the front to say *hello*.

"Hi, Jonas," I said, walking up to him.

"Miss Quincy! Been a long time since I seen you, girl." He rose and reached out his hand to shake mine. "You sure have growed up."

"How are you doing?" I asked, taking his hand.

"Ain't doing nothing much."

"I guess pretty soon the grass'll be growing like crazy and you'll have to be mowing up a storm."

"Yep, pretty soon." He took a cigarette wrapper from one pocket and a packet of tobacco from another. He tapped tobacco onto the wrapper. "If 'n we don't get more rain, we won't be doing too much mowing, though." He rolled the wrapper around the tobacco and licked the edges to stick them together.

"Guess not."

"How's your Aunt? Ain't seen her around much lately."

"She's in New York working on the new book."

"The new book," he repeated.

My hand flew to my mouth. "Oh, my gosh. I wasn't supposed to talk about the new book. Please, please Jonas, don't say anything."

He pulled a matchbook from his pocket. "Don't you go worrying about me, now, you hear. I know's when to keep my mouth shut. I been doing that for a long time now. Keeping my mouth shut."

About what I wondered. However, the subject of what Jonas kept his mouth shut about would have to be explored another day. Earlene would start to worry if I didn't get home soon. "Well, I better be going. See you later, Jonas."

"You come on back and see us sometimes, you hear?"

"Sure will." I started away, but stopped when an idea struck me. "I'm doing an English report on Nathan," I said, turning back to Jonas. ". . . and I need to finish my research, but Pearl stands over me breathing down my neck. She makes me so nervous I can't get anything done."

"Ah, Pearl don't mean no harm."

"When does she leave the house? She must have to go out sometimes, grocery shopping or something."

Jonas sat down, stretched out a leg, and took a drag from his cigarette. "Well, now . . .

"Help me out, Jonas. I have this handsome English teacher and I want to impress him." I grinned the way I thought people expected silly sixteen-year-olds to grin.

He nodded as though he understood. "She goes out shopping ever' Thursday after lunch, about two o'clock, and don't come back for three, four hours. She goes out in the evenings sometimes, too. Down to Jake's.

243

But the house is all shut up then. You'd best come on a Thursday if you want to avoid Miss Pearl. I'll let you in the back door."

"Thank you, Jonas. You won't tell anybody about the book?"

"No'm, I won't tell nobody."

❧ ❧ ❧

"I was about ready to send the police out after you." Earlene was waiting on the front porch, her face layered with frowns on top of frowns.

"I told you I was going to Nathan's after school." I kept walking — up the steps, across the porch, into the house. She followed me.

"It's done near five-thirty. You been there all this time?"

"Of course, I've been there all this time." I paused at the foot of the stairs and scowled over my shoulder at her. "Where else would I be?"

"You ain't practiced and your supper's sittin' there, getting cold."

"All right." I knew I sounded grumpy. "I'll put my books away later."

I dumped them on the bottom stair and went to the kitchen. Starved, I gobbled up potato salad and ham, but shoved the collards to the edge of my plate. I wasn't *that* hungry. Lunch had been those big white beans — I never knew what to call them — and shoe leather chicken.

"You ain't going to eat them collards?"

"I don't like collards." I pushed my plate away. "You never talk to me much, Earlene. Why don't you sit down and talk to me?"

"Ain't you gonna practice?"

"Soon. Sit down for a minute." I held out my hand, palm up, inviting her to take the seat opposite me.

She trudged over and sat down, the whole time casting me a look that said: *How come you want the household help sitting at the table with you?* The

244

truth was that sometimes I forgot she was black. Or rather, I forgot that being black mattered.

"So, I'm here."

"When did you start working for Addy?"

"A good long while ago."

"Did you meet Nathan?"

"Of course, I met Nathan. He come here for supper every now and then — him and his long hair. But he was a right nice man in spite of that. Sometimes, a bunch of people be here, drinking their wine, smoking their cigarettes, and him his pipe. Ever' body else loud and noisy, including Miz Addy, but he just listened. When he had something to say, he spoke so soft everybody had to get quiet to hear him." She brushed crumbs from the table into her palm and then closed her fist around them. "Sometimes, he'd be here alone with Miz Addy. He sure did like your aunt. And he sure was a polite man, always mannerly, and all." She rubbed at a spot on the table. "I declare, no matter how much I scrub this dang table I always miss a spot or two." She rose, grabbed a dishrag from the sink and jabbed at the spot. "It sure was a sad day when Mr. Waterstone died. Miz Addy, she beside herself. She went running off and . . . Ain't you gonna practice?"

"Yes." I shoved my plate aside. "Will you tell me about Nathan's death sometimes?"

"What's to tell? He died." She picked up my dishes and took them to the sink.

"I'm going back to his house on Thursday afternoon. I still have a lot to do. Do you know Jonas?"

"Course I know old Jonas. I'll whip up a batch of divinity for you to take him."

"Did Reverend Stewart and Fiona ever come here for dinner at the same time as Nathan?"

"Yes'm, they did. For someone who's always so anxious to practice you ain't in no hurry tonight."

"Just wanted to talk to you, Earlene. I'm going now."

ꝛ ꝛ ꝛ

I walked to the piano as though crossing a stage. I bowed my head to an imaginary audience the way Mrs. Rich had taught me. I sat down, folded my hands in my lap, closed my eyes, and heard the opening bars of the Mozart sonata as I wanted my audience to hear them. I played the sonata, and then I played my other recital pieces. I listened for rough spots; for places where I was too extravagant with nuances of rhythm, diminuendo or crescendo; for places where I was not extravagant enough. When I finished, I stood, bowed, and then sat back down to work on problem areas.

Around nine I turned off the piano lamp and went into Addy's study. Exhausted, I flopped down on the sofa. My homework could wait a few minutes. Or until morning.

I looked around the study, rubbing my arm absently. The typewriter sat silent. The stack of papers that made up the new manuscript were gone. The desk gave no sign of having been a work place. Without Addy, the room seemed cold and lifeless. Only the corner where the armoire stood seemed alive. *Come, open me,* the armoire beckoned. *Look. See what mysterious contents await your meddling.* I knew the armoire would be locked, but I went over anyway and pulled at the handle.

The door opened. In her haste to get away Addy had forgotten to lock it. My blood pulsed with the thrill of possible discovery.

The shelves contained stacks of files, yellow legal pads, an empty manuscript box with its lid sitting askew, letters still in their envelopes and

246

rubber banded together. A few fraying newspapers lay on the bottom shelf. On one of the middle shelves lay a single handwritten sheet. I looked at it, and realized that the sheet was the one Addy had shown me as an illustration of Nathan's bad handwriting. Where was the rest of the manuscript? I searched the shelves, shoving things around, but then carefully putting them back in place. I didn't find it. Had she taken the manuscript with her, and accidently left this one page behind?

As I struggled to read the first few sentences on the page, I didn't envy Addy having to decipher a whole manuscript of Nathan's handwriting. The portion I read described a hiking trail and sounded like some of the descriptions in *Himalayan Adventure*. The new book obviously had something about mountains too. Scottish mountains, this time, not Himalayan. I put the page back where I found it.

Then, shoved behind a box of pencils, I found a little book . . . . A diary?

A diary!

≈   ≈   ≈

Fully conscious of doing wrong, I looked into someone else's soul that night. I took the diary to my bed and read, stealing what my aunt had chosen to keep to herself, stealing her privacy, her pride, and her innocence.

I began at the beginning.

> *Warren has gone off to fight even though this is not our country's war. Loving fighting more than he loves me, he had to go. I know that Germany's invasion of Poland and annexation of Austria is grievous beyond all understanding. As is the division of France. I know this terrible man, this Jew hater, needs to be removed, and I*

247

know how strongly Warren feels about the loss of civil liberty, but still . . . Oh, God, I'm being selfish. But I feel abandoned. I am abandoned, and at the moment I find it awfully hard to love Warren.

A few pages later:

> *I've moved to London. Mama sends me letters urging me to return to the U.S. She begs and pleads, but how can I leave Warren in danger on the other side of the channel? What if he's injured and needs me? What if . . . No, I won't think of that. Bad things happen to other people.*

I continued to read about her loneliness, the progress of the war, how she filled her time with museum visits, reading in the library, attempts to find a meaningful job. And then:

> *The most interesting thing happened today. I met a fascinating man at Parry's Pub. He's an American from Macon, Georgia. He was seated at the table next to me. As soon as I heard his southern drawl I went over and introduced myself. He's a writer who has just published his first novel,* Highland Deception. *He's working on another — working under a great deal of pressure, he claims, because he promised his parents he'd attend medical school, although he seems extremely reluctant to do so. He listened patiently while I went on and on about Warren having left me alone. I'm glad he just listened and didn't pass judgment. He offered me a job and I gratefully accepted. I can hardly wait to start.*

Two days after meeting Nathan, Addy described spending an evening with him:

> *Oh my, but he was interesting. All evening, and into the night, I sat listening to his stories of traveling in Burma, Nepal, Thailand, India. Just hearing the names of those countries thrilled me. How I'd like to travel in Asia! For almost four hours I forgot about the war and Warren.*

How does one forget a husband?

Homework lay unfinished on my desk. I'd plead a headache when they asked for my assignments; I'd say I'd been sick; that there was an emergency in the family; that I had to go to the hospital to sit with my sick aunt. Or I'd not go to school at all.

I rolled onto my side, and, pulling the covers around my ears, snuggled the diary close to my chest and continued reading. Addy described how she went to work for Nathan, editing and typing his manuscript, handling correspondence, and whatever else that needed doing. The dairy entries became sketchy:

> *Typed eight hours today. I'm too, too tired to write a thing.*

Entries describing her work followed for the remainder of that week.

> *I like this book better than the last. He's titled the book:* Himalayan Adventure. *However, Nathan does get carried away with descriptions. He spent much too long describing the cure for a stinging nettle. I persuaded him to shorten the scene. No news from Warren.*

There was a gap of several days before the next entry:

Nathan wanted me to do some research about Freak Street in Kathmandu. He has a terrific memory, but even the best of us forgets facts here and there. My assignment was to find out exactly how long the street extended. I went to the British Library and ensconced myself there for a couple hours but never found out how long the street was. Is the length of the street really important? Still, no news from Warren.

I kept nodding off, but perked up when I read the entry where Addy met Reverend Stewart:

I went to the British Library again today. Actually, I didn't quite get there, so I shall have to go tomorrow. On the way, I stopped at a book store to buy a copy of Burmese Days. *Nathan says he enjoyed the book immensely. I headed for the library then, but only got as far as the steps. Rain had fallen sporadically throughout the day and, of course, wet stone becomes slippery. A very handsome young man came springing down the steps and, upon reaching the bottom step, slipped. He crashed into me, sending me sprawling. My new book flew into a puddle and I landed on my bottom, resulting in a thorough soaking of the back half of my skirt and a ruined book. Naturally, my anger flared. My book budget is minimal at best, so I'm afraid my anger got the better of me. He apologized profusely and kept offering to pay the cleaning bill for my skirt. Eventually, he realized that the ruined book was what had me in a snit. He proposed that we go*

250

back to the bookstore, where he'd gladly replace the book.
On the way, I learned that he — his name is Robert
Stewart — was a student in the divinity school at the
University of Aberdeen in Scotland. He has come to
London to do research for his dissertation. He's comparing
early Christian writings to the early writings of Buddhism
and Hinduism. The British Library has a substantial
collection of early monastic works, he explained. When I
told him I worked for a writer who had traveled where
those religions are practiced, his eyes lit up. "You wouldn't
possibly be referring to Nathan Waterstone?" he asked.
Then he told me how he and Nathan met in Nepal on a
trek up Goripani. Robert was most anxious to resume
their friendship. What a coincidence that we should meet
like that!

Would Addy's diary be the source that proved Fiona had been the Lady? Excited, I read on.

Very busy today. My back hurt like heck from
bending over the typewriter for so many hours. Nathan was
overjoyed that I'd run into Robert Stewart. He rang him
up straightaway, and they arranged to meet for tea at
Piccadilly Pickles.

I spent the day working with Nathan on chapter
7. He goes off on too many tangents. I know how
interesting trekking in the Himalayas must be,
experiencing the ragged beauty, interacting with villagers,
watching Sherpas lug heavy loads up steep mountain

251

passes, but Nathan is writing a story, for Pete's sake, not
a travelogue. He gets too carried away with details and
descriptions.

I continued reading. Midnight came and went, and then one o'clock. Wanting to find Fiona's name, I skimmed over entries about the war and the bombing of London. Addy mentioned Robert Stewart several times, but there was nothing about his wife.

The pages fairly dripped Nathan's name, while references to Warren became rare. An uneasy feeling began deep in the pit of my stomach and grew and grew. Once, unable to hold my eyes open, I dozed for a short while. When I awoke I read the following entry:

I should be too tired to write tonight for we sat
together until an extravagant hour. Huddled in a booth in
too-cold McGraw's Pub, we warmed ourselves with the
heat of each other's bodies — a delicious warmth. We
forgot, for a while, that a war waged across the channel and
that the world stood on the brink of disaster. We engaged
in the composition of silly rhymes, using other customers as
subjects. Nathan is so very good at that sort of thing. My
contributions were pretty awful. e.g.:

"Good man Chubb,

entered the pub,

wearing his tie and bowler.

He sat on a stool,

Acted the fool,

Then left with Hildy, the Hooker.

Silly, I know, but how else does one banish these
illicit longings?

She spoke of *illicit longings* while the name *Warren* had practically disappeared from the entries? The uneasy feeling became dread, and dread turned to nausea. In my disgust, I abruptly sat up from where I'd been lounging against my pillows. The diary slipped from my hands and fell to the floor. When I retrieved the diary, the pages fell open to the worst entry of all.

> *He gave me a beautiful gold locket embossed with a heart. "My heart is yours for always," he said when he fastened the locket around my neck. When I looked inside . . . Oh, I shall never let anyone see inside! He is my soul! My heart! My life!*

Her locket! The one she wouldn't let me touch. The one she claimed didn't open. The one she still wore. I continued reading while the sick feeling mounted. Nathan had a bout with pneumonia. The air raids became more and more intolerable. Robert returned to Scotland. He'd finished his research and was to be married. Then I fell asleep again. I don't know how long I slept, but once again I awoke and kept reading.

> *What shall I do? What shall I do? Is my heart to be ripped into a million pieces? Months ago I should have done the right thing and ended my marriage. I'd have broken Warren's heart, but is that worse than breaking other hearts? How can I live without this man whom I have come to love so? Whose presence inflames my passion near to the point of no control?*

I ran to the bathroom and retched in the toilet. I vomited again and again. When my stomach had emptied, I sat on the floor and leaned my head on the toilet seat. The tiles were cold against my legs, and the air stunk of my vomit.

I didn't understand. Fiona was the Lady. Yet Addy pointed the finger at herself. In a trance of self-loathing at what I was doing, I went back to bed and finished the diary, as though finishing the abominable thing was a punishment I forced on myself for reading the diary in the first place.

Addy seemed to have lost interest in journaling for the entries, in a rapid decrescendo, became shorter and shorter. One page before the end contained the entry:

I'm going up to Scotland today.

And then the last page:

Warren is dead.

CHAPTER 16

Earlene shook me awake. "Didn't you hear the alarm? Come on, you be late for school."

My eyes refused to open.

"I done made your breakfast."

"I'm sick."

"You ain't sick."

"I'm sick, Earlene." I must have sounded sick; she remained quiet for a few moments. I almost dropped off again, but then I felt her hand on my forehead.

"You *are* a bit warm."

Go away and leave me alone, I wanted to plead, *so I can cry*. A corner of Addy's diary pressed into my ribs.

"You ain't been absent except that one time," she said. "I guess another day won't hurt. You want some orange juice?"

"No."

I slept again. Deeply, from exhaustion. Twice I awoke and remembered that Addy had deceived her husband. That she was an adulteress. When I awoke for the last time and felt the diary jamming my ribs, I thought I'd vomit again. I ran to the toilet, leaned over, and retched.

255

Only foul-tasting saliva came out. There was nothing left in my stomach.

While Earlene shuffled around the kitchen, preparing chicken noodle soup and milk toast to comfort my "illness," I replaced the diary.

I'd thought Addy perfect. So perfect. How could I ever again look her in the face?

ȣ   ȣ   ȣ

I returned to school the following day, trudging from class to class as if I wore iron shoes. When I was supposed to be reading or following along in my textbook, the words made no sense. I drew circles on my paper when I was supposed to be taking notes — circle after circle after circle while the world swept past me like a river, leaving me stranded in a stinking, slimy swamp.

"Your face is flushed," Jessie said at the end of French. "You must still have a fever."

I shrugged, gathered my books, and headed for History. I hated History more than ever. I hated all my subjects. I hated life.

"Do you think Hestor Prynne's adultery was forgivable?" I asked Mary Watson after English class.

"I suppose. Isn't everything?"

"No." I must have sounded bitter. She raised her eyebrows.

"In the Bible . . ."

"Since when did you become religious?" I snapped at her.

Her eyebrows rose higher. "I'm not religious. You are."

"I am?" Snappishness gave way to sarcasm.

"I thought . . .," she said, hesitating before she continued, ". . . that you were very religious. I mean, because of your father." She paused. "Aren't you?"

"I don't know what I am."

We'd come to our lockers. She gave me a searching look before opening hers. I looked away, seeing, but not seeing, the river of students swirling past in the current of the corridor. I heard the snap of Mary's locker door shutting, and waited for her to go through the routine of insuring her locker was locked.

"Maybe you don't know what you are because your parents aren't here to tell you what to think," she said when she finished and we moved toward our next class. "People believe what their parents tell them to believe. And parents believe what *their* parents told them to believe. It's like lining up dominos. You push the first one, and all the others fall over, one by one. Generation after generation believes what they've been told, and hardly anyone ever stops to question what's really true. You'll do the same to your kids. Do you believe in the Devil?"

"I don't know. Do you?"

"Hardly. That play we talked about, *Faust* — well, the play was symbolic of other things. Goethe didn't mean the story to be literally true."

"You hadn't even heard of Faust a few weeks ago."

"Well, I have now. I read about the play. I like to find out things for myself. I don't believe everything I'm told. I have to stop at the toilet. See you later."

I wasn't able to concentrate in my next class any more than I had in the others. While Mr. Mann went on about some assassination in Sarajevo, I puzzled over the picture I'd seen in Fiona's drawer and over the other things that fit the description of Lady Isabelle Duncan: the golden hair, her being a nurse, the opal pin. I found only one explanation: Nathan tried to hide Addy's identity by describing her as she wasn't. Sometimes Addy had streaks of gold in her hair from the sun, but that was different from actually having red-gold hair. She had a necklace with an opal pendant, not an opal pin, although the pendant could have once been a pin. She wasn't a nurse, and she'd never mentioned volunteering in hospitals like many Londoners had during the war. But was that another of her secrets?

If Addy had lied about being the Lady, had she also lied about the things Alice accused her of? Taking money that didn't belong to her? But the suggestion that someone had drugged Nathan . . .

I felt an overpowering need for adult comfort.

I stood outside his office door and watched Reverend Stewart for a few moments without being noticed. He worked on his sermon. I'd grown up seeing Daddy do the same thing — scribbling; stopping for a moment to think; looking over at an open book and running his finger along a passage before scribbling again. Reverend Stewart had more books than Daddy. They lay scattered on his desk, some open, some closed. His reading glasses hung low on his nose. A cup, half-full of pungent-smelling tea, sat within reach. The used tea bag lay on a stained tissue.

I stepped closer.

"Quincy," he said looking up and smiling. "I'm glad to see you." He stood and extended his hand. I gave him mine. "Have a seat." He motioned to one of the chairs opposite his desk, but I remained standing.

"What brings you here?"

"I wanted to ask a favor." I hoped he'd forgive my unannounced visit. "I'm writing a paper about Nathan Waterstone."

"Yes, I remember.

"I want to come up with something original." I shifted from foot to foot.

He nodded, waiting for me to go on.

"There're lots of snapshots in Nathan's house. I don't suppose you have time to go over there with me and tell me who they are, do you? I mean, I thought I might like to hear you talk about his friends, and who they were, and what they did. You know, stuff like that."

Afterwards, I wondered if he realized how troubled I was. Or if he saw something else in my face. I'd invented such a silly reason to pull him away from his work. *Looking at photos.* Yet, he consented without hesitation.

"I'd be happy to. To tell the truth, I'm sort of stuck on my sermon." He motioned to the books and papers piled on his desk. "A break might help. Did you walk here from school?" Moving from behind his desk he rummaged in his pocket for car keys.

"Jessie dropped me."

"Ah, yes, Jessie. How is she these days? Still having problems with Devilstiltskin?" He stuck his glasses in his shirt pocket.

"How did you know she called her brother that?"

"I'm like Santa Claus; I know all sorts of things. Well, let's go take a look and then I'll drive you home."

Halfway there he turned to me, frowning. "You look tired. Are you working too hard?"

"I *have* been working hard," I said. "Maybe I'll go to bed early tonight." I almost cried. I wanted so badly for someone to console me over the loss of my aunt as I had known her. But that would have meant sharing what I'd learned and admitting how despicable I was for reading her diary.

Pearl met us at the door with a big smile for Reverend Stewart — she *could* smile after all. We went from room to room looking at photos, Reverend Stewart identifying people and telling me what he knew about them. Standing next to him made me feel warm, and I wanted him to hug me, not like a lover, but like a Daddy.

"You're trying to find out who the Lady was, aren't you?" he asked

259

finally. His eyes teased.

I wasn't. Not anymore. But I nodded and felt my face flush.

"Nathan went to great length to conceal her identity. You didn't think he'd have her picture here for everyone to see, did you?" He looked amused.

"You were with him so often. I thought you'd know."

"I spent the occasional evening in his company. Mostly I was hunkered down in the British Library. I didn't have much time to finish my dissertation before having to serve as a chaplain in the RAF. Besides, when I wasn't focused on research, my mind was filled with thoughts of my own lady, not Nathan's."

My hands tightened until my fingernails bit into my palms. The length to which they went to conceal her identity angered me. Would anyone ever understand that to learn the truth suddenly — Bam! There's the truth. — was devastating?

"They obviously planned very carefully when they went out in public not to be seen by people they knew," he said. "Anyway, they probably weren't out together that often. Remember, she was married."

"Was Addy the Lady?" The question just popped out. Without thinking. Without considering the consequences. My throat felt dry and my tongue salty.

His mouth fell open. "Of course not," he said after an interval. "Why would you even ask that?"

I saw that he didn't know. Caught up in his own upcoming marriage and in writing his dissertation, he'd failed to see the signs. But now I'd planted the seed of suspicion in his head. I saw the expression on his face; I saw how he took what I said, twisted my words, turned them, looked at them from this angle and that. What had I done?

❧ ❧ ❧

Reverend Stewart drove me home. I went to the piano, but after a few minutes, abandoned the attempt to make beautiful sounds. My music had lost its soul. I worked on technique instead, setting the metronome and thudding out each note. I played difficult phrases over and over, thud, thud, thud. Then I changed the speed on the metronome to practice the phrases again. Thud, thud, thud, a bit faster. I played until my fingers ached, sometimes forgetting my hellish discovery for a few seconds, but still with the hollow feeling of something being wrong.

"Miss Addy will be home tomorrow early afternoon," Earlene said when I started up the stairs at bedtime.

"Oh, good," I said. *Horrors,* I thought. How would I greet her? *Not only do you smoke and drink, dear, sweet Addy, but you were an adulteress. And if Alice Worthington is right, there's more.*

❧ ❧ ❧

When I came home from school, I found Addy in the chaise lounge on the back porch basking in the warmth of an April afternoon. Elizabeth Walker sat in a rocking chair. I stiffened when Addy jumped up to give me a hug.

"Oh, dear," she said, drawing back. "You don't look well."

"Could be mono. Teenagers get that, you know," Mrs. Walker said, eying me with the vast array of child-rearing knowledge the childless have.

"I had a little bug. I'll be fine."

Addy ran her hand over my cheek and frowned.

261

"I'm ok, Addy. Really, I'm fine." I tried to brighten my smile, or rather I tried to smile, period.

"Come, sit beside me." With one hand, she motioned toward the chaise lounge, while she put the other on my back to steer me over to sit beside her, shoulder to shoulder, hip to hip. "I missed you," she said, taking my hand.

I wanted to pull away; I didn't want her to touch me. Bit by bit I slipped my hand from hers and inched my hip and shoulder away. When we no longer touched, I almost cried. Right there in front of Addy and Mrs. Walker, in front of God and anyone else who wanted to look, I almost cried. I'd missed her. Even knowing what I now knew, I'd missed her. She'd been the bright spot in my life, and now she'd become a stranger.

I sat quietly while Addy told Mrs. Walker a story about losing an opera ticket one evening in New York, and another about a haughty waiter serving her pork tenderloin instead of the beef tenderloin she'd ordered. While she talked, Addy glanced at me periodically with a puzzled look, and then she'd reach over and squeeze my hand, or pat my leg, or make some other loving gesture.

Reverend Stewart stopped by. I watched to see if my question about Addy being the Lady changed the way he looked at her, but I detected nothing different.

"I brought back some new books," Addy said when I rose to practice. "They're on the kitchen table. Someone smuggled the manuscript for one of the books, *Dr. Zhivago,* out of Russia recently. Adam got me an advance copy. I read the book while I was in New York. I think you'll like it."

I nodded and walked toward the back door, but then stopped and looked back over my shoulder. "Is *Dr. Zhivago* about adultery?"

She gave me a puzzled look. "That's part of the story. How did you know?"

"I didn't." I went inside before she could comment.

๑ ๑ ๑

Addy began work on the final version of *Dunfermline*. I'd walk in the house every day after school to the sound of clacking typewriter keys. After putting my books away I'd stick my head through the door of the study to let her know I was home.

"How was school?" she'd ask, giving me a brief look. I was glad to have her preoccupied and too busy to notice my distress. "Great," I'd reply and then say quickly: "I'm going to practice now." I'd close the door so I wouldn't hear the typewriter, and she wouldn't hear the piano. Then I'd settle down for two hours of uninspired practice. Inspiration had died.

I couldn't forget, even for a minute, what I'd learned. While practicing, I thought about the contents of the diary; when I did homework, or ate, or helped with some chore around the house, I thought about the diary; when I went out with friends, I thought about the diary.

I'd been curious before about where Addy's money came from, but now the question burned my insides like hell fire. If Alice Worthington was right, my aunt had been involved, not just in adultery, but in something criminal.

I avoided Addy as much as possible, but I couldn't avoid her all the time. She typed with such ferocity she'd get all knotted up and have to bend and stretch to unkink. Then she'd head for the backyard swing for a few minutes relaxation. "Time for recess, honey," she'd call from the back door. "Come out and talk to me."

I'd go out. She'd be stretching her arms and rotating her neck and shoulders, loosening knotted muscles. I'd sit down beside her, trying not to touch, and saying little.

"You're not very talkative, lately," she said one afternoon.

"The end of the year is crashing down on me. Projects are due. Papers are due. Then finals. And the recital." Instead of looking at her, I looked over at Mrs. Thompson's fish pool, and watched Lucifer balancing on the bridge as he looked for a golden snack.

"How's your paper coming?"

"OK." I shrugged. Shrugging, I discovered, worked as a good substitute for words. "When will you be done with the book?"

"I think the manuscript will be done by the end of the summer, and then . . ."

"By the end of the summer!" I did look at her then. "I thought you'd finish sooner."

"There are a lot of revisions to make. Is it important when I finish?"

"I wanted to write about the book in my paper." Expecting to do well on my paper had become a habit — sort of a mechanical priority, not one of the heart.

"I'm sorry, honey, you can't." She patted my hand. "I'll take you to Nathan's house and maybe we can come up with something interesting. I'll tell you everything I know about Nathan."

"That would be great." *Everything?* I wanted to ask. *How he was as a lover? How much money he gave you?* My stomach heaved, and the taste in my mouth turned bitter. "I need to finish practicing." I stood up and, before she could see my distress, bolted for the back door.

~ ~ ~

A few days later, Mr. Feldman asked us about the progress on our rough drafts.

"I'm finished," Mary Watson bragged. "It's thirty pages long."

Gasps erupted around the room.

"Has anyone else written their rough draft?" Mr. Feldman looked around the class. No one answered. He looked at me. "What about you, Miss Bruce? How is yours progressing?"

My paper *wasn't* progressing. My paper was dying. I wished I'd never heard of Nathan Waterstone. I wished I'd chosen Mark Twain, Ferlinghetti, Steinbeck, Hawthorne — anyone other than Nathan Waterstone. Someone in the back of the room thumped his knuckles on his desk, a low drumbeat signaling boredom. Feet shuffled. Mary Watson looked at me in that maddening way she sometimes did. Miss Superiority. She galled me enough that I managed to smile sweetly at Mr. Feldman. "My paper is coming along just fine," I said. "I'm doing research from original sources."

In a wild flight of fancy, I imagined Addy's reaction if I wrote about the new novel in spite of her saying I couldn't. Or if I announced she'd been the Lady. Or that *some* thought she'd taken money willed to Pearl. Did Mary Watson have the vaguest clue that rumors included her father in a conspiracy to cheat Pearl? Strangely, I felt no sympathy for Pearl. I thought her cold, calculating, and unfriendly.

Mr. Feldman, sensing none of my nasty thoughts, ploughed cheerfully on. "I look forward to reading your paper, Miss Bruce. I can hardly wait to see what new information you have."

ல்   ல்   ல்

I tried to organize my notes that evening, but after attempting to bring order to the mess of note cards, I gave up, set them aside, and sat down cross-legged on the floor to think.

That Addy had been the Lady was now firmly entrenched in my head and no longer shocked me. I even began to think I could forgive her eventually. Adultery ranked high on the list of *Most Sinful Sins*, but if I took into consideration that Warren abandoned her to fight the Germans, that she was all alone in London, and that she'd had polio and almost died, then maybe someday I might not be so repulsed.

The other things frightened me, though. *They're rumors; they're rumors,* I repeated over and over, trying to convince myself. But I needed to know. The following day was Thursday. Pearl would be gone and I'd be free to snoop. I rose and went downstairs.

"I'm going to Nathan's house tomorrow," I told Earlene. "Do you want to send divinity to Jonas?"

"I sure do. I'll whip up a batch right now."

I'd let Earlene tell Addy where I was.

❧   ❧   ❧

"Hi, Jonas," I said, stepping through the gate into Nathan's backyard. Jonas was bent over a flower bed pulling weeds. I hoped he'd been right about Pearl being away on Thursdays.

"I do believe you done come back like you said." He straightened and wiped one hand across his brow, leaving a streak of muck.

I held out the paper bag with the divinity. "Earlene made this for you."

"Well, I do declare. What do we have here?"

"Divinity."

"Earlene made me some of her divinity?"

"Just for you."

266

He opened the bag and sniffed. "My, my, that candy sure do smell good." He held the bag toward me. "Here, you have some, too."

"No thanks. I want to go inside and get to work."

I flipped on the light in the study, removed the key from underneath the pipe rack, and unlocked the file cabinet. A file cabinet seemed a likely place to put important documents. I sorted through the contents of the bottom drawer again, in case I'd missed something the first time. I still found nothing but a jumble of receipts, notepads, broken pencils, typewriter ribbons, an old driver's license, and used envelopes.

I decided that Nathan must have kept his important papers somewhere upstairs. His bedroom, maybe. Nevertheless, I decided to explore the desks. Each had a shallow center drawer and a larger drawer on the left side. The smell of stale tobacco seeped out when I opened the center drawer of Nathan's desk. Inside, I found index cards, rubber bands, an old pipe, photos, Scotch tape, notes scribbled on bits of paper, and spilled tobacco. Nothing worth examining.

Several large envelopes, each marked with the name of one his books, were in the side drawer. The envelope labeled *Highland Deception* contained newspaper clippings, an article from *The Atlanta Constitution* praising the first novel of a native son, a similar article from a Yale University paper, reviews torn from magazines, letters from the editor leading up to the book's publication, and a couple of letters referring to his beginning a new novel. The contents of the *Himalayan Adventure* envelope were similar. I couldn't bear to look at anything relating to *The Lady*, so I set that envelope aside.

I was surprised to see several letters from a disappointed Adam Johnson in the envelope labeled *Runaway*. "What has happened to you, Nathan?" Adam wrote in one. "A high school student could have done better. We can't publish this. Re-submit when you won't be wasting my time with such trash." In another letter: "I'm sorry, Nathan. The book still isn't publishable. Go back to the drawing board." Then finally: "Hurrah, you've done a hell of a rewrite. Your style has matured, and at the same time evolved into one more accessible to the general public. Your writing is more readable, yet at the same time wonderfully artistic. Congratulations."

I took a quick look at some of the reviews for the book. "Nathan Waterstone's book will become a modern classic," the critic from *The Atlanta Journal* said. "*Runaway* marks a turning point in his career. While *The Lady* achieved popular success, this book achieves literary success." A reviewer from *Swanee Literary Review* wrote: "*Runaway* succeeds on so many levels. What a book! What a woman. I was riveted from start to finish. The story is a smart, quirky, and satisfying tale of revenge. An absolute must read."

The reviews for the next two novels, *Game of Chance* and *Mary Lucas*, also glowed with enthusiasm for Nathan's writing. I still hadn't found the handwritten manuscripts for those two novels, and I wondered again how much handwritten manuscripts were worth. I thought of the conversation I'd heard between Addy and Adam behind a nearly closed study door. *We'll be ruined . . . I made no promises . . . It isn't fair . . . Look at what you've gotten out of this . . .* But I couldn't make out how Adam fit into Alice's accusations.

The stash of papers inside the envelope for *The Mistress* was similar to the others — reviews, letters from Adam, financial statements. Only this time, the reviews were mixed. ". . . a profound story. A story for our times," Sam Matts wrote in *Swanee Literary Review*. "This book does not deserve to win the GFC Award," wrote a critic in *The Atlanta Journal*. "While I was delighted by the prose, I was disgusted at the immorality." Irvin Hooper from *The Atlanta Constitution* differed. "*The Mistress* is richly deserving of the recent award," he wrote.

But reviews and letters weren't what I was after. I moved over to Addy's desk. The top drawer contained items similar to the ones in Nathan's but with the addition of an old tube of lipstick and minus the pipe and tobacco.

When I tried to open the large drawer, the hair on my arms stood up: the drawer was locked. I jerked at the handle but the lock held fast. Something revealing lay inside. I was sure of that. Something to prove or disprove Addy's alleged crimes. Jonas probably had a tool that I could use to break the lock. I looked out the window and saw him still busy in the flower bed. Was there a hammer or a wrench in the house?

But did I want to see what was inside?

No one else hinted at rumors. Only Alice. But who would have told me? My new friends in Wilson? Hardly. *Guess what Quincy, we heard your aunt was an adulteress, and she has money that doesn't rightfully belong to her; and to top that off, Nathan Waterstone might have been murdered. They say his eyes looked strange when they found him dead at the bottom of the stairs.*

I jerked at the drawer again. The drawer didn't budge. I squeezed my eyes shut. What now? I'd have to find something at home to pry open the drawer. That meant one more trip to Nathan's. How many times could I come and snoop without Addy or Pearl getting suspicious?

The key to the file cabinet was still in the keyhole of the top drawer. I needed to return the key to the envelope so Pearl wouldn't know someone had been in the study. When I tilted back the pipe rack to replace the key, I noticed a smaller key taped to the bottom of the rack. My heart pounded as I peeled back the tape. I guessed, correctly, that the key fit Addy's desk drawer.

My hands shook as I removed several bulging files, each labeled with letters that made no sense. From one marked *XX*, I removed a stack of papers. A letter in Addy's handwriting, addressed to Magnolia

Convalescent Home, lay on top.

Madam. I enclose a copy of the check with which you were paid in full for Mr. Wasserman's stay in your facility from March 3, 1949 to September 10, 1949. Why do you continue to send bills when we have already paid? Please correct your records, and do not bother us with any further bills.

Puzzled, I reread the letter. Addy had never mentioned anything about Nathan having health problems. His heart attack surprised everyone. So why did he spend six months in a convalescent home? And why was Addy so snippy? This wasn't the Addy I knew. Or the Addy I'd thought I knew. Then I realized the name wasn't *Waterstone*, but *Wasserman*.

I heard the thud of the front door closing. And footsteps. I crammed the papers back in the envelope, tossed the envelope in the drawer, and closed the drawer, trying not to make any noise — there was just a tiny kiss of wood against wood. I replaced the key, grabbed my notes, and tiptoed to the door to peek out. Pearl stood in the hallway, very still, as though she'd heard something. I didn't breathe. After a few moments I heard her continue down the hall and into the kitchen. Then, I heard the thump of grocery bags being set on the counter.

I escaped through the back door.

CHAPTER 17

Rain spattered my face as I hurried home. By suppertime, the spattering had turned into a downpour, pounding on the roof and cascading in gunnels down the sides of the house and over the windows.

"Chicken 'n dumplings, probably the best storm food there is," Earlene said. She stood at the window watching the deluge while Addy and I ate. "This rain going to wash Miz Thompson's flower seeds right out of the ground."

Addy's gaze drifted to the window. Preoccupied, she hadn't commented on my absence. I wondered if she'd even noticed. "How was school?" she asked. She didn't sound like she had any real interest in hearing my answer.

"OK."

"How's the research paper going?"

"So, so." I scooped up a dumpling.

"I promised to take you to Nathan's house. Shall we go this weekend?"

"Sure."

I felt her eyes on me.

"Whenever you're ready for me to proofread, I'm here."

"Tell me about Nathan's death." From the corners of my eyes, I watched to see if she flinched.

"He had a heart attack." She held her fork motionless. "You knew that."

"He was so young."

"Only forty-five"

"Did he have heart problems before?"

She shook her head. "His death came as a big blow."

"What time of day did he die?" I asked, even though I knew. I remembered Addy's flight to our house that day, and how she sobbed on Mama's shoulder. But I wanted to test her. See her reaction to my questions about Nathan's death.

"Around eleven. I'd been taking care of correspondence." She stared down at her plate. With her fork, she pushed a dumpling from one side of her plate to the other, and then back again. "When he finished breakfast that morning, he came to the study and looked aimlessly around. Then he said something about not feeling well and went up to his room."

A crash of thunder jarred the window.

"Lordy Mercy," Earlene said, and backed away. "This turning out to be some storm. I better make sure all the windows are closed tight."

"I'm sorry," Addy said, when Earlene's footsteps faded away. "I'm tired. Can we talk about Nathan's death some other time?" She gave a little sound, like the beginning of a laugh. "I really should get up from that typewriter and go for a long walk every now and then."

We continued to eat without talking until Addy abruptly put down her fork and folded her hands in her lap.

"What's wrong, Quincy?"

"I guess I'm tired, too. Maybe we both need to take a break and go for a long walk when the rain stops. I'm going to practice." I escaped before she could ask more questions.

⁓   ⁓   ⁓

Mrs. Arness tried to teach us about perspective by drawing a house and showing how lines drawn from various points of the house come together in one spot on the horizon. She called that spot the vanishing point. She directed us to draw a barn with lines going off to a vanishing point in the field beyond. Alice's barn looked like a barn; mine looked like something hit by a Luftwaffe bomb.

"I want to talk to your uncle," I whispered to Alice.

Her pencil stopped moving. "He won't talk to you."

"Why not?"

"He doesn't want to get in trouble."

"How can he get in trouble by talking to me?"

She bit her lips and resumed sketching.

"Alice, please. I want to know."

"We can't talk here."

"Everyone else is talking. We've talked here before."

"And this is the only place you'll talk to me."

"That isn't true."

She ignored me. I sat idle, watching her draw until Mrs. Arness came and stood over me. Her smock stunk of turpentine. I couldn't paint or draw to begin with, but with her breathing down my neck I might as well have been trying to draw with my toes. Finally, she sighed and moved away.

"Did you make up everything?" I asked.

"Are you calling me a liar?" Alice glared at me.

"I'm just questioning why you don't want me to talk to your uncle."

"What I said was, he won't talk to you. He's not crazy enough to go repeating rumors to Adelaide Simmons' niece."

I clamped my mouth shut and scowled at my drawing. My art work was like my life: horrid. I jabbed at my barn, crisscrossing the drawing with lines going in all directions, and then I slammed down my charcoal, crossed my arms, and sat back on my stool, glowering.

Alice giggled. "You're hopeless in art."

I didn't answer, but stared straight ahead. How dare she hint at horrible things but not allow me to find out everything her uncle knew? Or what he *thought* he knew.

"You must have heard the rumors from other people," she said, relenting.

"Nope. You're the only one."

She gave me a long look before bending over her drawing.

I'd ruined my sketch, but I resumed work, leaning in close, faking indifference. I didn't want Alice to see how desperate I was to learn more.

≈   ≈   ≈

We were having a run of bad weather. The following day dawned warm, sultry, and overcast. As the morning progressed, the sky grew darker. By lunchtime, a downpour carved channels in the schoolyard.

We still worked on perspective in art, or rather pretended to. For a change, Mrs. Arness sat at her desk, ignoring us. Except for Alice who actually worked, the rest of us watched the deluge and talked. Alice bent over her barn drawing and, with ruler and pencil, drew lines that met at the vanishing point.

"You really haven't heard the rumors?" she asked, when I glanced at her during a lull in the conversation I'd been having with someone else.

"No."

"That mulatto . . ."

"Pearl."

"Yeah, her." Alice stopped and looked out the window. My gaze followed hers. The rain looked thick enough to drown in.

"What about Pearl?" I prompted.

"Sometimes my Daddy goes to that place on the edge of town," she said. ". . . the one they call Jake's Joint."

"I thought only Negroes went there."

"Sometimes white people go there." She ran her finger along her barn roof. "My Daddy goes there and sometimes my uncle. The one that drove the ambulance. He doesn't drive the ambulance anymore; he has an ice plant now. When he needs to hire help, he goes out to Jake's, sits at the bar, and finds niggers to work for him. He hears gossip down there. You people with maids have your business spread all over town. Anyway . . ." Alice rubbed absently at a line. "Pearl goes to Jake's. She has a boyfriend who goes there, and he talks a lot. He told everybody that Pearl got cheated out of a lot of money." She put down her pencil. "And they say . . .," she leaned closer to me, ". . . that they killed him."

"He died of a heart attack." What kind of a twisted mind would invent such an absurd story? But my heart raced, and beads of sweat dribbled from my armpits.

"Someone drugged him."

"That isn't true. My aunt was there all morning the day he died."

Quickly, too quickly, Alice shifted her eyes away. A shiver ran down my spine. "Who else was there?" My voice quivered and my knee had begun to jerk.

"Just that old man, the gardener. He was in the back yard. Pearl was out." Alice frowned at her drawing, pretending to examine her vanishing point.

I packed up my art supplies and, with every cell in my body gone numb and every thought in my head paralyzed, I sat until the bell rang to end the day.

∫ ∫ ∫

The rain had almost stopped when Jessie drove me home. "You're quiet today," she said when we arrived in my driveway.

"Yeah, I guess." I wanted to invite her into the kitchen, offer her a Coca-Cola and cookies, and share my pain. Only she wouldn't feel the pain, just the scandal. Besides, Addy would be in her study typing. I couldn't talk with her in the house.

"There's nothing wrong between you and Fulton, is there?"

I shook my head. "Did you ever discover something you didn't want to know about one of your relatives?"

"Don't think so. Did you?"

I nodded.

"What?"

I looked down the tunnel of oaks, leaving Jessie's question hovering for a few seconds. "I hate my father," I burst out finally.

"Your father?"

"I hate him. And my mother. And Aunt Mildred. I hate them all. They're all so righteous, so right, so . . ." What was I talking about? What did they have to do with anything?

"I never heard you talk like this before."

I tried to retract. "I didn't really mean what I just said." Although, I did. I hated their judging, judging, judging. "What do you think of Hester Prynne in *The Scarlet Letter*?"

Jessie frowned. "What do I think of her?"

"Do you think people should forgive adultery?"

She shrugged. "I never thought much about adultery. Adultery happens mainly in books, doesn't it? Did your father do that? Or your Aunt Mildred?" Jessie looked concerned.

"No, they wouldn't dream of committing adultery. They're too righteous." I opened the door and slid out. "See you tomorrow." I forced a smile.

"Wait," she said. "I want to know what's going on."

"I'm just in a bad mood. Sorry. None of my relatives is having an affair. All that English stuff got to me." I turned and left Jessie staring after me, probably wondering which English stuff she'd missed.

ꝛ   *ꝛ*   *ꝛ*

"Well, hello Miss Sunshine," Earlene said after one glance at me. "Your face looks like that storm we just had."

I slammed my books down on the table. "Mary Watson made a better grade than I did on the history test." A lie. I'd made one point higher — at least one bright spot in the dark, dark day. But how else to explain my bad mood? "Are there any cookies?"

"No cookies." She stirred something on the stove that smelled like black-eyed peas. I hated black-eyed peas.

"Well, I'm hungry and I'm tired of peanut butter on vanilla wafers. Isn't there anything good to eat here?"

She cocked her head at me. The sound of the spoon clanking on the side of the pot raised my hackles. Clank, clank, bloody clank. I let out a huff.

"What got your tail in a dither?"

"I'm not in a dither. I'm hungry. We had canned ravioli in the lunchroom and it tasted like cat food." I marched to the cupboard, jerked open the door, and stared at the shelves.

"Ain't nothing there that weren't there yesterday."

I slammed the cupboard door, turned around, and stopped short. Addy leaned on the doorframe, arms crossed.

"What's wrong?"

"Nothing."

"Come to the study." She turned away, leaving me to follow.

"Sit down," she said, motioning to the spot on the sofa next to her. I sat in the armchair instead. Surprised at my rebellion, she studied me for a few moments. "What's wrong?"

"Nothing."

"Something is wrong." Hands on her lap, she tightened one over the other.

"I'm hungry."

"When have you not been hungry?" Her mouth curled at one corner in a poor attempt at a smile.

I took a deep breath, exhaled noisily, and then clamped my mouth shut. She stared at me. I stared back at her. A staring contest: *Who's going to talk first?* She did.

"Quincy, you're not yourself lately. Please tell me why."

I shook my head.

"Is something wrong at school?"

"No."

"Is everything ok with Fulton?"

"Yes."

"Are you having a fight with one of your friends?"

"No."

"Are you pregnant?"

"Addy!" I almost shouted. "How can you ask such a thing? You don't think I'd do . . . that?"

"No, I know you won't do *that*, but something is wrong, and I want to know what. You've been different since I got back from New York."

I gritted my teeth and stared out the window at Mrs. Thompson's roof.

"Quincy, please tell me." Her voice almost broke. When I saw tears filling her eyes, something in me relented.

"I'm sorry." Then, I lied. "My recital is coming up. Final exams are close behind. I'm afraid I'll get pimples for the prom." I wasn't afraid of getting pimples, but everybody else worried about pimples, so I threw that into the mix. "My paper about Nathan isn't shaping up the way I wanted, and I really am hungry."

She laughed and wiped her eyes. "OK, let's take care of these problems one at a time. You're prepared for the recital. I don't know why you'd even worry about that. You're supposed to be a little nervous; nervousness helps you play better. Final exams, well, why don't you worry about those when the recital is over. And pimples. Good heavens, Quincy, you haven't had a pimple in years. The research paper — I'll help you with your paper. Adam Johnson can just wait for his bloody manuscript. And the last problem is easily solved. Let's go find something to eat."

ન   ન   ન

Mrs. Ethridge, from across the street, dropped by as we were finishing supper. She wanted Addy to pass judgment on fabric samples she was considering for new living room curtains. Addy went back across the street with her to look at the samples while I had dessert. Earlene must have been standing in the middle of the kitchen for a couple minutes before I realized she was scowling at me.

"What are you doing to your aunt?"

I let my fork clink onto my plate. "What do you mean?"

"You know what I mean." I'd never seen Earlene angry before. "You been going around like you wished *she* was the one off in the Congo. She ain't done nothing to you. You been listening to that Alice Worthington, ain't you? I know you been sneaking off down to her house."

I didn't know what to say.

"There's always them that spouts rumors. They spouts them out like one of them things at that Yellowstone park."

"Geysers."

"Don't you believe none of what that girl says. Your aunt is handing you your future on a silver platter and here you are treating her like a leper. Ain't nobody handing my James his future. He might not never get what he wants just because he's the wrong color."

When she turned around and began slamming dishes into the sink, I crept away.

I was tired when my alarm went off the next morning. Thinking about Alice's rumors had exhausted me. I had to stop thinking. I had to stop feeling. I was slipping down, down, down. I needed something to hold on to.

Trying to save myself, I let a sense of wild abandon grab hold. So what, my mind sang as I stepped into my panties; so what? Addy had an affair, and Alice Worthington is a jealous kook with a wild imagination. By the time I had my clothes on and my hair brushed, I felt ditzy — like I wasn't all there. I didn't want to be all there.

"I never saw you so silly before," Jessie said as we walked to French together.

"It's National Silly Day."

I was still silly when I got to art class. I sang and hummed under my breath and giggled at the slightest excuse

"Will you stop that!" Alice complained. "I can't concentrate."

"But you're so good, you don't need to concentrate." I slapped a paintbrush at my painting, not caring what color I painted things. Mrs. Arness had taped pictures to the blackboard — houses, barns, churches — and ordered us to draw a building or group of buildings using what we'd learned about the vanishing point and then to color in our pictures with water colors. I chose to do Aunt Mildred's farmhouse with hell fire glinting off the roof and Uncle Roger's barn off to the side. Somewhere in their cotton field was the vanishing point. Mrs. Buzzard and her infamous vanishing point! I wanted to vanish right out of the class.

It was Thursday. Should I return to Nathan's house? Should I look for something to verify Alice's accusations? Should I look for something to refute Alice's accusations? Should I ignore her accusations and always wonder what the truth was? With lips pinched and jaw clenched, I dabbed alizarin crimson on the farmhouse roof. The muscles across my chest and shoulders tightened like a drawn slingshot.

"Not a good color," Mrs. Arness said. The old crow had been standing a few feet behind, spying on me.

I pretended I didn't hear and painted the barn roof cobalt blue and the chicken house lemon yellow. My picture looked like a Disney cartoon — a Disney cartoon painted by a three-year-old because my arm jerked every time I laid paint brush to paper. Mrs. Arness slithered closer. Her breath smelled like something that had been in the refrigerator too long.

"You seem to have forgotten what we've learned about colors."

"Yes, Ma'am. I just thought painting the roofs bright colors might be fun." I gritted my teeth.

"Roofs aren't those colors."

"No ma'am. But I don't like ugly brown roofs."

"I hear you're such a good student in your other subjects, Quincy. Why don't you do as well in art?"

"I guess I'm just not very good at art." People turned to stare. But not Alice. She kept right on painting her perfect picture, pretending not to hear.

Mrs. Arness sighed and walked away.

"You can fix the roofs," Alice said when Mrs. Arness was out of hearing. "Wet a brush and remove some of the paint. Then you can paint over them with better colors."

"I don't want better colors. I hate this class." I ripped off the tape that fastened the paper to the water color board, wadded up my despicable painting, and threw the monstrosity across the room, almost hitting Mrs. Arness.

"I'll see you for detention this afternoon, Quincy Bruce," she snapped. Her eyes shot daggers.

      ҩ   ҩ   ҩ

I should have won an Oscar for my after school performance. I cried; I moaned; I faked sad faces. "I miss my parents. I haven't seen them for almost a year," I whined. Then I cried some more. Mrs. Arness managed an *oh-you-poor-thing* look. "And I'm bad at art." I shed more tears. "It bothers me so much to be bad at something, and if my parents weren't all the way across the ocean in Africa I'd probably be able to draw and paint better, and I'm so sorry for ripping up my painting, and I'm new in school this year, and that isn't easy." I wiped my tears and hung my head in shame. The tears were real; the shame was fake. If Addy could pretend to be what she wasn't, then so could I.

Jessie waited for me in the parking lot.

"Well? Did she really lash into you?"

"No. I cried, and she felt sorry for me."

"All right! Did you really cry? Real tears?"

"Yes, real tears." I'd been banking them for weeks. They'd been accumulating since the night I read Addy's diary. "Can you drop me at Nathan's house?"

"You're really into researching this paper, aren't you?"

"Yeah." The research was no longer about my English paper, or the Lady; the research was about Addy.

છ   છ   છ

I trudged around to Nathan's backyard, carrying the weight of the world on my shoulders. Sin is heavy — even when the sin belongs to someone else. Jonas, his back to me, pushed the lawnmower through the tall grass and didn't see me when I opened the gate and slipped in. I stood inside the fence waiting for him to get to the end of the row and turn around. He stopped when I waved.

"Hi," I said, walking over to him. "The lawn looks real nice."

"Yes'm, that rain sure helped."

"Has Pearl gone shopping?"

"Yeah, she done gone a couple hours ago. How's Miss Earlene doing this week?"

"She's doing fine."

"You tell her now, I sure did enjoy that divinity."

"I'll ask her to make you some more."

He grinned. "Miss Earlene makes the best divinity I ever did taste."

"I agree."

"I think the sweet peas are just about ready to come up." He nodded toward the empty flower bed. "I thought I seen little green heads poking their way through the dirt." He left the lawn mower and went over to look. "Yep, they's coming up all right." He motioned for me to come and see.

I obliged. Bending over, I saw small green knobs running in even rows through the soil.

"Pretty soon the yard'll look real good. Those ladies will probably come again this year and let everybody in to see Nathan's flowers."

"You mean the Garden Club tour?"

"Yes'm. I'm going to be real busy between now and then. Nathan always liked to have his yard pretty. Said there weren't nothing better than a well-kept yard."

"He liked flowers?"

"Use to be he'd come out here and wander around. Then he'd sit down in that swing over yonder and smoke his pipe and enjoy his flowers."

I looked to where the swing hung from an oak tree, the chains bolted to a limb. "I guess I better go in and get to work," I said then. "Talk to you later, Jonas." I wiggled my fingers at him and started for the back door.

With clammy hands, I unlocked the drawer in what had been Addy's desk. Sweat puddled under my arms, and my heart pounded as I huddled on the floor in front of the drawer and reached inside. Putting aside the files I'd gone through the previous week, I shuffled through the remaining contents, throwing things to the floor after a brief look. A paper island began to form around my feet.

I found a stack of receipts showing payment to various convalescent homes. No two names were the same. One was for Timothy Nelson; another for Nathaniel Brown; another for Lawrence Stone. Who were these people? Chewing at my lower lip, I opened file after file, rifling through the contents and searching for evidence of . . . Of what? An extended family that he supported? A charity?

A bulging envelope contained bank statements and canceled checks. I held my breath as I looked through them, dreading to see large sums made out to Addy, but only one check per month was made out to her, and the amount was always the same — a modest amount. *Salary* had been written in the note section on each check.

A flat metal box lay in the back of the drawer. Inside I found Nathan's birth certificate, an old passport, a social security card, his parents' marriage license, and their death certificates. There was no will and no death certificate for Nathan.

Something told me this was my last chance to discover secrets. How long before Pearl returned? How long before Addy started to wonder where I was? I leaned back on my heels in the middle of my paper island, my shoulders drooping. Then, sighing, I rose and went to the window. The lawn mower stood motionless while Jonas busied himself rolling a cigarette. As I watched him reach into his pocket for matches, I had an idea.

By the time I got outside, Jonas was sucking at his cigarette. "Jonas," I said, ". . . I was just wondering something."

"Yes'm, what you be wondering your pretty head about?"

"When Nathan died, what time of day did he fall down the stairs?"

I expected Jonas to say something like: "Why Miss Quincy, he didn't fall down no stairs; he died of a heart attack."

"It was done near 'bout lunch time. Miz Addy, she be in there.

285

Miss Pearl was gone."

My breath caught. He *had* fallen down the stairs. "Addy was there? Not Pearl?"

"Yes'm. Miss Pearl was out at the dentist's. I heard Miz Addy screaming and I went running in. I seen him at the bottom of the stairs." He stopped for a moment before continuing in a barely audible voice, "Miz Addy was standing over him. 'Oh my god, what have I done? What have I done?' she kept screaming."

My right arm began to shake uncontrollably, and I could barely control my jerky breaths enough to ask the next question. Finally, I managed to gasp out: "How long did the ambulance crew have to wait outside?"

Jonas' mouth twitched. "A long while," he said finally. "They made me go out and wait too. Dr. Whiddon came. Then Mr. Watson, he come and they let him in, and we had to wait some more." Jonas hurled his cigarette to the ground. "She didn't ought to give him that stuff." He shook his head as though trying to shake away the memory. "Opium." He spit out the word and then grasped the handle of the lawn mower. "Got to mow this lawn. Got to git going. Ain't got no more time to talk."

I have no memory of how I got there, but I found myself once again in Nathan's study, sitting on the floor, dumping out the contents of files and envelopes I'd already gone through, adding them to the pile of paper around me. A light green certificate with a raised seal at the bottom fell from one. How had I missed the certificate before? I scanned the page. *Commonwealth of Georgia. Local Registrar's Certification of Death.* A number printed in red. *Full name of deceased. Residence.* I skipped over the unimportant details, and looked down to the part labeled *Medical Certificate. Part I: Death was caused by: severe head trauma from fall down stairs (a) blank (b) blank (c) blank. Part II. OTHER SIGNIFICANT CONDITIONS: contributing to death but not related to the immediate cause given in Part I (a). under the influence of opium.*

The front door slammed, but the sound didn't register. Not until I heard Addy calling my name. I snatched at the scattered contents of the drawer and tried to cram everything back in. But I wasn't fast enough.

CHAPTER 20

Lightning struck a tree two houses away and sizzled like a soul burning in hell. Thunder exploded. I was glad for a noise that drowned out the pounding of my heart. Addy and I ran to her car and hurled ourselves inside a few seconds before the sky opened to pour out a river.

The six blocks between Nathan's house and Addy's stretched to ten thousand miserable miles. Addy stared straight ahead as she grasped the steering wheel in a death clench and navigated through the blinding rain. Cars glided along the street like ghost cars, as cold rain met warm engines causing a mist to rise around them.

We had no umbrellas. The rain drenched us to the skin as we dashed for the house. Addy, leaving a wake of rainwater behind, stormed off to her bedroom. I crept away to mine.

We ate separate suppers — I in the kitchen; she in her study. Then she demanded my presence.

"What were you doing?" She sat on the sofa in the den, arms folded, eyes riveted on me. Her fingers made white valleys where they pressed into her upper arms. Her supper dishes sat on the coffee table. A piece of fried chicken had one bite missing and the potato salad appeared untouched.

I looked down at my shoes, at my smudged, muddy saddle oxfords.

"I trusted you, Quincy."

And I trusted you, Addy.

"Why were you snooping?"

"You gave me permission to look at Nathan's stuff."

Silence from the sofa. I refused to meet her eyes. I looked down at my shoes. They had become most interesting. *Too many layers of white shoe polish. That's the reason they get so splotchy in the rain.*

"I did not give you permission to go through either Nathan's desk or mine. Why didn't you tell me where you were going?"

"I thought I did," I lied.

Another interval of silence. Then a sobbing sound. I looked up. She wiped away tears but my heart had become a fossil.

"What were you up to?" Her voice broke. She swallowed and then took a deep breath. "What did you think you were going to find?" Then she narrowed her eyes. "What *did* you find?"

I bit my lips.

"Quincy?"

I shook my head.

She waited for what seemed a long time and then, giving up, rose and brushed past me as she left the room.

What was I to do? My aunt wasn't who I thought she was. How could I remain in her house? I could spend the night with Jessie, but one night wasn't enough. I needed a week to think things out. Or two weeks. Or forever. The only place I knew to go was Aunt Mildred's. What would be my explanation to her? *Aunt Mildred, you were right about Addy. She was the Lady. But it gets better. Someone drugged Nathan Waterstone with opium and then pushed him down the stairs. Addy was the only one in the house that morning. She stood over him, calling out, "What have I done? What have I done?" And she has more money*

289

than she earned as an editorial assistant. Her husband left her nothing. Uncle Samuel
left her very little. She has no war widow's pension. Nathan's will left a bunch of money
to Pearl. Pearl never got that money.

I wandered into the hall and stood there for a few moments before my feet, from habit, took me into the living room. I looked at the piano. But something inside me had shut down. I couldn't play.

$$\wp \qquad \wp \qquad \wp$$

Addy and I didn't speak for the remainder of the week. Ignoring Earlene's questioning eyes, we passed in silence; we ate in silence. Addy's typewriter no longer went *clickety-clack*. She sat in her study with Beethoven's *Tempest* sonata playing in the background and sank deep into a world that only she saw. She played the sonata over and over. When she emerged to eat or sleep, I saw her uneven gait. She no longer bothered to hide her limp.

I didn't practice. Several times I saw her looking at me as though she wanted to ask why I'd abandoned the piano, but she never did. She knew I'd learned something. I suspected she was afraid to ask for fear of revealing more.

At school I tried to behave as the Quincy Bruce everyone knew. I laughed and gossiped. I complained about teachers and homework. I talked to Fulton between classes. But the whole time my mouth was set so tight that my jaw ached, and my neck became so stiff I could barely turn my head.

I had to make a choice. My aunt, my formerly beloved aunt, my formerly trusted aunt, appeared to be guilty of murder. Knowing that, I had to also believe Alice's accusations that Addy took money rightfully belonging to Pearl. I shuddered at the idea of living in the same house with an adulteress, murderer, and thief. But where could I go? Desperately, I sought a solution, but in the end I knew there were only two choices — the same two Mama and Daddy fought over before they left.

If I lived with Addy, I'd become more and more bitter. But I could go to college or to a conservatory and study piano.

If I moved in with Aunt Mildred, I'd never play the piano again.

I missed my parents. Would they leave Africa and come home to me if I told them how miserable I was?

I knew they wouldn't.

I carried on for the remainder of the week, wanting comfort, but not knowing where to find it. "What are you doing after school?" I asked Fulton on Friday when we walked together to algebra.

"Nothing. Want to do something?"

"Sure."

"You aren't practicing?"

"I need a break."

"We can grab something to eat and then go for a ride."

"Sounds good."

We drove down a winding country road with pine forests on both sides, coming finally to a dirt lane leading into the woods.

"There's a pond down there," Fulton said as he turned into the lane. "We used to go fishing there."

I said nothing as we bumped along, eventually arriving at a small pond. The area was heavily wooded and shielded from view. We got out and walked to the water's edge. For a few minutes we watched minnows and tadpoles darting about. Fulton tossed a stone and we watched the ripples.

"You like to fish?" I asked.

"I used to fish a lot. We'd bring a picnic down here and stay the day sometimes. Seems like there's never any time for that anymore." He looked around. "There's where we ate." He pointed to a large oak. "Come on. I have a candy bar. We'll picnic on a Snickers."

He grabbed my hand and pulled me toward the oak. We sat at the base of the tree. Fulton unwrapped the Snickers and broke it in half. He leaned back on one elbow to eat his share. I gazed at the pond while I ate mine. When I finished, I wiped my hands on the grass.

"Come on. Get comfortable," he said, and tugged at my arm.

I lay back. He rolled over on his side and ran his forefinger lightly over my face. "You're pretty," he said.

I didn't reply.

"What's the matter, Quincy? You look sad."

When I still didn't reply, he leaned down and kissed me, barely brushing my lips. Then he kissed me again. I put my hands on his shoulders and then around his neck as his kisses became more passionate. His breathing quickened, and he put one leg between mine. I thought of what Aunt Mildred said the day I went to live with Addy: something about winding up in the same fix as Mama.

Addy and I didn't talk to each other on the way to my piano lesson.

Not talking to each other had become a habit. I rested my head on the seat, closed my eyes, and felt the wind from the open window blow over my face and tried not to think about having to tell Mrs. Rich that today's lesson was my last.

My stomach was in my mouth when I walked into her studio.

"Good morning, dear," she said.

She was half-turned away, reaching for her lesson book. While I put my music on the music rack, she opened the book to the place where she'd written last week's notes, and then turned around and motioned for me to sit down at the piano. I hesitated.

"What's the matter?"

This was the time to tell her. *I won't be coming back, Mrs. Rich. I'm going to live with Aunt Mildred and she doesn't like music. Actually, I don't like it so much myself anymore. You see, my Aunt Addy, whom I dearly loved, and trusted, and who was my champion, has turned out to be someone I don't know.* "You've taught me so much." I said, and struggled not to cry.

"You're an excellent student. You listen. You work hard. Just imagine how you'll sound this time next year."

There won't be a next year, Mrs. Rich. Not even a next week. I couldn't speak. I'd break apart, if I tried.

She held out her hand, palm up, toward the piano bench. "What would you like to play first?"

I sat down and rubbed my hands together. They were so cold. Lately, I seemed to be cold all the time. I curled my toes inside my shoes and took a deep breath. I'd tell her later. At the end of the lesson. I stood on the edge of a cliff and couldn't jump. Not just yet. I played a b-flat. Why a b-flat? I don't know. I played the note again, listening to the reverberations until they died away. B-flat, the first note of the Schubert Impromptu.

It's hard to describe what happened then. For nine months I'd been working on phrasing, timing, fingering, wrist movements, staccatos, legatos, . . . But I forgot all that. I shut down my brain and played with my ears. And the music was beautiful.

My hands slid into my lap when I finished, and I sucked in a quick breath. For a few moments I sat in awe of what I'd just done. When I heard a sniffle, I turned to see Mrs. Rich wiping her eyes.

She gave an embarrassed laugh and wiped her eyes again. "Forgive me. I'm so thrilled at your progress I can't help but shed a few tears. I want you to audition at Julliard."

I struggled to remain composed while she went on about a future that was never to be. At some point, I found myself standing between her and Addy while they both talked about me, about auditions, about Julliard — things that were never going to happen. The opportunity to inform Mrs. Rich that this was my last lesson slipped away.

❧   ❧   ❧

When we arrived back in Addy's driveway — another wordless journey — I reached up to open the car door, but she held up her palm to stop me.

"Wait," she said.

I looked down at my lap, letting my hair fall over my cheeks to veil the sides of my face. I clasped my hands to keep them from shaking. Sooner or later we'd have to discuss what I didn't want to discuss. Apparently, that was going to be now. My stomach clenched.

"You stumbled across something when you were at Nathan's house. Or did Alice Worthington repeat some rumor to you? She told you something, and you were you looking for confirmation?"

294

My whole body tightened.

"I know there are rumors," she continued when I didn't answer. "There are things that can't be told, and there are good reasons for . . ." She stopped short. I turned to see why she'd stopped and then followed her gaze to the front porch.

Reverend Stewart sat in a rocking chair, his elbows propped on his knees and his face resting in his hands. We got out of the car and hurried toward him. When we came to the porch, he looked up with such a look that Addy stopped short. But for only a moment. She went to him, put her hand on his arm urging him to stand, and then led him toward the front door.

"Come inside," she said softly. Then she looked over her shoulder at me. *Leave us alone*, her look said.

I went to my room, sat down on my bed, and rubbed hard at my forehead, trying to rub away a headache. I assumed Fiona had taken a turn for the worse. And I'd thought she was the Lady! Hah! Next week I'd be back at Ellerbie Baptist, with the congregation praying for me after my brush with sin. They'd thank God for my safe deliverance back into the hands of a Baptist Church. After condemning Addy, they'd pray for her soul.

I brought out my suitcases from the closet. What, other than my toothbrush and the autographed copy of *The Lady*, remained of the things I'd come with? Nothing. I'd have to wear clothes Addy had bought with stolen money or leave naked.

৶   ৶   ৶

Addy woke me. I didn't even remember lying down. Tearful, she sat on the edge of my bed, and at that moment, I probably loved my aunt more than I ever had. I remembered the wonderful things about her, the things she'd done for me, her spirited outlook on life, her fight to overcome her disability. I remembered her as she had been. Or as I thought she'd been. She wouldn't understand when I left. Or maybe she would. I couldn't bear to think of her never loving me again.

"She's dying," she said and shook her head as though in disbelief. "Fiona's dying."

"Is she in the hospital?"

"No, she's at home. They're just trying to make her comfortable now."

"Oh." *Oh, oh, oh.* That's all I could think of to say.

"I'm going over there. Honey, do you mind having supper alone?"

I shook my head.

At bedtime, Addy still wasn't back.

"Fiona died last night," Addy said when I came down for breakfast. Her shoulders drooped. She pushed her bowl of uneaten cereal away. "I'm going to dress for church," she said at length and left the table.

I was surprised to see Reverend Stewart in the pulpit. His wife, the woman I'd been so sure was the Lady, had died; yet, he was there. I decided he must have come because he felt the need to grieve with those who loved him. His voice broke from time to time as he gave a short sermon about how people come into this life as babies, crying, protesting, and then exit the same way, crying and protesting. "But we move on to better things. God is gracious," he said. "He has prepared a far better place for us, one where we shed the pain and suffering of the earth. This morning Fiona is there, in the place God prepared for her." He finished in a voice that was almost a whisper. "A better place. For eternity."

A better place. Eternity was such a long time. Was what they said about Heaven and Hell really true? Daddy, with his pulpit theatrics, his threats, and his thunder, had created doubt in my mind, but Reverend Stewart made heaven sound almost real. But still, even if Heaven existed, were we supposed to spend so much of our time worrying about the afterlife instead of concentrating on this one?

I sat close to Addy. Our shoulders touched and she held my hand. I cried inwardly, but not for Reverend Stewart and Fiona. I grieved for Addy and me. After church, she dropped me at home. She was going to the manse. "To help feed people," she explained.

I knew I had to call Aunt Mildred while Addy was out of the house and while Earlene was busy in the kitchen preparing food to be sent to the Stewart's. In my stocking feet, I tiptoed to the phone and dialed Aunt Mildred's number. My insides had turned to cement. Darrell answered.

"I'm coming to live with you. Tell Aunt Mildred she can pick me up around three."

❧　　❧　　❧

Slumped in the swing, I waited for Aunt Mildred on the front porch. But I dreamed, didn't I? I squeezed my eyes shut. Wasn't I still sitting in our front porch swing in Ellerbie waiting for Addy? With my two suitcases and a cardboard box at the top of the steps ready to go into the trunk of her car? Mama and Daddy busied themselves inside, packing for the Congo. I was about to begin a new life. Addy was going to help me become a pianist.

I opened my eyes to see two squirrels scampering across the yard, one chasing the other. They leaped onto the trunk of an oak and then clambered up to disappear in the branches — branches that hung over Addy's yard, not our yard in Ellerbie; hundreds of branches curving and crooking through the leaves and moss like a secret script. I tried to read what they said, but theirs was a language I didn't understand. Not that I understood anything anymore.

How could I have been so wrong about Addy? How could Aunt Mildred have been so right? I hated her for that. *Hated her,* adding that to my other sins. I'd disobeyed; I'd snooped; I'd taken what wasn't mine — even though I'd returned the diary, I'd stolen what was inside; I'd been proud and arrogant, thinking I could do what I wanted in order to impress Mr. Feldman and to satisfy my curiosity. Now I had to pay by giving up my dream. The dream collector shambled in my direction.

A question had been growing in the shadows of my mind, which I'd tried to ignore. But the question was there. Knocking. Begging for entry. Must I tell the police that my aunt might have murdered Nathan Waterstone and taken money he'd willed to Pearl?

But how could I destroy Addy? Did the good things about her not outweigh the bad? Was killing one person worse than waging war and killing thousands? Was taking money from Pearl worse than denying livelihoods, dreams, and dignity to a whole race of people? Aunt Mildred, and the other *she's* and *he's* like her, didn't have pure white souls either.

I remembered the discussion about *The Scarlet Letter* and what Mary Watson said when she gave her synopsis: *To Hawthorne, the greatest sin wasn't Hester's adultery, but Roger Chillingworth's attempt to master the soul of Arthur Dimmesdale.* Somehow, I'd always felt that Aunt Mildred was attempting to master my soul when she spoke for God. And why did she hate me so much that she said those things the day I went to live with Addy?

At three-fifteen, Aunt Mildred hadn't come. She was more often late than not, so I had no reason to hope she *wasn't* coming. But the dream collector was. He crept toward me, fingers twitching, ready to snatch away my dream to bury beside Mama's. He drew closer. He smelled like rotten leaves and week-old fish; like dirty socks; like a putrid swamp; like cowardice. Mary Watson believed that people didn't think for themselves. The dream collector smelled like that too. Like people not thinking for themselves. And giving up. Addy thought *Devil* meant anything that prevents a person from following his rightful path. Did that make her my devil?

I pressed my fingers to my temples. Hard. There were too many questions and too few answers. Addy had once told me that life was messy. I understood now exactly how messy it can get. I had questions, but no answers. I wanted to escape from myself. Or at least escape from the questions. I went inside. To the piano. I closed my eyes and played.

ဢ ဢ ဢ

I didn't hear the front door open and then close. I didn't know that Addy had come home, or that she stood behind me until some small sound — a breath, perhaps — alerted me. I stopped playing, rested my hands in my lap, and looked straight ahead.

"Why is your suitcase on the front porch?"

A lump the size of an orange filled my throat. Addy sat down on the bench so that we faced in opposite directions. Our arms touched. A sob erupted. I bit my lips to hold back the other sobs, straining to break the dike. She put her arms around me, pulled me to her, and the dike broke.

She didn't try to stop me. When I finally did, the shoulder of her dress was soaked. I raised my head, and she brushed back a strand of hair from my face, her hands gliding over my skin like a swan on a glass pond.

"I was going to live with Aunt Mildred," I said, finally, and saw a wave of pain wash over Addy's face. "If you tolerate sin in other people, that makes you bad, too, doesn't it?" She drew back. "I thought I couldn't live with you when I found out you lied. But, I can't live without music either. I know that you were the Lady."

Her mouth fell open, and her hands fluttered up like baby birds looking for a vanished nest. She rose from the bench, turned her head this way and that. I saw how she tried to find words but couldn't. At length, she went to the sofa and sat down. "Come here," she said. Her voice shook. I didn't move. She motioned for me to come, insisting. I went and sat beside her.

I felt lighter. Or at least a little lighter now that I'd told her that much.

She grasped her forehead as though trying to wrench away a headache. "I've always been afraid that some might think I was the Lady. But I didn't think you would." She dropped her hand to her lap. "I knew you suspected something. But that I was the Lady! Whatever made you think that? Alice Worthington didn't tell you I was the Lady."

I looked down at my hands and rubbed at the rough spot playing the piano had made on the side cuticle of my right thumb. "I read your diary," I whispered.

"My diary?"

"You left the cabinet unlocked when you went to New York." I had become the despicable one and wondered why sneaking around to read someone's private thoughts suddenly seemed as odious as adultery.

The quiet between us crept on and on. I heard the voices of

300

neighborhood children on the sidewalk outside, riding past on their bikes, roller skating, living normal lives. "I'm sorry," I said at length.

She made a sound and covered her face with her hands for a moment before looking up again. "Quincy, I sinned grievously. Warren was gone. I felt abandoned. Then I met the love of my life, the only man I've ever truly loved. But why did you think that man was Nathan?" She studied me with narrowed eyes. "You didn't read the whole diary, did you?"

I was about to say I'd read the whole thing when I remembered dozing off and the diary falling to the floor. Had I skipped pages when I started reading again?

"I wasn't the *Lady*, Quincy."

"But you just said . . ."

"I said nothing about being the *Lady*. I said I met the love of my life."

"But, who . . .?"

She gave me such a look of longing. Her cheeks glowed, and her lips parted. "I did love Warren," she said. "But there is love, and then there is love that saturates every cell, every breath, every . . ." She let her gaze wander. I wasn't sure if she spoke to me or to herself. "A few people have the good fortune and the bad fortune to meet the one person in the world meant to be their soul mate."

"Bad fortune?"

"I was married; he was promised to someone else."

"He was engaged?"

She nodded and looked down at her feet. "We had only a few months together to become best friends and lovers, to have fun and share our pain, to laugh and cry together, to learn that neither of us could ever be a whole person without the other."

"He wouldn't break his engagement," I said, remembering the

301

opening lines from the new book: *Once again I've crossed the ocean, my love. I have come back hoping that nothing has changed, or that everything has changed.*

"He would have. His intended would have been hurt, but he knew she'd eventually find someone she deserved — someone who loved only her and not another woman." She frowned. "It was me. I thought I was doing the right thing, but I was wrong. We would have been happy together, and she . . ." Her gaze wandered to the window. For a few seconds I thought she wouldn't finish her sentence. "She would have gotten over him in time," she said then.

"Who was he?"

"Robert."

"Reverend Steward?"

She nodded.

It took a few seconds to sink in. But then I was surprised that I wasn't surprised. It was as though I'd known all along. *They fit*; they drew together like magnets. Remembering my own semi-crush on him, I laughed. Not knowing why I laughed, Addy gave me a funny look. "I understand," I said, containing my laughter. "He's the one I would have chosen for you . . . I mean, if he hadn't been married."

Her eyes glistened with tears. "You need to know, Quincy, that we never committed adultery. When I said we became lovers, I mean only that we loved each other dearly. There were so many times . . ." She stopped. "There were times," she began again, ". . . when I wished we had. There were times when I wished we'd had a child. I could have brought our child here, and no one would have known. People would have assumed the child was Warren's. But that didn't happen and I should never have said that to you."

"He gave you the locket?"

She nodded.

"What will happen now?"

"Don't ask that." She inhaled deeply, calming herself. "He's become my best friend. When he married Fiona, he was faithful to her in every way. He sends me flowers sometimes — *a thank you* he says, for being Fiona's friend. He made himself forget how we once felt about each other." The color drained from her face and she whispered, but not to me. "He made himself forget."

"Surely he must remember."

She shook her head. "He's forgotten. And he's angry with me."

While I was puzzling out her last statement, a car backfired. I jumped, and then froze, afraid Aunt Mildred had arrived. I'd forgotten about her. But the vehicle passed.

"This is what you've been so unhappy about?" She asked before I could ask her why Reverend Stewart was angry.

I nodded.

"I wish you'd told me. We could have talked."

I had to know about the other things. But when I asked, would she turn her back on me, lock herself in her room, and insist Aunt Mildred come and remove me from her house? How could she endure the sight of me after such questions?

She stood and walked to the window that looked out across Mrs. Thompson's yard. She leaned one shoulder against the panes. "What else do you need to know? My diary gave away no other sins. At least that I remember. But you've talked to Alice Worthington."

"Was Fiona the Lady?"

Her mouth fell open and she stared at me. "Fiona? Wherever did you get that idea?"

"Her hair. I saw the picture in her bureau drawer when I went to fetch a shawl."

"Oh, that bloody picture! I thought she'd destroyed the thing." She touched her fingers to her temple and let out an exasperated sound. "That bloody picture!" She narrowed her eyes. "But Alice didn't tell you that. What did Alice tell you?"

"That Nathan didn't die of a heart attack and that he left everything to Pearl." The words tumbled out leaving me breathless, like I'd run for miles and miles.

She didn't answer for what seemed a very long time.

"I think I have to tell you everything," she said, finally.

My stomach knotted into a thousand knots. The clank of a dish reverberated from the kitchen. Earlene busied herself preparing a Sunday evening meal that would probably not be touched.

"Nathan didn't die of a heart attack." Still leaning on the window, she looked out.

"It was a lie?"

"Yes, a lie. To you. To everyone. You see, Quincy, to perpetuate the lies we'd already begun, we had to lie about his death."

"What lies? And who is *we*?"

"Dr. Whiddon announced that he died of a heart attack. We didn't want people to know what really happened."

I interlaced my ice-cold fingers, squeezing them until they hurt. I had to ask one question before she told me more, and I was afraid to hear the answer. "Were you the only person in the house that day?"

"No."

Jonas had told me Pearl was away. "Who else was there?" I didn't breathe, dreading to hear her say Pearl's name.

"The nurse," she said. My breath exploded from my lungs, but she didn't seem to notice. "We'd hired a nurse. Mamie Fletcher. Mamie came from Memphis so we shipped her home right away with a bribe and a promise not to tell what happened."

"What happened?" I leaned forward.

"I'm so tired of keeping secrets." She folded her hands over her throat and let out a ragged sigh. "So tired." She moved away from the window and began to pace. "You wanted something new and sensational for your English paper. I'm going to give you something. I'm going to tell you everything."

"And will you tell me why Reverend Stewart is angry?"

"Yes. But what about Aunt Mildred? Is she on her way to pick you up?"

"Oh my gosh. I need to stop her."

Addy motioned toward the hall where the phone was.

I dialed, knowing I was probably too late to stop Aunt Mildred. Even if she hadn't already left, she'd come anyway. She wouldn't be able to resist the opportunity to snatch me from the jaws of hell and be rewarded with a lifetime of pleasurable gloating.

Darrell answered.

"Darrell?"

"Oh, hi, Quincy."

"Where's Aunt Mildred?"

"Over at the Church."

"What's she doing there?"

"They're having an all afternoon Woman's Missionary Society meeting to pray for . . ."

"You didn't tell her what I told you? About . . ." My mind raced. "You didn't tell her that she and Uncle Roger are supposed to come here for dinner next Sunday?"

"You didn't say that. You said . . ."

I interrupted him. "That's exactly what I said — they're invited to come next Sunday. For dinner. And you and Patsy and Bobby, too. Don't forget to tell her."

"OK. But I thought you said something about moving in with us."

"Good heavens, why would you think I said that? Just tell her about dinner."

❧   ❧   ❧

"Part of what I'm going to tell, you can reveal," Addy said when I returned to the living room. "The remainder must be kept secret for a long while yet. I wish this were a novel where we could tie things up and say "the end." But we can't. Some things have to wait. You'll become the guardian of my secrets."

"Not to excuse what happened later . . .," she said as she left the window and walked over to settle on the sofa. ". . . the whole sorry story began when I lay in a hospital bed for two long years. No one thought I'd walk again. No one, that is, except for me. I knew I'd walk. I'd not only walk, but I'd run, and jump, and fly. I imagined spreading my wings and flying away from that sterile white room filled with beds, and needles, and the sound of weeping, and the smell of medicine, and of praying and cursing, and of hope and lack of hope. I drew picture after picture of me soaring over the world. I wanted to go everywhere, see everything. I wanted so much, and I was impatient." She stopped, waited a few seconds, and then continued. "I recovered, and soon enough I began to go, and see, and have. Then one day I went to London. I met Nathan and . . .

She talked, and I listened. When she finished, I sat in stunned silence. In retrospect, I realized the evidence had been around me the whole time.

While I tried to absorb what she'd said, she rose and went again to the window and gazed out into the yard until, suddenly, she burst out laughing. She beckoned me with one hand while the other pointed toward something outside. I went to see and looked out in time to see Mrs. Thompson dragging Lucifer from her fish pond.

"Finally, that cat fell in." Addy laughed again. Her laugh, missing for a long time, was the most beautiful music I'd ever heard.

Mrs. Thompson put Lucifer, a sopping wet and bedraggled pile of black fur, on the lawn beside the pool. He looked like he'd been anesthetized and for a few seconds sat so still he might have been a lawn statue. Then he shook himself and slunk away to hide beneath a japonica bush. I was sorry Earlene had missed seeing Lucifer's fall. Addy obviously thought the same thing. "What a shame, Earlene wasn't here to see," she said.

"Quincy . . ." She put her hand on my cheek. ". . . why in the world would you even think of giving up music?"

"It left me," I said, my voice breaking. "Music disappeared from my head and heart for a little while, because . . ."

"Because you thought I was the Lady? Because you thought I lied about Nathan's death?"

I nodded.

She let her hand drop away from my cheek and closed her eyes for a moment. "I *did* lie about Nathan's death."

"You told me once that life can be messy."

She nodded.

"Daddy would say that I've been very sinful. Disobeying you when I went to see Alice; sneaking around in Nathan's house; reading your diary."

"Oh, good heavens. The only people who don't sin are those who do nothing. Certainly all those gossipy ladies in Sunday hats sin." She put her hand on my shoulder. "Quincy, you have a talent. Talents are meant to be used. Remember the parable. In your lifetime you're going to sin a lot more, just as I and everyone else will, so get over it. Play the piano."

CHAPTER 19

We handed in our research reports the first Friday in May. I saw Mr. Feldman put mine on top when he collected them. Mary saw too. "You must have convinced him you actually have something new and wonderful to say." She didn't look at me, but tightened her mouth and began organizing her books and papers for the next class.

I no longer cared whose paper was better. My life had been restored, and I'd discovered English research papers were no longer that important to me. I collected my books and swung my legs around to the side of my desk, ready for a quick exit when the bell rang.

"When are you going to tell the rest of us what you found out?" Jessie asked.

"As soon as you throw me a party with champagne and caviar." Not that I'd tasted either. Or that caviar even appealed to me. But I wasn't about to divulge the information until I was sure Mr. Feldman had read my paper.

"Come on," Jessie urged. "Just a hint."

"Not a chance."

The bell rang, and I dashed off to talk to Fulton. I'd been afraid he'd be angry with me after I pushed him away at the pond that day, but he wasn't. He even apologized for getting *fresh*. I liked Fulton, but someday I wanted to have a great passion like Addy had had. However, unlike hers, I wanted a happy ending. I shuddered when I thought how close I came to possibly ruining my future, both in music and in love, by letting an immature boy make love to me — one who set typewriters on fire and started fires in chemistry lab.

I hadn't wanted to reveal what Addy told me. Having her back — the Addy I loved — meant more to me than impressing Mr. Feldman or outdoing Mary. I told Addy I'd explain to Mr. Feldman that I wouldn't be able to share *something new about Nathan Waterstone at this time*. If that disappointed him, as I expected it to, then . . . Well, he'd just have to be disappointed. But Addy insisted. "I'm tired of secrets," she said. "Tell the one thing now; many years from now, you'll tell the others."

As for secrets, Mr. Watson would be speaking with Alice's daddy and her uncle that very morning, using his lawyering abilities to stop the rumors they'd been spreading. He wouldn't tell them everything — not unless they persisted, in which case, he'd threaten them with a libel suit. Whatever Mr. Watson said to Alice's daddy would be passed on to Alice. I expected to get the cold shoulder in art class.

♥　　♥　　♥

Mr. Feldman must have spent every minute and every second of the weekend grading our reports. When we walked in Monday morning there they were: twenty-five research reports in a stack on his desk. He stood with his back to us, writing a review list for our final exam on the board while he waited for the bell to ring. Once, he turned around and gave me a quick look before turning back to his list.

You'd have thought I was about to perform in Carnegie Hall. I was

310

that nervous — a lot more nervous, in fact, than I'd been on Friday evening for my recital, which, by the way, went superbly. I had spent hours and hours mastering technique, but I'd also learned to play with my ears. When I finished my last piece, the Schubert Impromptu, I rose from the piano bench, bowed to the audience, and in the midst of their enthusiastic applause, understood for the first time that I really would be a pianist.

Mary ambled in, trying to look casual. I knew her casualness was a big act, because Mary never ambled. I think she actually worried that my paper was going to outshine hers. I wanted to tell her there were more important things than having the best paper. Knowing the unhappiness Addy had endured, hearing her laugh again when Lucifer fell in the pool, shedding the bad feelings between us — *that* was important.

The bell rang. Mr. Feldman turned and glanced at me again before surveying the class. Something caught his attention in the back. Frowning, he plunged his hands in his pockets and stared. The entire class looked around to see Buddy Simms emptying sand from his gym shoes onto the floor.

Buddy looked up. "Whoops," he said.

"Please put you shoes back on, Mr. Sims." Mr. Feldman waited while Buddy slipped his feet back in his shoes and tied them. "Maybe we can begin now." Mr. Feldman walked to his desk, took a report from the top of the stack and returned to the front of the class. He held the report up, looked at the first page, but then lowered the report to his side.

"This is very unusual," he said and fell silent.

Jessie nudged me in the back. "That's yours," she whispered. "What in the world did you write?"

"You'll see," I whispered.

Mr. Feldman's forehead knitted, not in a frown, but in perplexity. "Is this true, Quincy?" He held the paper toward me.

311

Looking him directly in the eyes, I nodded.

"I'm going to read part of the report to the class. You know that what you've written here will get out?"

I nodded again.

"Does your aunt know?"

"She gave me permission to write what I did, and she'll verify the information."

"Very well, then." He turned to the page he'd marked. After giving me one last glance, he began to read.

Shortly after the publication of The Lady, *Amanda Blakely interviewed Nathan Waterstone on BBC radio. In the course of the interview, he admitted that his novel was based on truth, that he had had an affair with a woman whose husband was away, engaged in something having to do with the war.*

The admission created a furor in London. Bombs fell almost nightly, and each morning Londoners awoke to destruction and death. Yet while brave Englishmen were dying in an effort to save London, Nathan Waterstone flaunted an affair with a married woman by fictionalizing the affair in a novel.

Who is she, they wondered. Because Nathan Waterstone used the word "Lady," everyone assumed her to be someone important. Book sales soared as people attempted to identify her. There were a few hints: her hair, which she wore pulled over one shoulder, ranged somewhere between red and blonde; she volunteered as a nurse; she spoke English with an accent from some other English-speaking area; and Nathan gave her an opal pin as a birthday gift.

Perhaps the furor over who she was had to do with the state of mind people found themselves in because of the constant bombardment. For a few moments, Londoners could divert their attention from death and destruction to something else. At any rate, the book made Nathan Waterstone both rich and famous.

In succeeding years, the furor over who the Lady was died down, but there still remained a strong interest in learning her identity. Literary scholars have, from time to time, quizzed Mr. Waterstone's editorial assistant, Adelaide Simmons, as well as his closest friends, in an attempt to find out.

Three people have known all along who she was. Or rather who she wasn't. She was no one. Mr. Waterstone created her. From a picture of a friend's fiancée, he adopted the hair style and hair color. The friend's fiancée seldom wore her hair pulled over her shoulder, but had once had a photo taken with her hair arranged like that. Mr. Waterstone saw the photo during a visit to his friend's apartment. After the publication of the book, she hid the photo, afraid that someone would see it and think she'd been the Lady. The pin, which Mr. Waterstone describes in the book as a gift from him, was actually a gift from the grandmother of the woman. Several events in the book were retellings of things that happened to or with other women. In particular, his search for the Lady at the end of the book happened to someone else.

It is disappointing to learn that the tremendous sales for one of the most popular books of the decade was based on a publicity stunt.

Mr. Feldman stopped reading. You could have heard a pin drop. He opened his mouth to say something, but then stopped. I glanced at Mary. Her mouth hung open as she stared at me. I actually felt sorry for her.

"Well, Miss Bruce," he said, after clearing his throat. "I know you plan to be a pianist, and I look forward to hearing you perform some day, but your first bit of fame is going to be outside the musical arena." He raised his eyebrows. "There aren't any other interesting tidbits about Nathan Waterstone that you're going to surprise us with, are there?"

If you only knew, I thought. "Isn't that enough?" I smiled at him. Directly into his beautiful blue eyes.

"Oh, quite enough."

"If you stick around until the turn of the century . . .," I joked, even though it wasn't a joke, ". . . I might come up with something else."

CHAPTER 20

The Turn of the Century

January, 2000

Philadelphia, PA

I'm doing this for Addy. She chose the time — one week before a documentary commemorating Nathan Waterstone's literary career. They'll need to rewrite their script after they hear what I'm going to say.

The make-up woman is trying to make me presentable for TV. She's using more mascara than I ever thought possible. Certainly more than I use for my performances. The eyeliner is going on so heavy; I believe I'm in danger of looking like a raccoon.

A skinny woman with stark black-hair, who is both official and officious looking, trots around with a clipboard in one hand and a cell phone in the other. She has a frantic look on her face. My guess is that the frantic look molded itself to her long ago and remains even when she ceases to be frantic. Poor woman. I'd like to play her something soothing.

Chopin's *Raindrop Prelude,* perhaps.

It's too warm. The lights glare and smell of burning. People rush about. Camera and sound crews fiddle with equipment. I prefer the quiet that prevails backstage before a concert.

Now the make-up woman is applying some shiny white stuff beneath my eyes which, she claims, will "pull up" my face, or at least make my face appear to be "pulled up." I suppose I should look my best, and, lord knows, my face definitely needs pulling up lately.

It's almost time. The woman with the clipboard waves her bony arm at me, and then holds up three fingers, indicating that I need to be seated in my interviewee chair in that many minutes. The make-up woman aims a last gush of hair-spray at me, and then brushes an errant strand back in place.

"This way. Quickly," a man wearing a red sweat shirt says, and hurries me by placing his hand on my elbow. *Mt. Everest* is stamped above a picture of a white peak on his sweatshirt. Underneath the peak is something written in English — I can't read the words because of the glare — and underneath the English is something written in whatever language they speak in Nepal. Nepali? Why I'm paying attention to a sweatshirt as I'm walking onto a platform surrounded by TV cameras is unfathomable. Will they stick one of those cameras right in my face?

Lydia Hopkins is seated in the interviewer chair. She rises and shakes my hand.

"One minute. Are you ready?" Her red hair flashes neon from the lights.

"I'm ready." I've been ready for years.

I compose myself before playing a concert by standing backstage and hearing in my mind the first piece I'm going to play. Tonight, what I choose to hear instead is Addy's laughter the day Lucifer fell in the

315

fishpond. Every cell in me relaxes as I recall the music of her laugh. We sit down and wait a few seconds until, in response to a signal, Ms. Hopkins smiles into the camera.

"Tonight, our first guest on *Talk America* is . . ."

I wait, nodding and smiling, as she goes through the preliminaries, explaining to the audience who I am. *Quincy Bruce Hollander, concert pianist, distinguished professor of music at The University of Pennsylvania, and niece of Adelaide Simmons, who was the editorial assistant to Nathan Waterstone. The Quincy Bruce who revealed the Lady's identity. Or rather lack of identity.*

I feel sweat starting to dribble down my bosom. Will the make-up run?

Ms. Hopkins finishes her preliminaries. "We pause now for a commercial," she says. "Right after the commercial, we'll be back with Quincy Bruce Hollander."

Someone steps up and conducts a murmured conversation with Ms. Hopkins, leaving me free to think my own thoughts for the duration of an antacid ad.

Not even Mama knows what I'm going to tell tonight. She has become one of my biggest fans, attending my concerts whenever she can. Years ago, when I accused Mama and Daddy of abandoning me, I discovered I'd misjudged Mama almost as badly as I misjudged Addy. Addy eventually made me aware that Mama went along with Daddy's plan to go to Africa because Mama knew that if I went to Wilson High School, with their higher academic standards, I'd have a better chance of getting a scholarship to college. She didn't want me to miss what she'd missed.

Daddy won't be watching. He died in Africa fifteen years ago. Mama left him alone there, returning to the States after less than two years. She returned in time for my high school graduation. With Addy's help, she went to college, earned a teaching certificate, and taught English until she retired. Now she writes poetry.

Some people's dreams come true, but not everyone's. I think of Alice Worthington whose father punished her for spreading the same rumors that he spread. He ordered her to never again take another art class, and to never — at least while she lived under his roof — paint or draw. One of my hopes has always been that Alice left home after graduation and found a way to pursue her art.

Someone whose dream *did* come true is Earlene's son, James. He became an orthopedic surgeon and now lives and practices in Baltimore. Earlene lives with him and glows with pride over his accomplishment.

The commercial is about to end, and Ms. Hopkins is reviewing her notes. Other than Addy and my husband, there are only two others who know what I'm going to tell: Mr. Watson and Adam Johnson. I'm sure they're glued to their screens, waiting. Dr. Whiddon died seven years ago, so he isn't around to hear.

The commercial ends. Ms. Hopkins turns to me. "Your aunt, Adelaide Simmons, worked as Nathan Waterstone's editorial assistant, from the outbreak of World War II until his death in 1950."

"She goes by the name of Mrs. Robert Stewart now," I say.

"Ah, yes. She married a minister, I believe." I watch my interviewer cross her legs in the opposite direction before continuing. "She surprised the world when she permitted you to reveal in a high school research report that the woman in *The Lady* didn't exist."

I nod.

"I'm intrigued and also quite curious . . ." Ms. Hopkins wrinkles her brow. ". . . how this happened. Why did she allow you to make known the Lady's identity, when people had been trying for years to find out?"

"She decided the time had come for people to know."

"She wanted people to know that Nathan Waterstone engaged in a

317

cheap publicity stunt to stimulate sales?"

"There was more." My hands shake. I take a deep breath to calm myself.

"More?" She looks puzzled. Three days ago we rehearsed what she was to ask and what I was to say, and now I'm changing the script. "What do you mean *more?*"

"May I tell you a story?"

I detect a doubt in her nod. I've thrown her off-kilter.

"At the beginning of the war, my aunt was studying in Heidelberg, Germany . . .," I begin. "When her husband joined the French Resistance, she moved to London where she met Nathan Waterstone. She worked for him during most of her stay in London, typing and editing two novels. After the war, Addy moved to Wilson, near where she'd grown up."

Ms. Hopkins, not wanting to hear my aunt's history, since the subject of this interview is Nathan Waterstone, not Adelaide Simmons Stewart, looks like she's ready to halt my monologue. She puts up her hand and starts to say something, but I turn to the camera and, disregarding her, talk to the camera.

"Before Addy met Nathan, he spent time in Nepal, Thailand, India, and . . ."

"Ms. Hollander . . ."

I ignore her. "While in Nepal, he developed a bad habit." I flash a glance at Ms. Hopkins. The mention of a *bad habit* has gotten her attention. "Nathan Waterstone learned to like opium." I say this to her instead of to the camera, but then I turn back to the camera. "In London, he managed to secure opium infrequently, but shortly after moving to Wilson, he began to show signs of addiction. Those closest to him, the ones who knew, tried to discover his source, but couldn't. Eventually, he had to be sent to a facility. This happened several times. Each time he entered a facility, he used an

318

alias. His publisher didn't want the public to know that their profitable author was addicted to opium. Nathan would detox, return home, remain clean for a short time, but then after a few months, he'd fall back into old habits. No one knew who supplied him with opium."

I stop for a moment to catch my breath.

"On the day Nathan died, Addy was working in his study. After breakfast, he came in briefly. Then, after saying he didn't feel well, he went up to his bedroom. Later in the morning, my aunt heard him falling down the stairs. She ran out to find him dead at the bottom of the staircase."

Ms. Hopkins emits a small gasp, but I continue.

"In the days following his death, Addy suffered agonies of guilt because she'd ignored his complaints of not feeling well. I think she never got over feeling that she was to blame for his death."

"He had a heart attack and fell?" I hear the puzzlement in Ms. Hopkins' voice.

"He didn't have a heart attack. He died of a head injury. He'd gone to his room, smoked too much opium, and then attempted to come down stairs."

I hear her quick intake of breath. The time has come for another commercial, but she touches her ear to hold the ad, and motions for me to continue.

"My aunt called an ambulance," I say to the camera. "But when the ambulance arrived, she realized that other secrets were in danger of being discovered if the ambulance crew and the coroner reported what happened."

"Other secrets? What . . ."

"Addy kept the ambulance crew outside on the front porch until after Dr. Whiddon came." I *will* tell the story. Addy and I rehearsed what I'll say. She's at home watching. She lives with me now. My husband, Tad, and my two grown children sit with her, holding her hand, rubbing her back, all the things she used to do for me. When Addy declined this interview, sending me instead, her refusal had nothing to do with her age — she's ninety-four — but rather with not wanting to display emotion in public. And she will be emotional when I tell the other thing in a few more seconds.

"Dr. Whiddon was Nathan's doctor. He came and filled out the death certificate, and then he accompanied the ambulance to the mortuary. He filed the death certificate. But contrary to what he'd written on the certificate — that Nathan died of a head injury — he announced that Nathan Waterstone had died of a heart attack."

Ms. Hopkins is staring at me. I swallow. My throat is dry. I realize that a glass of water sits on the table beside me. I take a drink. The whole studio — Miss Hopkins, the camera people, the audience — remains stone still.

"You said that other secrets were in danger of being discovered. What secrets?"

"Shortly after Nathan moved to Wilson, he hired a housekeeper, Pearl Odum. At some point in the afternoon following his death, Pearl presented Nathan's lawyer, Mr. Watkins, with a will in which she was to receive everything. A previous will provided that Nathan's wealth be used to set up a foundation. He wanted his house maintained as a museum. When Mr. Watkins contacted Addy about the new will, she understood what she hadn't previously been able to figure out. She realized who had been supplying the opium. She searched the one place she'd never searched: the kitchen. She found opium in the flour canister.

"Threatened with the possibility of arrest, Pearl admitted everything. She confessed that she'd supplied the opium and had bribed Nathan to rewrite his will, threatening to cut off the supply if he didn't make her the heir to his fortune. Nathan's lawyer and his agent made a deal with Pearl. They'd not call the police if she promised to keep Nathan's addiction a secret. They kept her on as housekeeper to keep tabs on her."

"But why?" Ms. Hopkins interjects. "Why didn't they just arrest her? Did it matter that the world knew he had an addiction? Many writers had addictions. Many writers *have* addictions. Their addictions don't change their literary contributions."

"Nathan's did."

She raises her hands in a question. "I'm not following you."

"After *The Lady* Nathan ceased to be a writer."

"Ceased to be a writer? He wrote four novels after *The Lady*. From a literary viewpoint, every one of them is considered to be better than *The Lady*."

I shake my head, smile, and look into the camera. "*Runaway* was the first novel to be published after *The Lady*. When Nathan finished the manuscript and sent it to Adam Johnson, his agent, Adam sent back a letter of rejection."

"Obviously, Nathan rewrote the book."

"Addy rewrote the book."

"You mean she helped him edit the manuscript?"

"No, she rewrote the entire book — with no input from Nathan. Except for a few plot elements, the published novel is completely different from Nathan's original creation."

Miss Hopkins looks as though she doesn't believe me, and why should she?

"Nathan provided fragments of the plot for *Runaway*, but for the remaining four novels he didn't even do that. Adelaide Simmons Stewart wrote them from beginning to end, plot and all."

The audience has come alive. They're shifting in their seats, talking, emitting sounds of surprise.

"This is quite a claim to be making, Mrs. Hollander. Do you have proof?" My interviewer has raised her voice. She sounds accusatory. The audience becomes quiet again.

"The proof is in writing, and Nathan's editor is still alive. Ask him. Adam Johnson retired to Martha's Vineyard. He can be reached there. Before she turned over the manuscript for *Dunfermline,* my aunt made him sign a document stating that she wrote four of the novels attributed to Nathan. The document guaranteed that she'd eventually get credit for them, although not until the turn of the century. Beginning this year, the novels Addy wrote, the ones that now bear Nathan's name, will say: *by Adelaide Simmons, originally attributed to Nathan Waterstone.* The man my aunt later married, Robert Stewart, insisted that she require this agreement from the publisher before handing him the manuscript for *Dunfermline.* From the beginning, Robert knew Addy wrote the novels. This was a source of friction between them. I remember them arguing over this once, although at the time I didn't know what their argument was about. They were in her study, and then he went storming out of the house. He wanted her to have credit for what she'd done. I'm sorry to say Robert died two years ago, otherwise he'd be able to tell this story, too. He was very close to Nathan Waterstone and was one of four people who knew that Addy had written the books. The other two were Nathan's lawyer and his doctor. The lawyer, Mr. Watson, will verify what I've told you. He drew up the contracts for the four books Addy wrote using Nathan's name. Those contracts stipulated that Addy would receive half the royalties while the other half went to Nathan, and after Nathan died, to the Nathan Waterstone Foundation."

Ms. Hopkins, clearly thrown, is moving her hands around trying to decide where to put them; I think she's trying to regain control of both herself and the interview. I'll let her do that now. She faces the camera and motions to the camera man to focus on her.

"We know," she says in her polished camera-voice, ". . . that Adelaide Simmons wrote several novels beginning with *The Season of Hope*, published in . . . When exactly was that novel published?" She glances at me.

"1960."

"*Season of Hope* was published in 1960," she says, looking back at the camera. ". . . and was followed by others."

"Seven others," I interject.

"What I don't understand," she says, turning to me, "is why she agreed to do such a thing in the first place. Obviously, she's a talented writer." Then, seeming to forget the audience and the camera, she addresses me directly, and for the first time, we have a real conversation between us, not an interview. "When she's such a capable writer herself, why did she allow her work to be published under Nathan Waterstone's name?"

"She chose money over the long and uncertain struggle to establish herself as a writer." What I don't say is that, in the beginning, Addy thought money might replace the hole in her life created when she gave up Robert. "I guess, in a way, that choice was like selling her soul. Like Faust."

Ms. Hopkins gives a little laugh. "I suppose you could say that." She drops the conversational tone and, becoming once again Lydia Hopkins, hostess of *Talk America*, addresses her TV audience. She's confident, professional, and quite aware that on tonight's late news, and in tomorrow's newspapers and TV broadcasts, this interview will propel her to a few minutes of fame. Those few minutes will, I'm sure, incline her to forgive me magnanimously for hijacking the interview.

Ms. Hopkins is once again in control. And that's fine. I'm tired. Tomorrow evening I play a concert for the Lansdale Community Concert Series, so I need to get to bed at a decent hour. I want to go home, give my children a hug, kiss my husband good night, and hold Addy's hand for a little while. Then I want to play the piano. It's still my solace as well as my livelihood.

THE END

Acknowledgements

I am deeply grateful to all the people who helped me achieve the goal of publishing my first novel. Many, many thanks to: Jesse Sisken, my writing buddy for the past two years; Jan Isenhour, of the Carnegie Center in Lexington, KY; Dr. Timothy Clark, who, among other things, helped me get rid of a few thousand extra words, and who also taught me piano (Alas! I'm not as talented as Quincy, my heroine); Shelly Culbertson, a fellow writer who gave me valuable insights; Julia Pezzi, who claims she knows nothing about writing, yet gave me excellent advice; Mitzi Geese, my long-time friend and a great writer herself; and Jane Warner for drawing my attention to several details I should have thought of myself, but didn't. Erin Higgins did a fabulous job of line editing and making sure all my changes made sense.

Nat Jones designed an amazing cover as well as entertaining me with amusing emails when I was overcome with the stress of publication details. Thank you, Nat.

Many thanks to Stephen Higgins for formatting and setting up my website, a task more formidable to me than that of writing a novel.

Julia Pezzi and Stephen Higgins advised me on many different issues related to this book, as well as enduring my endless whining when I thought I should probably just delete the whole thing and start gardening instead of trying to write. This book really would not have been possible without their support.

I am particularly beholden to the Amazon Breakout Novel Contest. When the rough draft of *The Lady* was named a semi-finalist, I was inspired to continue working on it.

Finally, I am indebted to my writers' group in Qatar who listened to the first painful attempts at bringing this story to life: Shelly Culbertson, Tim Clark, Celia Flynn, Doug Lane, LuAnne Ktiri-Idrissi, Ellie Holte, and Corbin Smith.

Made in the USA
Charleston, SC
15 December 2013